Raashh Decisions
Xxan War #2

Brenna Lyons

Fireborn Publishing Copyright Statement

us know at sales@firebornpublishing.com or via the author's personal email.

This book is written in US English.

PUBLISHER

Glossary of Xxan Terms

Dominant- Xxanian males with Dominant personalities and larger bodies

elder- the head of a Xxanian nest — this is always a Dominant male, usually the oldest and wisest Dominant male in a nest, even if younger males are stronger ("The elders" can also refer to all the older members of a nest as a group.)

first- the first lover a Xxanian female experiences; this male is usually chosen by her *seir* when the quickening strikes or is decided by fate when a female unexpectedly hits her quickening in close proximity to Xxanian males (Xxanian Dominants will fight for the right to sate a quickening — to the death, if necessary — and the one left standing will be her first.)

gran-Hauaa- grandmother

gran-seir- grandfather

gran-vvaash- granddaughter

gran-vvaashee- grandson

gran-vvaasheen- grandchildren

Grea Elders- ruling class of the Xxan, comprised exclusively of the strongest elders

grippers- lightweight shoes that allow engineering division military to grip to wet decks and oily machinery

Hauaa- mother (Unlike other family relationships, Hauaa is always capitalized, no matter whether the person is speaking about or directly addressing the Hauaa.)

Hauaa zhhaaia- young mother

High Xxan- one of the seven forms of Xxanian martial arts; considered the most advanced form, this form is usually only taught to Dominants and is only practiced regularly by *Grea* Elders

IAC- Inter Agency Command, a panel of the heads of all military and government offices concerned with alien affairs

Interstellar War Pact- an interstellar Geneva Convention, covering war and treatment of prisoners (For the record, the Xxan do not practice or recognize it.)

nest- home of a Xxanian family; typically an armored underground bunker populated with gardens and pools of water

pregnancy block- a drug to prevent pregnancy, given to both men and women

quickening- a Xxanian female's sexual maturation, as experienced in a mating frenzy with her first

ripen- the process of making a female fertile by way of mating (An unripened female is usually unable to conceive a child, which ensures no offspring for Xxanian females until they are bonded to their mates.)

Saahaal- a clove-like spice that grows on the Xxanian home world, a sacred part of their religion (They use clove instead on Earth.)

scaly/scalies- an offensive term for Xxanians

scaly-lovers- an offensive term for those sympathetic to Xxanians

seir- father

Seir-God- the Xxanian deity

sister-moon- Xxania Hethhh; the Xxanian home world is actually a moon in the Xxanian solar system, and Xxania Hethhh is the twin moon to the home world, sharing an orbit with the home world.)

s'saahhta- a sickle-shaped weapon carried by Xxanian warriors

s'sanuea- preparation room; akin to a locker room (Inhabitants of and guests of the nest change clothing in the *s'sanuea* before entering the nest proper.)

S'shuuaih- a general word, signifying clothing, in general, both for males and females

S'suuhhea- female Xxanian clothing

S'suumea- male Xxanian clothing- comes in formal and informal styles

STD block- a drug to prevent STD transmission from person to person; can be administered to both males and females

Subdominants- Xxan males with beta personalities and smaller bodies; Xxanians identify Dominants and Subdominants by scent

swamp skin- an offensive term for the Xxan

tongue-scent- using the tongue to collect more scent information than the nose gives; the Xxan have slightly-roughened tongues with a way array of scent receptors

Xxan- the collective Xxanian people; also, their language is called Xxan

Xxan-Dree- one of the seven Xxanian martial arts

Xxania Hethhh- the Xxanian sister-moon; a twin moon to the Xxanian home world

Xxania Uuaahth- the Xxanian home world

Xxanian- adj referring to the Xxan

z'hhabe- a drug that helps stall Xxanian labor

Zhigaaah- female sex hormone

Zhigaaal- male sex hormone

zhirrakkah- a Xxanian insult, comparing a person to a carrion eater from the Xxanian home world

zuahhhbeahhh- a spiked weapon used by Xxanian Dominants

z'haahn- the spiced meat the Xxan and crossbred Xxan eat daily

Section 1:
The Founding

Raashh
Elder

Prologue

"Do you understand what you're getting yourself into?" Stephen Rayn asked.

Marie smiled at him. "I've read all the files, Doctor. I've gone over the psychological and medical information with your staff in great detail. I've met with all the members of Daahn's nest. I fully understand that I'm agreeing to bind with Raashh for life."

The second in command of our new Xxanian allies. She'd always had a thing for powerful men, and he was sure to be more powerful than any unmated or unmarried man she'd ever met.

"And this doesn't bother you?" Captain MacNair inquired, one brow raised in what she would assume was disbelief.

"Did it bother Emma?" she countered.

The military liaison winced. "Emma was illegally infused with Daahn's *Zhigaaal* and was launched into a mating frenzy for him. Raashh is willing to allow you to be similarly infused before he approaches you, if you would be more comfortable with it."

"I don't think so. I would much rather meet Raashh with a clear head and let him know I came to him willingly, as one of his own females would have."

The two men exchanged looks that said she didn't know what she was in for.

"If there's nothing else you need to tell me, gentlemen..." She hinted that they should be on their way to Raashh's nest.

Rayn cleared his throat. "You may want to reconsider, Ms. Kade. At least let us infuse you first. Raashh is—"

"Emma compares him to a cargo van, Doctor. I know he's much larger than Daahn is. I know Daahn and Emma are concerned that no human female would choose to bind herself to Raashh. I am happy to say they are incorrect. I fully intend to bind to Raashh." *Today, if they stop wasting time.*

In fact, she was counting on it. What could be more Dominant than a warrior race with clearly defined Dominant and Subdominant classes? Especially a leader of their kind?

They shared another long look. At last, Rayn spoke. "Very well. Let's get your bio-tracker on and take you to meet Raashh."

* * * *

Raashh paced the length of the center nest, his emotions in a riot. They'd done it. Rayn and Mac had found a human female willing to bind to him.

She may not once she meets me. He knew the chance of finding a female comfortable with his size was unlikely. *She will most likely take one look at me and change her mind. She'll beg to be given to one of the others. One of the smaller males.*

Unless they've infused her. His primary ached at the thought of her arriving, already anointed with his *Zhigaaal* and in a frenzy for him as Emma had been for Daahn. He'd agreed to it, praying to the *Seir*-God that the human female would not come to her senses until he'd bound her to him and proven himself a worthy male to her unique sensibilities.

Everything he'd done—from building this lush nest to stocking in human delicacies—had been designed to seduce her senses and impress her nesting instincts. *Please, Seir-God, let it be enough.* He'd been without a female for more than six Earth years. Raashh wasn't sure how much longer he could last.

A tone let him know Mac's shuttle was inside the blast shields. It would only take him a few moments to unload Rayn and the female.

I should go to meet her.

No. I should meet her here, so she sees me after she sees what I offer.

Which would be better? It was enough to drive a male mad.

The sounds of them descending from the shuttle pad had his cock hard and ready. Raashh listened closely, picking out the feminine tones mixed in with those of Rayn and Mac.

It didn't sound as if she had been infused. Raashh bit back a dozen harsh curses at that. If she hadn't been infused, she was sure to refuse him.

At least I will meet her. Perhaps she will look kindly on what I offer, if not on me personally.

They entered the center nest, the two men walking side-by-side in front of the female, blocking his view of her. It was a weak mirror of the way a female's *seir* and brothers might bring her to a male to sate her quickening. Still,

Raashh knew the real reason for this. It was a warning to him to rein in his instincts. She was a human female and too fragile to handle him at his most sexual and Dominant.

They should have infused her.

Mac and Rayn came to a halt just outside Raashh's reach. Each man took a step apart, revealing the female to him.

Mac didn't hesitate. His Xxan was smooth and near-perfect, despite his human birth. "May I present Marie Kade, Raashh."

Raashh fought for the ability to respond. The yellow-haired female barely reached Mac's broad shoulders, and the springs of curl cascading around her face and shoulders reminded him of old vids he'd seen of child actors from a bygone age. "This must be what humans call a *joke*, Mac. She cannot possibly be my mate."

The female answered before Mac had a chance to...and in even smoother Xxan than Daahn's brother warrior could manage. "Am I displeasing to you, Raashh? You haven't even scented me yet."

"It is not a matter of pleasure." As humans went, she was a delicious little morsel. *And therein lies the problem.* "You are much smaller than Daahn's mate is. You are too small to handle a male of my size." Though her facial structure appeared adult and her breasts and hips well rounded, her stature was that of a prepubescent human in height and width. Raashh was certain he could cover three-quarters the span of her narrow waist with one hand and talons combined and span her hips with both.

He'd heard the sounds Daahn's mate made when Daahn lay with her. If those pitiful sounds were any indication, Emma could hardly take Daahn's length and girth. Raashh might well split this poor, tiny female in two in the attempt. Human or not, harming a female went against a Xxanian male's ethics and instincts.

Her smile was disarming. It warned that the discussion was not nearly over as he'd believed it would be after his protest.

She padded to him on bare feet, her *S'suuhhea* swishing around her body. "I don't believe you are correct, Raashh." She went up on her tiptoes, and her lips pressed to the musk well high on his chest. Her tongue prodded at it, bringing his primary cock up again and making his musk flow.

Raashh was too stunned to react. He wanted this more than he could remember wanting anything since he'd been captured.

"If you gentlemen would excuse us?" she suggested.

"The tranq pad—" Rayn started to offer.

"Won't be necessary," she countered.

The two human males left the center nest, and Marie reached beneath his *S'suumea*, taking his primary in her hand. She moaned.

"Your purpose, Marie?"

"Proving that I'm not too small to handle a male your size."

She stroked him to his full length, making him ache for more.

5

"And once I do, will you still refuse me?"

He growled, warning her not to challenge him. He was a Dominant. *I am not to be trifled with.*

The sound that escaped her lips could only be classified as a purr.

Raashh untied his *S'suumea*, let it drop, and then untied her *S'suuhhea* and let it flutter to the grass. Her ready scent went to his head. Marie wasn't simply aroused. She was in the human time of fertility. As he understood it, that meant she would ripen for him quickly if he claimed her as his own, as Daahn's mate had caught for him immediately.

She turned, rubbing up and down his body, enticing him as a Xxanian female in the quickening would.

So that's what she wants. Raashh brought her to her knees beneath his bulk and started working the length of his primary cock into her tight little body.

Moans and hisses left her lips, and he bit back foul curses at the fact that he'd been correct. She couldn't take him. That a given, he withdrew.

"Don't you dare," she warned.

"I don't understand. I am too large for—"

Marie turned on him, glaring as Emma did when Daahn angered her. What had he done to anger Marie? He was being solicitous, attentive, concerned with her well-being. He'd thought all females appreciated such care.

She climbed astride his lap and worked her body down the head of his primary, encasing him in delight. Her sounds were sharp, and she bit at her lower lip, her eyes sliding shut.

Raashh wrapped his hands around her waist and stopped her, rumbling out a soothing sound. If she couldn't take him, she couldn't.

Marie smacked at his hand, stunning him to momentary silence.

"You will only hurt yourself," he protested.

"What in the wide, beautiful universe makes you think you're hurting me?"

That succeeded in rendering him speechless for a longer period of time.

Marie beat him to coherent speech. "You think the sounds I'm making mean you're hurting me. Don't you?"

"They don't?"

"You'll know if you hurt me."

"How will I?" It seemed he couldn't rely on her sounds to be an indicator.

She pushed further down on his length, stealing his breath. Marie guided one of his hands to her breast, licking her lips when he stroked the soft mound.

"You feel how hard my nipple is?"

He nodded, his head spinning in pleasure.

"And how wet and hot my *pussy* is?"

"*Pussy?*" It wasn't a term he knew.

Her inner muscles tightened around his primary. "*Pussy.*"

"Yes. Very hot and wet," he agreed.

"Those signs mean I am not in pain. I am aroused and in need of you. *Desperate* need of you."

7

Marie pushed further down his length, more than halfway sheathing him. "More, Raashh," she urged him.

"I could climax with this little of you," he admitted.

"You are going to give me all you have to give, and I am going to love every millimeter of your cock."

His Dominant instincts stood up and took notice. "You are *ordering* me?" *Me? Second in command to Daahn?*

"Perhaps you should show me what my place will be as your mate," she suggested.

He considered that. Did she want him to Dominate her or did she wish him to play the part of a submissive human male for her pleasure? No female was worth that. *I am Raashh. I am Dominant, and if that does not please her, she had best find a human male.*

That in mind, he dragged her hands over her head and pinned Marie to the grass. Raashh thrust deeper, retreated, and came at her again...and again...and again. She wiggled against him, her sounds rising. He peeked down at her nipples, and his cock bucked at the sight of the hard buds of deep pink.

Thank the Seir-God! She does enjoy the Dominant in me.

That freed him to thrust harder and deeper. At last, he was fully-seated, and she still gave every indication that she was enjoying his sex.

Marie arched under him, venting screams that would have made him think she was in dire

8

discomfort. Her climaxing pussy convinced him she was experiencing nothing of the sort.

He followed her over with a roar of possession. His fluids jetted into her body, setting off a quickening of Marie's climax in response. She gasped out his name, pulling lightly against his hold on her wrists.

Marie lay beneath him, panting hard, her nipples still hard and inviting. Raashh lowered his head and licked at one, wondering if Marie would produce the sweet milk to feed their young, as Emma had for Daahn's young.

She shimmied, her breasts bouncing and swaying. He hesitated, meeting her gaze, uncertain if she was asking him to continue or asking him to stop.

"Use your tongue, Raashh. Use it everywhere. I love it."

The invitation was too sweet to pass up.

* * * *

The rough surface of his tongue was sublime. All the better was the way the forked tips played counterpoint to each other, wrapping around her nipple, tugging lightly at it, rasping against the sensitive nubs. Raashh moved from one nipple to the other and back again, making his stillness inside her nearly unbearable.

His cock was still hard and lodged more than halfway inside her pussy. Marie wanted him deeper. She wanted him pounding again. Moreover, she wanted both cocks staking his claim on her.

Her heart sank as he withdrew. Marie stared at him, begging him silently not to refuse her.

He offered a soothing rumble. "I am simply giving my future mate what she so desperately needs." There was a hint of a taunt in that.

Before she could question it, he'd turned her and positioned Marie on her hands and knees again. He spread the globes of her ass and traced the ring of her anus with his tongue.

Marie went weak in the knees, and moans escaped her throat. Visions of his secondary, pushing past the ring and into the depths of her ass had tantalized her in her dreams for weeks.

She stiffened at the abrupt thrust of his rough tongue into her ass, thankful that she'd used an enema to clean herself out for whatever play he wanted to engage in. He went still at the change.

"Yes," she gasped. "Taste wherever you want to, Raashh. Please. Touch me."

He came at her more avidly, piercing her ass over and over. Just as she felt she might come from his exploration, he moved on to her weeping pussy. The rasping of his tongue sent her to a second climax in moments, and his lazy tasting of her clit set off aftershocks.

Marie came to her senses, cradled in Raashh's arms, her body vibrating in awareness. They stared at each other, and she wasn't certain which one of them was more stunned.

She swallowed hard, terrified that he would see her weakness in pleasure as a risk. "Will you refuse me, Raashh?" she asked. Her heart ached at the fact that he could. *He could, and I would pine for more of him for the rest of my life.*

"Tell me you wish to be my mate, and I would not deny you, little one." He stroked her hair between his thick fingers.

"I do wish to. Now. Please."

"First I will feed you and bathe you. Then I will make you my mate."

Marie nodded, gasping out her agreement.

* * * *

Marie moaned at the stroke of clove oil against her clit. She shifted her hips, riding the slick length of Raashh's finger, seeking closer contact. She licked her lips, wondering how much longer he would keep her in this sexual limbo.

"You make me crazy to make you mine," Raashh rumbled.

Closer inspection showed his muscles were strung tight, probably in misguided restraint.

Marie smiled. "I was ready when I got off the shuttle."

He didn't argue it. Raashh scooped up her right hand and guided it beneath the surface of the water. His primary was rigid, and she started to stroke it. He shook his head and moved her fingers lower. She gasped in the realization that his secondary was already the length of her little finger.

"Make me ready to anoint you."

11

Oh, yes! Marie started using two fingers to stroke him. In moments, he was long enough to use three. Then all four.

Guttural sounds escaped his throat, and Raashh shivered in seeming delight. "Be sure, Marie. When my *Zhigaaal* starts to flow, I will anoint you, and I will not rest until you are bound as my mate and full of my young."

"Oh, yes. That is what I want."

His secondary moved against her hand slightly. A light burning sensation said his *Zhigaaal* had started to flow.

Her heart rate rose a dozen beats a minute and then more. Already, the need to have him between her thighs was maddening.

Raashh lifted Marie by the waist, and she let his cock slip from between her fingers. He settled her on a warm boulder at the edge of the pond.

Before she could question him, his fingers started working at her nipples, spreading the stinging *Zhigaaal* over her. Marie arched into his touch, at a loss for the words to encourage him. Her supporting arms trembled beneath her.

He traced a line of heat down her abdomen, retreated, and came back with what could only be a fresh coating of the pheromone. Marie pressed up with her heels, opening herself to him for more. Hot trails stole her thinking mind, leaving her aware of only a patchwork of pleasure as Raashh worked the *Zhigaaal* into her clit, her swollen and hungry labia, and finally into the ring of her ass.

She was on fire, needing more that only Raashh could offer. Marie didn't question that

Emma's memories of being anointed were correct. If another man touched her now, she'd try to kill him. *With good reason. I am Raashh's woman.*

Raashh set out to drive her mad. He spread his pheromone along her inner thighs, coated her mound with it, even painted a line of it between the globes of her ass, as if assuring himself that every possible erogenous zone was liberally coated in his potent scent.

As if proving her assessment correct, he did the same along the line of her collarbones, down the pulse points of her throat, at the soft, sensitive spot behind her ear, and finally brought a healthy helping to her mouth. Marie trembled as he spread it along her lips, thirsty for more, ravenous for what would come next.

She sucked his finger in, talon and all. Raashh went still, watching her drinking every drop with a moan, his eye slits narrowing.

"Do you...suck as I have heard other human women suck?" he asked.

Marie released him and licked her lips. "Anytime you want me to," she vowed.

He hesitated long enough to make Marie wonder if he wanted it or was repulsed by it. At last, Raashh rose to his feet and brought his cocks to her lips. "Suck me, Marie."

She engulfed most of the primary, working the broad column in and out. Raashh let her fellate him, his hand playing at her curls lightly but not pulling her in for more. He would learn in time that she liked that.

"The secondary. Suck the secondary." There was no mistaking the bark of order.

Marie released his primary and sucked the secondary in. The *Zhigaaal* was like spice on her tongue, and she moaned, seeking more of him. Before she quite knew what was happening, his secondary was sliding in and out of her throat without a hint of her gag reflex.

Raashh's roar spurred her on. She was going to make him come. She was going to drink down every drop, and after that, she would be his forever.

His second roar was accompanied by a hand holding the back of her head, his secondary deep in her throat. He erupted, shooting a load of *Zhigaaal* in; she swallowed it greedily. Her head spun, and her arms folded. Raashh supported her weight, laying her on the boulder as his secondary slipped from between her lax lips.

There was no mistaking his next move. Raashh positioned himself so she could see him stroking up more *Zhigaaal*. His expression said she was his, and he would kill anyone who stood in the way of him finalizing that connection between them.

Thank the stars! He's what I've always wanted.

* * * *

Raashh had never seen anything more beautiful. Marie was splayed out on the stone, drunk on his *Zhigaaal*, already well on her way to being his forever.

Quickly. Females fight when the stunning wears off.

Just as Marie started to move, he positioned his secondary at her delicate pink seam and thrust into her, spreading his pheromone the full length of her lovely channel.

The channel I'll be pounding for the next three days. And then the rest of our lives, as it pleases us to do so. He hoped Marie would continue to be as receptive as she'd been thus far, as the years passed.

It didn't take much to make him climax again, especially since his first thrust pushed her to the delicious contractions and sounds that announced her climax.

All that time, I thought Emma was in pain. Daahn has been blessed to have so responsive a mate.

But not as responsive as mine, it seems.

Marie went still beneath him again, the momentary pause in the binding that the *Seir-God* had graciously built in to allow the biding to progress unimpeded. Raashh didn't waste it. He massaged the base of his secondary, pouring as much of his *Zhigaaal* against her barrier as he could. The iris of muscle spread wide to the relaxing effects of the pheromone, and Raashh worked his secondary through it carefully, mindful that human women might tear at too-rough handling.

Marie moaned, and her hands came up. Raashh winced in the expectation of her human talons biting skin, but that didn't happen. She stroked her hands up his chest, closing her legs around him, wrapping herself around his bulk as best she could.

The first whisper of movement up and down his secondary nearly stole Raashh's thinking mind. He grasped her hips and aided her, his careful thrusting becoming more manic as she vented cries that he now recognized meant she was in desperate need of his sex. Since the bio-tracker would let Rayn know if she was in any physical danger, and the medic would intervene, Raashh let his drives loose, staking his claim as he would on a Xxanian female as a test.

Marie's sounds became more frantic and encouraging, and there was no sign of the human males. It was more than Raashh had ever dared hope for. He planted the next course of *Zhigaaal* deep in her womb with a prayer that she would ripen and give him young.

With Marie relaxed in his arms, loosely wrapped around him, he considered giving her one more infusion into her womb. Memories of her sounds and movements as he tongued her ass made his cocks throb for other delights and a quicker end to the torture of his secondary jetting useless cum into the center nest when it could be finding a home in his mate.

Later. I will fill her womb with Zhigaaal *and cum for three days. Moving on now will not prevent her from being my mate.*

She moaned out a protest when he left her body.

"Only a moment, my little mate. You wish to be mine?" *Of course she does.*

"Yes. Yes. Please, Raashh."

Hearing her say it was almost more than he could bear.

Raashh pressed his secondary to the ring of her tight little ass, moaning at the slight bite of the muscles against the head. He massaged up more *Zhigaaal*, using it to relax the muscles as he eased inside. With every forward motion, Marie made little sounds of encouragement or pleasure. With every slight withdrawal, she tightened her grip on his arms as if in protest. At last, he was deep enough in her ass for his primary to tease at her seam.

"Yes. Oh, yes, Raashh. I'm burning. I need your primary."

That broke his self-control, and Raashh thrust both cocks deep into her. Marie didn't scream. A litany of pleas left her lips. It took only a moment for him to realize they were pleas for him to keep moving. Her legs tightened around his hips again.

Another sign that she needs my sex. He committed it to memory.

One thrust led to another and another and another. Her tight little pussy ensured he wouldn't last long, but he lasted longer than she did, which was a relief.

Again, Marie went lax in his arms. Before Raashh could decide what to do with her next, she was already coming out of her stupor.

So soon?

To his surprise, she didn't fight him. Marie's arms and legs tightened around him, and she rubbed her body up and down his, moving his cocks minutely inside her.

"I need more, Raashh." It was a breathless little whisper of sound.

"More like this?" Or was there something else she wanted?

"Yes. This. Then...everything."

His heart pounding, Raashh brought her into the water with him, working both cocks hard, to the sweet music of Marie's sounds.

* * * *

Marie woke in the shelter of Raashh's body, snug on his dreaming mat. She was on her left side, her head pillowed on one large arm. His chest was pressed to her back, his primary cock stirring lightly against the curve of her ass.

Her body came to life that quickly. Three days of carnality, broken only by a nap here and there and Raashh feeding her to maintain her strength, and the burn to have him buried inside her hadn't subsided in the least.

His grumbled curse said he was more than aware of her state of arousal. One big hand covered her breast and kneaded. "Your nipple is hard, and you are wet and hot. Are you in desperate need of me, Marie?"

"You know I am." It came out as a gasp of sound.

His hand moved to her inner thigh, and Raashh spread her legs a bit. He shifted, bringing his primary to her sensitized labia. In the next heartbeat, he was inside and thrusting hard and fast.

Her body exploded in pleasure, and she vented screams of release, swiveling her hips to heighten Raashh's pleasure. He came with a grunted curse in the Xxan language.

They were still for a moment, panting hard in the aftermath of the best quickie Marie had ever had.

Who am I kidding? Raashh is, in every way, the best I've ever had. He'd learned quickly that she liked being dominated by him, having Raashh position her for both their pleasure, being lightly restrained by him, having him order her to suck him or to remain still for his maddening touching.

Just the memories of his handling fired her for more.

He left her body in a rush and turned Marie beneath him, bringing his mouth down on hers with brutal efficiency. For a race that didn't kiss as part of mating, Raashh had taken to the art and mastered it within a day.

It had started when she'd suggested she would like to try *z'haahn*. Raashh had fed it to her in the Xxanian manner, the mating male mouth feeding his female. When Marie had continued the kiss well after the meat was gone, he'd questioned it, then experimented with kissing. In short order, he'd been back inside her. Then the feeding had continued, resulting in more mating. They'd shared several meals of *z'haahn* since, all with roughly the same results.

Raashh broke off the kiss and cupped her chin. "Food for my mate," he grumbled. "And then we will let Rayn take his damned tests, so they can leave the nest and allow us to set about scenting more of it."

Marie smiled at the sentiment. *"Z'haahn?"* she suggested.

"Tease me much more, and you will be drinking my *Zhigaaal* before the shuttle departs the nest." It was a challenge he wanted her to take him up on.

"Do you wish me to drink it now?"

"Little tease." In a whirlwind, Raashh was thrusting hard inside her again, reinforcing his claim. "I will not give them any reason to tarry. You will be sucking my secondary the moment they depart the center nest."

Her climax neared, a promise of another three days of mating frenzy. Or six. Or a dozen. "Oh, yes."

Section 2:
The Business of Love

Daveed

Dominant

Chapter One

Twenty-nine years later

"The files are on your desktop, Mr. Raashh," Celeste informed him with her usual military efficiency.

"Thank you." He tried to keep the edge of irritation out of his voice, but that was difficult. One thing Celeste had never understood was his single-minded approach to design. When he was creating, no interruption was welcome. Not even one I knew was coming at some point today.

Celeste puts up with my moods and distraction. How many personal assistants would be so understanding?

Of course, when I have another designer working with me, I can have many interruptions handled by him. That would be a blessing of the *Seir*-God.

The creative spark successfully derailed, he dropped the electronic pen to the shelf on the inclined drawing table and pushed the button to save the design he'd been working on. He pushed away from his preferred workspace with a sigh and headed for the desk.

The idea of holding a contest to choose the new designer had been Arren's, and it was a stroke of genius. The very idea of Daveed spending days or weeks interviewing prospective candidates had convinced him not to take on another designer for more than a year. This way, he had minimal contact with them and only had to interview those whose work he felt would fit with *Spice*'s existing line best.

The first three designers' offerings held his attention for less than five minutes each. At that, he was being kind, seeing if anything they offered might fit with his image for *Spice*.

The fourth left him shocked speechless for a moment. The designer's Neo-Xenolithic style went beyond the usual flounces and ragged edges and straight to the heart of some two-year-old's idea of Xxanian culture. The skin-tight silken creations covered from neck to ankle, some with hoods, and included long gloves, complete with fake talons. The entire line was in green, blue, and black scale designs.

Daveed considered stopping right there. Clearly, he wasn't going to find what he wanted this way.

Something convinced him to go on. *Just one more.*

He was glad he did from the very first outfit that appeared. The designer had produced long, flowing gowns that draped the female form in elegance, short gowns that enticed without being vulgar, and blouses that would show a Xxanian female's fertile stripe clearly.

"Perfect," he decided. How could any designer's work be so perfect for *Spice*? *Maybe he is another Xxanian. That would certainly explain it.*

Excited by the prospect, Daveed skipped to the artist's introduction of himself. His breath caught, and he gulped in shock. The designer wasn't Xxanian. She wasn't male, either.

Her dark honey-colored hair was pulled up in a simple style at the top of her head, and errant curls surrounded her face. She wore one of her own designs, a deep blue that matched her eyes, and she moved gracefully on stiletto heels.

Daveed barely heard the details she imparted to the vid-recorder. The only one that stuck in his mind was her name.

"Joy." It was also the name of her clothing line.

He paused the feed and summoned Celeste with the push of a button. She appeared in the doorway and waited to hear what he needed from her.

"I wish to interview number five...Joy."

"Joy Patterson," she replied. "Any others, Mr. Raashh?"

"Just the one for now." *Seir*-God willing, he would have no need to meet the others.

"As you wish."

When she'd disappeared from view, Daveed started Joy's vid again, from the beginning. He wanted to know everything about Joy and her line he could before the interview with her.

He made a mental note to have Arren do a background check on the artist in question, in the meantime. One could never be careful enough with anti-Xxan guerrillas on the prowl.

* * * *

Joy scooped up the phone, growling at the interruption. "Yes?" she asked.

"Ms. Patterson?" the woman on the other end asked.

"Yes." Since it was her work phone, there was no sense denying it. It wasn't as if she had a staff. *Yet. I will have my own staff. Someday.*

"Good afternoon, Ms. Patterson. This is Celeste Banks from Mr. Raashh's office at *Spice Industries.*"

Her heart thudded in her chest at that pronouncement. If they were calling, it wasn't a refusal of her proposal outright. *I'm still in the running.* "Yes, Ms. Banks?"

"Celeste will be fine."

"Celeste." Her tongue felt thick in her mouth.

"Mr. Raashh would like to interview you. I have openings in his schedule on Friday afternoon and again on Monday afternoon. If that's not convenient, I can try to move another appointment to —"

"Friday. I mean, Friday works well for me." *Keep calm, Joy. Don't make them think you're desperate.*

But she *was* desperate to win a position with *Spice.* Any position would do, even if she failed to get the job as Daveed Raashh's assistant. *Spice* had a name for advancing from the inside; even if it took years to advance, a job like this could make her entire career.

"Very well." The click of keys in the background let Joy know Celeste was making the appointment for her.

"The...contest details said you would provide transportation?" It had been one of the reasons she'd snapped at the chance to enter. There was no way she could afford the trip to Virginia on her own.

"Yes. You can meet the *Spice* shuttle at noon at the airport. Go to the cargo terminal area and park at *Spice's* hanger. Mr. Raashh's private shuttle will meet you there. The pilot's name is Karl."

She swallowed a lump of surprise. "I will. Thank you, Celeste. Should I bring samples along?"

"There's no need for that, but if you have any new designs that are not on the vid, you may want to bring the files to view here."

"Yes. Absolutely." Her mind spun. Which designs would Mr. Raashh like best?

"Until Friday, then. Good luck, Ms. Patterson."

Celeste was gone before Joy could find the words to thank her again.

She hung up the phone and rushed to the racks of clothes. What would be the best outfit to meet the Xxanian designer in?

He's already seen me in the short wrap dress. Nothing too formal. Her hand closed on a knee-length evening dress that was cut deep between her breasts and to the center of her back. *I can couple it with a suit coat and remove it, if I need to.* "Perfect."

* * * *

"Two minutes, Ms. Patterson," Karl called out.

"Thank you."

She took another sip of the white wine. She'd tried to tell the Xxanian male she didn't need anything for the short cross-country flight, but he'd insisted on providing refreshments for her.

The shuttle was decadent. A far cry from the public transports students took to space stations on field trips, the interior of Daveed Raashh's private shuttle would look at home in a five-star hotel.

The vehicle touched down with a whisper of sideward motion, and the engines wound down. Joy took a calming breath, unfastened her seat harness, and stood.

Karl rushed past her and opened the door. He stepped out and offered his hand to help her down the stairs. She climbed down carefully and looked around.

They were on the rooftop of the *Spice Building.* The sideward movement of the shuttle had brought the vehicle's door under a reinforced overhang.

"This way, Ms. Patterson," Karl instructed. He led the way to an elevator.

It opened as they reached it, and a child that looked to be about twelve years old exited and headed for the shuttle at a trot, a riot of bright blond curls bouncing around his face. He wore jeans and a t-shirt with high-top tennis shoes and sunglasses. He was thin but muscular.

Karl turned to him with a smile. "Just a moment, Arren."

"Okay." He hopped into the shuttle and disappeared from view.

Joy watched him, confused by the interaction.

"Raashh's younger son," Karl explained.

He's not hairless. She hadn't known first-generation crossbreeds had hair. Arren didn't have a light dusting of hair, either. He had a full head of golden curls that many girls would die to possess. Or to run their fingers through, if he was a little older.

"Board the elevator. Celeste will meet you. Good luck, Ms. Patterson."

"Thank you."

He loped away almost before she could get that much out.

Joy stepped into the elevator. She snapped her head up as the engines started ramping up again. Karl was securing the door, which meant the child was piloting. *Is that even legal?*

The elevator doors closed, and it moved smoothly downward. Moments later, it opened.

Joy's smile faltered a bit at the sight of the man standing in the doorway, muscular arms crossed over a broad chest. He stood at least two and a quarter meters tall, bald, imposing, and wearing sunglasses indoors.

She raised a quaking hand. "Mr. Raashh, thank you for inviting me. I'm Joy Patterson."

* * * *

"Karl says they're coming in now."

Daveed heard Arren's shout of excitement. He didn't doubt the boy was on his way to the roof for the flying lesson Karl had promised him.

He didn't understand why their *seir* spoiled Arren as he did, though he suspected Raashh saw his dead mate in his younger son's face and was uncharacteristically soft on him for it. The old buck had never been soft on Daveed. That much was certain.

"On my way," he grumbled. Daveed rose and buttoned his suit coat, then headed for the elevator. Just in time to see Arren disappear into it.

He couldn't wait to meet Joy Patterson. Everything Daveed had learned about her had roused his interest further.

The elevator returned with the lady in question aboard. She focused at his chest level, then her head tipped back and she looked up into his face. Her smile went stiff. It eased again, and she raised her hand.

"Mr. Raashh, thank you for inviting me. I'm Joy Patterson."

Daveed hesitated before he took her hand and kissed the back of her knuckles. Women seldom invited a male's touch in such a manner.

Especially the touch of a Xxanian male. I will not waste such a gift.

"Welcome to *Spice Industries*, Ms. Patterson. May I escort you in?" He offered his arm as his *Hauaa* had taught him to.

Her cheeks darkened in a blush. "Yes. Thank you." She took his arm and accompanied him down the corridor toward his workroom.

"Was your flight in pleasant, Ms. Patterson?"

"Joy," she invited.

His heart skipped a beat in excitement.

30

"Lovely. Thank you. Karl made sure I was comfortable."

A niggling of jealousy ate at him, and Daveed pushed it away. "This is our design department. You understand that the job would be here and not in Oregon, where you currently live?"

"Yes."

"We would, of course, relocate you."

By her easing muscles and exhalation of air, Daveed guessed she was relieved to hear that.

He ushered her into his office. She sucked in a startled breath and surveyed his workspace. Daveed took pride in her reaction.

"Your office will be here." He motioned to the adjoining door.

Joy looked up at him, seemingly confused. "My... I thought I was here for an interview?"

Daveed smiled. "Xxanian Dominants are decisive. Your designs are a perfect complement to the vision I have for *Spice Clothing*. That a given, I fully intend to offer you the position."

"Of...of assistant designer? You're serious?"

"Is there a problem?" It seemed there was.

She hesitated a moment, then answered. "I entered the contest on the off chance you might like my style and choose to offer me a lesser job in the company. I supposed..."

"Yes?" Daveed prompted her.

"I supposed that there were other contestants with much more experience than I have."

"Experience is not as important to me as vision. You match the direction I am seeking to take *Spice* in, and that is the most important factor." That and the fact that Arren found not a single indication that Joy might be affiliated with or susceptible to coercion from any anti-Xxan groups.

"You're offering me the job of assistant designer?" It seemed she was still having problems believing he was offering her an executive position.

It was time to shock her with the truth. "Actually, you will be the head designer of *Joy by Spice* line, the sister line to the one I head. I trust that would be acceptable to you?"

"You're keeping my name on the line?"

He raised her hand and kissed her knuckles again. "Why interfere with perfection?"

"You're serious. Aren't you?"

Daveed furrowed his brow. Hadn't he made himself clear yet? "The job is yours, Ms. Patterson. The only question is... How much will you make me pay to secure your services as a designer for my company?"

Her face went scarlet, and she seemed to have trouble forming words.

Knowing he had the upper hand, Daveed took advantage of it like the Dominant he was born to be. "I know what I will do. I'll offer you more than any other firm would consider proper. Then you cannot possibly refuse the job."

She swallowed hard.

Daveed leaned down and whispered a figure in her ear. He could go much higher, but he suspected she'd believe anything higher a joke.

She gasped. "That is more than fair, Mr. Raashh."

"Daveed," he invited her. "I assume we will be on a first-name basis when we are working together."

"Joy." Her hand tightened slightly on his fingers. "I think I should see the contract."

"Of course." Daveed left her side, punched the salary amount into the contract Arren had finalized that morning, and collected it from the print tray. The intricacies of legal agreements were something Daveed wished he could live without, but business demanded it. For that reason, Daveed was glad his younger brother was a prodigy in the minutia of legal and contract terms.

Joy sat on the chair he used to design, one shapely leg crossed over the other. She was silent, but her breath heaved in and out at certain points. Daveed tensed every time it happened, certain that Arren had put something in the contract she'd find unacceptable.

At last, she looked up at him. "Do you have a pen, Daveed?"

* * * *

Joy drank down half the glass of wine in a single swallow, containing her need to shout in triumph. She'd done it. She'd signed a contract with a major fashion house.

But not just any contract. *I've signed a contract as lead designer of my own signature line, produced by said house. And at a huge salary. With bonuses.*

She'd come away from the non-existent negotiations with everything she'd ever hoped for and ten times the money she'd expected to be offered at this stage in her career.

Daveed had introduced a budget and advanced the idea of her choosing an assistant designer from the remaining contest entries. By his tone, she guessed he wasn't sure she would find any complementary designers in the group.

Of course, she had to pack and buy her way out of her lease over the next two weeks before she was due to start work at *Spice*. Daveed had informed her that the moving service would be at her disposal, whenever she was ready for them. Her packed belongings would be transported by van to the airport and by shuttle to Virginia.

Daveed had arranged for immediate transfer of three months of her salary as a signing bonus to "offset the financial and emotional burdens of her move". *Spice* even maintained a secure building, and she'd been granted the penthouse as part of her contract.

He'd made the choice to sign the contract painless for her. The only thing that bothered her about the entire thing was her attraction to Daveed.

Don't mix business with pleasure. Remember that, Joy. It's bitten you in the rear before.

* * * *

Daveed sat behind his desk, smiling at the signed contract. The moment he'd met Joy's eyes, he'd known he had to have her with him in the office.

That had been confirmed for him shortly before she'd left for home, when she'd suggested a change to one of his new designs that transformed a simple dress into a work of art. As he'd believed, her design sense was precisely what *Spice* needed.

Precisely what I need. Of course, there was no saying Joy would be more than a worker to him. Despite her maddening scent, her body language, and her stunning looks, she might simply be a sensual woman, in general. Her arousal and subconscious invitations hadn't necessarily been aimed at him.

As always, the choice of mate is the female's.

Celeste appeared in the doorway. "I take it the interview didn't go well?" she inquired.

His smile widened. "It did. A copy of Ms. Patterson's contract is in the files."

Joy. She invited me to call her by her given name. But Joy will be an executive of the company; there is no reason to extend that invitation to the secretarial and personal assistant staff.

I should let Celeste know what I need from her. "She'll be using the penthouse, so a cleaning crew should be assigned to prepare it. And...flowers when she is expected to arrive. She will need a personal assistant. The adjoining office will need to be outfitted to match mine."

"In every detail?"

"If Ms. Patterson wishes to change her furnishings, she may. To begin with, the two offices will match precisely." Joy had liked the design of his office, so assuming she wanted a matching office wasn't a stretch of the imagination.

Celeste's jaw tightened, but she didn't voice whatever she took exception to. "Right away, Mr. Raashh." She was gone before he could decide if he was overreacting to her expression and the weight in her step or not.

Chapter Two

Joy strode onto the stage behind Daveed, Andre at her heels. The head of PR, Lyle Nelson, was already at the podium, giving the details of the contest *Spice* had run.

"It is my pleasure to present the winners of the *Spice Clothing Design Contest*: Ms. Joy Patterson, head designer of *Joy by Spice*, and Mr. Andre Banna, assistant designer of *Joy Juniors*."

He made an expansive arm movement, and Joy and Andre took positions on either side of him while the audience politely clapped. Daveed made his way to Joy's side. On the screens behind them, the newly-designed logos and a handful of product pictures from their entry videos rotated.

The media in attendance started asking questions immediately.

"There was supposed to be a single winner. Is there a reason two were chosen?"

Daveed answered that one. "I was so impressed by the Joy line, I decided to acquire it and the design services of Ms. Patterson nearly immediately. It might have stopped there, but I'd instructed her to hire any other designers she felt would fit well with the existing lines. She chose Mr. Banna."

Another spoke up. "So Ms. Patterson asked to award another of the designers in competition with her?"

Daveed waved Joy on, indicating that she should answer that for herself.

"It only made sense to begin my search for an assistant from the existing contest entries. Andre brings something to the mix that had been missing before."

"And that is?" the reporter continued.

"A children's line that would appeal to both Xxanian mix and human children. Until now, the *Spice Clothing* for children line has been primarily *S'suumea* and *S'suuhhea*, designed for Xxanian children. Why don't you tell them about the *Joy Junior* line, Andre?"

He spoke up in his deeply accented voice, laying out the range of products the *Joy Junior* line would offer. The way Andre shifted from foot to foot made it clear that he was much less comfortable with public speaking than he was with designing clothing.

At last, Lyle called for another question.

"Ms. Patterson, how are you enjoying work at *Spice Industries*?"

She smiled. "It's a dream come true. I've never been in the company of so many highly talented individuals, all working as a team. The feedback makes for a very...nurturing and creative environment."

Before Lyle could move on, the same reporter launched in with another question. "Have there been any problems?"

Joy was sure her smile faltered a bit. "I'm not sure I know what you mean. What kind of problems could I possibly encounter?"

"As a woman working in a Xxanian company. Have you had any difficulties?"

"A large portion of our workforce is female," she replied, unsure of what he was hinting at. It wasn't like there was any lack of women at *Spice*.

"Forty-five percent," Lyle offered smartly. "Only two of the female employees are Xxanian, which means the human female employees are well over forty-four percent of our workforce."

The reporter persisted. "Working so closely with a Xxanian male, are there any—?"

Joy cut him off. "I'm not sure what you're insinuating or why, precisely, but the answer is 'no'. I have not had any interracial or interpersonal difficulties with the Xxanian males at *Spice*. Can we move on, please?"

Lyle motioned to another of the reporters, who asked Andre a question.

Joy tried to focus on his answer, but something about the earlier reporter kept drawing her back. Something about him made her nervous, uneasy...even slightly afraid.

Daveed moved closer to her, and he whispered to her. "You are safe at *Spice*. There is nothing to fear here."

She looked up at him, offering a smile. Camera flashes went off all around them.

Chapter Three

It was nearly seven, and Joy was still at her desk, slaving over new designs for the spring season. Her honey-colored hair made enticing curls around her face when it was down, and Daveed had dreamed of combing his fingers through them for the last month.

"Dinner?" he offered.

Joy looked up from her designs, checked the clock, then checked her watch with a shake of her head. "You want to talk to me, Daveed?"

He smiled. "If you wish to discuss business, we can. I just thought you might enjoy having dinner with me."

She shied a bit on the chair, her expression wary. "That's probably not a good idea."

Daveed tried not to let his disappointment show. "Really? We both need to eat. Is there a reason we shouldn't eat together?"

"I would hope Lyle explained that to you." Her voice was calm and even, but her hands shook.

"The so-called news?" That didn't bother her, did it?

"Daveed, the news will say you're being inappropriate."

"By having dinner with a colleague?" It burned to call her that when he wanted so much more from her.

Joy sighed. "The anti-Xxan guerrillas have attacked for less, you know."

"What if...?" *By the* Seir-*God, I have never had problems talking to a woman before.*

I've never wanted a woman like I want Joy before.

"Daveed?"

"What if I want to be very *appropriate* with you?"

Her eyes widened a bit, enticing him with the blue highlights that matched her jacket. "How...appropriate?" Fear wafted off of her in waves.

I'm scaring her away. I need to retreat. "Never mind. This is the wrong time, I suppose."

She straightened in her chair. "Daveed..."

He waited for her to find the words.

Joy cleared her throat. "Relationships... I mean sexual relationships in the workplace don't often work out, and when they don't, it becomes very difficult to work together in the aftermath. And with the perception problems—"

He nodded grimly, then tipped his head. "Have a good night, Joy. Don't work too late."

"I won't."

Daveed made his way out of the office. He stopped at the security office and ordered the guards to walk Joy to her vehicle. Then he ordered one of them to follow her back to the secured building, just to make sure she arrived safely.

That accomplished, he made his way to the nest, nursing what he suspected was a broken heart.

* * * *

Nine days later

Joy snapped awake, her heart pounding and her breathing ragged. The sweet edge of climax still sang in her body. She moaned at the pull of the sheets against her peaked nipples.

The dream had been like dozens of others she'd had in the last week or a little more. It seemed they'd started when Daveed made the enigmatic statement about being "very appropriate" with her. She still wished she knew what that meant.

The dreams were persistent. In them, Daveed kissed her, touched her, thrust into her, hard and fast.

How many times had she woken, wanting him? At least four times every night, it seemed.

This wasn't smart. Not smart at all. Hadn't Tristan taught her that office flings were a bad idea?

But what if he wants more than a fling? Xxanian men mated for life. *Was that what he meant by "very appropriate"?*

Just the thought sent a zing of pleasure through her. If she was certain Daveed wanted more, there would be no stopping her.

At least she was fairly certain about that.

What if he was saying he wasn't interested in a relationship with her? She wasn't about to suggest one, just to see what his answer would be. If Daveed Raashh wanted something from her, he would have to make a move.

Chapter Four

Joy entered the lobby of the *Spice Building* and smiled to the guards at the desk. She'd nearly reached the elevator when the alarms sounded. She looked back at the desk, dismayed to see the guards dispersing toward the doors with weapons in hand.

"Get aboard the elevator," one of them shouted at her. "Get aboard before the shields come down."

Weapons fire cracked and sizzled, and Joy ducked. The elevator didn't open. She closed her fist on the Identi-chip, wincing as a shot struck the wall above her.

Someone shouted, then cursed fluently. She forced herself not to look. She didn't want to know if the injured party was friend or foe.

At last, the elevator doors started moving. Joy prepared to scramble inside.

She didn't have a chance to. An arm reached out of the half-opened doors and dragged her inside. Joy's scream of fear ended at the sound of Xxan trilling from her rescuer's mouth.

Daveed.

The doors reversed, starting to close when they were only half-open. He pressed her to the wall and shielded her with his body.

Daveed shoved her hard against the wall, and pain sliced along her chin and cheek. The doors slammed shut, the elevator dropped faster than it usually did...then stopped with a jerk, and what could only be blast doors shut around them.

"You're...you're safe, Joy," he breathed. "Safe with me."

Hot liquid streamed down her neck and chest, soaking through her clothing. Realization that he was bleeding hit her hard. How badly was he hurt?

Joy looked up at him, wincing at his dilated eyes and gasping breaths. Daveed opened his mouth as if to say something, then collapsed, landing hard on the floor of the elevator.

She looked down at Daveed, her heart stuttering at the sheer volume of orange blood soaking through his shirt and jacket. Joy launched for the emergency cabinet and dragged it open. There had to be an emergency medical kit inside. She pulled it out, then snatched up the cell phone from the sheath beside it and opened it.

A voice came over it before she could figure out what to dial. "Stay calm. You are inside the blast chamber."

"Daveed has been shot. What do I do?" She knelt to his side and started pulling supplies out of the small duffel.

"How bad is it?"

Blood made lazy tracks from beneath his shoulder. Most likely the entry wound. "He's bleeding out fast, I think. What do I need?"

"The green bag." In the background, she could hear other voices relaying the information.

Most likely to first responders or SLAL. *Or both.* Joy rifled through the pile, found the green bag, and ripped it open. "What now?"

"Pull out the yellow pouch. Place the medicated towels over the worst of the wounds and press hard on them. It will slow his bleeding."

Turning Daveed to his side to find the entry wound wasn't easy, but she managed to get a towel on each side before she let him drop again. Joy squeezed tight, hoping for the best.

"Done?" the voice asked.

"Done, but he needs help. He's already lost a lot of blood." A trickle let her know that she'd only slowed the flow and not stopped it. "And he's still bleeding."

"On its way."

The blast doors shifted, and the elevator started to rise.

Joy pressed down harder, cursing aloud at the fact that Daveed continued to bleed faster than she was comfortable with. "Don't you dare die on me, Daveed. Don't you dare."

The elevator stopped, but the doors didn't open.

"Where is that help?" she demanded.

"Five minutes away."

"I don't know if he has *two* minutes."

There was a moment of silence. Even the voices in the background went still.

A buzzing voice on the other side of the phone had her breathing a sigh of relief. "Twenty seconds." It wasn't the same man she'd been talking to moments before, but it was giving the answer Daveed needed.

The doors started opening, and Joy held her breath. She looked over her shoulder and sobbed at the sight of Karl loping toward them.

He vaulted across Daveed's legs, landing smoothly on the opposite side of his body from her. "Keep pressure on," he ordered.

Joy nodded, and he lifted Daveed from the floor as if he weighed no more than she did. She rushed to stay even with him. They jogged to the shuttle, Daveed between them.

Her heel caught on the edge of a roof tile, and the shoe whipped off her foot in mid-step. She hobbled along without it. At the step up into the shuttle, she levered the other shoe off and went in barefoot.

They lowered Daveed to the floor, and Karl spun away to the door, barking out orders in Xxan. He looked back at Joy, wide-eyed. "Your shoes," he shouted.

"Don't be stupid," Joy replied. "Just get Daveed to a doctor."

The shuttle rose and turned, and Joy gasped at the sight of the building rushing away as the door closed. She took a calming breath as it locked. Air rushed past her as the craft pressurized.

"Go, Arren," Karl ordered.

The sudden movement jerked Joy to one side. Then the anti-grav systems kicked in, and she shifted back into a comfortable position.

Karl was already in motion, pulling down medical supplies. He landed hard on his knees, then reached for her face with a cloth in hand.

Joy recoiled. "What is wrong with you?" Daveed was injured, and he was trying to clean her face?

"You're bleeding. A female —"

"Daveed is bleeding *out*. We don't have time to waste on this."

He hesitated, then set the cloth aside. Karl threw himself fully into his work. In short order, he had an IV of what she suspected was crossbred Xxanian blood hooked up. Moments later, he'd placed wrist bands on Daveed. By the tones they were emitting, Joy guessed they were tracking his vital signs and transmitting them to SLAL.

The overhead speakers came to life, and a mixture of Xxan and English overlapped. Mostly Xxan, which left Joy more than a little lost.

"Three minutes," Arren yelled in response to something in Xxan.

He can't mean when we'll be there. It's usually a forty minute or longer trip to the space station.

It is an emergency. Maybe they cleared lanes.

The shuttle came down on its struts with a light bounce, and Karl had the door open a few heartbeats later. Human and crossbred doctors poured into the shuttle. Two of them took over for Joy, and she moved to the far corner to let them work.

The five doctors and Karl hefted Daveed out and onto a gurney. They sprinted away fast enough to make her head spin.

Joy sat on the plush floor of the shuttle, stunned. She wasn't sure what to do or where to go. The last thing she wanted was to end up in their way. *Or somewhere on the space station I shouldn't be. It* is *a military station.*

Arren made his way out of the cockpit, his dark glasses hooked onto the neckline of his t-shirt. He offered his hand to help her to her feet. "Come on. We should have someone tend to you too."

"Can they?" It was out before Joy reasoned it was a stupid question to ask.

He smiled widely, showing his human front teeth and Xxanian rear ones. "Sure. They can treat almost any type of life up here."

She took his hand and allowed Arren to help her up with a whispered "Thanks."

The landing bay was all but deserted. A lone soldier appeared and disappeared again between the stacks of supply crates. They crossed it in silence.

A warning alarm sounded moments before another shuttle bounced in harder than Arren had. Joy winced and glanced around, anticipating the rush of a second medical team. They didn't appear.

The engines screeched to an unnatural stop, and the door burst out. Joy took an unsteady step back at the sight of the hulking pureblood Xxanian stalking their direction.

Raashh. He had the look of a father who'd been told his son had been grievously injured. The fact that Raashh was here and not cleaving those responsible in two surprised her, given what she'd learned about their race in school.

The string of Xxan rumbling from the elder started halfway across the landing bay from them. Whatever Arren said in response resulted in a snort and a bark of order from his *seir.*

The change in mood came in a heartbeat. The moment Raashh looked Joy's direction, his entire body tensed. His ridge plates rose, as did the frills atop his massive head. Raashh roared, showing his hunting teeth, and his frills shook in warning.

Joy pressed to the wall behind her, shaking hard. There was no question he intended to rip her to pieces, and she had no idea why. *Am I too close to Arren for his comfort? Is protecting his young instinctual for him?*

Arren stepped between them, growling and grumbling. Hisses and trills followed. The noises Raashh made in response implied he intended to go through Arren if he had to.

The young Xxanian snapped and switched to English. "She couldn't order Daveed not to bleed. Neither can you. She saved his life. Don't forget it."

Joy hoped that was true, but considering the amount of blood Daveed had lost, that wasn't certain.

The elder's frills folded in, and he tipped his head to Joy. One big hand came down on Arren's head, and he ruffled his son's hair, leaving his curls in disarray. Then Raashh stalked down the corridor.

"What did he say?" Joy asked, trying to reason that the crisis was over and her knees could stop shaking. Her knees weren't listening, it seemed.

"He warned me not to fly into a war zone again, even if my brother dies next time. I'm a Subdominant. I would not make a good warrior."

Joy rolled her eyes. "And?" *About me?*

"He told me to see to your care and comfort. Raashh—and I are in your debt, Ms. Patterson."

She didn't know what to say to that, so Joy resisted the urge to question it. Instead, she followed Arren to a medical bay.

There was already a doctor waiting for her. She motioned to the bed and the clear plastic bag next to it. "I'll need you to remove your clothing and put it in the bag. There is a shower through that door—you can change in there—and a clean medical gown hung in there for your use. After that, we'll get you patched up."

"Can the clothing be cleaned?"

"I'm afraid it's evidence, miss. But we'll—"

"I'll take care of clothing, Ms. Patterson," Arren interrupted whatever the doctor was going to say. He started to turn away.

"You don't have to," Joy called out after him.

Arren offered her a smile. "I own a clothing company. It's really no trouble at all."

Before she could answer, he was racing down the corridor. Thankfully, he wasn't going toward the shuttles. If he went back to *Spice* now, his *seir* was sure to hurt them both for it.

* * * *

The doctor returned to the room with a garment bag. She'd disappeared at a comm a few minutes earlier. "This was just delivered for you, and Arren informs me that Karl is ready to take you home in Raashh's shuttle, at your convenience."

She nodded and took the bag. With it laid out over the examination bed, Joy unzipped it and started parting the tissue inside.

"If you would like to speak to a cosmetic surgeon, there are several I can recommend. Raashh will pay for it, of course."

"What? No. You can hardly see the scar." Even a bit of face powder would cover it completely. Someone who didn't know about the attack probably wouldn't even notice it.

She pulled out the dress, swallowing a gasp of shock. It was the most expensive dress *Spice* made, one of Daveed's early commercial successes in the human market. It was a full-length evening gown that was nearly backless and had a long slit up to the center of her left thigh. A quick check showed it was her size. Moreover, there were underwear and shoes to match it in the bag.

"That's pretty," the doctor noted.

"Yes. It is." It was the also the inspiration of her entire line. She'd adored Daveed's sense of style and had wanted to make clothing as beautiful as his.

"If you'd rather have privacy..." the doctor hinted.

"I would. Thank you."

She left with a smile, and Joy dressed. Every touch teased her body with sensual awareness. Though her new salary would allow her to purchase clothing like this, Joy had never dreamed of owning this dress.

Her senses scattered, Joy left the room. Arren was waiting for her in the hall, and she offered him a smile.

"I hope the dress is to your liking," he offered in a tone that felt far too formal for a child to utter.

"It is. Thank you, but really... This is too much."

He snorted. "It's nothing." He turned away, leading the way to the landing bay. "Besides, I know it's your favorite."

Her heart stuttered. "How could you know a thing like that?"

Arren chuckled. "When you look at it...even an image of it, your eyes linger, your scent changes. You wanted this dress, so that's what I ordered for you."

Words stuck in her throat. "Thank you, Arren. It's lovely."

"It is," he agreed.

There was a comfortable moment of silence between them.

Arren broke it. "If it wouldn't be too intrusive to say something?" he hinted. "I don't want to offend you."

Joy stared at him, shocked by a child of eight saying something so adult. "I'll try not to be offended."

He looked up at her, his expression starkly serious. "I've seen the way you look at Daveed."

Her cheeks flamed at that. "Arren, romances in the workplace aren't really professional...or smart."

"I've seen the way Daveed looks at you too. I don't think it would be sex between you. If you let him, he would be a very good mate."

Words deserted her. Joy stopped cold in the middle of the hallway, finding it hard to make eye contact with Arren.

"It wasn't an accident that Daveed was on that elevator with you. It wasn't fate. He was on his way to the shuttle with me, ordered to evacuate by our *seir*. He chose to come back for you. He demanded it. Daveed all but threw me at Karl and told him to get me out of there. Then he ordered the elevator to take him to you."

She realized her mouth was hanging open and snapped it shut. "I don't..."

"You do understand, Joy. Any other woman, my brother would have let the security forces do their jobs. Not you."

Her nerves rattled, she started walking again. Part of her wanted to protest that Daveed couldn't feel that way about her. Another knew Arren wasn't lying. *The Xxan don't believe in lying.*

What did that mean for her? Joy shivered in realization. Daveed had risked death to save her, when he was halfway to escape.

At the shuttle, Arren took her hand and bowed over it, bringing the back of her hand to his forehead. She suspected it was a Xxanian sign of respect of some sort.

"Rest well, Joy. Please...don't try to come to work tomorrow. Allow us time to institute new security measures. When you come back... I've ordered your driver to use the secured level of the garage for you, from now on." He hesitated. "Think about what I said?"

Answering that was difficult, though Joy didn't think she could think of anything else. "I will, Arren. Thank you."

He disappeared with a smile and a wave.

Karl stepped down the stairs from the shuttle. "If I may be so bold, Ms. Patterson?"

"It seems to be the day for it."

"Beg your pardon?" His brow creased in confusion.

She managed a weak smile. "Go on."

He raised her hand and pressed his forehead to it, just as Arren had. After a whispered Xxanian phrase, he stepped back and offered his hand to help her onto the shuttle.

Joy hesitated. "What...? Arren did the same thing. What does that mean, precisely?"

Karl cleared his throat. "It means we respect your courage and strength, Ms. Patterson. What you did for Daveed—"

"What about what Daveed did for me?"

His expression said she was being a fool, though Joy didn't understand why he would think that.

Chapter Five

Three days later

Daveed left the driver in the bunker and took the elevator up to his office suite, his mind and emotions in a riot. Who knew what awaited him? The certainty that Joy had resigned cast a pall not unlike the loss of his mother over him.

But this wasn't illness. There is no fighting a sudden, acute illness. Joy was shot at, attacked in a building I'd assured her was secure. I wasn't fast enough to shield her. Of course, she'll leave.

All too soon, the doors opened on the thirty-second floor, and Daveed exited the elevator with a confident stride that belied his inner torment.

If she's gone, I have to hide my emotions. He steeled himself for the worst at the sight of Celeste rushing toward him. *I should have asked about Joy before I got here.*

Stupid! It would have told Celeste too much.

"It's so good to have you back, Mr. Raashh." She pivoted neatly, reversed course, and matched his stride.

"Quite good to be here." It was. *Five millimeters to the left and I wouldn't be here. If Joy had been slower or Arren hadn't broken with our* seir's *orders, I wouldn't be.* "What is my schedule for this morning?" *Please let it be light.* Pretending his healing wound didn't pain him was difficult enough. The uncertainty over Joy was worse.

"Mr. Rowe sent over new contracts for your signature."

"I'll look over them tonight." Actually, Arren would. At eight years old, his younger brother had displayed a tremendous aptitude for business. *Someday, he may be in charge of* Spice Industries. That day would be a relief for Daveed.

She tapped at the screen on her tablet computer. "Ms. Patterson is setting up the presentation of the new line in conference room three. She said to let you know it would be ready for your perusal any time."

His heart stuttered, and the healing tissue in his chest pulled and ached. "Now?" *She's here.*

"Is it a problem? I can reschedule her to—"

"No." *It's not a problem at all. It's a...joy. A delight.* He composed himself. "I was simply verifying my schedule for the day." He was lying. It was the only reason a Xxanian *would* lie—to protect a female or child.

"Ms. Patterson is your only meeting today, so it is no problem to move her, if you want me to."

Suspicion made his blood burn. "Is it? Why so light?" He suspected he knew. *Damned doctors and my* seir.

"Your doctors' orders," she confirmed for him.

Rayn, you are a damned interfering man.

Forget it. It gives me time to talk to Joy.

"Is there a problem, Mr. Raashh?"

"No. I'll see Ms. Patterson now. Handle any calls. I do not wish to be disturbed." He left Celeste far behind and marched into the conference room she'd indicated.

The door swung open noiselessly, revealing a lush ass encased in silk and—he was sure—nothing else. He closed the door, his primary hard and heavy behind his trousers.

Her scent was potent and alluring, and she shifted further, still folded over the table.

She wants me. Is she inviting me? If she was, Joy would be his only appointment...and not because Rayn insisted on it. In fact, it was a sure bet that Rayn would be irked that Daveed was considering such hearty exercise.

"How are you, Joy?"

* * * *

His voice sent pleasant shivers down her spine, and Joy considered her position. She hadn't intended to meet Daveed in such a provocative pose, but her body heated at the idea of him taking advantage of it.

He didn't, and she turned to face him. Daveed stood, his ankles slightly parted, as imposing as always, despite his injury.

His cock was hard and pressing out against his trousers. Joy licked her upper lip slowly, and he breathed in deeply.

Scenting me. He knows I want him.

She leaned back on the table, seeking something solid to support her when her shaking knees weren't helping much. "I should be asking you that question." Her voice was breathy and lacking the conviction she'd wanted it to carry. *How can I think with his cock so ready, let alone speak?*

Daveed stepped toward her, his expression solemn. "My injuries are nothing."

"Nothing? You must be—"

Her lungs and throat seized at the brush of his fingers against the line of scar tissue on her chin.

His words caressed her lips with heat. "Yours is intolerable to me." He traced the line again.

"Just a scratch," she whispered. "You could have died."

"I would willingly die to save you from harm. *Any* male would willingly die to save a female from harm." It sounded like he was correcting himself.

"Not any male." Her ex certainly wouldn't have put himself in danger to save her.

"Any *honorable* male would."

"Yes. I believe that," she agreed.

They stood there, close enough to kiss. When Daveed didn't make the first move, Joy's nerves deserted her.

She motioned to the display. "The proposed line will be—"

"Is that what you want to show me?" There was nothing coy in that, nothing teasing.

Words failed her. Joy shook her head slowly.

"Then it can wait." Still Daveed made no move toward her.

I refused him. I need to do something he can't mistake as interest. She wrapped her arms around his neck and rose on tiptoe, pressing her lips to his.

Daveed didn't hesitate. His arms encircled her body and drew her flush to his chest. His scent made her head spin, and Joy opened her lips to gasp.

His tongue dipped inside, and she moaned at the taste of him in her mouth. *Musk and spice.* She'd always thought it was cologne, but it was his natural flavor. Joy entwined her tongue with his, drinking in the potent flavor of Daveed.

He caressed a hand down her shoulder and arm. His hand angled away, and the sound of the doors locking shut followed.

He has a button to secure the doors. It wasn't unexpected. Many corporate meeting rooms had such security features.

The sound around them muted, and she shivered in understanding. He'd also soundproofed the room.

Daveed drew back, and she stared at him blearily. He'd dimmed the lights in the room and removed his sunglasses. His eyes were narrowed, and the pupils were widened until they almost formed circles instead of slits.

He stroked at her throat, making designs with his smooth thumb. "Do you want this, Joy?"

She nodded, managing a gasped "yes" to go along with it.

Daveed slipped his hand under the shoulder of the low-cut dress she'd worn, eased the fabric off her shoulder, and massaged her bare skin. "If I do this, I am not content for it to be one time."

Her heart thundered in excitement. "I don't want a one-night stand either." She blushed in the realization that he hadn't said that. Xxanian men were a sexual lot. He could mean he wasn't going to stop with one quick fuck but wasn't offering a long-term relationship. What if Arren was wrong? Not lying but reading his brother wrong?

He cocked his head to one side. "I intend to claim you as my mate, if you have the least interest in—"

"I do."

That seemed to surprise him.

"I've always believed that casual sexual relationships between coworkers or employee and employer don't work. If you're not in a committed relationship with the other person, it's a recipe for disaster." With humans, it could *still* be a recipe for disaster, but once a Xxanian mated, it was forever. No nasty divorce scenes.

"Are you saying you're willing to mate with me? Now?"

"Yes." Saying it was easier than she'd anticipated it would be.

Daveed looked around. "That would be problematic."

Her hopes sank a bit.

His body pressed to hers. "I suggest we take the edge off of our need here and go somewhere safer to mate."

She nodded. "Safer. Yes." His scent drew her in, and Joy worked his tie open, then the buttons on his shirt. She had to find the source of that enticing scent.

She parted his shirt, tears filling her eyes at the sight of the healing wound. He'd nearly died for her.

"Joy?"

She pressed her lips to the line of healing tissue, and he shivered.

Daveed guided her head to one side, situating her at his male nipple. "I believe this is what you really want."

The spice against her lips made her moan. Joy licked her lips, and he gasped. She sucked at him, and Daveed's hand closed in her hair. She didn't question that his musk was an aphrodisiac. And she didn't care. Joy sucked more avidly, then moved to the other side.

Daveed drew her back, then brought his mouth down on hers. The kiss left no doubt that they were going to finish what they'd started. Here and now.

He broke away, and she opened her eyes, staring up into his. Once he had her complete attention, he started talking.

"And now, Joy, I will sample your musk."

Her breath caught in her throat at that pronouncement. She reached for the zipper at the back of her dress, but his hands were there first. Letting Daveed strip her clothes off was a decadent pleasure, and Joy settled back, indulging in it.

The silk eased down her body, and Daveed sank to one knee, keeping pace with it. His tongue circled one nipple, and Joy grasped at the back of his head, enjoying his smooth skin. His tasting touches became sucking so avid she felt love bites rising on her skin.

He pushed her dress up her thighs, baring her. This dress wasn't meant to be worn with underwear. She was glad that she chose it.

Daveed left her breasts, and his hot breath teased at her sensitized skin. He lifted her by the waist and settled Joy on the edge of the table, then pushed her knees apart.

The first puff over her core wrenched a moan from her. His tongue came next, more mobile than a human man's. He traced her, inside and out, then started thrusting inside her, the slightly-roughened surface of his tongue propelling her into bliss.

Her sense of balance deserted her, and Joy reached behind her, hoping to brace herself up. The stacks of folded silk went sliding across the top of the table. She landed in the midst of it, silk tantalizing her back and thighs, while Daveed drove her toward release.

She abandoned her attempts at quiet in the realization that he'd soundproofed the room. Moans turned to pleas, then to shouts, as Joy catapulted over the edge of reason.

Still Daveed didn't stop. He was ravenous, determined, but what he was determined to accomplish, Joy couldn't say.

At last, he rose to his feet between her spread knees. Joy trailed her gaze to his cock, erect and weeping pre-cum already, his trousers spread just enough to allow her a peek at his hairless balls. His shirt was open wide around his chest, and his jacket was off, probably dropped to the floor. She licked her lips, wondering if all of him tasted of that hint of spice.

Daveed groaned. "Not now. If you do, I'll start claiming you here, and this is definitely the wrong place to begin that process."

Joy nodded her agreement. In the office wasn't even appropriate for what they'd done so far, but that didn't mean she was going to stop him now.

He reached out and turned her until she was bent over the conference table, her legs quaking lightly beneath her. There was a moment of stillness.

"Daveed?"

He slipped to the hilt inside her, his silk-mix trousers teasing at her buttocks as he started thrusting. One large hand closed on her hip, holding Joy's midsection away from the edge of the table. The other closed on a breast, kneading lightly.

Joy gasped, her body rocketing toward another release. *By the stars, I should have done this weeks ago.*

"You're mine," Daveed grumbled. His thrusts came faster and harder, as if in a physical representation of that proclamation.

Her body tightened, then shot into climax. Joy was vaguely aware that she was shouting.

Daveed's cock erupted, filling her with a glorious wave of heat. He was growling, every muscle taut against her body. He eased her against the edge of the table, then started laying kisses on the back of her neck and shoulder.

He eased out of her, then turned Joy to the edge of the table. Just when she thought he was going to kiss her, perhaps even thrust into her again, Daveed started drawing the dress up her body. He reached around her and eased the zipper up, bringing their bodies in close contact again.

"Daveed?"

"The sooner we dress, the sooner I can claim you properly."

"At your home?"

He hesitated for a moment. "No. We'll want privacy. Your penthouse is in the secured building. Would you mind going there?"

She shook her head.

Daveed lifted her from the table and settled Joy to her feet. He smoothed her dress down her thighs. Then he scooped up his jacket and held it up for her to ease her arms into it. Joy complied, and he buttoned it for her. She cuffed up the arms twice, and still her fingers peeked from the edges.

He buttoned his shirt, leaving the top two buttons open and the tie hanging loose down the front. Then he tucked his cock into his trousers and fastened them, blousing his shirt slightly.

Daveed held out his hand to her.

Joy glanced around at the destruction they were leaving behind. Her face heated. Between the way they were dressed and the state of the conference room, there would be no question what they'd been doing in here.

He placed his fingertips beneath her chin and tipped Joy's face up. "We'll be leaving on my personal elevator. No one will be in this room until we come back again."

She nodded, though she wasn't sure where the personal elevator might be. She'd never seen one in his office. Maybe it was a hidden elevator. Joy looked around at the walls. "Where?"

Daveed laughed heartily at her question. "There are three. I'll show you how to access them all. But, for now..."

He strode to the far side of the room, where a Van Gough that she'd always suspected was the original hung on the wall. Daveed spoke in smooth, trilling Xxan. Then he waved her over to him. Joy made her way to his side.

Daveed tipped his head down and whispered in her ear. "Say your name and the words 'transport now'."

"Joy transport now."

Another order in Xxan left his lips. Was he training the elevator to respond to her?

"Say it again, but this time, say your full name."

She looked up at him, questioning. "My name as it is now or...?"

"My woman is quick and intelligent," he breathed. "But I knew that. The name you will use once we are mated."

She nodded. "Joy Raashh transport now."

He smiled. "Again. The same words."

"Joy Raashh transport now."

Daveed pressed a kiss to her lips. Joy turned her head, amazed that the elevator door was halfway open, moving silently; one section of wall pulled forward and slid aside in front of another.

"Anytime you feel the need to call the elevator—in an emergency or just to move about the building without going through the public areas of it, you will use those words. It is keyed to your voice, and once we have mated, I will key the interior controls to recognize your biological signature."

He guided her onto the elevator, and the door closed behind them automatically. Daveed pressed a button marked RG.

"RG?"

"Raashh's personal garage area. The vehicles transporting members of our nest park in a secured area."

"Understandable." The area her driver dropped her in at the penthouse had the same security, as did the one her driver had taken her to that morning. Was that Raashh's personal garage? Something told her it was.

Another question occurred to her. "So, if I pushed the button now, before you've keyed the controls to me?"

"The elevator would lock down and summon our security team."

"And you can't key it to me now, because...?"

"Your biological signature will change slightly during mating. Not significantly, but a bit. It's best to wait and not confuse the system."

The door opened, and Daveed took her arm. Their leisurely stroll across the garage ended at a streak of what could only be a Xxanian bodyguard coming their way.

Daveed barked an order in Xxan.

The bodyguard came to a halt. He tipped his head to Daveed. "My apologies. When I saw you coming down, I thought there was something wrong." He tipped his head to Joy. "Ms. Patterson."

Joy wondered how he knew her name.

Her limo pulled up behind his, and her driver vaulted out. He rushed to open the door for her, looking more than a little rattled.

Daveed waved him off. "We won't be needing you, Beel. Joy will be with me for the rest of the day. You're relieved."

Her driver tipped his head, though his expression said he was confused. "Very well, Daveed. Call for me if Ms. Patterson requires my services today."

Her cheeks heated. From what she understood, she wouldn't require his services for several days. Beel's eyes narrowed, and he withdrew.

Daveed led her to the back door of his limousine, and his bodyguard moved to open it for them. Joy slid onto the seat. Halfway in, she looked up at the bodyguard and went still. He'd stiffened, and his tongue peeked past his lips.

Tongue scenting. He knows we've had sex. The other male's cock stirred behind his uniform pants.

An order from Daveed had him straightening, backing off a step, leaving her field of vision.

Joy moved across the seat, and Daveed joined her. The bodyguard closed the door and rounded the car to the driver's seat.

Once he was settled, he questioned Daveed. "The nest?" he asked.

"No. The penthouse in town."

"Your *seir*—"

"Now," Daveed snapped.

"As you wish, Daveed."

Once they were in motion, Daveed closed the panel between the driver and themselves. He sealed his mouth to hers.

The arousal was scorching, and Joy climbed astride him. She reached down and stroked his cock through his trousers. Even if they didn't have time to have sex again, she wanted to touch him.

Daveed didn't argue it. His moan said he wanted precisely what she was doing.

Joy gasped at the feeling of a narrow column, growing next to his cock. *Two cocks. It must be his secondary.* She stroked more avidly, bringing him up.

He pulled back from the kiss, his breathing ragged. "You shouldn't. If I come, it's begun."

She stroked harder, gasping at his length coming up, surpassing his primary cock in length.

"Be sure, Joy. My secondary will bind us, nearly at the first touch of my *Zhigaaal.*"

"Good."

Both cocks jerked beneath her hand. Joy wanted to open his trousers, but something told her he wouldn't allow that. She went back to stroking, watching the secondary grow avidly.

A wet spot appeared at the head of the secondary, beneath the waistband of his trousers.

So long.

Joy's mouth went dry in the memory of Daveed's warning. It was her choice to bind with him. She touched the spot, her fingertips tingling. His secondary twitched, and she went back to rubbing, bringing up more of the stinging liquid.

She trailed her fingertips in it, her attention rapt on the growing spot. Some primal voice in her mind urged her to rub it on her clit, on her slit, to let Daveed lick it off. Somehow, Joy knew he would. It was madness. How could she know such a thing?

Her heart thundered and her head spun pleasantly. She wanted him inside her. *Now.* A glance at the darkened window showed they were nearly to the penthouse. *Soon.*

The scent rising between them was sublime. Joy licked her lips again, visions of her returning the favor of him eating her to climax running a sex tape looping in her mind.

"You need me already. Don't you?" Daveed breathed. "I knew you would."

"I want to suck you," she admitted. "Now. And then—"

"In a moment. I promise you, I'll let you suck me."

"Your secondary," she qualified.

"Most definitely."

The car's engine turned off, and she eased off of Daveed's lap and to the seat, pulling down at the dress. She glanced at the dual ridges pressing to the front of his trousers.

"Joy?" he prompted.

"There is no way we're going to hide that."

Daveed laughed. "There's no reason *to* hide it." He pushed the door open and stepped out. Then Daveed reached a hand in for Joy.

She stood, shooting a sideward glance at the bodyguard. He didn't look their direction, though she had no doubts he was more than aware of precisely how far they'd gone in the car.

They were in the elevator when the bodyguard spoke again.

"I will have to tell your *seir* where you are, Daveed. He will be expecting you."

Daveed raised Joy's hand and kissed her palm, making her heart race. "Tell him."

The elevator door closed behind them, and Daveed swept Joy into a heated kiss that made her wonder if they would even make it out of the elevator before the mating started.

She reached for his trousers, and he let her unfasten them, though he held her tight to his body so she couldn't slide to her knees as she wanted to. Joy worked her hand between them. She wrapped it around both cocks, then released the primary and stroked just the secondary. It was the secondary she wanted to explore. It moved against her hand as a cat's tail might, making her gasp.

The pre-cum on his secondary was more potent when it touched her skin directly, and she moaned. Air scorched in her lungs, and heat licked down her inner thighs.

The elevator door opened, and Daveed backed her out of it, their lips parting and meshing over and over again.

"Please, let me suck you, Daveed." They were inside the penthouse now.

"You want to now?" He wasn't teasing. It seemed the idea inflamed him. "You're already mine, Joy. If you do this now, you will be fully committed to the binding, lost in the thrall of my *Zhigaaal*. We can stop for a moment. Eat. There won't be time again for quite a while."

"No. There's only one thing I want to eat, and that's you."

He didn't release her immediately. Instead, he unzipped the back of her dress. "Take off your dress."

He took a step back, his expression hot in promise, while she accomplished that task. Daveed pushed his trousers away, letting them fall to his ankles. He toed off his shoes, then kicked his trousers away.

"Unbutton my shirt."

His tone of command caused a pleasant clench of her sheath. Joy stepped toward him, wearing only her heels, feeling sexy. She undid the buttons, sucking at his chest as it appeared in the opening.

"That's right," Daveed urged her. "Feed yourself on my musk."

"It's an aphrodisiac. Isn't it?"

"Not as much as the pure *Zhigaaal* from my secondary is." As if in demonstration, he reached down and massaged the base of the long, slim secondary cock, bringing more of his sex pheromone up. It trickled down the head, thick and creamy.

She pushed the shirt off his body, letting it fall to the floor. Daveed brought up one foot and then the other, pulling off his socks, leaving them both nude, save her heels.

Come fuck me heels. Oh yes, come fuck me, Daveed.

He stood there, every muscle taut, his blue-gold gaze stroking her body like a physical caress, both cocks swaying her direction, as if begging for her touch. Joy reached for him.

"Be still a moment. I want to look at you."

To look at what is his.

Screw that. I want more. "Daveed, please."

"Very well. Suck." There was a challenge in that.

It was a challenge Joy intended to take him up on. She went to her knees between his ankles, the thick rug cushioning her. She didn't question that he wanted her to suck his secondary, in specific. "I want to suck the primary later," she informed him.

"Anytime you want." His hand cupped the back of her head and guided Joy closer to his body.

She didn't want to suck the primary right now. The scent of spice and musk from his secondary was too enticing.

Joy sucked in the head, gasping at the acid burn against her lips and tongue. It went to her head and her slit, increasing her urgency while it scattered her thinking mind. The only thing that was clear to her was the idea that the sooner she sucked him off, the sooner he would be inside her body again. *Where he belongs.*

Another spurt of the *Zhigaaal* filled her mouth, and she swallowed it. Then another. It took Joy a moment to realize Daveed was massaging it up for her, getting her drunk on his aphrodisiac fluids.

It's mine. I want it. Joy sucked him deeper, reveling in Daveed's groan, in his hand tightening against the back of her head. He thrust into her mouth, testing her ability to take more. She tensed for the gag reflex, but it didn't come.

Joy pushed her face to his hairless body, groaning at the feeling of his secondary pressing deep into her throat. She started to pull back, but Daveed held her there. He roared, his body tensing. His musky cum filling her throat and setting off her instinct to swallow it.

Her muscles went lax, and Joy crumpled into Daveed's waiting hands. He scooped her up and bolted for the bed. Everything around her was disjointed, blocks of color and snips of sound and sensation.

The burn against her nipples had her arching off the bed. Daveed pinned both her hands to the mattress with one large hand.

His secondary trailed up and down her sensitized core, between her widely-spread legs. She gasped at the sensation of it turning and stroking, snakelike. The burning came a moment later, his *Zhigaaal* coating her. She dimly noted that he wasn't just massaging it up for her. He was stroking himself off to provide a full climax of the pheromone on her body. That accomplished, he started rubbing it into her, heating her blood further.

Her breathing went choppy, and her body burned. She need him inside her. *Now. Now. Now!* Joy climaxed, screaming, then begging him to take her.

The secondary scorched a trail up her vaginal walls, and she bucked. The need for his primary hit her hard, and she tried to ask for it.

Daveed pressed her hard to the mattress, his body a delightful weight on her. "Soon, Joy. Let me anoint you with my secondary. Then you'll be ready for my primary."

He thrust the narrow column inside her, filling her body with the stinging pheromone. Joy screamed in the mixture of pleasure and pain. Her muscles failed her again, and she lay boneless beneath him, half-hearing Daveed's soothing words.

"Again, Joy. Once more. Then we move on."

He was thrusting again before she regained use of her muscles.

Deeper. Deeper than she'd ever felt someone before, she was sure.

He climaxed again with a growl.

Joy whimpered at the sensation of the burning spreading out, lighting up her abdomen in the sublime pleasure-pain. Then the muscle numbing sensation overtook her again.

Daveed left her body in a rush. The sting at the ring of her anus made Joy want to protest, to move, but none of her muscles were responding yet.

He didn't tell me this was part of their mating. It was an intrusion.

He stretched her, pushing just inside her body. The spurt of *Zhigaaal* caused the iris to loosen, and he pushed deeper, withdrew until only the tip breached her, and thrust deeper again.

Her muscles gained strength slowly, but Joy didn't move to unseat him. There was something about him fucking her ass, something possessive. He owned all of her, and Daveed could make even this appealing to her. She'd never allowed a man to do this to her before, but she wanted to let Daveed finish. She was sure even this would be mind-blowing.

As if in confirmation of that, his primary pressed to her seam. He held there, teasing her with double penetration. She wiggled against him, urging him on in movements when words deserted her.

"Are you comfortable with this, Joy? I can anoint your ass and leave it. It's only required this once."

"More. Please. More." It was the most coherent thing she could manage.

He pressed deeper, filling both holes together. His primary and secondary brushed on either side of the barrier between the channels, crowding each other, filling her as she'd never been full before.

Joy moaned, raising her hips to play the two cocks inside her. That was all the encouragement Daveed needed. He pounded hard and fast, his noises rising. It took her only a moment to realize this was a particular sexual pleasure for him, something he liked to do but feared she wouldn't permit him to.

The end came quickly, and his cum was soothing against her burning tissues. Again, her body went weak beneath him.

Daveed didn't withdraw. He lay inside her, his secondary stirring slightly against her. He waited for her muscles to recover before he questioned her.

"Tell me what you want, Joy." There was near plea in that.

"Release my hands."

His brows went up in surprise, but he complied. His muscles tensed as if in expectation of some sort of attack.

Joy ran her hands down his chest, around his lower rib cage, and to his ass. She grasped at his buttocks and pulled him tight to her body, forcing her hips down to meet him with a groan.

He didn't take the hint. "Tell me what you want, Joy."

"Don't you dare leave my body, Daveed."

"Both cocks?" he asked, seemingly employing the last of his self-control. "Do you want both?"

"Oh, yes. Now."

He thrust deep, moving minutely inside her, a gentle rocking that had her digging her short nails into the meat of his buttocks. She wanted him like this. Deep, hard, and filling all of her.

In moments, his heat and soothing cool were playing counterpoint inside her, forcing Joy to another climax with him. She was recovering from the stunning effects of it faster each time now, as if she was becoming accustomed to his effect on her.

"More," she begged. "Daveed, please. Give me more."

"Until you beg me not to, you'll have both of my cocks, Joy. Both of them making you mine."

"I am yours." There was no question of that.

* * * *

Daveed thrust into Joy's body, more alive than he'd ever felt. *She is mine. Mine.* Topped off by his secondary a half dozen times already, there would be no separating them. Andy Daahn had proven that, and Daveed reveled in it.

He couldn't wait until the first time she woke from sleep. He already knew what he wanted. Her mouth, moving from cock to cock, maybe even taking both into her heat for the climax, her tongue pressing to the sensitive underside as she swallowed.

But for now, he'd promised to give her both cocks and nothing less.

A tickle on his chest brought his gaze down to search out the cause. The riotous sex had opened the liquid stitches a bit, and a trickle of blood wound down his chest. Daveed ignored it. His mate was in a frenzy and would be for the next three days. His wound would wait.

Joy pressed up to him, her body releasing against his primary again, her hair in disarray on the pillow, her cries echoing off the walls. Anything but the woman beneath him could wait.

Daveed climaxed, and a pinch announced the wound widening slightly. Joy wrapped her arms around him, seeking out his mouth for a kiss, and the drive to sate them both kept him hard and ready for her. He cycled his hips, thrusting into her. Though he knew a change of position—like Joy on top—would be less stressful on his healing wound, he wasn't ready to abandon the Dominant position yet.

A growl brought his head around, and he glared at his *seir*. He'd known coming here was a good idea. At the nest, Raashh would have forbidden him from binding them in his state. Now that they'd progressed so far, there was nothing Raashh could do to stop it.

"You know Rayn ordered you not to strain yourself. I only allowed—"

"Out!" Daveed pulled the sheet around Joy, attempting to shield her from his *seir's* sight.

She grasped at his now-still hips, her breathing harsh. "Daveed, please."

Daveed pushed deep inside her, and Joy cried out in pleasure. She moved a little beneath him, rocking her hips to ride the dual lengths buried inside her.

The old buck's eyes widened, and he stood there, tongue scenting. He turned his back with a series of curses. "Bring her," he ordered.

"What?" They were in the midst of mating. Surely he'd scented that much.

"I will bring you to SLAL."

"My mate is in no need—" he started to rage.

"*You* are."

Daveed wanted to argue it but couldn't. He'd already decided he would risk himself to finish mating with Joy. *Putting myself at risk is no longer an option. We are bound already. If I die, Joy dies shortly after me.*

"Withdraw for a few moments. We will follow."

"A few moments," his *seir* reminded him. He left the room.

Daveed focused all his attention on Joy, driving them both over in heartbeats. When her hands loosened against his hips, he left her body, aching at the loss, momentary though it was. He wrapped her in the sheet and lifted Joy into his arms.

His *seir* nodded at them as they reached the elevator. "I will get you there safely."

They entered the elevator and took it to the roof. Halfway there, Joy pulled Daveed into a kiss that promised more.

Raashh hurried them aboard his shuttle, and closed it up in a rush. He paused to look down at Daveed and Joy, seated together on one of the plush oversized seats in the passenger compartment. She was trying to work her way out of the sheet already.

"Let her take the dominant until we reach SLAL," he ordered.

"Gladly."

His *seir* disappeared into the cockpit and closed that door as well. The engines ramped up.

Joy pushed the sheet away and straddled him, standing on tiptoe in her high heeled shoes. She lowered herself over his secondary with a gasp, her back channel accommodating him. Daveed positioned his primary at her seam, then eased her down both cocks. Before they cleared the rooftop, he was back inside Joy fully.

My mate.

The trip to SLAL passed in a blur of sexual congress. At last, his *seir* called out a warning that they'd arrived. Daveed wrapped her in the sheet again and growled his *seir* in.

Damn, this is not the way a mating is supposed to progress. Too many interruptions.

Raashh led them off the shuttle, Daveed joining and parting from Joy in kisses. He promised he would be back inside her with as little delay as possible.

Joy pressed against him and gasped. Daveed raised his head, growling a warning at Rayn. The human doctor was far too close to Joy for his safety.

Her eyes slid shut, and Joy collapsed in Daveed's arms. He roared, showing his hunting teeth in warning. Whatever Rayn did to Joy, he would pay for it.

Raashh restrained him lightly. "A sedative. It will allow Rayn to tend to you without your mate suffering the wait."

He wanted to argue it, but he couldn't. He had to be tended to, and it might take hours for Joy to succumb to sleep of her own accord. Daveed glared at the doctor. "Do not attempt to do so without my permission to again."

Rayn tipped his head in agreement. "It won't last long. If you would give her to your *seir*."

"*No one* touches my mate but me."

"Mating," his *seir* grumbled. "Get them into a room. He won't leave his mate until the cycle is complete. Perhaps not even then. She has already been endangered once."

Rayn nodded, his jaw tense. "Bring what we need to room three." He turned on his heel and led the way.

Daveed settled Joy in the middle of the mattress, and sat with his back to her. Rayn raised an eyebrow, and Daveed looked down at himself, cursing his state of undress. In the fever of mating, he hadn't even considered pulling his trousers back on.

"Your head clearing a bit?" Rayn asked.

"Just repair the damage." Daveed snarled at him.

"Before his mate wakes," Raashh added.

"Joy," he insisted. Daveed met his *seir's* gaze. "May I present my mate, Joy Raashh, formerly Patterson."

He grunted. "The designer who saved your life. I know well who she is already. Now I know why you insisted on risking yourself for her."

Daveed nodded. "I would have died for her the first time I met her." Before, perhaps.

Joy shifted in her sleep, and Rayn hurried to make the repair. It was accomplished quickly.

"I wish you had waited another week to do this," the doctor grumbled. "But I understand why you didn't wait."

Daveed didn't answer him. Nothing he said would be courteous, and the doctor was helping him. *I should be courteous.*

Rayn held up a hypo. "There will be three of these in the drawer. You will wear the bio-tracker. If I open the speakers and tell you to administer a hypo to Joy, you will...at the first possible break between sexual exploits. We will treat you and allow mating to continue. If you refuse the order, we will flood the room with a mild sedative and force you to be treated. Am I understood, Daveed?"

The Dominant in him wanted to argue it. His rational mind reasoned that it was for Joy's protection. *If I die, she dies.* "Understood. I won't refuse that order. Joy depends on it."

"Daveed?" Joy's voice shocked him into motion.

By the time he was laying beside her, the door was closing behind the other males.

"Where are we?" she asked.

"Somewhere safe."

Joy nodded.

"Do you need anything? Food? Drink?" He was sure Rayn was arranging for everything they would need to finish mating.

Her smile was the lazy smile of an aroused woman. "All I need is you."

"You'll have that." As much of me as you can stand, until you ask for a reprieve or lapse into sleep.

Chapter Six

Four days later

Daveed nodded his thanks to Karl and opened the outer door into the secure landing bay at the nest. He lifted Joy down, smiling at how perfectly the *S'suuhhea* suited her.

Almost as if she was born to be my mate.

Karl whispered the blessing of many daughters and secured the door. He waited until Daveed led Joy out of the bay, then started the engines again and made his way back to *Spice Tower* and his flying lessons with Arren.

There was no question that Raashh would be waiting for them in the center nest. He knew Daveed had mated with Joy, and he knew they were on their way home to the nest.

Raashh bowed to Joy. His English was stilted. Since Marie had come to him speaking Xxan, Raashh hadn't had to learn to speak it fluently for her. "Wel-come, daugh-ter."

She seemed to have trouble forming words for a moment. "Thank you, Raashh."

Daveed scented her shock and noted the nervous little movements of her feet. *"You've met before."* He didn't question it. Though he wasn't sure what the details were, it was clear his *seir* had not made a good first impression on her.

His *seir* tucked his frills in a clear show of embarrassment. *"When you were shot... I am afraid I was not gracious to your mate. Seeing her covered in your blood rattled me. You ignored my orders and were injured. Your brother ignored my orders and endangered himself. I was...not kind to her. I have many debts to pay to her."*

"Then I suggest you start as soon as possible." Daveed didn't try to hide his irritation.

"Is there a problem?" Joy asked.

"No problem," Daveed assured her. "My *seir* was simply explaining his deplorable behavior to me. I guarantee it will *not* happen again." He shot his *seir* a warning look.

Raashh snorted, then tipped his head to Joy again. *"Does your mate understand our customs?"*

Daveed nodded. *"I've explained them to her. She is...willing to respect them."*

"It really is rather rude for you two to continue speaking Xxan, when I don't understand it."

"I will have to translate for you until you learn Xxan," Daveed explained. "My *seir* doesn't speak English very well, though he understands it. We typically speak Xxan in the nest."

She darkened a notch. "Oh. I see."

Raashh took a step toward her and motioned toward Joy.

Daveed nodded. "My *seir* is going to take in your scent, to add your scent to his family memory."

Joy nodded shakily. "I think I understand."

Raashh took the last step that separated them and wrapped his hands around her waist. He lifted her, bringing Joy face to face with him. She didn't shy from him or raise a fuss at the move.

Daveed smiled at that. *My woman is brave. She is strong. But I knew that already.* He'd seen the vids of her tending to him in the elevator.

"Don't you dare die on me, Daveed."

He secretly wondered if he'd heard that in his unconscious state and followed his mate's orders.

His *seir's* tongue extended. He drew in Joy's scent, then stroked his tongue along her throat gently. Joy gasped, but she didn't strike out or withdraw. She didn't even shudder or shiver at the move as many human females did.

Raashh nestled Joy to his chest, tucking her head beneath his chin. He rumbled his welcome, and her arms crept up to circle his neck. His *seir* shot Daveed a look of surprise, then he tucked her tighter beneath his chin.

There was no need for explanation. Joy was the only female in their nest. The fact that she accepted Raashh was a boon. It would be difficult to protect Joy if she shied from the huge elder at every turn.

"We're going to bathe you now," Daveed informed her.

Joy nodded slowly, and a tremor worked its way through her body.

"Tell her we will be gentle."

"She knows that," Daveed grumbled.

Joy shot him a questioning look.

"We will be gentle. Trust me."

She nodded. "I do."

Daveed stripped off his *S'suumea* and put his arms out for her. Once Raashh deposited Joy in his arms, Daveed made his way into the pool with her.

"Remember what we will do," he soothed her.

She nodded. "Remove my clothing in deep enough water that Raashh cannot see my body. Bathe me. Then Raashh will leave the pool, and we will..." Her cheeks darkened in a blush.

"He won't watch. It's tradition to welcome a new female to the nest this way. If you enjoy it, we can do it again. If not, we don't have to do more than bathe you when you present a baby to the nest or when you're injured." His muscles tightened a notch. "Which I do *not* intend to allow to happen again."

The water reached his upper thighs, and Daveed turned and went to his knees, lowering her to hers. Joy tensed, then relaxed. A moan left her mouth.

He smiled. "You like the pool?"

"Do you know how much money women pay at spas to use pools like these?"

"A fortune." Daveed worked the *S'suuhhea* up her body and pitched it out of the pool, then he brushed the water droplets out of her hair. He leaned toward her and pressed a kiss to her lips. "Now you're so rich you own your own."

His *seir* entered the pool, nude. He cocked his head to one side, listening to their discussion as he crept closer to them.

Joy shook her head. "No. This is Raashh's. I mean...we'll *live* here, but it's—"

"You'll find that everything in a Xxanian nest is designed for the comfort of the females of the nest or to entice females to join the nest. Perhaps

I should have brought you here long ago. Would that have *enticed* you, Joy?"

Words seemed to desert her, then she forced them out. "The dreams I've had of you had nothing to do with mineral pools. They usually involved our desks. Or the bed in the penthouse, though I admit those weren't anywhere near the reality."

His smile widened, and his primary came up at the idea of her having sex dreams about him. "We will talk about those dreams later. For now... The truth is Raashh's private sleeping area is his own. Other than that, your comfort will come first. If you wish to swim nude in the pool, only I will be welcome in the area while you do."

Raashh reached her back and went to his knees. Joy shifted closer to Daveed in response, took a deep breath, and settled between them. Daveed offered her a smile.

His *seir* poured out a handful of the clove oil he'd brought into the pool with him. He passed the bottle to Daveed.

Joy's eyes closed at Raashh's massage of her neck. After a moment, he moved to her shoulder and repeated the kneading.

Daveed started at her neck, stroking clove oil down to her collarbones. By the time he reached her chest, her nipples were hard and begging for his touch. He had little doubt the sex between them in the pool would be well-received.

His *seir* massaged his way down her back. *"Your mate saved your life, Daveed. You will bathe her with* Saahaal *every day. You owe your life to this female. We all owe your life to her."*

Daveed swallowed the lump in his throat.

"What did he say?" Joy's voice whispered between them.

"The Xxan show respect for our females by bathing with the *Saahaal*—the clove oil. We use it in apology, for healing, but most commonly for respect."

She nodded.

"When a female joins a nest, she is usually bathed daily by her mate for a week with *Saahaal*."

Joy moaned and arched into his hand, driving him from her lower ribs to her mound.

"Raashh orders me to use the *Saahaal* at every bathing. Every..." He circled a finger against her clit, smiling at her gasp. "...day of your life, unless you request for me not to use it, of course."

She pressed to his body, her breath teasing at his throat.

Raashh's hands were at her hips, spreading the last of the *Saahaal* he would before retreating. *"She will be fertile very soon. If she agrees to carry for you, the next week will be ideal."* With that, he rose to leave.

Joy tipped her head back, inviting Daveed's kiss. He sealed them together, his body in overdrive, their tongues dancing against each other. He thrust two fingers into her and started pumping them, hinting at what he intended.

She widened her stance and pushed back at him, moving forward, climbing astride his legs when he settled to his heels. He took her hint and eased his fingers out of her body.

Joy didn't wait for him to lift her. She pushed up and used one hand to position his cock at her slit. She started working her way down his length, her mouth leaving his completely as she approached the root.

Daveed thrust up, pushing himself to the hilt. Joy shouted, holding to him, her legs circling him.

"I intend to give you everything you want, Joy. Tell me what you want."

Her lips trembled a bit. "The same way you bound us."

His secondary responded. "You want me inside both holes? Filling all of you at once?"

She moaned, then nodded. "Yes."

He reached down past her bottom, stroking his secondary hard for her. "It's not the usual way we complete the first bathing, but I would give you anything, Joy. Anything."

"What did your *seir* say before he left?"

Daveed hesitated. "He suggested the best time for us to conceive, if you would be willing to carry for me now."

"The new line—"

"There will always be a new line, but we don't have to leave our children to see to it. Did I ever mention there is another room behind our offices?"

She shook her head. "What is it?"

"A bedroom, but we can add a crib to it...a full play area."

Joy shivered in his arms.

"What is it?" he asked.

"You just gave me fodder for a whole new set of fantasies."

"I can take care of those," he assured her. His secondary pressed at the ring of her anus, and he started massaging up the *Zhigaaal* to loosen the ring of tissue for him.

"When?" she breathed.

"You tell me."

Joy laughed, then gasped, as he pushed inside her ass. She moved back and forth, her clenching muscles stroking the secondary up further.

"No," she gasped. "I mean...when will it be possible?"

"Sometime within the next week. I can use condoms if you—"

She levered herself up slightly and then down, making him moan. His cocks were sensitized from binding, and Joy's tight body milking him was delightful. In moments, she was climaxing around him, her screams echoing off the walls. He followed her over with a roar.

They sat together, Joy wrapped around him, their bodies brushing against each other.

Joy kissed his chest. "If you dare do anything differently than you are right now, I may have to hurt you."

"As my mate requests."

* * * *

Joy sat on the biggest, softest pile of cushions she'd ever encountered, wearing a clean silk *S'suuhhea*. Daveed fed her piece after piece of food from a series of trays that contained everything from sashimi to blocks of cheese and slices of meat, from fresh fruit to chocolates.

She smiled at him. "You're spoiling me."

"I intend to keep doing that."

"Well, then—"

Arren rushed into the room, looking all limbs in his *S'suumea*. Daveed shot him an irritated look.

"Sorry. Sorry," Arren apologized.

"It's okay," Joy assured him.

"If you don't mind, Arren," Daveed hinted.

"It's sort of important."

"Whatever game—"

"It's *not* a game. You cannot take Joy back to *Spice*. Not yet. Give me three days."

They both turned to look at him; Joy folded her legs beneath her.

"Go on," Daveed invited.

"I've been looking into the attack. The code the guerillas used to get through the outer shell of security is the same one *Spice* gives to access executive areas on your floor. I *told* the security team everyone should have a separate access code." He visibly fumed at that.

Daveed scrubbed his hand across his mouth. "How many people have that code?"

"Counting the assistants who use it, seven. I can positively clear four of them. I did the security clearances on Joy and Andre myself. We know the two of us aren't guilty. That leaves the three executive assistants on the floor. Give me three days to run new clearances on them." He shifted from foot to foot nervously.

"Do it," Daveed ordered. His ridge plates were extended.

Arren nodded and started to turn away.

"Thank you, Arren," Joy yelled after him.

He stopped at the entryway to the room, seemingly uncertain. "Anything to keep you safe, Joy."

He was gone before Daveed could protest the comment.

Chapter Seven

Five days later

Joy and Daveed stepped off elevator three...directly into a plush bedroom decorated in dark colors.

She laughed heartily. "You weren't joking."

He pressed to her back, wrapping his arms around her, his primary hard against her lower back. "Not at all. Do your fantasies do it justice?"

"Not even close."

"Good. Should we...?"

"Later. We really do have to do some work, Daveed."

He groaned. "The horrors of owning a company."

Joy turned toward him. "It's not all bad. Who else has a bedroom to take lunches together in?"

Daveed's brow rose. "I will take that as a promise."

She strode toward the door opposite the elevator. "You better."

Daveed rushed to catch up to her, showed her how to check for someone in the office, and how to let herself out of the bedroom and into the office. In moments, they were head-to-head, checking the progress reports on the new line.

A light knock at the doorframe brought both their heads up. The woman in the doorway was matronly, not quite old enough to be Joy's mother but nearly so, if she got an early start to child-bearing.

"Yes?" Daveed inquired.

She smiled. "I just wanted to introduce myself. My name is Mallory, and I will be your new assistant."

He rose, towering over Joy. "Yes. Arren told me he hired you. My mate...Joy." There was a warning in his tone.

Joy winced. Yes, Arren had hired Mallory, and he'd proven Celeste had been the one who'd helped the guerrillas gain entrance. In fact, she'd had them target Joy, in specific. Shooting Arren had been a coup they hadn't expected.

Beyond that, Arren had determined Joy's former assistant—Lauren—was compromised and open to blackmail of some sort. He'd reassigned her to another department.

Arren had asked them for two more days to fully check on the candidates for a replacement assistant before they returned to work. Not that Joy and Daveed had complained about the delay. Once Daveed and Raashh had determined Joy was fertile, it had been hard to keep Joy and Daveed apart. The last two days had been comparable to their binding.

Raashh was pleased they were staying at the nest, not only because they were busy trying to conceive his grandchild, but also because they were both safe in the nest, and Daveed was getting more rest than he would have at work. With his wound still healing, that was just what the doctor ordered. Literally.

Mallory continued. "I understand the two of you enjoy quiet to work and dislike interruptions. Is there anything at all I should interrupt you for or should I handle everything that comes in? I find it best to set the expectations right away. That way, you can do what you need to, I can do what I need to, and everyone can be most productive."

Joy smiled. "If there's a family emergency, something with Arren or Raashh, disturb us."

"No business concerns?"

Daveed shook his head. "Contracts go in a pile for me to take home to Arren. Suppliers submit samples, which we will go over at our leisure. Distribution hubs go through Leon George in sales. Requests for interviews and similar items go through Lyle Nelson in PR. You can schedule appointments they request of you, but no one comes to us unless they have gone through the other department heads first. We prefer morning appointments when possible. That gives us the rest of the day to design, with no interruptions."

"Each of you prefer—"

"No. Joy is my mate. She takes no appointments without me."

There was a moment of tense silence. Mallory nodded. "Understood. Anything else I should keep in mind?"

Daveed crossed his arms over his chest. "Whatever Joy requests, she gets. Whatever she orders is done immediately. There is no higher consideration than her safety and comfort."

Joy had decided days earlier that hearing Daveed say things like that was one of the greatest aphrodisiacs she'd found. She crossed one leg over the other, more than aware of her arousal.

Mallory glanced from him to Joy. She smiled. "I can handle that. I have already changed the contacts in your desk phones. Number one still reaches security. Number two now reaches me."

Joy offered a smile that felt strained. "That's wonderful. Mallory, would you mind locking the door on the way out? We have a lot of work to do. Lunch at noon, please?"

"Yes, ma'am. Right away." She turned and made her way out without question. The lock clicked behind her.

Daveed sat on the desk, blocking her view of the computer screen. "Do you want to start making those fantasies come true now or later?" he asked.

Joy pulled the fabric off her shoulders, baring her breasts.

For a moment, Daveed was still and silent. "I believe this is one of *my* fantasies," he breathed.

"Then we should definitely get to work on it."

Section 3:
Subdominant Son

Arren

Subdominant

Chapter Eight

Eighteen years later

"Is that one of the Xxanian males?"

Zondra looked around at Sandy's purr, picking out Arren Raashh across the restaurant. "Yes. That's Arren." It shouldn't have surprised her that Raashh's younger son was in the posh little restaurant. It was only three blocks from the *Spice Industries'* main offices and served food fit for both Xxanians and humans. It was probably an ideal place to host business lunches.

By Sandy's rising scent and the slow, sensual lick of her red-tinted lips, Zondra could guess that her college friend was highly interested in Arren. Of course, like most Xxanian crossbreeds, he was tall and muscular. Those were appealing qualities in both Xxan and human. Being human, the fact that Arren was a Subdominant wouldn't be off-putting to Sandy.

"Would you like an introduction?" she rushed to offer.

Zondra knew what she was doing, of course. In Sandy's heightened state of arousal, introducing Sandy to Arren was practically arranging the pair a hot one-night stand. Fresh from a breakup with her boyfriend, maybe this was just what Sandy needed to feel appealing again.

"Would you?" Her pleading eyes were all it took to convince Zondra she was doing the right thing.

"If that's what you want. Of course."

And she did. There was no question that Sandy wanted Arren between her legs as soon as he could get himself there.

If he has his usual car with him, that won't take long at all.

* * * *

Arren tipped his head in respect at Zondra Duncan's approach, swallowing down longing at the sight of her rounded womb. If the rumors were correct, her latest pregnancy was a young female.

Of course, it wouldn't do to touch her or to sample her musk to test it for himself. She was a mated female. Evan Duncan had risen to head of the technical department of *Spice Industries'* assorted companies. Zondra had been attacked by a male before. And if Evan and the Xxanian males of Daahn's nest didn't kill Arren for such an unseemly move, Arren's *seir*—Raashh himself—would.

With good reason to. It's not as if I will ever be worthy of a Xxanian crossbred female of a nest as important as Daahn's. Probably not of a Xxanian crossbred female of any nest.

"Zondra... So nice to see you."

He didn't offer his hand. One did not touch another male's mate. One did not handle a mated female, unless her safety depended on it and her mate was not around to protect her personally. In such a case, he offered apologies to the mated male for the offense...and typically a gift of spice to help wash the scent of a rival male away.

Not that I am much of a rival. Daveed is fond enough of pointing that out.

"And you, Arren. Arren Raashh, may I present an old friend of mine, Sandy Butler. Sandy, this is Arren Raashh."

He focused on the very human female at Zondra's side, taking a deep breath to scent her. That quickly, his primary surged up. She was in the human version of quickening, a fierce arousal.

Aimed at me. Thank you, Zondra, for the introduction.

Sandy's hair was a warm reddish brown, and her eyes were blue-gray. The entire package was appealing, from her high, tight breasts to her rounded hips and long legs. Visions of those legs wrapped around him while he sated them both were stark and searing.

He extended his hand, hinting for her to place hers in it. Touching a female socially was a joy he denied himself as seldom as possible. "A pleasure. Can I interest you in joining me?"

Sandy shot Zondra a look that said she was sorry for considering ditching her friend but torn because she really wanted to do so.

Zondra smiled. "I should be going. Evan and I have a shuttle to SLAL in an hour."

Thank you, Zondra. Arren owed her for this kindness. He would find a way to repay her somehow.

Sandy placed her hand in his. "Then I would love to join you."

Arren raised her hand to his lips and kissed her knuckles tenderly, holding her gaze solidly with his own. Her pulse rate surged against his lips.

"Do you want to eat?" he offered. Arren wanted to eat her, but if she was hungry, he would rein in his arousal long enough to see to her physical needs.

Her expression said she wanted to eat him as much as he wanted to eat her. "Not particularly," she lied.

Oh yes. You want to eat, but you want something other than base sustenance. Thank the Seir-*God!* "Then perhaps I can drive you somewhere."

"Sounds good." She eased her hand from his and turned to hug Zondra. That accomplished, she focused on Arren and took his offered arm.

Walking with a woman on your arm was something far too many human men took for granted. Arren had decided that long ago, and so far, nothing had changed that opinion of them.

At his car, Arren played the gallant: he held her door, helped her into the bucket seat, then closed her in. He settled behind the wheel and set the engine purring. "Would my apartment be acceptable to you?"

Sandy darkened in a demure little blush. "Yes. That would be fine."

Something in her reserve sounded alarm bells in Arren's head. "Perhaps you should tell me what you hope will happen next." If she wanted someone to dominate her, he could play the game, but it wasn't in Arren's base nature to do so.

Her eyes said she wasn't entirely certain what she wanted.

"Is sex with two cocks what you want to experience?" Many human women were intrigued by the idea.

Her blush deepened. "Is that true?"

It's not curiosity then. Arren turned on his seat to face her more fully. "Why did you choose me, Sandy?" He kept his voice low and soothing.

Her eyes were wide and innocent. "I..."

"Go on," he urged her.

She swallowed what appeared to be a lump in her throat.

"Is it my family's money?" He'd met women that wanted to tap into that commodity before. If that's what she wanted, he wasn't sure it was worth the time to bed her at all.

"I guess you have money, based on this car, but no. It has nothing to do with that."

Her scent said she wasn't lying to him. Sandy intrigued him.

"Then what?" When she didn't offer an answer, he considered telling her that he wasn't willing. *Libido be damned.*

"Xxanian men..."

He cocked an eyebrow up and waited for her explanation. Perhaps it was her hesitation that made him decide not to order her out.

Her face went a deep scarlet. "I want a man that isn't a dog."

It wasn't remotely what he thought she'd say. "In what way?"

* * * *

Sandy took a calming breath. *Well, I've come this far.* "Human men all seem to want to trade up. Anytime something shiny comes their way, they go sniffing and—"

She reached for the door handle at the muscles tensing beneath his fitted suit. She'd angered him. "Never mind." This was crazy. Sandy wasn't sure why she'd thought this was a good idea in the first place.

Arren wrapped a hand around her upper arm and slowly drew her back. She could just make out his eyes through the sunglasses Xxanians wore. There was no amusement in those eyes...and no anger. If anything, she'd say he was concerned. That was enough to relax her.

One smooth hand stroked down her cheek. "Are you saying you want to mate with a Xxanian male to find a man who won't cheat on you as human men have?"

Sandy considered her answer carefully. Xxanian men didn't get a chance to mate often. There weren't enough of their own females yet, and human women didn't choose to be bound physically to a man nearly often enough to provide mates for all the men who needed them. If she said that's what she wanted, she'd be leading him on. "Maybe. If it's the right man."

"I am not a Dominant." That sounded like a warning.

Her breathing eased.

His head cocked to one side. "You're relieved that I'm not."

"The idea of a Dominant is rather frightening."

His lips curved in the shadow of a smile. "Is it? Why would a Dominant scare you?"

She shrugged. "Too many BDSM books I've read?"

He laughed heartily. "Some Dominants do tend to insist on a bit of bondage and domination. I assure you, that is not to my tastes." Arren leaned across the gear shift, his breath hot against her mouth. "I am a Subdominant. I like long, slow seductions and hot, sweating sex with a very willing partner."

Her breathing hitched at his pronouncement.

"Are you, Sandy? Are you a *very* willing partner?"

"Yes."

He slipped his tongue through her parted lips and invited her into potent passion. His tongue was rough and—she realized after a moment of exploring it with her own—slightly forked. She moaned at the thought of what that might feel like against her clit.

Arren slid back into his own seat and offered her a stunning smile. "Please tell me you don't have to be anywhere else later today."

"Nowhere."

He focused on the road and put the car in gear. "Good." Arren pulled into the flow of traffic and maneuvered through it expertly, intent on the task of getting them to his apartment.

Sandy shifted on the seat, aroused already. Just watching his single-minded attention to getting her to his home set off visions of his single-minded attention to other details to come.

He groaned. "You are so wet. Aren't you?"

"Yes."

"What do you want first? Tell me." He shifted into a higher gear.

Sandy looked at his mouth, memories of his tongue setting off shivers of delight. "Your mouth. Your tongue."

Without a word, Arren pressed a button on the dashboard, and the windows went dark. He yanked off his sunglasses and tossed them onto the dash.

"Arren?" she questioned.

"No one outside can see us."

She nodded, at a loss for what he had in mind. He was still driving, after all.

"Take off your panties. I plan to lick you in the car, if you're willing. If not...in my personal elevator."

It was bold, shocking...and made her wetter still. Sandy pulled her skirt up to her waist. She kicked off her heels and worked her pantyhose and underwear down together.

Arren didn't watch her do it, but his tongue peeked from between his lips, and his nostrils flared.

Tongue-scenting. She'd heard that's what they called it.

"Which will it be, Sandy? In the car or in the elevator?"

She pulled the pantyhose off one foot and then the other. "The car." It was wild, reckless, and appealing on a level nothing she'd done sexually in her life could compare to.

He hissed out a breath and slid a glance at her. "Recline your seat and turn to face me."

Sandy fumbled around for the switch to recline the seat. When it was halfway back, she turned and raised her left leg, planting her foot on the back of the gear shift.

The position put her on display for him. As if Arren agreed, he placed his right hand on her raised knee and guided her leg back to the seat, exposing her further.

His eyes flicked toward her and away several times. His voice emerged, rougher than she'd heard it so far. "We're almost there, Sandy."

Her legs trembled, but it was a pleasant sensation, a need that she hadn't experienced before sex with other partners. The wait was delicious. It was intolerable. She moaned.

"You want to touch yourself. Don't you?"

"I want you to touch me."

His hand slid down the length of her inner thigh to her seam. One thick finger trailed along her slit. "Where do you want me to touch you? How do you want me to?"

"Inside. I want to feel you finger fucking me." She'd never been so bold with her demands, but something told her Arren would give her precisely what she asked for.

He did. His skin was soft, and his thrusts were masterful.

Sandy gasped in delight, shifting on the seat restlessly. She fisted her hands, needing to do something with them.

I want him inside me as quickly as possible. That a given, she started unbuttoning her blouse, hesitated a moment, then unhooked the front clasp on her bra. Sandy spread them, baring her breasts.

Arren groaned. "You won't regret offering them." He twisted his finger inside her and stroked little circles, matching the motion over her clit with his thumb.

Sandy arched up with a shout, climax beating at her.

His hand retreated abruptly. "Not until we're in my private garage."

Just as she was about to protest, he pulled off the street and stopped at a security gate that looked like it would stop an urban pacification tank cold. She didn't question that it was the entrance to his garage.

After a moment, the gate rose smoothly, and Arren maneuvered the car down the ramp. She looked back, watching the gate close behind them.

"Identi-chip?" she asked.

"Coupled with bio scans and weapons scans."

He stopped at a blast door, then proceeded through when it came up as well. That allowed him to go down another level, and the blast door started down when they'd barely cleared it.

Wow! She'd heard the Xxan lived with security, but this went beyond any concept of personal security she'd heard of.

Her more mundane concerns faded away at the sight of Arren placing the fingers he'd been using for foreplay into his mouth. He sucked them clean with a moan that started a pulse of anticipation beating in her sheath.

He pulled into a parking space next to the elevator, and put the car in park, switching off the engine in the same sweep of his hand. Sandy looked around, startled to see there was only one other vehicle on this level. The level above had been half full.

"My private garage," he answered her unasked question.

Before she could focus on him, Arren was in motion. The lick up the line of her labia brought her off the seat with a scream of pleasure.

His tongue slid deeply inside her, rasping against the walls of her sheath in delicious little strokes. Sandy buried her hands in the wealth of his silky curls, gasping for breath as he licked her toward a frenzy.

His tongue was longer than she'd anticipated, nearly as long as a slightly below-average cock, she was sure, but prehensile...and covered in slightly-roughened nubs that reminded her of a kitten's tongue. The combination shot her toward climax when she wanted the moment to last.

Arren didn't pull away when she climaxed. He continued, taking what might have been a simple climax and stretching it out into a mind-altering experience.

And this is just his tongue.

Her senses swam, and she forced a deep breath. It left her body on a scream.

At last, he raised his head. Arren stared at her, his expression starkly serious. "Have I convinced you I'm a worthy lover? Will you accompany me to my apartment?"

"Yes. Yes, I will. I want you inside me....as soon as possible."

A smile lifted one side of his lips. "Do you mean that?"

"Every word."

Chapter Nine

Arren's primary took notice of her plea. Not only did she want him, Sandy wanted his cock inside her as soon as physically possible. He intended to deliver on it.

"Not in the car," he promised.

She looked around. "Too cramped," she agreed.

Arren nodded. "Then you won't mind me getting you out of it before we go further."

Sandy turned on the seat, then slid her feet into her modest heels. Her manic movements made him smile. Arren got out of the car and shut his door. He rounded the vehicle to her side and opened hers. The sight of her—her lush breasts bracketed by her open shirt and bra—had his cock complaining.

She put one shapely leg out of the car and took his hand. Sandy hesitated a moment, halfway to her feet, and stared at the ridge of his cock through his trousers. Her hand cupped him, and she straightened. But her gaze stayed locked on the view of him.

"As soon as possible?" he repeated.

"Oh, yes."

His length jerked at the tone of invitation. "Not in a filthy garage," he vowed. "But we may not make it off the elevator."

Sandy gasped. "Oh, yes," she repeated.

Arren reached past her, pulling a small box of condoms out of the glove box. Sandy didn't hesitate. At the sight of them, she started working his trousers open. Arren pulled a condom sized for his primary out and held it up to her. She snatched it, then eased his cock out of his trousers. Sandy ripped it open, pulled the condom out, and started rolling it down his length.

Oh, Seir-*God, this is going to be hard and fast, and it's not going to end at once.* That in mind, he tucked the box of condoms into his pocket.

When she reached the base, she looked up at him. Arren guided her to the elevator and called for it.

Her fingers trailed up his length, and Arren pulled her into a kiss. She parted her lips, inviting him in, and he took full advantage of the offer. By the time the elevator arrived, they were fully engaged in each other, so much so that the doors started to close without them.

Arren threw his hand out and slapped it open again. Then he backed Sandy onto it.

He parted from her long enough to hit the button for the penthouse. Then he lifted her and pressed Sandy to one of the mirrored walls.

Inspiration struck. "Pull your skirt up. All the way to your waist, Sandy."

She complied, her breathing ragged.

"Now look at the mirrors. Watch my cock."

He didn't question when she'd found the right angle. Her breathing hitched, and she raised her legs a bit, hooking them over his waist.

Arren eased inside, millimeter by millimeter, savoring her grip against his cock. Whoever she'd been with before him had obviously been a smaller man than he was.

Her eyes closed on a groan.

"Watch," he reminded her.

Her gray-blue eyes slid open, and she focused on the mirror again, her breathing harsh and her body trembling lightly.

The elevator stopped, and the doors slid open. Arren withdrew slightly, smiling at her moan of protest. He eased her down again, savoring every clenching muscle.

The doors slid shut, and Sandy gasped. Her eyes went wide.

"What is it?" he invited, withdrawing again, a long, slow glide that ensured he wouldn't miss a single sensation.

"The..." She gasped again, as he reversed direction. "...elevator."

"My *private* elevator," he reminded her. "No one else can open it or call for it." Well, no one but Raashh's security team or members of Raashh's nest, but there was no reason for them to come here.

Sandy nodded.

Arren slid back and forward, his heart pounding at the little mews of need and whimpers of protest escaping Sandy's lips. Her sounds enflamed him.

She was rapt on the mirror image, her lips slightly parted. Visions of her sucking him down nearly forced him to climax.

Not without her. But he needed to bring Sandy to climax again soon, or he wouldn't be able to live to that.

"I have more mirrors in the penthouse, Sandy." He didn't speed his thrusts, but he pushed deeper.

Her breathing went ragged. "Over the bed?"

Deeper. *She likes that.* He chuckled. "Nothing like that. There's a big mirror in the bathing room. Would you like to watch us in it?"

The clenching of her sheath said she did. "Later."

So close. "There are mirrored closet doors in the bedroom. I would very much like to sit on the edge of the bed with you astride me, both of us facing that mirror."

She shot into climax with a scream, and her eyes closed.

Arren pushed deeper. "Watch." *Seir*-God, but he wanted her to watch. The game was a delight.

She complied, and little sounds left her lips at every forward motion of his hips. Arren couldn't hold off any longer. He climaxed, his heart aching in the certainty that she'd had what she wanted and would choose to leave him.

They parted slowly. Arren eased her to her feet, then straightened his trousers a bit over his half-mast length. Sandy's rapt attention on the move made his heart stutter.

"What do you want, Sandy?"

She took a deep breath. "I think you should show me where the bedroom mirror is."

His primary jerked at the invitation. Arren hit the door open button and waved her into his apartment. "Anything the lady wishes."

It wasn't a line. If it meant the possibility of convincing Sandy to be his, he would offer fantasies and make those she'd harbored for years come true.

* * * *

"You don't really have to walk me to my door." Sandy's blush was deep, but he didn't sense that she had something to hide.

Arren smiled. "A gentleman would," he countered.

She smiled at that, the same shy little smile she'd been shooting him all afternoon. "Okay, but I warn you, my apartment isn't nearly as impressive as yours is."

He stroked the backs of his fingertips along her cheek. "You don't think that matters to me, do you?"

"Considering the day so far..."

He raised an eyebrow and waited for an answer.

"No. Of course not." She wasn't lying.

Arren was relieved. He let himself out of the car and circled to her door, opening it before she had a chance to. Sandy offered a smile and led him inside, then up the stairs to the second floor.

There were two apartments on this level, and the building wasn't a large one. Arren did calculations. It was most likely a single-bedroom unit of thirty or forty square meters, adequate for one person. Or a very cozy couple.

He committed her address to memory, as he'd been committing every detail to the same, sexual tastes and more mundane likes and dislikes. It had surprised him to find she worked for the law firm *Spice* used, *Tasker and Rowe*, but that could work out well for them.

Sandy hesitated at the door, then looked up at him. "It's not much, but would you like to come in?"

Was she kidding? Being invited into a female's home was something Xxanian mix males dreamed of. "I would. Very much."

Her lips quirked up in a smile. "Good."

He was still reeling at that single word when she opened the door and led the way inside. Arren didn't dare ask what she meant by it. They barely knew each other. She hadn't made decisions about him beyond the moment, he was sure.

Sandy closed the door behind them, and he looked around. The entryway was narrow and full of furniture that looked like antiques, all in matching dark wood. She pulled off her coat and hung it on an old-fashioned wooden coat rack. Then she deposited her keys in a ceramic bowl set on lace-covered table that also supported a lamp with a shade of what appeared to be a patchwork of colored glass.

"What do you think?" she asked, her smile strained.

He reached for the lamp, then hesitated, certain that this was not a reproduction. It was museum quality, he was sure. Raashh had insisted on museum quality art for *Spice Tower*, so he'd seen his fair share. "May I?"

"Yes. Of course." She reached around him and turned it on.

The glow was mesmerizing. Arren touched the glass, his fingers shaking lightly, afraid of breaking it. "It's beautiful. Antique, I presume?"

"Yes. It has been passed down in my family from mother to daughter since the nineteen-fifties."

His jaw dropped at that pronouncement. "Seven hundred years?" These things were worth a fortune. If anyone knew about them, they might kill Sandy to own them.

"Unbelievable, isn't it? The power supply and light source have been updated, of course, but the entire lamp body and shade are original."

"I think it's fantastic. One of the things missing in my penthouse is a sense of history." Then again, even Raashh's nest hadn't had a sense of history, since he'd been separated from his home world and trapped on Earth. Daveed and Joy's sons were only the second generation to spend their entire lives in the nest.

His heart lightened at the idea that Joy could provide that sense of history to his home if they mated. He would love to have her precious belongings surrounding him. "Is there more?" He had to know.

Sandy smiled widely. "Some. Over the centuries, pieces have been split up. My great-great grandmother got these pieces, while her younger sister got the dining room set. Over the years, that's happened. The lamp is the oldest of the pieces I inherited. Most of the others are between a hundred and three hundred years old. The table and coat rack are three hundred. But this..." She touched the lamp, her expression soft. "This is the one thing I hope I never lose."

If we're together long enough, I'll convince her to let me put in a security system to protect her and her belongings. "May I see the others?"

"Of course." She turned with a spring in her step and rushed through the kitchen into the living room. "The coffee table matches the set in the front hall, and the bookshelves are from my great-great grandmother, to replace the ones given to her sister. They match the other pieces well, I think."

"They do," he agreed.

She waved him along and fairly sped out of the room.

Arren stopped halfway to the doorway. There was a male scent in the room. It might be a relative of Sandy's, but he couldn't be sure. The cologne or aftershave the man wore was too overpowering for him to identify the scent of the male beneath it.

"Arren?" she prompted him.

He followed her voice, tongue scenting as he made his way down the hallway toward her. "You never told me about your family," he noted. "Do you have any sisters or brothers?"

"No sisters. I do have a brother."

His heart eased a bit.

"We don't see each other often. Noel's military, so he's offworld most of the time."

The scent got stronger as he approached her, but he could tell now that the male scent was old...stale. Whoever he was, hadn't been in her apartment for days. Perhaps a week, considering the after shave. But still, another male's scent in Sandy's home was unacceptable. He marched through the doorway...into her bedroom.

"The bed is a reproduction, made to match the bureaus. They are two hundred and fifty years old, and the jewelry stand is five hundred years old."

The latter floored him. "You have strong family ties."

He'd never felt as strongly about his own. His *Hauaa* had died when he'd been too young to remember her, and his *seir* didn't like to talk about her passing. Or about her in general. His *seir* had always been distant, and his brother hadn't been close to him, in age or in temperament.

And that was before you took into account that Arren was a Subdominant. His *seir* was ashamed of him, and his brother looked down on him.

Moving out of the nest hadn't been a hard choice for Arren. It certainly hadn't been nearly as difficult as most Xxan made it seem it would be.

"Not so much these days. To be honest, I was never close to my father. My mother... Well, she's been gone since shortly after I started college. It's just me and my brother, and like I said—"

"He's not around much," he repeated.

She smiled weakly. "Yes. I see him nearly every time he's on the planet though."

"Is he now?"

"No. He's been deployed for the last six months, about half his typical tour. I can't wait for him to come home again."

The scent wasn't her brother. Was it a former lover? *Most likely.* A casual acquaintance wouldn't have left his scent in her bedroom, and a maintenance man wouldn't have spent enough time to leave such a potent scent.

"Arren?" she prompted him.

"My mother died when I was too young to remember her." *And I don't see my brother often.* Maybe that's why they were so drawn to each other.

The scent irritated him, reminding him that another male had been here, probably within the week. Arren replayed what he knew about the last male in her life.

He cheated on her. Whoever he is, he isn't welcome here, because he went sniffing after something he found more appealing. The idiot.

"Arren?" She touched his cheek.

"I want you. Here. Now." He had to eradicate that damned scent. No male scent but his own was allowed near her. *None but her brother. That is right. That is proper.*

She didn't hesitate. Sandy rose on tiptoe and kissed him. Arren led her toward the bed, thankful that the scent was not as potent there. She'd changed the sheets, wiped away the other male's scent as best he could.

I can do better.

Chapter Ten

Her alarm blaring dragged a groan from Sandy, and she reached around for the offensive piece of machinery. It turned off at her slap, and she burrowed under the covers.

The enticing scent of sex had her licking her lips. Her body came to life a little at a time. Pleasant twinges brought vivid memories of the marathon of sex she'd indulged in with Arren, first at his apartment and then at hers. Her nipples came to hard points, and her sheath wet and pulsed in want.

That's it. I'm calling in sick today.

Sandy turned toward...the empty side of the bed. "Arren?"

There was no response, and she flopped down onto her pillow, cursing under her breath. When he'd stayed in bed after sex, she'd had fantasies of waking with him, but he was gone.

"Typical male," she grumbled. They were all the same, human or Xxanian, and any hope for variation in the breed was a pipe dream.

Her arousal waning—*Too much to ask to have a hot morning climax of my own making, I guess.*—Sandy threw the covers back and lumbered out of bed. *Might as well go to work, since my day is already ruined.*

She tried not to obsess over the fact that she'd never cared when Jason had left after sex. *Jason never made me come like Arren does. That's all it is.*

Sandy knew she was lying to herself. Arren was like the fairy tale knight: gracious, chivalrous, and attentive. *But hot in bed. The Brothers Grimm never wrote that into their bedtime stories. A lot more adults would read them, if they had.*

There is a lot to fall in love with there, beyond that talented cock and mouth.

She grumbled a sacrilegious oath and called herself a fool for even thinking something so stupid. *What? I live to have my heart broken?*

Probably so.

In the kitchen and still naked, Sandy reached for the coffee pot. Paper crinkled under her hand, and she squinted at it. It took a full minute for the neat penmanship on the note paper she kept next to phone to take shape. Her hands trembling, Sandy opened it.

Dear Sandy,

My apologies for leaving this way, but I had an early morning meeting to attend to. I didn't want to wake you, since you no doubt have a long day of work ahead of you.

Last night was wonderful. I hope it was the same for you.

I would very much like to see you again, if you're willing.

Willing? Is he kidding? What part of last night did he find me unwilling? She read on.

I have left my business card on the counter. My private line is on the back. If you would like to see me again, please leave a message for me at your convenience, and I will get back to you as soon as my schedule permits.

Arren

Her heart melted. Okay, so he wasn't like human men. *No human man would have left a note like this.* No human man would have even explained why he'd left, let alone apologized for leaving without waking her. For that matter, how many human men would have left a direct number? Most of them took a woman's number and gave lip service to "I'll call you."

She considered calling him right away, then dismissed the idea. If he left early for a meeting, he was either getting ready for that meeting or involved in it. Waiting for a while might mean she'd reach him after it and be able to talk to him directly instead of leaving a message.

And if I call now, it will look desperate. As if she didn't already look desperate to him. Sandy had abandoned anything short of that when she'd admitted why she wanted to sleep with him.

Frustrated with herself, she filled the coffeemaker, started it, then headed off to the shower. Maybe that would clear her head.

It didn't. Sandy emerged from her morning bathroom routine no less conflicted than she'd been before it.

But at least I have coffee to help me recover from the sleep deprivation, and I intend to savor it.

Thirty minutes later, dressed in a skirt suit, she slipped her feet into her pumps and reached for her purse. The business card caught her eye, and she lifted it from the counter.

It was better to call Arren from here than work, she supposed. If it meant leaving him a message, it did.

Sandy pulled her mobile phone from her pocket and dialed the phone number on the back of the card. It rang once. Twice.

A voice answered with a cheery, "Mr. Raashh's office. How may I direct your call?"

"I'm sorry," Sandy blurted out. "I thought I was calling Arren...Mr. Raashh directly."

"You are. He is in a meeting at the moment. Can I take a message for him?"

His secretary? I don't think this is what Arren meant by leaving him a message. "Uh...I guess n—"

"Oh. Is this Miss Butler? I've been expecting your call." There was clicking of keys on the other side of the phone. "Are you free for a meeting this evening?"

Meeting?

Well, he's not going to tell his secretary he's having her schedule his sexual liaisons. "Yes. This evening would be fine."

"What time is convenient for you?"

"I beg your pardon?"

"What time do you finish work? And do you need me to send a car for you?"

Words stuck in her throat. He had his secretary schedule his dates so often it was considered normal? Sandy considered telling Arren to go stuff himself.

Memories of his mouth meshing with hers nixed that. There had been nothing perfunctory in that. "F-five. No, I don't need a car. I tend to take public transport where I need to go."

More keys clicked. "If you'd prefer it, but I can send a car. It's no trouble."

"Thank you. No."

"Do you need the address?"

"To where?"

The secretary laughed, but it wasn't a mean sound. "My apologies. That is your choice. You can meet Mr. Raashh at his apartment or at the *Spice Industries* building, of course. I should have said that first." The last part sounded like a reminder a distracted person gave herself.

"Uh... *Spice*, I suppose." It was closer than his apartment was, but it would also be less conspicuous than meeting Arren at his apartment. If she said the apartment, it would be akin to admitting they were having sex, and since she didn't know if his secretary could be trusted, Sandy wasn't incriminating Arren or herself in any way. "Yes. I know where it is." *Who doesn't know where the* Spice Tower *is?*

"Very well. When you arrive, just go to the front desk. They will direct you from there."

"Thank you. That's very helpful."

"That's my job. Call me anytime, Miss Butler. I am at your disposal."

"You are?" What in the world was she talking about?

"I am. Mr. Raashh has told me to arrange anything you need me to."

Her heart pounded at that pronouncement. "When I'm scheduled to meet him, you mean."

"He didn't say that, and I've learned to take Mr. Raashh literally. Most Xxan say precisely what they mean."

Sandy tried to brush away the feeling that she was being bought and paid for. A kept woman.

"Is anything wrong, Miss Butler? Can I help you with anything else?"

"No. No thank you." She hung up before she could call off their "meeting" for tonight.

Her thoughts troubled, Sandy looked up at the clock, startled, then rushed off to catch the train to work.

* * * *

"I had really hoped to meet with Daveed." Li Ross's disappointment was palpable.

"It is no insult to you, Mr. Li," Arren offered smoothly in the human elder's own language. "My older brother is a genius in design, but business is my art."

A slight tip of the oriental businessman's head preceded his answer. "Of course. We all have our strengths and weaknesses."

Arren's typical Subdominant strength of patience was wearing thin. It was ten o'clock in the morning at the main office, and there was still no word from Sandy. Had she decided not to call him? Had he offended her or disappointed her already?

He sat at the table, calmly discussing prices and delivery dates for Li's best silk, but his nerves jumped beneath the surface. An hour later, he stood and sealed the deal with a thumb print on the negotiation board and a handshake.

Finally, he was free to turn his handheld computer on again and check for messages. His heart skipped a beat or two at the sight of the new entry on his schedule. Betty had even flagged it for him.

As if I would miss it?

Sandy Butler: after 5:00 pm at Spice Industries

A smile pulled up at his lips. As soon as the meal Li had offered was over, Arren would have the shuttle pilot take him back to *Spice*.

"You seem to have gotten good news," Li observed.

"A meeting I'd been hoping to arrange has fallen into place," he explained in a half truth.

"Ah. We all have our strengths. Yours serve your family well."

In this case, possibly. Raashh has never expected me to bind a female to me.

* * * *

Sandy rushed off the train and up to street level. Of course she was late. *Story of my life.*

Jason, the rat, had made sure she had work that "just had to be completed today". She didn't question that it had been his doing, though she wouldn't give him the satisfaction of seeing her rattled.

Rattled definitely described her state of mind. It was after six, and though she hadn't given Arren's secretary a time for her arrival, they'd probably anticipated her earlier than this.

Rain pounded against her rain slicker and made a rushing stream of the sidewalk and gutter. Though the weather report had called for rain, she hadn't expected this downpour.

As if reinforcing that, she slipped and crashed to the ground. Sandy planted a hand on the slick pavement, panting in and out, waiting for the first slice of pain to pass.

Great. Just great. I should go. I'm a mess.

Sandy chided herself for being shallow. Even if she had to go home to change, Arren was expecting her. She owed it to him to tell him she had to call their date off in person. Gingerly— and none too comfortably—she levered herself off the ground and limped toward the lobby of *Spice Tower*.

The security guard's bored expression turned to a frown. "Can I help you, miss? Do you need me to call the staff physician for you?"

"Do I look that bad?" she quipped in return.

He didn't reply to that.

"I have a meeting with Mr. Raashh."

"Which Mr. Raashh?"

"Uh..." *There's more than one at the company?* It wasn't exactly a common name, she was sure. "Arren Raashh."

"Name?" He focused on the screen before him, and the clacking of keys said he was checking Arren's schedule.

He must be very important if the guards check before letting someone come up.

Or maybe they do that for everyone. Spice *is a highly-guarded company.* In fact, they were a cornerstone client of the law firm she worked for, an account that only the senior partners worked with. She couldn't be sure what a company like that had in place for security measures, but after the terrorist attacks, it was probably iron-clad.

"Sandy Butler."

His eyes widened. "Oh, I am sorry to keep you waiting, Miss Butler." He rushed out from behind the desk and pressed an Identi-chip into her hand. "This will clear you for the elevator. Mr. Raashh is on the thirtieth floor. Straight off the elevator. You can't miss his office."

His gaze went to her legs. "Uh... Are you sure you don't want me to call the staff physician to take care of that knee first? It won't be any trouble at all."

Why did he keep saying that to her? Sandy glanced down at herself and winced at her ripped nylons and bleeding knee. *Oh. He's probably afraid of a lawsuit.* "Thank you, but no. I'm sure there's a restroom I can use to freshen up somewhere?"

"Mr. Raashh has one in his office."

In *his office? He must mean on that floor or in the office suite Arren shares with other employees.* She offered a smile. "Thank you. Thirtieth?"

"Yes, ma'am."

She made her way to the bank of elevators and searched the signs until she found the single one that accessed the twenty-seventh floor of the tower and above. Under the watchful eye of the guard, she used the Identi-chip to call the elevator and again inside to unlock the floor she needed.

Arren must be very important to work on a locked floor. The image of the executive keeping a mistress niggled at her thoughts again.

The trip to the thirtieth floor was fast and smooth, without the typical inner ear discomfort that long elevator trips usually caused. She stepped off and started down the corridor as the guard had instructed.

An empty desk dominated a lush waiting room. The door beyond it read:

Arren Raashh
CEO, Spice Automotive
Vice President of Operations, Spice Industries

Very important doesn't cover it. No wonder he thought I might be after his money. With titles like those, he's swimming in it.

* * * *

The phone on Arren's desk rang, and he pounced on it. "Yes?" Too late, he realized he sounded harried. *I am harried.*

But I shouldn't sound it. It's unbecoming.

"Front desk, sir. Your guest has arrived and is on her way up, Mr. Raashh."

Arren breathed a sigh of relief. "Good."

"I offered to call the staff physician for the lady, but—"

"What? Why?"

There was a moment of silence, followed by hemming and hawing.

"Why?" he demanded.

"It looks like the lady took a fall in the rain and—"

"Send the physician up. Now." Arren dropped the phone back on its cradle without waiting for an answer and bolted for the elevators.

Sandy startled at his headlong rush out his office door and dropped back a step. He came to a halt behind Betty's desk and assessed her appearance. Sandy's hair was damp and her rain slicker dripped water onto the imported offworld rug in his office suite.

Fuck the rug.

Her nylons were torn, and a trail of blood wound down her leg. She shifted, taking more of the weight off that foot.

She's favoring the leg. Blast it!

Sandy straightened her rain slicker. "I should go home and change," she breathed. "I'm so sorry, Arren." Her eyes pleaded with him.

For what? He didn't understand her concern. "Don't be silly." He strode to her and lifted Sandy into his arms.

"You'll be soaked," she protested miserably.

"I can change clothing as well as you can." He carried her through his office and to his private bathing chamber. "There is a robe on the hook here. Take off your wet clothing, and give them to me."

The fact that she didn't balk at the idea was heartening.

Sandy drew her coat off and handed it to him. Arren hung it on the furthest hook and reached to take her suit jacket. The cuffs were soaking wet, probably from her pushing herself up after her fall. Her blouse came next, similarly affected.

She lifted her injured leg to toe off her shoe, and Arren went to one knee and slipped it off for her. Sandy hesitated and settled that foot on the floor; she raised the other and offered it to him. Arren obliged her.

Her move to unfasten her skirt ended when he reached the hook and eye first. Sandy watched him slide the zipper down and unhook the waistband, and her scent teased at his senses. The skirt plummeted to the floor, sodden and dirty, and Sandy stepped out of it, releasing it to him.

Her panties were wet, and so were her pantyhose. Arren started sliding them off together. Her breathing went ragged, and her scent intensified.

Not now. The doctor is coming to treat her injury.

Arren removed the clothing, sliding it off each foot as she raised them in turn to aid him. That accomplished, he stood to reach for the robe.

Sandy wasn't finished yet. She unfastened the front closure on her bra and peeled it away, releasing her lush breasts. Arren's mouth watered to taste them.

The doctor is on his way.

She raised the bra and draped it over his shoulder in a blatant offer. His cock was hard and demanding.

The doctor!

Arren forced himself to wrap the robe around her, and Sandy pushed her arms through, though her expression questioned his wish to cover her.

I don't want to cover her.

A knock at the door saved him the trouble of explaining. Sandy startled and pulled the robe closed around her body, and Arren took his time tying it shut for her. She snatched the bra from his shoulder and tossed it on one of the hooks. When she was covered, he took her by the arm and led Sandy to the plush sofa.

"Enter," he shouted at last.

One of the human doctors *Spice* employed to care for their staff bustled in, took one look at Sandy, and tipped his head to her. "If you would?" He motioned to the sofa.

She sank to the surface of it. "It really isn't that serious," she sighed.

Arren shot her a look of warning. "Let the doctor care for you."

Sandy nodded and uncovered her knee.

The doctor started asking questions about how she fell and where. He cleaned the cut, prompting a wince from Sandy.

In the meantime, Arren looked at the tags on her clothing and sent a message to Betty by computer, asking her to have something to replace them sent over immediately.

"What would you like to eat?" he interrupted the ongoing discussion.

"I'm hardly dressed for a restaurant, Arren," Sandy replied with a tone that might be teasing.

The doctor placed a large self-stick bandage on her knee.

Arren smiled. "That goes without saying, but you *must* eat, so what would you like to eat?"

"Chinese? Japanese?"

"In specific?" he inquired.

"Well...sashimi? Tuna and salmon?"

Something I can eat as well. How considerate of her. "Anything else?" Something told him she was holding back.

"Miso soup, please."

He shot her a smile. "That's better." At least she hadn't stated her wishes as a question this time.

She blushed deeply, and he focused on his computer. Betty had already responded that clothing was on the way, and he sent the request for food. He followed it with a promise that he wouldn't bother her further that evening.

The reply came in moments.

Food is on its way, Mr. Raashh. Anytime you need me, just let me know.

With the money he was paying her, that would be true of any executive secretary, but Betty was more than that. The woman was middle-aged, widowed, and seemed to view Arren as the son she'd never had. She pampered him mercilessly.

Another message followed, proving that she knew him better than he wanted to admit.

Good luck with your lady friend. I hope your evening goes well.

In other words, she hopes I find a mate. Thank you, Betty.

Across the room, the doctor was preparing a hypo. Sandy pulled the oversize sleeve to her shoulder, baring her upper arm.

Arren's heart stuttered. "What are you doing?"

The older man paused and looked his way. "The lady hasn't had a tetanus shot for quite some time. For her safety, I should give her one."

Arren grunted his agreement and went back to the keyboard, though he had no reason to. For some reason, he found watching the doctor inject the medicine into Sandy disturbing. Still, he was aware of the small sound of distress she made and tensed in response.

Calm down. It is for her safety. A female's safety must always come first.

The injection accomplished, the doctor gave a few instructions about signs he considered a danger and took his leave with a tip of his head to her and then to Arren.

Arren, in the meantime, was busy committing the instructions to memory. As long as Sandy was his woman, it was his responsibility to see to her health and safety. It was a duty all Xxanian males took very seriously.

The door closed behind the doctor, and Sandy rubbed at the injection site, scowling. "I told you it wasn't serious," she grumbled.

Arren crossed the room to her and settled on the sofa. "You aren't really going to hold seeing to your health and safety against me, are you?" If she would, there was little chance she would accept mating with him.

Sandy opened her mouth, closed it again, sighed, and then answered. "No. I suppose that would be ungrateful of me."

He stroked his fingertips along her jaw line. "I don't want you injured or sick, Sandy."

She nodded and managed a weak smile. "I suppose you also want to make sure I don't file suit or something like that."

The undertone of hurt shocked him more than her words. "Why would you think something so ludicrous?" Too late, he realized being dismissive of her feelings wasn't a good choice. Arren opened his mouth to apologize.

"Well, everyone is so concerned over a little cut. What other reason—"

Arren dipped his head and sealed his lips to hers. *How could she question why I want to protect her? I must have failed to make my intentions clear.*

Sandy hesitated, then threw herself into the moment.

She understands this, at least.

It wasn't enough. Arren broke off the kiss, his cock protesting the premature end to what they both clearly wanted.

Sandy pressed to him, her scent enticing.

"You think this is all I want," he breathed.

She pulled at his tie, loosening it. "You don't?"

Arren bit back a series of curses. "If you want me to bed you, I won't deny you, but you are deciding something I will do everything in my power to convince you of."

Her eyes widened.

"You are deciding whether or not you will let me bind you as my mate. If you believe a few days or weeks of a woman in my bed will ever be more important to me than having you specifically as my mate, you are sadly mistaken."

Her breaths came in little puffs of air. "Are you saying you already know you want that?"

If I asked her now, she might agree. It would be said in haste, not a considered choice. "I am fairly certain...if you prove willing, but we can't make that choice without learning about each other."

Sandy nodded, her eyes heavy and slumberous.

Arren stroked the backs of his fingers over the bandage on her knee. "That means I am going to treat you as much like you are my mate now as is appropriate. I am going to protect you from all harm possible. Do you accept that proposition, Sandy?"

She gasped out an affirmative response.

"Then we are going to eat, talk, perhaps touch..."

Sandy rose against him. "And then?"

"As always, it is your choice." There was a moment of potent silence. "Any other concerns?" he prodded.

"Just one." Her voice was low and breathy.

Arren raised a brow. "And that is?"

"You're all wet. I think you should remove your shirt."

He smiled at that and started to work the buttons open.

* * * *

Sandy set her food aside, full nearly to discomfort. Arren smiled and tipped his chopsticks to her, chewing a bit of sashimi.

She ranged her gaze over his body. He was still shirtless, and after the guards had brought up the food and other packages, he'd removed his shoes and socks as well. Sandy licked her lips, considering what lay beneath his trousers. Unless the previous day was an anomaly, the trousers were the only thing he was wearing.

Arren went still. He turned his head, staring at her, the muscles in his arms and shoulders bunching as if he was preparing to pounce.

On me. The thought delighted her.

He leaned to her, brushing his lips across hers. Sandy cupped his face in her hands, tilting her head to open her mouth to his fully.

The kiss was full of promise and heat, and a heartbeat later, Sandy was in Arren's lap. She untied the robe and pulled the sides apart.

He left the kiss, shaking his head. "Somewhere we can move freely," he grumbled.

Arren stood, lifting Sandy with him. Just when she thought he was going to place her on the desk, he rounded it and went to the couch instead.

Their lips parted, as he deposited her carefully on it. He stood next to the piece of furniture, working at the button and zipper on his trousers. He let them fall, confirming that commando was his usual state of dress.

Sandy eased the robe off her shoulders, leaving herself nude. His gaze scorched her senses, moving from her feet to her face and down again.

Arren ripped open a condom without looking down at it and rolled it down the length of his cock. In a heartbeat, he was between her ankles, spreading Sandy's legs around him. Then she was upright, in his hands, poised over the head of his cock. He lowered her onto him slowly, stretching her around his girth.

She grasped at his shoulders, her body on fire. One thrust led to another and a third. Sandy held to him, her head swimming in pleasure. Stars, but she'd never felt like this before.

The pressure built in her, coming to a keen edge before she pitched into the abyss. Arren followed her over, his muscles tensing. A growl escaped his lips.

They held to each other, breathing hard. Sandy settled her head to his chest.

"You are so beautiful," Arren complimented her.

She shivered in the memory of Jason, when she told him it was over. Every word out of his mouth had been the opposite of that compliment. Jason's words had been ugly.

"What is it?"

"Nothing. Just...bad memories."

His lips caressed her forehead. "The man who hurt you?" he guessed.

"Yes." She managed a smile that felt brittle. "But I don't want to think about him."

"I agree." His voice went gruff. Before she could question him, Arren continued. "There are so many better things we could think of."

Sandy pushed back a bit and looked up at him. "Like?"

"There are still a few places in your apartment I haven't managed to make love to you yet."

He was teasing, but her heart rate picked up at the comment. "That *is* a much better thing to think about. Or to do."

His smile told her she'd made the right choice.

Chapter Eleven

Six days later

Sandy hooked her purse over her shoulder and headed for the elevator, her heart light. After her fall in the rain, Arren had all-but demanded to have a car available for her at the end of her work day.

He'd tried to insist on a driver for all her needs, but she'd balked at that extravagance. Unless she had errands to run for work or herself, there really wasn't much for the driver to do. Why pay someone full time wages or more to sit around and wait for Sandy to find some work for him?

She'd halfway expected that Arren would try to offer her a car and city parking for it instead. Perhaps even he realized that would be too much, considering they didn't know where their relationship was going from here.

She punched the call button and smoothed her jacket, hoping she looked passable for an evening out.

Or in. Sex with Arren was fast becoming an addiction. Sandy found herself daydreaming far too often for her sanity or comfort.

The elevator opened, and she hurried aboard. The way down seemed to take far too long, and she realized she was already anticipating seeing Arren.

I am hopeless. He was sending a car for her. Arren wasn't picking her up himself. It might be half an hour or more before she saw him, and she was already wet and ready.

And I'm early. She sighed. It would be even longer until she saw Arren, since she'd worked through lunch. The driver wouldn't be there for the pickup until five, and it was only four fifteen. Sandy made a mental note to get the driver's direct number, so she could let the man know if she would be early or late for his usual pick-up.

The elevator doors opened, and she headed for the front doors. The building had a small garden at every door, and it would be a nice place to pass the time until the driver arrived.

Again, Sandy cursed herself for not thinking to get the driver's number. If she had it, she could just call him and let him know she'd be taking the subway over to *Spice Industries* today.

Maybe I could get the number from Betty. That was even more ridiculous. Sandy knew from experience that the last thing a secretary wanted was someone calling with nitpicky little questions they could have answered for themselves. *Oh well. It's a nice day, and sitting in the garden won't be a hardship.*

That thought came to a screeching halt at the sight of Arren's hired driver vaulting from the car and rounding it to the passenger door.

She went to his side, taking his offered hand. Sandy slid into the car, and he closed her in.

The driver took his place again. "Where to, Ms. Butler?"

Now that he'd mentioned it, she wasn't sure. "I don't know. Arren won't be finished with work for a while. Maybe you should just drop me at home, and he can meet me there later?" It wasn't the way she'd wanted to unveil her surprise for him, but it would have to do.

"Just a moment."

"Of course."

He opened a cell phone and spoke in Xxan into it. After a moment, he nodded and shut the phone. He pocketed it. "Arren is ready to leave now. I can take you to the *Spice Tower* and leave you in Arren's care."

"Yes. Please." This was much more like it. Sandy knew how she wanted to reveal her surprise to Arren.

It didn't take them long to reach *Spice Tower*. The driver pulled into the garage, through a blast door, and down into a nearly-deserted area in the garage.

"Arren's parking area?" she asked.

The driver nodded.

Arren appeared from an elevator. He came to her door and opened it for her. "Thank you, Beel. That will be all for today."

The driver tipped his head. "Have a good evening."

"We will," Sandy answered. Her cheeks heated at saying something so bold in front of another Xxanian male. She didn't even know if he was mated. What if he wasn't?

Arren laughed and swung the door shut. Beel left them there.

He leaned down and laid a kiss on her lips. "So, where do you want to go for dinner?"

"Let's go to your apartment." That's what she'd planned all along. Sandy reached out and touched his cock, needing him. *And I will have him.*

* * * *

Arren shivered at the stroking of her fingers along the line of his primary. "You do need to eat," he reminded her.

"Later."

The promise of more was all the enticement he needed. Arren took her arm and led Sandy toward his coupe. "That's good. I wanted to take you to the penthouse. I have a surprise for you."

"I have a surprise for you too." There was something smug in that, something he couldn't identify.

"Let's go. We can get dinner later."

"I agree."

He helped her into the passenger seat, then took his own. By the time he was settled, she'd removed her suit jacket and deposited it and her purse on the floor. He darkened the windows and took off his glasses, just in case that was a sign she'd intended for him to pick up on.

They were halfway to the penthouse before he spoke again. "You really have a surprise for me?"

"I do."

He ranged his gaze up and down her body, postulating on what it might be. "Please tell me you're wearing some really interesting underclothes."

Sandy chuckled and leaned closer to him. "I'm not wearing any."

His primary came fully erect, and he ached to find out if she was telling him the truth. "Is that your surprise?"

"No." She opened a button on her blouse. "Do you want to see?"

Arren licked his lips. "You know I do."

Keeping his attention on the road was difficult. Button after button slid open, and Sandy's pupils dilated in arousal. Her scent was sublime. Sandy spread her blouse, showing him her bare breasts.

Memories of their first day together made his mouth water. "Do you want me to eat you in the car again, Sandy?"

She pulled the blouse off and dropped it on top of her jacket. "I want you to eat me, but not in the car."

A glance at her, wearing her skirt and stiletto heels...and reportedly nothing else, made his primary jerk against his trousers. "If you walk into my home dressed that way, I will eat you wherever you wish. However you wish."

She opened the car door and stepped out. "You'd better," she teased.

Arren followed her, his cock complaining at the wait. *Just a little longer. Just until we get to my surprise.*

In the elevator, Sandy started undoing buttons on his shirt. Holding still and letting her do it took all his self-control. When she had it opened, Arren shucked the shirt off and let it fall.

The elevator door opened, and Arren guided her off of it. "So... Where am I going to be eating you?" he asked.

Sandy smiled. "The bathroom, I suppose."

He tried to make sense of the request.

She rose on tiptoe and nibbled at his chin. "The mirror."

"Then maybe I should show you my surprise."

Her eyes lit in interest. "Maybe you should."

Arren led her to the bedside.

Sandy looked around the room. "I don't see anything different."

He reached to the side of the bedside table closest to the bed and pressed the button. Sandy's gaze snapped from the button to the ceiling at the sound of the panel moving aside.

Her eyes went wide, and she gaped at the sight of the mirror above the bed appearing from behind the panel. Her scent took on a potent edge.

"I take it the bed is acceptable for whatever you have planned?" he teased.

"Oh yes, it is. It's perfect, Arren."

It was the thing every Xxanian male lived to hear. Making his female happy with him was a dream come true.

"I can just picture it...all those golden curls between my legs." A tremor of what he hoped was anticipation worked down her body.

Arren bit back a grimace at her description of his hair. It was so fine, he didn't dare cut the curls off, lest he look like a toddler who hadn't grown in adult hair yet. Still, he'd always felt the curls were too feminine. Oddly, his *seir* seemed fond of them, for some reason Arren couldn't begin to fathom.

And it doesn't matter. Clearly, Sandy likes my hair this way. If she likes it, it stays. Forever.

Or as long as she is my woman. Losing her might well convince him to shave his head in despair.

Sandy stared at the mirror, lost in whatever daydreams and plans it engendered in her.

Curiosity ate at him; Arren had no clue what her surprise for him was, and he wanted to know. He needed to. "Sandy?"

She snapped her gaze to him, seemingly dazed.

"Your surprise?" he hinted.

Her cheeks went an enticing shade of red. She worked the button and zipper on her skirt open.

That made no sense to Arren. She said she wasn't wearing panties, so it couldn't be that. What else could lay beneath her skirt?

He wondered if she'd gotten a tattoo, but he dismissed it immediately. Why would she think such a thing would be for him? No Xxanian male would ask his female to endure such useless pain for his enjoyment.

She dropped the skirt and stepped out of it daintily.

It took a moment for what he was seeing to make sense. Arren trailed his fingertips over her bare mound, at a loss for words.

"I shaved for you."

But why had she? "You do not have to make yourself like a Xxanian female to be enticing to me," he breathed. Still, the sight of her hairless mound was strangely appealing to him. His mouth watered to taste her.

"Obviously. But..." She shifted closer to his hand, her scent intensifying in her arousal. Her nipples came to hard points that begged for his attention.

"But?"

"I've heard it makes a woman more sensitive. I wanted to test that rumor."

"Then we shall."

Arren lifted Sandy by the waist and laid her in the middle of the bed, centered beneath the mirror on the ceiling. He kicked off his shoes, climbed between her ankles, and forced her legs wide with his.

She looked up at him, her breathing already ragged. "Arren?"

He sank over her, tasting every millimeter of her outside before he thrust his tongue inside her. Sandy's moans deepened, and she closed a hand in his hair, drawing him closer to her body.

"Oh, yes. Stars burn, yes. This is perfect."

He didn't doubt that she meant both the mirror image of them and what he was doing to her.

The clenching of her sheath stole his breath, and her full climax followed close on its heels. Arren grinned, pleased with her sounds and her heightened taste.

"The rumors were true?" he asked.

"They certainly are with you."

Arren took pride in her praise. "We should continue to test that."

"What —?"

She gasped in surprise as he started eating her again.

Enjoy, Sandy. We have as much time as you grant me to enjoy the mirror in every possible way it can be used.

Chapter Twelve

Three weeks later

The restaurant was dimly lit, and plants grew in planters and hanging pots everywhere. It took a moment for the significance to hit her.

A Xxanian restaurant. She nibbled at her lower lip, uncertain what was required in such an establishment.

Two men rounded her, went to the side of the carpeted foyer, and removed their shoes.

Lesson one. Remove your shoes before passing through this room. Sandy hurried to comply, trying to keep the two men in her sights to use for more cues.

They approached the desk, spoke to the human maître d' in what she was sure was the Xxanian language, and shook hands with him before following the server to their table.

Sandy took a calming breath and approached. She couldn't speak Xxan, but she could offer her hand and tell the man why she was here.

The maître d' looked up, his smile of welcome fading at the sight of her. His gaze panned down her body and froze at her feet. "May I help you, miss?" he offered in a voice that said he was welcoming her, when his expression countered it.

Something told her not to offer her hand. "I am here to meet Arren Raashh."

His next glance at her feet said she'd done something wrong. His cheeks darkened, and he cleared his throat.

"I saw the men before me removing theirs and—"

"It is a female's choice to remove her shoes or not, miss. If you would rather not, I will wait to show you in, of course."

"No. It's comfortable. If it's not a problem, I believe I'll leave them off."

He tipped his head. "Yes, miss. Of course." With that, he waved for a server and spoke to the man in Xxan.

The Xxanian server slanted a glance at her feet, and the maître d' snapped a command that had him stiffening and looking to the far side of the room. With a quick tip of his head, he hurried away.

Sandy squirmed in place. "If it's a problem—"

"Not at all, miss," the maître d' replied gracefully. "We have two empty private dining chambers this evening. It is not an imposition at all."

Private dining chamber? What the blazes is he talking about? She glanced at the two men in the main dining room, wondering what was causing the stir developing.

* * * *

"If you would, sir?"

Arren looked up at the waiter, confused by the request for him to leave the table. "I beg your pardon."

The Subdominant switched to Xxan for his reply. *"Your female guest has indicated her wish for a private dining chamber, sir. Please accompany me, so you can escort her in properly."*

His shock was so profound that Arren hesitated a moment before complying. His cock was hard beneath the layers of human clothing, and he fastened his suit jacket for the sake of propriety.

The Subdominant motioned for another to clear their table and ready the private chamber, then he led Arren toward the maître d's desk.

One look at Sandy confirmed that she had no idea what was going on. She shifted from nylon-covered foot to foot, her color high. At the sight of him, she managed a weak smile.

Arren slanted a nod her direction and addressed the maître d'. *"I presume you did not tell her what bare feet meant?"*

"Certainly not, sir." He was understandably affronted by the suggestion. *"Do you believe it wise to—"*

"No. Set up the private dining chamber, and she will make that decision for herself, once she understands it."

"Is there a problem, Arren?" Sandy asked.

"No. Just a slight change in plans."

"If you'd rather have me wear my shoes—"

"No. I don't prefer that." *At all. Seir-God, you have no concept what walking through here with you shoeless means to me.*

Her smile was more heartfelt, and the muscles in her shoulders relaxed.

Arren offered his arm, and she took it. It was a simple courtesy. Considering what removing her shoes would typically signify, it was the least a male could do to escort her properly.

Discussions at neighboring tables quieted at their approach. Males sneaked hurried assessments of Sandy, then turned away before Arren could voice his offense.

Sandy was thankfully oblivious to all of it. Her attention was on the Xxanian artwork hung on the walls, the many plants, and the filtered lighting.

One selfish corner of his mind reveled in the fact that the other men were jealous of him, the Subdominant. Another argued that not telling Sandy what a female being shoeless meant was dishonorable.

She may be angry. She has a right to be, but I will make amends, if she is.

The waiter drew a heavy curtain back. "Here, sir."

Arren grumbled out his thanks and guided Sandy into the chamber beyond. The walls, floor, and ceiling were padded, and freshly laundered cushions were stacked in a raised box that took up half the room. Aside from the lights and the cushioned box, the only thing in the room was the long, low table the food would be deposited on.

Sandy looked around, seemingly uncertain as to where to sit or how to. Though she clearly had questions, she didn't ask them.

She's probably afraid of looking foolish in front of the staff. Or making me look bad in front of other Xxanians.

The waiter closed the drapes carefully. "Would you like to order now, sir?"

"A few moments, if you don't mind."

"Of course, sir."

At the sound of a throat clearing on the other side of the drape, the waiter reached through and brought the wine and glasses from their original table back. He arranged them on the low table, then took his leave.

The moment he disappeared, Sandy looked up at Arren. "I did something wrong. Didn't I?"

He sighed. "I don't see it that way, but you may. I apologize, but there was no way to explain it without causing you unease, so I let it continue until I could do it properly and privately."

Her glance toward the curtain spoke volumes of the fact that she didn't find this arrangement private.

"The staff is very discrete."

Sandy nodded. "What did I do wrong?" She seemed fixated on that concept, and Arren wished he could convince her it was unwarranted.

"All men remove their shoes. I can only assume you saw a man do so and thought everyone did."

Her cheeks flamed. "Two men. So...what does it mean when a woman removes her shoes?"

Arren motioned to the room. "You are requesting a private dining chamber."

"Just that?"

"Not precisely. It means you are...receptive. You are inviting your dinner partner to seduce you."

Her eyes went wide and wild. "So they think...?"

"That we mean to have sex in here? At the moment, yes. If you decide you want that, the servers will close the doors after they deliver the food, and no one will disturb us until we let ourselves out."

"And if I decide I don't want that?"

His heart sank, but Arren forced a smile to his face. "I tell the servers it was an error, because it is your first time at a Xxanian restaurant, and the doors will stay open. Everyone in the restaurant will believe we simply wanted comfort and privacy and not an intimate encounter."

Sandy stared at the cushion box. "And people do this often?"

"The cushions are laundered after each meal served in here," he assured her, though Arren feared that wasn't her concern. "Yes. These rooms are often used by mated couples, often bearing couples. Ones that are traveling and far from their nests find this an indulgence. Sometimes, unmated couples come here for pampering and a bit of privacy."

"And have you...? Before me?"

If the Xxan could blush, Arren thought he might be capable of it for the first time in his life. "Once. The female saw it as something of an adventure."

"Oh."

"You are not an adventure to me," he reminded her. Arren had made it clear enough that he wanted her as his mate, hadn't he?

She was silent and still, and her scent was an uncertain mix.

"Sandy? Would you rather leave?" Perhaps she was too shamed by this mistake to eat here.

"No." She looked up at him with those stunning light blue eyes. "Tell them to shut the doors."

"This will be a night you never forget," he vowed.

Arren unbuttoned his jacket and slid it off, letting it fall to the padded floor. He scooped Sandy into his arms and settled her onto the cushions. Once he'd provided her with a glass of wine, he called the waiter in, hoping to make the most striking announcement of her decision he could.

* * * *

The server entered the room, his gaze averted, though Sandy was certain he knew precisely how she was arranged on the cushions.

"Your choices, sir?"

"The best for my lady," he announced. "And preparations."

"Yes, sir. *S'shuuaih?*"

Arren shot a heated look at Sandy. "Yes. Thank you. Informal."

He withdrew, and Sandy peeked at Arren over the rim of her glass. "What did he ask?"

Before he could answer, the server was back with an armload of deep blue silk. He handed it off to Arren with a slight bow and hurried away again.

Arren set the silk on the low table and started unbuttoning his shirt.

"What are you doing?" she whispered.

"We are going to dress more comfortably for dinner," he informed her.

"We?" Her heart pounded in anticipation. This was turning out to be something altogether different than what she'd anticipated.

He smiled wickedly. "We."

Sandy set the glass on the edge of the table and went to work on her suit coat. When she was down to her bra and panties, she looked up to ask him what she should remove. The question stuck in her throat at the sight of him standing nude, his cock at attention.

I guess that answers my question.

She watched, spellbound, as he wrapped a length of blue cloth around his waist and tucked it into itself. His cock tented the front, and a slight wet stain announced he was more than ready for whatever was about to happen.

"Take off the rest, and I will help you wrap the *S'suuhhea*." His voice was rough and low.

Her body wet in response. Sandy made a show of removing her bra and underwear, and Arren brought a second length of cloth onto the cushions and knelt beside her.

"Raise your arms."

She complied, and he wrapped the silk around her back, drawing her slightly closer with it. He passed one side and then the other around her hungry breasts and tied two knots to make a loose loop around her throat.

His fingertips tickled at her inner thigh, and Arren worked the thigh-high stockings down her body and off. The scene was so sensual, she was gasping for breath before he collected her clothing and piled it with his own.

Then he was back, kneeling between her spread thighs. "You want me already. Don't you? You want my tongue thrusting inside you. Or do you want my cock?"

She swallowed down a moan, shivering pleasantly. "Yes. Please."

"Which?"

"Both."

His eye slits widened in arousal. "We have a few minutes before the servers return to close us in."

She moaned out a protest. He couldn't make her wait. It would be cruel to—

Arren spread the sides of the silk, exposing her body. His rough tongue rasped over one nipple and then the other. "You are going to spend a good deal of the meal like this, being seduced by taste and touch and smell and sight."

He sucked the nipple into his mouth, and she gasped in response. Sandy had never wanted to have public sex, but right now, the servers could walk in and watch, and she probably wouldn't care.

He teased her, stroking his tongue back and forth between her breasts, tasting her nipples in turn, ranging higher and lower but never as far as her slit or her mouth. Sandy sank into the cushions, boneless in pleasure. She swore she could come from this alone.

Arren whispered into her collarbone. "The doors aren't closed yet, Sandy. Do you want to scream for me before they are or wait for their muting properties?" He paused only a moment to let her digest that. "No one will care if you scream in pleasure. No one but me. The urge to make you scream is so tempting to me."

He was tempting her. The question was, how bold was she?

Not that bold. "Not yet." She wanted to ask if they would be able to hear her scream with the doors closed. *No. If I know they can, I'm not sure I'll be able to go through with this.*

"Then you must control yourself, Sandy, because I am going to try to make you scream."

Before her head stopped spinning from that pronouncement, Arren's tongue was buried between her thighs, scraping pleasantly in and out of her sheath.

Oh, stars burn. Help me. Sandy tunneled her hand in Arren's fine hair and fisted it. She pulled him deeper, needing the climax riding her desperately. *What is it about Arren that makes me want him so intensely? I act like a wanton with him, though he treats me like a goddess.*

He spread her slit and undulated his tongue. Her hip and leg muscles tightened, and she bowed up from the cushions.

A knock at the entrance startled her. Arren started to pull away, and she dragged him back with a harsh "no". Sandy didn't care who saw them or heard them. She needed to come.

Now.

Arren thrust his tongue in and out fiercely, driving her over with a mew of delight and a surprised little shout. In the aftermath, she lay beneath him, while Arren licked leisurely, lapping at her still-contracting body and forcing her to continuing climaxes.

He drew away slowly, pulled the cloth closed around her body, and covered her with the final piece of cloth, a silk sheet. Sandy vaguely noted that the servers would know roughly what they'd been doing moments before.

Do I care? She didn't, which might have bothered her a few weeks earlier, but it certainly didn't tonight. *Like a wanton.*

"Enter," Arren called out.

The tone of warning in his voice brought a smile to her face.

* * * *

Arren barely looked at the servers bringing the food in. The sight of Sandy, lying sated and mussed, was too appealing to ignore.

She has never known sated as she will after this meal.

Platter after platter settled on the table, some covered and some not. The servers took their leave with a muttered prayer, and the doors closed.

Arren made a show of kneeling at her side and reaching for the first of the trays.

Sandy performed a leisurely stretch and smiled. "Mmmm... Smells good. What's for dinner?"

He couldn't have controlled his need to leer at her if he'd wanted to.

She laughed. "I believe you've already had me for dinner."

"I don't believe I'm finished with that."

He lifted the covers on the trays, displaying the wide array of foods he had ordered for them. There was sashimi and *z'haahn*, fresh fruits and vegetables, cheeses, chocolates, and petit fours. To his delight, Sandy's eyes widened and glittered in excitement.

"What would my lady like first?" he asked formally.

Her brow crinkled in confusion.

Arren bowed his head to her. "In one of these private chambers, whatever the female wishes is the command of her male."

She shot a hungry look up and down his body. "You know the old saying."

"Which old saying?" There were thousands of them, he knew.

"Life is short. Eat dessert first."

He smiled. "Chocolates or petit fours?"

Sandy wrapped a hand around his neck and urged Arren into the pile of cushions over her. "Who said anything about that sort of dessert?"

He parted her lips, ravenous for whatever she would offer him. *Once we are both sated, I'll teach her everything I can do with the foods.* He knew it wouldn't end at once. With what he intended to do, he was laying wagers at somewhere around three times before they let themselves out of the room.

Chapter Thirteen

Sandy pulled her Identi-chips from her purse and reached for the lock. Arren's heat against her back stopped her in mid-reach, and she was abruptly aware of every millimeter of his body touching hers, aware of his needs, needs that he rarely voiced.

"As always, it is the female's choice."

She could lay with him for hours and not say a word. He knew what she wanted and gave it effortlessly and selflessly. There had never been a man that put her so at ease and demanded so little from her in her life.

As if in answer, his hand cradled hers, and he guided the Identi-chip up to the lock. Her breathing hitched in her chest and escaped on a rush.

Sandy didn't doubt that he would want to have sex in her apartment. He always did.

In every room. In countless positions. Her exhausted body reacted as if it had been weeks since they'd had sex instead of an hour.

The door lock disengaged, and Arren raised his free hand and pushed it open. He didn't ask to come in, but Sandy read the question in his stillness.

"Yes." To nearly anything he asks for.

Arren guided her inside and shut the door. He unfastened her coat and drew it off her arms. He circled her body and hung the piece of clothing on the coat rack.

Sandy's heart hammered at her ribs. "Why...?" She gasped when he started working her suit coat open.

"Why what, Sandy?"

"What is it about my apartment that you like so much?"

He smiled faintly. "You."

"But you can have me anywhere." Too late, she realized what she'd admitted. Her face flamed.

Arren chuckled darkly. He sobered and met her gaze. "When I started coming here, your apartment smelled of another male."

Her horror at that thought probably showed on her face.

"It was unacceptable. It would still be unacceptable, if the scent returned. Xxanian males are...possessive of their women. Having our mixed scent surrounding me is soothing for me. It also makes me proud to have my scent in your living space. It probably doesn't make much sense to you."

"No. I think I know what you mean." How many times had she breathed in his scent on the pillow before leaving the bed? It made perfect sense to her.

He nodded, though he still seemed troubled.

"Stay the night, Arren. No early morning meetings. Or...anything." Sandy was lightheaded. She wanted him to accept.

He's a busy man. He's going to refuse. He—

"Nothing is more important to me than you, Sandy. I give my vow. Nothing will make me leave you tonight. Nothing. Do you mind if I let Betty know to cancel my appointments for tomorrow?"

A giddy laugh bubbled up. Jason would never have canceled a single appointment for her, let alone a day of them. She waved him on, unable to form the words to accept the gift with decorum.

* * * *

Arren woke with the first rays of the sun peeking around the slatted blinds that covered Sandy's windows. He reached around for the pile of clothing littering the bedroom floor and pulled his dark glasses out.

With them in place, he watched his lover sleeping. *My mate.* If the last few weeks with her were any indication, Sandy fully intended to choose to bind to him.

It's a permanent step. It's not one human women take lightly.

The Xxan didn't take it lightly either, but while Arren was certain he wanted to bind himself to Sandy, it would likely be some time before she made her decision and voiced it. Some humans dated for years before they agreed to the legal binding of marriage, let alone the physical binding the Xxan enjoyed. Humans found the concept frightening, he understood.

Years. Seir-God but the thought was disheartening. Arren wanted to bind Sandy to him. He wanted to share the portions of himself he'd been reluctant to rush her to, the non-human parts.

If we are still together in another week, I will broach the subject. Even if he had to wear a condom, Arren wanted to bring his secondary into their lovemaking.

It was more than the selfish wish to feel her touching his secondary talking. If she was going to make the informed choice of him as mate, she had to accept all of him, including the fact that the two cocks Xxanian men had was no rumor.

Sandy stretched and reached for him, her mouth curving into a smile when her hand settled on his chest. "Hmmm... I wasn't dreaming," she purred.

His cock came to life that quickly. "Spend the weekend with me," he blurted out.

Her eyes opened a slit. "What?"

"The weekend."

"But you have work every—"

"I told Betty to cancel everything for the weekend." He had. It had been a rash move, but Arren had been certain Sandy would agree to spend her free days with him. *Was I wrong?*

"Here or at your apartment?" she asked.

"Your choice entirely." *Give me this, and the weekend is yours.*

Her expression was uncertain.

"If you don't want to—"

"I do!" Her cheeks darkened in a blush, and her eyes glittered. "I—I mean—"

"But?" Whatever the problem, he would do his best to solve it.

"Well, I do have a few things I can't cancel."

Arren settled back to hear her out. On some level, it intrigued him that she had such pressing concerns.

"I do laundry on weekends. If I don't, I won't have work clothes to wear next week. It will only take a few hours. You could come to the laundry with me," she suggested.

It warmed his heart that she wanted to include him in the mundane moments of her existence. "I have a better idea," he offered.

Her expression crumpled. "Okay."

She thinks I'm refusing to spend time with her while she goes about the little details of life. It couldn't be further from the truth. "Do you really want to do laundry?"

"Arren, you can't just buy me clean clothing every week."

He laughed. "I could, but I'm not suggesting it. Do you like doing laundry?"

Her expression said she didn't understand the question. "Of course not. Does anyone? It's a chore."

"Which is why I have a service that does my clothing. In fact, they will be picking up a load this afternoon and returning it tomorrow afternoon."

Her mouth opened in an O of surprise.

"I propose you pack a bag and plan to stay with me...as long as you wish to. We'll take your laundry to my apartment. The service will be happy for the extra money, and you won't have to do that particular chore this week. Instead, we can spend time together doing something enjoyable."

There was a moment of silence. "That's a deal," she decreed. Sandy leaned toward him and planted a kiss on Arren's lips. Then she was gone, out of the bed and across the bedroom at a run.

He smiled and pillowed his hands under his head. *This is precisely what we need. Maybe we can make this a weekly agreement and spend every weekend together.*

No one else at Spice *works seven days a week. Why should I?*

Chapter Fourteen

Sandy set the file folders for the elder Mr. Rowe on Tasha's desk and shouldered her purse. Though she didn't doubt that Arren meant what he said about picking her up, if she didn't leave for lunch with Arren while her inbox was empty, she might get cornered by someone before he arrived. It was safer to meet him in the lobby.

Tasha called her back three steps away. Sandy took a calming breath and turned toward the desk, pasting on a smile.

"You need something before I leave, Tasha?" It couldn't hurt to remind the senior partners' secretary that she was on her way out. *I'll tell her I have an appointment, if I have to.*

"Did I hear you say you were headed toward the Square?"

"I am, but I have an appointment I can't miss."

"That's okay. It's not urgent." She hefted a manila envelope. "If you could drop this at the *Spice Industries Building* on your way back, I'd appreciate it. Jack went home sick and Stephanie is on vacation, so I don't have an office courier in today, and I'm swamped under."

Her heart pounding, Sandy took the envelope and glanced down at the address on it. It wasn't for Arren. It was for someone named Daveed Raashh. *There* is *more than one Raashh at* Spice Industries. "Sure. I can handle that." It would give her more time with Arren, since he'd probably offer to show her to Daveed's office. Overall, this was a stroke of luck.

Her cheeks simmered at the fact that she was acting as if she hadn't seen him for a week. *I was at his apartment this morning.*

The weekend had turned into five days so far, and Sandy was in no hurry to go home for more than the things she hadn't taken with her. *If he asked me to marry him—mate with him—I'd say yes today.* Sadly, there'd been no mention of it recently.

"Thanks, hon."

Sandy turned toward the elevator and narrowly missed colliding with Jason. She started to round him, her heart stuttering at his glance at the envelope she was holding. Feigning preoccupation, she tipped it away and slid it into her purse. Then she made her way to the elevator.

Jason reached out and pushed the button before she could. Sandy shot him a glare, then turned on her heel and headed for the stairs. It sounded like a good idea until his steps started echoing down the cinderblock stairwell behind her.

I should have said I forgot something in my office.

Oh, what does it matter? He's a junior partner and son of one of the senior partners. The sad fact was that Jason could and would follow her anywhere in the building he wanted to.

Besides the ladies' room. That thought brought a wry smile to her face.

"Sandy, you're not avoiding me, are you?" His voice was sickeningly sweet, provoking her anger.

"Just heading for some fresh air." That part wasn't a lie. She'd never noticed before how obnoxious Jason's aftershave was in an enclosed space. *That's probably the scent Arren was so intent on getting rid of. Oh, do I understand that!*

"If you have a minute—"

"I don't, actually. I have an appointment I can't miss." The more times she said it, the smoother the half-truth came. *And there's the lobby door. I can get away from his stifling scent now.*

"At Raashh's company? Is that where you met him?"

She hesitated with her hand on the doorknob and turned to look at him. Jason smiled a vicious little smile that reminded her why she loathed him so much.

"Met who?" she inquired coolly.

"Whatever scaly you're busy screwing now that I've dumped you."

Words failed her. Sandy pushed through the door into the lobby and headed for the desk. She'd wait for Arren there, where she'd have at least the security guards for witnesses.

"I asked you a question, Sandy." There was a bark of order in that.

"And the answer is none of your business," she informed him. *I don't need to answer him. Being the boss doesn't grant him rights to my private life. Being an ex-boyfriend doesn't either.*

For that matter, she didn't need this job. There were other jobs. The more she thought about it, working somewhere else sounded really good to her.

Other jobs and other choices I could make. If I mated with Arren, he wouldn't want me to have a job across town from him. Would he?

He hasn't mentioned it, but what if I did? She didn't know whether males always broached the subject of mating in Xxanian society or not.

That thought came to a screeching halt as Jason's hand closed around her upper arm and yanked her to a stop. Before she could protest, Jason whirled her toward him.

He glared at her, and Sandy's heart skittered in outright fear. She'd never seen him like this before. If anyone had asked her, Sandy would have claimed that it wasn't Jason's style to act this way.

Something is wrong here. Very wrong. But what it was, she couldn't say.

"Did losing me really hurt you badly enough that you decided you wanted to give up men?"

Her face burned in anger and embarrassment. "I'm not a lesbian, Jason. And you are offensive."

"Those swamp skins are not men." He hurried on before she could protest. "Maybe you get off on the idea of sex in a public place."

The restaurant! Someone must have seen us go into the private room and told him. Or seen us come out of it.

"Or maybe you like the idea of two cocks. Too bad I didn't know. I'm sure I could have found another human willing to fuck you while I did. That might have at least made you passably interesting in bed."

Her temper ignited. Arren was proof enough that the problem in bed hadn't been hers. *Well, it was my problem, since Jason wasn't giving me what I needed, but thankfully Jason is someone else's problem now.*

"A man doesn't have to have two cocks to be twice the man you are or more. I imagine two-thirds of the men walking the Earth, Xxanian or not, are twice the man you are."

"Cute. You really are a scaly-lover, aren't you?"

"At least I'm not a specist like you are."

"You need to let the lady go."

Sandy panned her gaze up and to the right to Arren's face, at a loss to explain this scene to him. She had no idea how much he'd heard or how it might be misinterpreted. He tipped his head, his expression making promises she couldn't comprehend.

"Piss off," Jason ordered without looking at him. "This is a private matter."

"It's about to become a police matter, if you don't let her go."

Jason shot a dirty look over his shoulder, his eyes widening at the sight of Arren. He shifted toward the Xxanian that towered over him. "Mr. Raashh? What are you doing here?"

"I came here to pick up my mate for lunch. Imagine my surprise to find out one of the partners in my company's law firm is a such a blatant bigot."

"I can expl—"

"And imagine my surprise to find that same male assaulting my mate for the heinous crime of loving one of my kind." His face tipped down, drawing both Jason's and her own attention to his hand ringing her arm. "I suggest you let Sandy go. Now."

It was delivered in what she was sure was a falsely calm voice. Jason had been given his only warning.

He was too stunned to comply, probably preoccupied with envisioning his future being flushed because of this scene.

When Jason didn't move, Arren did. He plowed the tips of all four fingers on his right hand, molded into a blade shape, into Jason's shoulder. Jason's grip on her arm released, and Sandy rushed to Arren's back.

She didn't see the next move, but she heard it. The punch sent Jason skidding across the marble floor. Arren didn't chase him. He stood there calmly, watching as the security guards rushed from their desk to the scene.

* * * *

The next few minutes were a confusion of shouts and demands. Arren answered each one calmly, well aware of the pleasant press of Sandy against his back.

Defending her had made him feel alive. It had felt good to plant his fist in Rowe's face. It had felt better to have Sandy run to him for protection when Rowe's stunned nerves caused his grip to falter.

To me. The Subdominant. It was something Arren had never anticipated the experience of.

"This one is going to need an ambulance," one of the two guards announced. "Looks like a broken jaw."

"I assume the police will be arresting him once it's patched," Arren suggested.

The guard looked around at Sandy, then up at Arren. "I suppose they'll have to. I'm sorry, sir, but they are going to have to arrest you too."

He nodded grimly. "I know, but it had to be done. He was hurting my mate." It was presumptuous of him to keep calling Sandy that, since he hadn't bound the lovely lady to him yet. *But I will. If she's willing to be bound, I will.*

"No," Sandy protested.

His stomach clenched, and he prayed to the *Seir*-God that she wasn't protesting his use of the title for her.

"No. You can't arrest Arren. He was only protecting me. Jason was the one that—"

Arren drew her to his chest and cupped a hand around her cheek. He rumbled out one of the soothing calls in Xxan, shaking his head. She sank to his chest, still trembling.

"I broke the law, Sandy. It's okay. They have to arrest me, but I won't be in jail long."

"Too long," she complained. "It's not fair. It was his fault."

"A man takes responsibility for his own actions. Rowe was hurting you. I chose not to wait for these men to intervene. I chose to hurt him in return to make him release you. I must own that choice and pay for it."

The closer of the two security guards cleared his throat. "I'm on your side, sir. And I'll say so too, even if it costs me my job here."

"If that happens..." He sighed. "I appreciate your honesty, sir."

Arren stopped short of offering the man a job. It might be seen as bribery of some sort. Though the Xxan didn't condone the practice, it might appear he was doing so, when he was simply taking note of a security guard with a moral center he admired. In that profession, it was a worthy attribute to possess.

The doors opened, and the police marched in.

Arren thought fast. He pulled the chain with his Identi-chips on it and pressed it into Sandy's hand. She looked down at them, then up at him, her innocent blue-gray eyes large and lost.

"I want you safe. When the police are through with me, take my car. Let yourself into my apartment and stay there. Promise me, please."

She hesitated for a moment. "Only if you promise to come directly there when they release you."

A smile pulled up at his lips. "Of course." Knowing she was there, where else would he want to go?

"Should I call anyone?" she offered. "Betty?"

"No." Her first step would be to call Tasker and Rowe to handle it anyway. "I am certain Tasker and Rowe will take care of this very quickly. The last thing they will want is to leave me sitting in a jail cell, and they will know about this within minutes."

She nodded solemnly.

That settled, Arren brushed a gentle kiss over her lips and turned to face the officers that would place him in handcuffs and—for the first time in his life—place him on the wrong side of the law's eye.

* * * *

Sandy strode into Arren's penthouse. The elevator door closed behind her. She ambled across the room and let the Identi-chips fall to the table from shaking fingers.

The sight of him in handcuffs had brought tears to her eyes. Even now, she wanted to cry at the thought on him in a jail cell.

And why? Because Jason was being an asshole, and Arren tried to protect me.

At least Arren didn't seem upset with me about it. Considering the horrible things Jason had been saying, some men might have believed Sandy shared those sentiments. *Or that I had shared them at some point before meeting Arren.*

She shed her purse and suit coat onto the dining room table and made her way further into the apartment. It was unnaturally still but not unwelcoming. In the distance, she could hear the water bubbling into the pond from the small waterfall at the back.

It feels like home. All that's missing is Arren.

He'll be here soon. He promised to come here after he was released.

Sandy toed her heels off and left them next to the bed. The bath was too enticing. She wanted to wash Jason's touch off. *Arren won't want* his *scent in our home.*

That stopped her cold for a moment. *Our home. It could be* our *home, if we mated.*

Protecting their home was abruptly important to her. Sandy rushed to the bathing chamber and peeled off her clothes. After dropping them in the collection bag for the cleaners, she slipped into the water.

The clove soap Arren preferred to use made her skin tingle, and Sandy luxuriated in the sensation. She lounged in the water, feeling slightly guilty that Arren was nowhere near as comfortable as she currently was.

The stresses of the day wore at her, and the heated water lulled her toward sleep. Regretting every move, Sandy eased out of the pool and dried off with a thick, soft towel.

A check of her discarded watch showed that it had been two hours since the police had taken Arren away. He'd said he'd be here soon. How long could they keep him?

At a loss for anything else she wanted to do—or thought she could realistically focus on—Sandy ambled to the bed. Their clothing, stripped off in the heat of the moment the night before, littered the floor. She scooped up Arren's shirt and inhaled his scent.

Sandy pulled the shirt over her head, and curled into the bed, determined that he'd find her here when he returned.

* * * *

"Rash," the officer called out.

Arren rose from the cot stiffly and nodded to him.

The bars rolled back, and the officer waved him out. "Bail has been posted. You're free to go."

He ducked his head to pass through the too-short doorway, then straightened as the door clanged shut again. The officer led him to a desk without a word, returned his belongings, got his signature on the sheet attesting that everything was there, then ushered him to the lobby of the cramped building.

His internal question of what would happen next died at the sight of Daveed.

Fuck me.

Arren had thought bail had been posted by the law firm when they heard what had happened between Rowe the Younger and himself. He'd expected one of the senior partners to be in attendance, sucking up to Arren to avoid losing their account.

It wouldn't have worked, of course. He still intended to send a very personal and costly lesson about the price of bigotry to Rowe, his family, and their firm.

But Arren hadn't expected to see his older brother, his arms crossed over his chest, looking wholly and completely pissed off. That was a most unwelcome sight at best.

Arren's body hummed in awareness of his brother's sheer bulk. Daveed was a Dominant. He was half a head taller than Arren and had twice the muscle mass. Though Daveed had been full grown when Arren had been born, and as such they'd never tussled as brothers often did, Arren had never been completely unaware of his brother's imposing size.

Daveed, like most first generation crossbreeds, was also nearly-completely hairless. Arren had always been the oddity in that. He looked more like a second generation than a first, though no one could say for certain why that was.

"Come with me," Daveed ordered.

That grated at Arren's nerves. "Where, precisely?"

"To the nest. Raashh wants to see you. Immediately."

"Too bad. I have somewhere else to be. Immediately." A foreign emotion rose up in him. His nest had little use for Arren. Why should he have more use for them?

Daveed's look of shock should have been comical. Instead, it made Arren angry. As usual, they expected Arren to take their orders and swallow down the shit they threw his way.

Not this time.

"The *Grea* Elder... Our *seir* has given you an order. Doesn't that mean something to you?"

"It means nothing has changed and I was right to move out of the nest," he countered.

Daveed took a step toward him, his fisted hands swinging at his side in promise of a pummeling. Arren considered warning him that attacking Arren here would result in both of them being tossed back in the cells he'd just exited. Since Arren didn't intend to lay down and let Daveed beat him senseless, that was a given.

"Do you have any idea how much embarrassment you've caused the nest? Rowe the Elder and Tasker showed up at the doors, full of apologies for some slight they believe Rowe the Younger caused you. They wanted to apologize to you personally. We didn't even know you were imprisoned until they told us. You get locked up in a common jail and don't even bother to call your nest? How do you think that made us look to them?"

Arren forced the muscles in his shoulders and back to ease before he answered, well aware that his ridge plates were stirring to life behind his forehead. "I *expected* them to handle bailing me out themselves, since it was Rowe the Younger's doing that caused me to act in the first place."

"You want to *excuse* this?" He sounded as if the idea was incredulous.

"I own the fact that I punched Rowe. If he'd threatened and manhandled your mate, you might have killed him. I chose to hurt him instead."

Daveed stared at him, seemingly shocked to silence.

"Mate, Daveed. The word is mate. And as soon as she's willing, I will bind her as such."

"But—"

"So you can tell our *seir* that he will not be seeing me today. Perhaps not for several days. Or a week. I cannot say how long with certainty, given the situation. I gave my mate my vow that I would return to her immediately upon my release. If you had given Joy such a vow, I am sure that you would tell Raashh where to stuff his orders as well."

Daveed's hesitation was palatable.

"The fact that you have to consider the answer is amusing, you know." A smile pulled up at the corners of Arren's mouth, and he didn't fight it.

His older brother glared at him. "Going to see Joy would not preclude me seeing Raashh. I'm not the one who moved out of the nest."

"I don't regret that move. I doubt I ever will."

"You have to come to the nest long enough to explain this to our *seir*."

"I don't. But you're headed that way. Have a good time." He started to round his brother. "Oh, and I am moving our accounts to another law firm. You should be aware of that fact. I will send word when I decide on a new firm, so you can let your personal couriers know."

"You can't," Daveed protested.

"I can. You forget that the one thing Raashh values me for is my business sense. I am the final word in business decisions like this one.

"*Spice* chooses its partners and employees wisely. Dealing with a firm that openly displays such blatant bigotry is contrary to the honor and integrity of our structure. Not to mention that it lays us open for Rowe the Younger causing us problems down the line."

His brother's eyes narrowed. "Bigotry? They said you took exception to how Rowe was dealing with a female employee...that you were offended by the way he talked to her."

"Then you were lied to. And perhaps they were, as well, though I doubt it. The employee in question was my mate, and Rowe left no question to his feelings about swamp skins, scalies, or anyone who dares to love one. I could go on, but I won't. *Spice* will not deal with such a bigoted employee or business partner. And I will not deal with a man that physically assaults any woman, let alone my mate."

Arren didn't give Daveed time to collect his wits and protest Arren's exit. He used his cell phone to summon the company limo and met the car at a jewelry store several blocks away.

Chapter Fifteen

Arren nodded to the doorman on the way into the building. If seeing him come through the front door instead of up his private elevator shocked the man, he hid it well.

The building manager's office was on the main floor. Arren coded himself in with his administrative password, pulled off his glasses in the dim light, and went to the safe. Inside, he picked up his spare set of Identi-chips. The safe secured and the wall closed again, he headed to the far side of the office and keyed his elevator.

The ride up seemed to take longer than usual, and he convinced himself that it was anticipation of seeing her again working against him. Arren had never been an impatient man, but he was today. It was yet another new sensation in a world full of new sensations.

The doors opened, and he stepped into the apartment.

Sandy wasn't in the living room, curled into the sofa or one of the chairs, reading a book from the library against the far wall. She wasn't in the kitchen, eating some of the food he'd had stocked for her in the cabinets and the fridge. There was no sound of splashing water in the bath.

His cock went hard at the fact that she was probably in the bedroom. Restraining himself was going to be a chore, but what a delightful chore it would be.

As he'd expected, she was there, asleep in his bed, delightfully tousled. Her red-brown hair fell in loose curls to her shoulders. Arren watched her sleep, heartened by the sight of his intended mate in his bed.

It took a moment for him to identify her outfit. She was wearing the suit shirt he'd worn the day before. He wondered at that. It was an anomaly he would have to investigate.

He toed off his shoes and started to remove his suit jacket. Sandy woke with a start and peered up at him with unfocused eyes. In the next instant, she was hurtling into his arms, reaching up to lay kisses on his cheek and lips.

Between kisses, words gushed from her. "I'm so glad you're home. Are you okay? I was so worried."

He smiled at that.

Sandy took a moment to examine his face, and her brow furrowed. "What?"

Arren wrapped his arms around her and reveled in the moment. "Do you want the full list?"

"Uh...yes. I think so."

He guided her toward the bed. "First of all, I am proud that you called this apartment home. It is an honor and a pleasure that you think so." *And it means she is more likely to accept my proposal.*

Her cheeks darkened in a blush.

"I love that you worry about me." He lifted her to fit Sandy to his body, groaning as she wrapped her legs around his waist. "And I really like that you're wearing my clothes."

She looked down at the shirt, and her blush darkened.

"Why *are* you wearing my clothes?"

"I...missed you."

"You missed my scent?"

Sandy nodded, her expression starkly serious.

He groaned.

"What?" she asked again.

"I want to ask you something, and I want an honest answer, even if it is that you need time to decide or that you aren't comfortable with it."

She swallowed hard. "I think I can promise that."

"I want you to carry my scent permanently."

The furrow in her brow deepened, and a slight scowl pulled the edges of her lips down. "I don't understand what that means," she admitted.

"I want you to become my mate. When that happens, your scent will change slightly. A bit of my scent will mix with yours, so any other Xxanians will know you're my mate and...steer clear of you or protect you, as the case may be."

She stared at him long enough to make his nerves jump in nervous energy. At last, she spoke.

"You want to make me your mate?"

* * * *

Sandy stared at him, waiting for his answer, terrified that she'd misheard him. He was asking to tie himself to her permanently, to commit to a lifetime of being hers and never looking at another woman? It was too good to be true.

"If you don't want to—"

"I do." Saying that was easier than she'd found saying anything in her life.

Her answer seemed to stun him.

"I mean... If that's what you're asking, I do want to."

Arren nuzzled her lips, parting them and delving between, seducing her with his potent taste. He broke away and lowered her to the mattress. Then he sank to one knee before her.

At a loss, she started to stutter out a question.

He motioned for a moment of peace. Then he pulled what was surely a ring box out of his front pocket and offered it to her. "I'm asking. I'm offering to marry you, to make you my mate, to share my life with you."

"Yes." What other answer would she give?

He smiled. "You haven't even seen the ring yet."

Sandy took the box and opened it, her breathing hitching at the sight of the pear-shaped aquamarine with two diamonds bracketing it in. "Beautiful," she gasped out.

"Like your eyes. Will you wear it?"

She hurried to pull the ring on, her hands shaking. Arren shucked his jacket and went to work on his shirt. Sandy looked up at him to find his eye slits narrowed. He flicked his tongue out, taking her scent in earnest.

"You haven't eaten." Arren didn't question it.

His jump of subject confused her. "Does it matter?"

"Do you want to mate with me today? Or do you prefer to wait?"

Another jump of subject. "Today. Please...today."

He scented her in earnest again. "Yes, you do. You would." His answer was cryptic, at best.

"Arren?"

"If you wish to mate with me today, I must make sure you are well fed before we begin."

"You should?" That meant he wasn't skipping subjects.

"Yes. I must. You won't want to stop to eat often during the mating cycle. Neither will I." His fingers trailed along her lower lip, arousing her. "I will need to make a phone call. Then we will eat. Then..." His eyes went hot in promise.

"Then?" She barely forced the word out.

"Delights the likes of which neither of us have experienced before."

She nodded. "Yes. Now."

* * * *

Sandy's head came up at the knock at the door. Arren waved her back to her meal and rose, striding to the door dressed only in his trousers. The urge to yell at the caterer for taking so long was strong, and he swallowed it down, wondering at his continuing lack of patience.

The Xxanian didn't presume to enter. He offered the receipt for Arren to sign, his head down so he wouldn't accidentally look at the prospective mate he knew was somewhere within the apartment.

Arren signed it, barely noting the amount he was paying for this indulgence. It wasn't that he had to worry about the expense, but usually he would hold himself accountable for what he was spending. Today, no expense was too much.

The blessing of many daughters was passed in a whisper, and Arren thanked the other Subdominant for his kindness. In the next moment, the rolling carts were inside the apartment, and the other Xxanian male took his leave with a final instruction that Arren should call to have the carts taken away when he was done mating.

He closed the door behind the delivery man and pushed the carts into the bedroom. After a quick look inside to familiarize himself with the contents, he went back to Sandy.

She looked past him. "Is everything all right?"

"Perfect." He hoped it was.

She licked her lips, spreading her legs slightly. Her scent was enticing, making him crazy for what was to come. His appetite fled, and he pushed his plate away.

"Arren?" Her voice was low and breathy.

"Eat," he ordered. This was the last chance she'd have until the first frenzy peaked and passed.

Her hand pressed to her shaved mound through his shirt, indicating her need. "But you're not—"

"Oh, I am." He slid to the floor and flipped the edge of the shirt up to bare her body to his ravenous mouth. She moved to the edge of the chair with a gasp, inviting him.

There was no question that Sandy wouldn't eat more, whether or not he continued. With his blood boiling to make her his mate, he couldn't wait longer to taste the musk coating her seam and thighs.

It was strong in her passion and in her body's timing. If the *Seir*-God was kind, she would be receptive to him within hours.

Or immediately. He'd only worn condoms this long, because the scientists at SLAL hadn't been able to determine yet if human women needed mating to ripen them to carry for a Xxanian male. They *had* proven that a single infusion of a Dominant's *Zhigaaal* was capable of irrevocably binding a human woman to him.

He suckled at her body, groaning at her hand closing in the back of his hair, urging him on. Her cries echoed off the walls, and her renewed cream filled his mouth and stoked the fire for more.

They hadn't tested single infusions of *Zhigaaal* with Subdominants, and to his knowledge, pregnancy block and condoms had resulted in no unplanned crossbred births. Half a century after the first incursion of Xxanian warriors onto Earth, there was still so much they didn't know.

It might take three days to bind her, the same amount of time it would take to bind a Xxanian female to him.

Or it might not. The first touch of my Zhigaaal *might bind Sandy to me.* The uncertainty was enough to raise his secondary a minute amount. The strain was too much, and he started working his trousers open.

"Arren, please. I want to mate now."

She didn't have to ask twice. He guided her chair away from the table, stood, and scooped her into his arms. He crossed the apartment to the bed in a whirlwind of motion and lowered her to the mattress.

Arren stood over her, unfastening his trousers to bare his cocks. Sandy lay on the bed, her legs spread, circling her hand over her clit. She licked her lips at the sight of his primary, and he shivered in delight. Perhaps it was instinct that led her to precisely what he needed her to do.

Her eyes widened at the sight of his secondary. Arren stroked it, bringing it up further for her. When it was a third of the length of his primary, he stopped and finished removing his trousers. Naked, he stepped toward the bed.

She reached up, touching his secondary, moaning as it wrapped around the curve of her finger and skittered up and down her knuckle. Sandy pushed to her knees on the mattress and licked the secondary's soft head. He released a spurt of *Zhigaaal* onto her tongue at that move.

It has started. Or is done. The need to see her bound to him was maddening.

Arren didn't have to tell her what to do. Sandy sucked the secondary, stroking the primary while she did. It grew in her mouth, exploring his mate, staking claim to her.

He fisted a hand in her hair and guided her up and down the length, shuddering at her moan of delight. More *Zhigaaal* released into her mouth, and he groaned.

I should withdraw and anoint her with the Zhigaaal. *It is normally done that way.*

Who says it has to be? All his adult life, Arren had balked tradition. Why should he stop now?

Resolved, he let himself go, allowed Sandy to carry him to the brink and over. He guided her stroking hand to one side, aiming his primary for the foot of the bed.

His *Zhigaaal* coursed into her mouth, and she swallowed, drawing his secondary into her throat, still jetting its potent, binding pheromones into her body. Sandy's eyes opened wide, then slid shut. Her body relaxed into his grip on her scalp, and he eased his secondary out of her mouth, painting *Zhigaaal* in a line down her lower lip to her chin.

Her breathing came in sharp little gasps, and her muscles twitched. Soon those twitches would be a concerted effort to throw him off, he knew.

She licked her lips, then stroked her tongue up the length of his secondary.

I have to hurry. She'll be in the full frenzy soon.

Arren massaged the base of his secondary, expressing *Zhigaaal* to begin the anointing. To his shock, Sandy moved, taking his length down again. The shock of it was too much for him, and Arren climaxed again.

He lowered Sandy to the mattress and worked more of his *Zhigaaal* up. Before she had time to do more than moan, he'd anointed her pulse points and erogenous zones.

Sandy reached for him, and he slid his secondary to the hilt inside her. She arched against him with a shout, and Arren savored her reaction. In minutes, he was emptying his *Zhigaaal* into her.

One climax led to another and a third. At last, Arren moved on to her tight ass.

Sandy moaned and pitched her head back and forth.

"One more step in the binding," Arren promised her.

"I'm burning," she breathed.

"Just for a few minutes."

She whimpered as he worked his secondary through the ring of muscle. Arren cursed at how good the compression against the head felt. He worked his cock in and out, deeper with every inward thrust.

At last, his primary reached her slit. Arren thrust deep, growling as both cocks partook of paradise.

Sandy cried out wildly. "I'm burning," she pleaded.

"That's my *Zhigaaal*, Sandy. That's my *Zhigaaal*, making you my mate."

She sobbed.

"Soon," he soothed her. "The burning will end soon."

She nodded.

Arren thrust deeper and harder, his breathing going ragged. At last, he released into her.

Sandy's scream echoed off the walls, and her moans were low and sweet.

"Better?" he asked her. *Seir* God, but he hoped it was. The last thing he wanted was to hurt her. No, the last thing he wanted was to have to call SLAL in for her, but hurting her nearly equaled it.

She laid a kiss on his chest. "Much better. Thank you, Arren."

He smiled at that. *Good. As long as the burning was fleeting, I'm not going to stop until Sandy is mine.*

Chapter Sixteen

Three days later

Sandy stretched against Arren, her entire body relaxed and warm. She knew she should get up and go to the bathroom, but moving out of the bed sounded like more work than it was worth.

"Good morning." Arren's voice was a rumble that was all male and very appealing. "I've been waiting for you to wake."

"Mmmm... I'm afraid I have to get up for a minute before we do anything else." She yawned, stretching again.

"How convenient that it is time for us to be out of bed then."

Sandy opened her eyes, staring at him. "It is?"

He trailed one smooth finger from her lip, down her throat, and between her breasts. "Absolutely. You are my mate, and it is time to show you the care a Xxanian male shows a new mate."

"That is intriguing." He'd definitely piqued her interest.

"I assume you need to use the toilet on the way?" he asked.

She sighed. "Yes."

In a dizzying move, Arren was on his feet with Sandy in his arms. She grabbed at his shoulder, then loosened her grip. There was no way Arren would drop her.

He settled her on the toilet, turned away, and started preparing the stone tub for a bath: raising the temperature, adding agitation, and increasing the filtration. A bath sounded good, and Sandy hurried to join him. Arren lifted her into the hot water, but he didn't join her immediately. Instead, he collected supplies into a small basket and brought it to the edge of the tub. Then he sank in next to her.

He stared at her solemnly. "You are my mate now, Sandy. You know what that means to me. Nothing in life will be more important to me than you, from this moment on."

She nodded, though the concept made her head spin. She couldn't remember a time when she was first in anyone's life, let alone a man's.

"After mating, the first thing a male does is bathe his mate with *Saahaal*. Clove is the English word for the spice."

"Okay." Something told her it wasn't as simple as it sounded.

Arren nodded. He plucked a bottle from the basket and opened it. The liquid pooling in his hand released the smell of clove into the room, enticing her senses.

The clove stung like his *Zhigaaal* had. In fact, the *Zhigaaal* smelled faintly of clove, which might explain the slight sting.

What started out as a simple bath turned to more quickly. Arren cupped her breasts and smoothed the oil over her nipples, bringing them up against his fingertips.

Sandy reached out and snagged the clove oil out of the basket. She poured a handful and started working it up Arren's primary cock.

His pupils dilated in pleasure. "I'm supposed to be bathing you." It wasn't a complaint. Clearly, he liked what she was doing.

"Maybe I want more."

"If you were willing, this was supposed to end with more."

She chuckled, working him more avidly. "Obviously, I'm willing."

Arren stroked his hands down her body, arousing her to a potent edge before he thrust inside her. Sandy placed her hands on the side of the tub, levering herself up and down on his cock, breaths rasping in and out of her lungs, scorching her senses.

It was over in moments, Sandy holding tight to Arren's shoulders, her harsh breathing stirring the steam from the bath. Arren followed her over, every muscle tightening, even the ones that raised his ridge plates.

Sandy laughed in the release of tension, her body going lax as it had when they'd been binding.

"Yes?" he asked archly.

"When do we...?"

One eyebrow went up, and he cocked his head to one side.

"When do we use the secondary and when do we use only the primary?"

"Any time we have the time and you wish to experience another frenzy, we can use the secondary."

"In that case..." Sandy reached for him, intent on stroking him up.

Arren guided her hand away, then laid a kiss in the palm of his hand.

"But you said—"

"The next time we have a frenzy, I intend to have you dressed in silk, as you should be."

"You have silk. I've seen it."

He shook his head. "Those are *S'suumea*. I'm going to buy you your own silk clothing. Today." He started working the clove oil into her legs. "But first we eat."

"What do you have in mind for silk clothing?"

Arren chuckled. "Conveniently enough, *Spice* has a clothing department, and you can have anything you want from our clothing line."

"Oh, can I?" she played along.

"I have it on good authority. I happen to know the owners."

* * * *

"Good afternoon, Mr. Raashh," the clerk called out, offering a smile that Arren knew was fake. Few employees liked to see the owners of the company walking through the door.

"Good day. Sandy and I will be shopping for her today."

The clerk scanned her gaze up and down Sandy's body. Just when he would have protested the rude behavior, she started speaking again.

"A medium, I would think."

Sandy nodded. "Usually, yes."

"And what sorts of things will you be looking to purchase today?"

"On my account," Arren interjected. "Sandy has no limits."

The clerk shot him a look of surprise. She focused on Sandy with a false smile that turned Arren's stomach. Sandy squirmed uncomfortably.

"Very well. Do you know what you're looking for, Sandy?"

"The S'su..." She looked at Arren for help.

The clerk beat him to an answer. "*S'suuhhea*?"

"Yes," Arren answered for her. "Also lingerie, bath products, and silk daily wear."

"Yes, sir."

"I really liked the blue and silver print that was in the catalog."

The clerk performed a turn around her, making an examination Arren wondered at. "Yes, the blue and silver...and probably also the green and gold. Let's take a look at what I have in the back."

She led the way, and Arren took Sandy's arm and accompanied her to the work room.

The clerk's eyes went wide. She looked as if she meant to protest. Her gaze snapped to Sandy's hand, and she composed herself. "I see. If you would." She motioned to a chair.

Arren kissed Sandy's cheek and obliged the woman. The clerk showed Sandy style after style of dress, robe, nightgown, undergarments, and assorted frilly objects he had no name for. Her eyes lit up, and she looked his way.

"Anything you want," he assured her. "Everything you want."

Sandy smiled shyly. "And if I want you to wear the S'suum..." Again, she faltered.

"*S'suumea*," he provided. Arren considered it. "I will wear the informal *S'suumea* for you, if you wish."

"The one that looks like a silk kilt?" she asked.

"That is the informal," the clerk supplied.

Arren tipped his head, and Sandy smiled.

"I'll add it to the order then?" the clerk asked.

"In colors to match whatever Sandy picks out," Arren instructed.

Sandy's smile said he wouldn't regret it.

"While we are making the order," Arren inserted, "I will need a case of *Saahaal* and a second sent to Evan and Zondra Duncan at Daahn's nest. I will write a note to include with it."

The clerk nodded to him in acknowledgement and went back to Sandy.

"You're thanking her for introducing us, aren't you?" Sandy asked.

Arren chuckled. "Do you think that's not warranted?"

"No. I agree with you. Maybe I should send her something, as well." She pointed out a scandalously brief nightgown that would fit over Zondra's very pregnant form. "This in green and gold to match her eyes?"

"As long as the note makes it clear it comes from you. If Evan thinks I picked that out, you would very quickly find yourself a widow."

* * * *

"Hello, Deidre," another woman called out. "What have we here?"

"Good afternoon, Mrs. Raashh. Mr. Raa... Oh, dear. Having more than one is rather confusing isn't it?"

Sandy looked around at the petite, honey-haired woman staring at Arren. The deep blue silk sheath dress caressed her body.

"What a surprise," the new arrival exclaimed. "I've never seen you in here, Arren."

He stood and offered a bow of his head to her. "Joy. A pleasure."

She turned to Sandy. "And this must be... I'm sorry. I don't know your name yet."

Sandy's heart stuttered at that. This woman was Arren's family, but she hadn't heard of Sandy? She forced a weak smile and mumbled her first name. *I don't even know what last name I should be using.*

Joy surveyed the dress, then focused on the ring on Sandy's hand. "Preparing to take Sandy to the nest to introduce her, Arren?" Her tone made it seem she was teasing him.

"No. Dressing my mate in a manner appropriate to her place in my life."

Sandy looked around at him. It hadn't been her imagination. The tease had irritated or angered him. Arren's eye slits were narrowed, and his ridge plates pushed lightly out at his pale skin.

Joy's brow furrowed. "But...you've mated now. Haven't you? That's why you haven't been at the office the last few days. Daveed said—"

Arren tipped his head. "Yes, but we are just becoming established in our nest. The moment to visit my *seir* will come in time."

If Sandy was gauging her expression correctly, Arren's announcement had caused Joy distress.

At last, Joy composed herself. "I understand."

His expression said she didn't, but Arren didn't correct her.

"Should I send your regards to Raashh and Daveed?" There was a note of formality in the response that put Sandy's nerves on edge.

"You may," he responded crisply. "Inform them that I will return to work in the next few days."

"No rush. Daveed doesn't expect you to leave your mate immediately."

Daveed... The name resonated in Sandy's memories.

"I won't be leaving my mate. Sandy will be joining me at *Spice* as a second personal assistant. Betty will enjoy the help."

"That's good. I find working with my mate wonderful."

"Daveed," she breathed. "Oh!" Sandy strode to the table she'd left her purse on and rifled through it. The manila envelope in hand, she turned to Joy. "I forgot in the excitement. I was supposed to deliver this to Daveed."

Joy reached to take it, but Arren's hand was there first. He took the envelope, opened it, and flipped through the pages inside. "Daveed would have sent this to me to deal with anyway. I will take care of it."

"But your mate," Joy protested.

"It will only mean a phone call." It was clear that had been a dismissal.

Joy didn't miss it. She offered a weak smile to Sandy and left the room.

At a loss to understand the intricacies of Xxanian families, Sandy returned to the clerk just in time to see the silk shoes that matched the dresses being set out for her to choose from.

* * * *

Arren knew whatever was preying on Sandy's mind was coming to a head. "What's wrong?" he asked.

She didn't look at him. "Are you ashamed of me?"

He nearly wrecked the car in surprise. "What? Why would you ask such a thing?"

"Joy had never heard of me before. Why wouldn't you tell your family about me? Why don't you want to take me to the...nest?"

The hurt in her voice made him want to beat his head against the steering wheel. "I don't speak to my family often."

"You work with Daveed."

"Not really. We work in the same building. Two floors apart, but we rarely make an effort to see each other or speak to each other. We send papers and memorandums back and forth by office courier and assistants. We rarely even pick up a phone."

Sandy turned to look at him, her eyes wide and wounded. "Why?"

It was his greatest failing, a disgrace.

"What happened to make you two hate each other?"

"I don't *hate* him. We just... I'm a Subdominant."

"What does that mean?" Her expression said she really didn't know.

Arren pulled over and stared at the steering wheel. He turned to look at her. "All my life, I have been...less. Less than my brother. Less than my nephews. *Less.* A disgrace that my Dominant *seir* produced a Subdominant son. I have always been too human for his tastes."

"But his mate is human," she protested. "It seems *all* their mates are human."

"My mother was. They are. He doesn't begrudge the fem...the women being human. They were born human."

"You were born mixed," she fumed. "How can he begrudge you that?"

"Because he is the typical Xxanian Dominant. Raashh doesn't take my mother's attributes and genetics into account. He is a Dominant that produced a Subdominant. It is his failure, and I am a reminder of it. The only value I have to my family is in running the business. So, I moved out of the nest and live alone."

She touched his hand. "You aren't alone."

He smiled. "No, I'm not alone anymore. Now I am the Subdominant head of my own nest. It's an odd situation. It would be unlikely to happen on *Xxania Uuaahth.*"

"And you don't want to take me to the nest because...?"

He forced his jaw to unlock and his ridge plates to retract. "Because I refuse to let them show me disrespect in front of you. I know you would feel bad because of it, and that would make me brutally angry. It would be...*unpleasant* for all of us.

"They would not disrespect you, of course. Any female added to the nest is an asset to them. In fact, being able to bind a female to myself may make me more worthy in their eyes, but only marginally so."

"Why?"

He cocked his head to one side, at a loss for what she was asking.

"Why only marginally more worthy? Oh, I hate that term."

Arren smiled. "I knew you would." He sighed and ran a hand through his blond curls. "I am a Subdominant. Though I might bring female young to the nest, any males I produce will likely be..."

"Subdominant."

He nodded.

"They aren't really that stupid, are they?"

Holding back a laugh at that pronouncement was impossible. "That's one way to put it."

"Just so I know... Are we ever going to visit your family?"

Arren would have liked to lie to her, but that would be dishonorable. "I suppose we'll have to. But not today."

Her smile was wide and heartfelt.

Chapter Seventeen

Four days later

Arren turned toward the trilling phone,
sighing. Back at work two days, and it seemed
the paperwork and calls never ended. He would
ask Betty to handle the calls while he caught up
on paperwork, but he'd asked her to teach Sandy
everything she needed to know about her new
position as his legal aide, and he hated to
interrupt that. The two women had bonded so
well, he wanted to encourage it.

The secretary Betty had left on her own desk
was knowledgeable enough to handle a pre-made
list of chores, but she wasn't knowledgeable
enough to handle calls for Arren.

He scooped the phone to his ear with a
greeting of "Arren Raashh."

"You cannot continue ignoring our *seir*,
Arren," Daveed informed him.

*I should have just let all phone calls go to the
message box. Betty could have gone through them
later.*

But who knew Daveed would call me?
Honestly, Arren couldn't remember the last time
his brother called him personally. Usually,
Mallory called and spoke to Arren or Betty, and
Arren or Betty spoke to Mallory. He would have
sworn, until that very moment, that his older
brother had never willingly used a phone.

"I'm not ignoring Raashh, Daveed. After
mating, which isn't something you interrupt, I

had the priority of seeing to the needs of the company. Raashh put me in this position, so things were not left undone or half done."

"You have a mate, Arren."

A smile curved his lips at the reminder. "I know. It is not something one is unaware of."

"I introduced Joy to the nest less than a day after mating ended, and I only waited that long because Rayn insisted on his blasted tests."

And we all know you are the perfect son, Daveed. But there was no need to antagonize him. Arren's problems were largely with their *seir.* Even Daveed's attitudes could be traced back to the elder's.

"It's been four days," Daveed continued.

"I am well aware of the time."

"Do you ever intend to introduce your mate to the nest?" He was losing his patience, by the sound of it. Arren was sure his brother's ridge plates were extended.

I have to. "Eventually. When other priorities have been met."

"Other... It's not as if the nest is on the other side of the world, and even if it was, you have a shuttle at your disposal. How many priorities can there be that make visiting Raashh a physical impossibility for you?"

Even when you "ran the company", most of the work I do was delegated to others...or to me. But Arren didn't say that. Even if Daveed acknowledged it, he wouldn't find it germane to the discussion. "We will get there in time. Joy knew all three of us before she mated with you.

For you, it was a matter of form to introduce your mate to Raashh."

Daveed lost what little patience he had retained thus far. "It isn't a matter of form. It is a matter of *tradition*."

Ah, yes. And Raashh loves his traditions. "In case you've forgotten, I don't live at Raashh's nest. My mate is fully comfortable with my nest. She's been bathed with *Saahaal* in my nest. Doing the same in a nest I don't live in is not my highest priority."

His brother growled curses in Xxan. "Consider it."

"I'll consider it." He had since before he'd bound Sandy to him. "I promise." But he wasn't in any hurry to go back to Raashh's nest, where he was always treated as less.

* * * *

Two days later

Sandy pulled her hair back into a ponytail and turned toward the bathroom. The cleaner would arrive soon, and she had to collect the last of their scattered clothing from the week into the bags.

A sound from the living room sent her that direction instead. She'd thought Arren was in the arboretum, collecting clothes with her. What would have sent him to the living room?

"Arren? We don't have—"

She stopped short at the sight of a huge, hairless male, carefully removing his shoes just outside the elevator doors. He straightened, coming to his full height of nearly a head taller than Arren was. She'd wager he carried at least another thirty-five kilos of muscle on his form as well.

His brows raised in surprise at the sight of her, and he took a step toward her. Sandy backed away from him, nearly toppling backward over the couch in the process.

He charged toward her, and she ran further into the room. Sandy could have smacked herself for that. There were no doorways to other rooms that direction. Just the windows. She pressed her back to one, and pulled down on her nightshirt, trying to make it cover more of her body. As it was, he'd probably gotten a great look at her ass as she'd run from him.

"Arren!"

The intruder stopped a body length away.

My body length. She would have been more comfortable with one of his.

His hands went up in a calming motion. "I mean you no harm."

"Arren!"

He bolted from the bedroom doorway, a nude streak against the dark wood walls, and hit the intruder solidly, taking him to the floor. The fight she expected didn't occur. Instead, Arren came to his feet between them, blocking the other male's view of her.

The larger levered himself off the floor. "I meant her no harm," he groused. He dusted off his clothing, though there was no dust to remove.

"How dare you enter without asking permission." Arren's voice was little more than a growl, a sure sign that his ridge plates were extended and his Xxanian teeth bared.

"I didn't enter the center nest."

"In our small nest, the entire nest is the center nest. Sandy and I feel free to wear what we like or not here."

"In a proper nest—"

"It is proper enough for us."

There was a moment of tense silence. At last, the other male spoke. "My apologies to you for frightening you. I only meant to help you when you fell."

Arren whipped around and took visual inventory of Sandy. "Are you hurt?"

She shook her head, still trying to convince her breathing to settle. *He doesn't see this male as much of a threat, or he wouldn't turn his back on him.*

He pressed a kiss to her forehead and turned back to the other. "I suggest you leave, Daveed. We are clearly not dressed for company. Next time, try calling before you enter our nest."

"I came to—"

"I know why you came. In good time, I will come to Raashh's nest."

Daveed's ridge plates extended at that. "With your mate, I assume." There was a challenge in that.

"That is my mate's choice."

"I see." He turned on his heel and stalked back to the elevator. Daveed didn't pull his shoes back on. Instead, he scooped them up and stepped into the elevator. He didn't look back as he punched a button.

Sandy took a calming breath, as the doors closed him in. "Your older brother." She didn't question it.

He turned to look at her, his lips twitching in a wry smile. "Yes."

"When will we be going to the nest?"

"When you are comfortable with it."

She glanced toward the elevator doors. "Not today." With her nerves jangled by Daveed's appearance, Sandy knew she wasn't ready for that.

Arren tipped his head and led her back to the bedroom. He lifted her onto the mattress, and she shook her head.

"We don't have time. The cleaners will be here soon."

He smiled widely, a dangerous smile that showed his hunting teeth. "And I will meet them with the collection bags. Then I will come back here to you."

Her heart pounded in excitement at his meaning. She stripped off the nightshirt and handed it over. "You should add this to the bag." She didn't question that they wouldn't be donning clothing again after the cleaner left with the bags.

Chapter Eighteen

Two days later

Sandy slid from the bed, her stomach growling. She'd had a full dinner with Arren, but they'd also made love for a good portion of the evening. If there was one thing she'd learned it was that she could work up a hearty appetite with her husband.

Mate. Just the thought of it still sent pleasant shivers through her body. She had a mate who would never stray and wouldn't stand for someone hurting her.

She didn't bother to pull a *S'suuhhea* or robe on. There was no chance someone would barge into the apartment again, and there was something sinfully sensual about walking around the nest nude.

The floors were warm against her feet, and the water sounds from the fountains were soothing to her half-asleep mind. Overall, the only more calming thing about the nest was the times they slept in the arboretum.

The air from the refrigerator raised goose bumps on her body, but the low-level light Arren kept in it was kind to her eyes. In the weeks living in Arren's nest, her eyes had become accustomed to the lower light levels, so much so that she now wore sunglasses in bright light, just as he did.

Sandy reached for a bag of cheese cubes, then withdrew. Item after item caught her attention, then was dismissed. She was hungry, but nothing looked appetizing.

Except that. She pulled out a bowl of spiced meat and sank cross-legged to the floor with the bowl in her lap. Sandy had eaten Arren's meals a few times, though he made sure she had everything she needed or wanted to eat, if that wasn't her choice.

The meat was cold, but her mouth watered at the taste. It would be better warm. She didn't doubt it. The juices would flow through her mouth rather than being trapped in the meat.

Cube after cube disappeared from the bowl. Sandy let the refrigerator door swing shut.

She closed her eyes and savored every bite. All too soon, the bowl was empty. If there was more, she would eat it, but the idea of preparing more meat sounded like too much work.

Moving is too much work. Sandy lazed on the heated floor and dropped back to sleep.

* * * *

Arren stretched, his hand extending to— Empty space. He raised his head and opened his senses.

With Sandy's scent permeating the nest, it would be impossible to track her that way. There were no sounds of her moving around or splashing in the pool. The air was still, save the currents the fans created.

She can't have left the apartment. I would have heard the elevator or the fire doors. "Sandy?"

There was no reply, and his heart pounded in preparation for battle. "Sandy?" Arren came up off the bed and marched through the nest.

The bathing chamber was empty, as was the attached arboretum. The library and living room were dark and still. Then he saw her, lying on the kitchen floor, her hand resting on a bowl.

"Sandy!"

There was no response. Arren bolted to her side, terror driving him. Had she slipped and fallen? Were her injuries serious?

He ran his hands over her body, looking for blood, broken bones, and bruising, but there didn't seem to be any. The blood on her fingertips confused him for a moment. The pungent smell of spice explained it.

Meat. Z'haahn. The bowl was empty, and he furrowed his brow at the calculation that she'd eaten enough meat to feed him for a day in a single sitting.

Then fell asleep on the floor. Deeply asleep.

She must be bearing.

Arren didn't attempt to wake her. Sleep and food were very important to bearing women.

Instead, he lifted her and carried Sandy to the bed. A wet cloth from the bathing pool took care of the blood on her hands and chin. That accomplished, he slid into the bed with her and covered them both with the silk sheets.

His gaze lingered on his sleeping mate. Sandy was beautiful.

And bearing. For me.

* * * *

The scent of spiced meat brought Sandy to consciousness. She smiled up at Arren and rumbled out "Good morning."

"Are you hungry?" he asked.

She was. "Ravenous."

He chuckled and settled on the bed, depositing the platter of food between them. Sandy pushed to sitting and looked down at it. The contents confused her.

"Sandy?" he asked.

"You don't normally assume I want to eat your food."

"Don't you? I'll make you anything you want. Or get it, if we don't already have it in the pantry. Name it, and it's yours." There was an urgent undertone to that.

Sandy plucked a cube of warmed meat from the tray. "No. I want this." Her mouth watered at the scent. She popped it in her mouth and chewed.

Arren had the next cube at her lips a heartbeat after she'd swallowed the first. She opened her mouth to question him, and Arren eased the cube in. He waited for Sandy to start chewing before he spoke again.

"You must let me know immediately when you are hungry, day or night. You must eat as much as you can."

Sandy nearly choked at that pronouncement.

Arren rubbed her back tenderly and kept talking. "I will prepare all your food for you. If you crave anything, I will provide it as soon as possible."

Crave? "Are—"

He raised another cube of meet. "You must sleep whenever you feel tired."

"Arren! Am I... Am I pregnant?"

"You throw all the signs of it. If I am correct, I will be able to scent it within the week." He motioned with the meat, seemingly ordering her to take it.

Sandy complied, though her stomach was squirming in excitement.

Arren smiled a brittle little smile. "Please, do not try to feed yourself again."

Her cheeks heated at the memory of her late night snack, and she swallowed the bite in her mouth. Arren offered another. Sandy took it and started chewing.

"Cold meat could give you cramps and cause you to vomit. And you could be injured if you fall asleep unexpectedly."

She swallowed the meat and raised her hand to motion for a moment without one so she could talk. He paused and nodded her on.

"How can we work if this is the way pregnancy progresses? I can't do mine, and you—"

"The same way Daveed and Joy did," he crooned. Arren caressed her stomach, a smile curving his lips.

The motion made her feel weak and sleepy. "And that is?"

"A bed in my office and food stores on hand. I may engage a Xxanian service to provide several shifts of food for us."

"Nothing will get done," she complained.

"Everything will. You don't need to worry about anything."

She believed that. Something told Sandy that Arren intended to take care of everything she needed or wanted.

Chapter Nineteen

Four days later

Arren looked up in surprise at Sandy's dipping head. He vaulted from his desk chair and lifted her from hers. She was asleep before he deposited her on the bed.

Stars take it! She pushes too hard. Sandy was more than willing to eat whenever their young one demanded it, but she refused to stop working to sleep.

Of course, she ate and slept more than he'd been told was normal for women in their first month of pregnancy. *Certainly more than Daveed said Joy did. This is more indicative of the final month than the first.*

Arren considered his options and came to the one he'd hoped to avoid. If this was a Xxanian anomaly he'd never heard of, his *seir* would know it.

He ambled to his desk and picked up the phone, cursing himself for failing as head of his own nest.

Daveed's personal assistant picked up on the first ring. "Mr. Raashh's office. How may I help you?"

One Mr. Raashh. He swallowed down his frustration. "Is Daveed in, Mallory?"

"Good afternoon, Mr. Raashh. Yes, he is. I'll get him on the line."

I'd rather leave a message. As usual.

Coward!

For that matter, why is she putting me through? To his knowledge, Mallory had orders not to interrupt Daveed's work for anything but an emergency.

This is *an emergency.* "Thank you, Mallory."

Two clicks were followed by soft music that he understood humans found soothing. In his irritated state, Arren found it anything but.

He stared at Sandy, reminding himself that this was necessary.

"Problem, Arren?" Daveed's voice came without warning, startling Arren.

"I need to see Raashh."

"You know where he is. If you haven't forgotten, I mean."

Arren bit back a dozen sarcastic responses. "There's a problem. If my family won't help me, I'll go to strangers." He reached out to hang the phone back on the cradle.

"You know we will," he snapped.

He settled the phone to his ear again. "Obviously, I don't know it."

The silence settled like a storm cloud. It grew more oppressive by the second.

At last, Daveed broke it. "When should we expect you?"

"I need to pick up appropriate clothing from home."

The resulting silence was potent.

"We can provide whatever you need, Arren," Daveed reminded him.

He's chiding me.

"Joy has a list of what I purchased for Sandy before. She really likes the blue and silver, if it's in stock. Two *S'suuhhea* and matching *S'suumea* for me."

"Done. I'll have Deidre send them up to your office. I'll see you at home."

Your home. Not mine. "Thank you, Daveed."

"We're family, little brother."

"Family." *I'm not sure I know what you mean by that.*

He hung up and buried his face in his hands. *I can live with "family" for a few hours if it means Sandy is safe.*

But they are going to be the worst hours of my life. Arren didn't doubt it.

* * * *

The nest looked no less imposing than it had the last time Arren had visited it. *Far too soon for my tastes.*

He sighed, resigned to this course of action. Arren got out of his car, circled to Sandy's door, and drew her sleeping body out.

The code pad at the front door still recognized his code. On some level, that surprised him.

Arren pushed the door open and stepped inside with Sandy in his arms. The door slid shut behind them automatically, and he shuddered in revulsion.

With no proper sleeping surface, he settled Sandy's blanket wrapped body on the floor and pulled the *S'suumea* out of the bag on his shoulder.

It took a moment for the cut of the cloth to resonate with him. *Deidre sent the informal* S'suumea. *Raashh is going to be pissed.*

Arren hesitated. Leaving was still an option.

Fuck Raashh. Arren pulled off his street clothes, hung them on his usual hook, and secured the *S'suumea* around his waist. That accomplished, he unwrapped the blanket and hefted Sandy from the floor.

The door to the nest slid open, and Daveed glared down at him. His brother's gaze moved to Sandy, and his brow creased in worry.

"In the center nest?" Arren asked.

"Yes. In the center nest." Daveed cleared the way.

Xxan. Of course. We only speak Xxan in Raashh's nest. He switched to his *seir*'s language reluctantly. "My thanks."

"I welcome the brother to the nest."

Brother. Not the brother warrior. The insults never stop. He tipped his head in answer to the welcome.

Arren led the way through the garden tunnels, his body alive to the lush home he'd left. Even if he chose to create what his *seir* felt was a "proper" nest, it would take decades to match this growth.

I didn't leave because of the nest. I didn't stay to enjoy it either. A nest is just a place. Sandy and I like our little nest.

The center nest opened around him, and Arren forced a calming breath.

Raashh rose from the throne set before the water wall, coming to his full height of nearly three meters tall. At two hundred and forty kilos, it made the elder appear more wall than man.

Arren flicked a glance at the throne, and his jaw tightened reflexively. *A throne like Daahn's. A water wall like Daahn's.*

"You bring your mate to the nest?" Raashh asked. Before Arren could reply, his *seir* continued. "And you come here in that?"

He didn't have to look down at himself to know what his *seir* had taken offense to. "It was what Deidre had sent up to me, and it wasn't worth the time to go back for another *S'suumea.* A man has his priorities."

"Daveed will bring you proper clothing."

"You're wasting my time with—"

"We wear the formal *S'suumea.* You know this, Arren."

"Because Daahn does," he snapped back, his ridge plates undulating. "Think for yourself and stop wasting my time when my mate is at risk."

It was out before Arren could rein his tongue. *Too late now. Apologizing shows weakness.*

His *seir*'s ridge plates didn't extend in the slightest.

Because I'm not a worthy opponent. That burned at his gut.

Raashh tongue scented, then focused on Sandy. "Your mate..."

"Sandy Raashh, formerly Butler," he offered formally.

"The risk to her?"

"She is bearing, but her food and sleep requirements are perhaps four times the norm. If this is a Xxanian problem, I need to know it...and know what to do for her."

His *seir* didn't answer immediately. Instead, he leaned down to take in Sandy's scent directly from her throat. "How long has she carried?"

"Less than two weeks."

"You are certain of that?"

"Yes, I am. And I am certain the young one is my get. Now is this something seen in Xxanian bearing women or not?"

The elder pressed his talons to her womb. He dragged them back and forth, stirring the *S'suuhhea*. At last, Raashh spoke. "No. I have never heard of such a failing in a Xxanian female."

Failing. I was his failure. Raashh views this as my failure. My child is no one's failure. "Perhaps I should just go to SLAL."

"You should."

Arren shot a glare at Daveed. *Of course Raashh will help. After all, we're* family. "I understand. Thank you for your precious time, Raashh."

He turned to go. There was a shuttle at *Spice Industries*. Arren could use it to get Sandy to one of the space stations.

His *seir* wrapped a hand around Arren's bicep and dragged him to a halt. He glared up at the old dinosaur, torn between turning his back on them all and taking the elder's own weapons to him.

Raashh's voice was slow and calm. "I do not think you *do* understand me. Yes, your mate is at risk. Grave risk, and I can do nothing to help her. Perhaps the scientists can."

The frank analysis nearly weakened Arren's knees. "I thought you said this isn't a Xxanian problem."

"It is not. Xxanian females' bodies selectively eliminate down to one fetus when two or more catch. Allowing more than one to gestate is a human frailty, and I cannot begin to guess how it will affect your mate."

Arren reeled at the news, and his *seir's* hand tightened. He stared up at the pureblood Xxanian elder, at a loss to reply.

"We need SLAL," Raashh informed him. "As soon as we can reach them."

"We?" Arren could hardly follow the conversation in his shock.

"My son's mate, my nest daughter, is at risk. My gran-*vvaasheen* are at risk. The entire nest stands with you, Arren." He looked over Arren's shoulder. "Daveed, prepare my shuttle. We will contact Rayn from orbit."

"Right away." Daveed loped away.

Arren forced his mouth to shut, swallowed a lump inexplicably stuck in his throat, and managed words. "Thank you...my *seir*."

* * * *

"Will my nest daughter and gran-*vvaasheen* live?" Raashh demanded.

Arren swallowed hard at his *seir's* fury. The elder's ridge plates and frills were extended, and he towered over Stephen Rayn, the head of Xxanian studies at SLAL.

The scientist seemed unconcerned. "I vow to do everything in my power to see to their survival, just as I did with your son."

Daveed and Arren stared at each other. His elder brother shrugged.

Raashh sank back a step, and his frills wavered.

Rayn sighed. "When Marie died, Arren should have died with her. You know the lengths we went to. And now your son is here, presenting you with *his* young. Do you believe I will give him any less than I gave you?"

Raashh's frills folded to his head, and his ridge plates disappeared. "We will not lose Sandy. I will not fail a female of my nest so grievously again. Now...tell us what you intend to do."

Carew threaded an IV into Sandy's arm. It was a testament to her condition that she didn't react to it. Arren had learned she had an intense dislike for needles and hypos.

Rayn broke the tense silence. "We can force enough nutrients into Sandy's body to support two Xxanian young, but the less she does, the better. Swimming or floating in a bathing pond will be preferable to walking. She cannot work."

"Of course not," Arren agreed.

The scientist tipped a head grimly. "We want to encourage her to carry as long as possible. As it is, it will be difficult to get her to four months."

"Four?" Arren protested. "Can a young one survive being born so soon?" The typical Xxanian pregnancy was five months. The typical crossbred pregnancy was almost six months. A rare few lasted just under five.

Rayn focused on him, his expression solemn. "Most probably. I want to keep Sandy in a nest environment as long as possible. At three months, we have to bring her here. We can arrange a low-gravity nest suite for you both."

Raashh interrupted. "I will provide plants from one of the satellite nests." He focused on Arren. "Choose a nest for your mate's care."

The words to refuse stuck in his throat. It was presumptuous to assume Arren would move back into the nest.

I don't have a proper nest, and I can't do this alone. "My childhood nest. It is most calming." *And close to the pool.*

A look of discomfort flitted onto and then off of his *seir*'s face. "Precisely why I chose it for you."

"Will you have space for one of my assistants?" Rayn asked.

Raashh straightened at the question, and his ridge plates undulated.

Rayn waved off whatever protest Raashh might have been about to voice. "I have a few unobtrusive males on staff. Tim would be a good choice." He motioned to the one he'd introduced as Carew. "He has dealt extensively with Evan and Zondra Duncan."

To Arren's surprise, Raashh looked to him for an answer instead of making a decree for the nest.

Arren considered it carefully, scanning his gaze over Tim Carew before he answered. "If it will keep Sandy and my young safe, I will agree to that, but he won't be sleeping in our personal nest."

"No. Nothing like that," Tim groused in English. He switched to Xxan to continue. "I'll only enter your personal nest to administer medical aid, run tests...or to administer IVs. The IVs will be timed. I'll have to administer at least one during the sleep cycle, but I'll try to disturb you as little as possible when I do it."

"We'll have to sleep in clothing then," Arren noted to himself.

Rayn took over. "We will be outfitting Sandy with a bio-tracker. Tim will carry the report plate."

"Should Arren also have one?" Daveed asked.

"Why?" he shot back. "I won't be leaving Sandy. Anything that requires my attention can be sent by courier or accomplished by electronic transfer from the nest."

He expected Raashh to deny the installation of electronics in the nest. His *seir* tipped his head in agreement. "See to it, Daveed."

Arren met his brother's questioning gaze. "My Identi-chips are in the *s'sanuea*. Everything on the desktop of my nest office will do for now. We can arrange with Betty to send whatever else I need later."

Daveed clapped a hand on his shoulder. "You know I will see to it."

"I'm...starting to."

His brother offered a tense smile and headed for the shuttle bay.

"Wait!" Arren shouted after him.

Daveed turned back in seeming shock.

"Her lamp. Sandy can choose whichever of her possessions she wishes brought to the nest later, but there is a lamp next to the bed that she must have near her. It's precious. Antique. It has been passed from mother to daughter in her family for seven hundred years, Daveed. Nothing must happen to it."

His brother hesitated for only a moment, then tipped his head. "I'm honored that you trust me to see to its safety."

"I do." He wondered at it, but it was true. Arren nodded, then turned back toward the bed.

Raashh came to Sandy's bedside and stroked the side of one large finger along her cheek. "We will not fail you, little daughter."

* * * *

Sandy shifted on the bed. She must have fallen asleep at her desk again. She mumbled Arren's name, her mind still too foggy to consider getting up.

Movement to her left announced Arren rushing to her side, and Sandy reached for him. The skin under her hand was covered in smooth, cool scales. She pulled back and opened her eyes.

The massive reptile sent her scrambling back to the headboard of the bed. Movement closed on them from every side, and Arren gathered her to his chest, soothing sounds rumbling between them.

"It's my *seir*, Sandy. Calm down. It's my *seir*."

She nodded. "Just startled me," she managed. Little details started sinking in, first and foremost the IV line in her arm. Sandy looked down at it, trying to work out why she'd needed one. She hadn't thrown up a single meal. How could she dehydrate?

Someone cleared his throat, and she looked that direction, meeting the eyes of the closest lab-coated man.

He offered a tip of his head. "Welcome to SLAL, Sandy. I'm Doctor Stephen Rayn."

"I'm in space?" *When did that happen?* Why had it happened?

A strained smile was his only immediate answer. "Raashh and Arren brought you here for medical care."

She peeked up at the Xxanian elder and nodded her thanks. "I'm sick?" Her heart pounded at a worse possibility. "Or there's something wrong with the baby?" She looked Rayn's direction, hoping for a negative response.

Rayn paused for a moment. "Ba*bies*," he corrected. "Carrying one Xxanian young one is difficult enough for a human *Hauaa*. Carrying two causes a few problems."

"You're not suggesting—"

"No," the scientist at Rayn's right cut her off. "If we try to terminate one, you would probably lose both. It's better to help you carry both as long as your body can tolerate it."

Her breathing eased a bit at that pronouncement. "But?"

Rayn took over again. "But you'll be on bed rest."

"I can't seem to stay out of bed for very long anyway," she groused.

"We'll have to live at Raashh's nest," Arren inserted. "I will be working from there."

Sandy chanced another look at the elder. "Is that...okay?" She stopped short of asking if Arren was willing to risk his family's mistreatment.

"Yes," Arren assured her. "It is."

Raashh snorted in a manner that said he'd found her question offensive.

He understands English. Does he speak it?

As if answering her, the elder cupped his fingers under her chin. "Li-ttle daugh-ter," he pronounced in stilted English.

She managed a smile for him. Raashh didn't seem so bad to her. *I may find he is in time.*

Rayn drew her attention back. "Let's go over the treatment plan, Sandy. After that, we'll let you get back to the nest."

Chapter Twenty

Two days later

The movement of air drew Arren's attention away from the quarterly reports. He tongue-scented, unsure who would enter his personal nest without calling out softly first.

"You need something, Raashh?"

As if he'd taken it as an invitation, his *seir* moved closer. "Looking in on my nest daughter and the young ones."

Arren turned from the desk and watched as his *seir* leaned over Sandy. Raashh massaged Sandy's quickly expanding womb and made cooing sounds that would soothe the young ones. He'd never seen his *seir* act so solicitous before.

Maybe now is the time to ask. "What did Rayn mean when he talked about saving me?"

Raashh went rigid for a moment, then relaxed. "Your *Hauaa* died when you were a young nurser, little more than a week old. I thought you knew this."

"I know I have no memories of her, but I didn't know when she'd died." *No one ever discussed it. Why would I?*

"It was my failing. Marie complained of pain, but I'd foolishly equated it to the pains Daahn's mate suffered after Andy's birth. I did not seek medical attention for her, as I should have. Marie was strong and healthy, and I was attentive to her needs. I told myself... If it was serious, we would know it, Marie and I. I would act to protect my mate. She chided me so often about being overbearing about little things." He laughed harshly. "You are the better mate, you see. When your mate and children are at stake, there is no such thing as a 'little thing'."

Answering that was difficult. "She died when I was very young, and I should have died with her. Rayn said I should have. But I didn't." Arren hadn't thought a young babe could survive without its mother.

Raashh didn't reply directly to that. He seemed lost in bitter memories. "She died when Daahn and his mate were visiting with young Aleeks. My killing rage was fierce. I thought I'd lost both of you, and I had no one to blame for it but myself."

The elder paused, stroking Sandy's womb as if he was as comforted by the move as she would be if she were awake. "Daahn had no choice but to incapacitate me. I woke with him standing over me, my mate dead. My younger son...gone."

That piqued his attention. "Where was I?"

"It took me the better part of a week to calm down enough to ask that question. It took almost another for me to calm enough for Daahn to trust me with an answer," Raashh groused. "Until then, he would only tell me you lived.

"Daahn had summoned Mac to take his mate and gran-*vvaashee* to his nest, while he handled me. He ordered Mac to take you to Rayn. If anyone could save you, he'd hoped it would be Rayn. I think he knew that losing both of you would end me."

Arren considered the moment he'd learned Sandy was seriously ill. It would have ended him, but he'd always thought his *seir* was stronger than that. "Go on."

"You were half dead when Mac carried you off the shuttle and handed you to the scientists at SLAL. Human milk substitutes nearly killed you. They put" —he motioned to the IV absently— "the tube in you while Rayn put out a call for anyone nursing a crossbred child.

"There were two. One was a human weaning her young one; the other was a crossbred female actively nursing. The crossbreed's milk was complementary to your needs, and Rayn synthesized milk from samples he'd taken from her."

His *seir* offered a slight smile. "Rayn's mate became your...suurahget...*Hauaa.* Eva carried you in a sling, skin to skin with her. They fed you with a human style bottle. By the time Daahn trusted me inside SLAL, you had bonded to her."

"Which meant I couldn't be separated from her," Arren guessed.

"Not until you'd weaned. I could not bring you to our nest for months after you were taken from it. Your health was too fragile. When I...we did, Rayn and Eva stayed here" —an encompassing motion to the personal cave Arren was sharing with Sandy— "in this nest. It was calming, one of Marie's favorite satellite nests, and it was close to mine."

There was more, Arren was certain. "You blame yourself for more than my *Hauaa's* death." He didn't question it.

A sound of mourning escaped Raashh's throat, and his frills tucked close to his body in a sign of shame. "You were a Dominant. My failures...changed something. I cannot know what. Perhaps it was the loss of the nest environment in your early weeks or the loss of your mother's changing milk...or our mixed scent carried in her milk. Perhaps it was the loss of family scent soaking into your skin and the addition of the scents from SLAL. Perhaps it was the trauma of nearly dying. I can never know precisely how I failed you, but I did."

Arren ground his teeth in frustration. "I am not a failure, and I am sick to death of being referred to as one."

Raashh offered a piercing glare not unlikely the ones he shot Daveed when his elder brother had offended Raashh. It wasn't an expression Raashh typically spared for his Subdominant son. On some level, Arren found it heartening that he did so.

"And, at times, you are so very like a Dominant, I believe the change in your scent and your diminished size is some error. It must be. Not even your brother would dare say the things to me you do."

A smile curved Arren's lips up. "You know what the humans say, my *seir*. The *runt* must fight the hardest to stay even."

Raashh's brow wrinkled, as if he hadn't understood that. "Which makes you the stronger man," he offered gruffly. "But do not presume too much. I tolerate much from you, like your appalling manner of dressing, but impertinence means I will test your strength as I would your brother."

"I welcome the test of a brother warrior."

His father paused as if he meant to say something more, turned, and strode toward the center nest. "You will not when you have tested me for the first time."

Arren bit back a laugh. If it meant his father saw him as an equal, he would nurse his bruises with pride.

* * * *

"You understand what will happen?" Arren asked.

Sandy nodded. Arren's description of the Xxanian custom of bathing a new female member of the nest didn't sound all that disturbing to her—certainly no more disturbing than communal steam rooms were and less overt than the private dining rooms at Xxanian restaurants were—but they seemed convinced she would balk at it.

Tim looked from the readout of her condition to Arren. "Honestly, not too stressed. If she crosses the line—"

"I know," Arren cut in. "You'll warn us from out of view, and we'll forego this for now."

Sandy rolled her eyes. "If you're done treating me like a barely-legal virgin..." She moved to stand.

Arren vaulted to his feet and scooped her from the lush sleeping mat.

She met Tim's gaze and motioned to her position. "Is this really necessary?"

He darkened. "Unfortunately... Yes. The less time you spend on your feet, the better. Arren will carry you wherever you need to go. If he's not there, for any reason, Raashh will. If it's an emergency, Daveed or I will carry you, but I can't imagine Raashh and Arren are both going to be gone at the same time while you're carrying."

"Not a chance," Arren agreed. "Tim... If you would..." He motioned toward the doorway to the center nest.

"On my way." He left their room.

"What is he doing?" Sandy asked.

"Letting Raashh know you're ready to be bathed."

"Oh. Okay."

Arren headed out after him.

Raashh waited for them in the center nest, but Tim was nowhere to be seen. Daveed and his sons stood to Raashh's left. Sandy wondered at that, since she knew they weren't permitted in the pool while she was bathed.

Daveed tipped his head in a formal show. "This welcome would typically start with a formal introduction of you to Raashh, but since that has already happened, we will skip forward a bit." He stepped closer and bowed deeply. "I welcome the sister to the nest. If you require any comfort or protection, know that every male is at your call to provide for you. You honor us greatly with your presence."

"Wow. That's...that's very nice." It was. It was an incredibly sweet vow.

He smiled as he straightened. "It is usually said in Xxan, but since you don't know enough Xxan to understand it yet, I wanted to be sure you understood what we promise you."

"Thank you."

He stepped aside and waved his sons forward. They bowed together, and the older started speaking. "We welcome the female to the nest. If you require or wish for anything, we are at your call. You honor us greatly with your presence and the young you add to the nest."

The younger added his comments. "May you carry well and safely, *Hauaa zhhaaia*." They straightened.

"What is Haa...?" Her cheeks heated. "Um..."

Arren laid a kiss on the top of her head. "It means young mother. We consider motherhood sacred. There are few higher compliments for a woman than being a mother."

"I take it that means you intend to pamper me even more than you usually do?"

His chuckle was low enough to send a shiver down her spine. "You have *no* idea."

Raashh appeared at her side. He put his arms out, and Arren settled Sandy in them. Before she could decide if she was uncomfortable being held by the huge elder or not, he'd tucked her under his chin and started a rumbling hum.

The hum was soothing, and in moments, she felt as if she might be falling asleep. It wasn't the abrupt sleep that pregnancy brought on, more a comfortable drifting.

The humming seemed to come from everywhere at once. Finally, her overtaxed mind supplied the information that all the men and boys were humming along.

Raashh shifted Sandy in his arms, and she settled her cheek against his chest. One hand smoothed its way down her abdomen.

The elder's rumbling forced her eyes open, but only for a moment. She was too tired to keep them that way.

"What did he say?" she managed.

Arren answered her. "He believes you may be carrying two daughters. There is no scent of male about you."

She nodded.

The humming rumble continued. Raashh started moving. The humming went softer. After a moment, Sandy decided it was Daveed and his sons moving away.

Raashh returned her to Arren's arms, and he turned away from his *seir*. The slight splashing of water announced he was entering the pool. The water lapped at her body, warmth tickling up her feet and legs...then her backside.

A heartbeat later, she was floating in Arren's arms. Raashh's hand feathered over her cheek. Discussion in Xxan passed between them.

Arren didn't remove her *S'suuhhea*. He didn't bring her to her knees in the water. Raashh's hands went to work, rubbing the clove oil into her neck and shoulders. Arren started at the front of her neck, then worked down her shoulders and chest.

Their discussion went on. Raashh moved to her feet and massaged the oil from there to her knees, while Arren started rinsing the oil from her upper body. Once they were done, Arren lifted her and started walking again.

Sandy licked her lips, trying to make sense of that. "Aren't we supposed to...?" Her cheeks heated at what she was asking.

Raashh smoothed a hand over her hair, rumbling Xxan she didn't understand.

Arren translated for him. "The pool will be here for you when you feel up to more. For now, sleep."

She tried to answer, but she was too tired to form words. Darkness closed around her.

Chapter Twenty-One

Three months later

Sandy sighed as Arren lowered her into the bathing pool in the center nest. The water wasn't the typical chlorinated water found in public pools. It was heavy in metals and a bit of salt. Though Arren was careful to wash her in a tub of fresh water after a long soak in the bathing pool, there was something soothing about floating in the salt water.

She sighed. "I'm going to miss this."

Her mate's brow furrowed a bit, and he rubbed lightly at the huge mound of her stomach. If Sandy didn't know how far along she was intimately, she'd have guessed someone in her state was due any day. She hadn't been able to see her feet for the last four weeks.

Not that anyone let her stand independently anymore. She was carried everywhere by Arren or Raashh. Daveed was willing to carry her, but unless it was an emergency, it was considered inappropriate for Arren's brother to take such liberties.

As it was, living in Raashh's nest had changed everything about how she and Arren lived. Living with so many people meant they couldn't walk around the nest naked as they had at Arren's apartment. The fact that Tim had to change out her IV in the middle of the night meant they couldn't sleep naked. Her soaks or floats in the bathing pool in the center nest couldn't even be accomplished naked. Arren had provided dozens of maternity *S'suuhhea*, and she went through at least a four every day, after they were soaked in the pool or had been slept in.

"The bathing pool in the center nest?" he asked, dragging her back to the conversation she'd started.

"Yes. I'll miss it when we go to SLAL." The readings from the scan plates had been so encouraging so far, Rayn had decided to give Sandy more time in Raashh's nest, on the assumption that the nest would be less stressful on her than the space station would be, but there was little doubt he'd order the formal move to SLAL at her next weekly visit. "Two more days."

"There is a bathing pool in the nursery nest at SLAL. We will have sole use of it for the duration of our stay."

Sole use? Did that mean she could bathe without the *S'suuhhea* there? That would be an improvement.

"But it won't be the same." If someone had asked her two months ago, Sandy wouldn't have envisioned she'd become so attached to Raashh's nest, but she had. To the nest and the family members in it. It seemed even Arren and his family were busy mending old wounds between them.

"As close as we can make it," he promised.

The babies started pummeling her again, and Sandy smiled. She couldn't help it. Their vigorous movements meant they were healthy.

Considering the circumstances, movement was good.

Arren touched her womb over one beating foot or hand, chuckling. "They are so strong."

She groaned in memory of them keeping her awake the night before. "I kn—"

"Arren!" Tim's voice was like a siren going off in a quiet park. He barreled across the still nest toward them and shouted Arren's name again.

Sandy swiveled her head, trying to get a better look at him. And it struck. The pain sliced through her, doubling her so that she took a faceful of water before Arren managed to scoop her into his arms.

Sandy screamed at the second pain, then panted in an attempt to avoid being swamped by it. Arren turned toward the stairs leading out of the pool, whispering assurances that everything would be fine.

Tim shouted out orders to someone unseen. "Get the shuttle ready. Now!" He launched into the pool in his clothing, readying a hypo for use.

Sandy winced at the injection, then ground her teeth at another pain.

Tim herded Arren out of the pool and toward the shuttle bay. The nest rushed past them at a rate that told Sandy the two men were running. The pains subsided, and she started taking deep breaths, reasoning her rattled nerves back a notch.

"How did this start so suddenly?" Arren demanded.

"I don't know. I've never seen labor start this way. Let's get her aboard the shuttle and worry about the how later. Hopefully the *z'hhabe* will give us enough time to reach the station."

"What is the usual effectiveness of it?"

Tim shook his head. "It varies too much to guess. It can last as long as two hours."

"Can? Or...what?" Arren raced onto the shuttle, and settled Sandy on a plush mat Daveed was smoothing on the carpeted floor.

Tim pulled down a kit he'd stored in the shuttle days earlier, every muscle tense.

"Carew!" Arren barked at him.

He hesitated in prepping a new IV. His expression told Sandy that this could end badly. "I've seen it wear off in fifteen minutes."

Arren gaped at him.

Daveed's hand closed on Arren's shoulder. "We can have you to SLAL in less than that," he vowed. "Go, Raashh!" He rushed away, secured the shuttle doors from outside, then thumped on the side of the shuttle to let his *seir* know they were ready to fly.

The momentary lightheadedness told Sandy that Raashh had engaged the anti-grav systems on land, probably in an attempt to spare her the usual gravitational pull of take-off. She supposed they were in flight just afterward, but with no sense of movement to cue her in, she couldn't be sure of that.

Tim hung the new IV, and Sandy stared at it, her heart hammering. It wasn't the yellowish color of nutrient base. The bag looked suspiciously like Xxanian-mix blood.

As if he was reading her thoughts, Tim squeezed her hand. "Calm down, Sandy. It will strengthen the three of you for labor and delivery. Your blood chemistry has changed, due to both being mated and carrying Xxanian young. Arren's blood won't harm you."

"Blood?" She'd never heard of them giving blood before someone was bleeding.

He injected something into the IV line, and heat raced up her arm instead of the usual chill of an IV. "We have to give you a shot of hormone. It will help mature the babies in the little time we have left."

To help them breathe. She nodded.

"We've been using small amounts of it for the last few weeks, but we'd hoped to have another month."

"Can't you stop labor?" Arren interrupted. "Human doctors can stop human labors."

"We can slow it down, if we reach the station before it's too late."

"Too late for—"

Sandy gasped at the feeling of something coursing down her thighs. She levered herself up, pushing past Arren's gentle attempt at restraint. There was no mistaking the Kelly green staining the mat. "The amniot. My water has broken."

There was a moment of tense silence.

"Too late?" Arren asked.

Tim nodded. "We have to reach the station as soon as possible. These babies are going to be born today, like it or not."

Arren helped Sandy back down to the mat. She took calming breaths, praying to any god that would listen that her babies were mature enough to survive. She didn't doubt that Arren's killing rage at losing one or both would be more than either of them could bear.

* * * *

Arren was certain they would reach SLAL without further incident when the situation took a turn for the worse. Sandy hadn't had any further contractions. The babies were moving lightly under his hand. He would have described the situation as stable. Until the moment Sandy screamed in pain.

Tim stared at her in shock for a single heartbeat. He whipped around and scanned his gaze down the tracking plate, shaking his head, muttering under his breath.

"What is it?" Arren demanded.

"I wish I knew. It's not contractions. It's—" He turned to look at Arren, but his gaze snapped to Sandy, and his face lost all color.

Arren followed his line of sight, his heart stuttering at the sight of Sandy gasping for breath. She grasped at his wrist, and Arren wrapped his hand around it, encouraging her to hold it if she needed to. Her grip surprised him.

Tim moved abruptly to one side, coming back with the medical kit. He rummaged through it, his hands unsteady. Arren's question of what was wrong ended when Tim shouted out orders to Raashh.

"Whatever speed we're at, double it. She's bleeding."

Arren snapped a look Tim's direction, focusing on the healing cloth he held pressed between her thighs. It wasn't a little blood. The cloth was soaked, and he was preparing a second.

In the background, he could hear his *seir* comming updates on Sandy's condition and their flight path to SLAL.

Fuck! Visions of losing his young and Sandy as well pushed him toward madness. "We're nearly there," he whispered. There was still time to save them.

Sandy's hand loosened against his, and Arren stroked her face, calling her name. There was no reply.

"She's doing fine," Tim assured him.

"Fine? This is fine?" he practically roared.

"She's stable," he corrected himself.

Arren didn't reply to that.

"Landing now," Raashh announced.

The engines wound down, and his *seir* rushed past them, working the exterior door with dexterity that surprised many humans.

"Lift her on three," Tim instructed. "Raashh, you'll have to take the IV bags."

The door swung wide, and Raashh turned back to them with a grumble of agreement.

"One. Two."

At "three," Arren and Tim slid to their feet, Tim holding the medicated pad to the bleeding. They maneuvered her out of the shuttle together, Raashh extending one long arm fully to take the rear position down the too-narrow ramp.

"Run."

Arren didn't need to be told twice. He sprinted for the emergency wing Rayn had pointed out to them on an earlier visit, Tim barely keeping up with his pace.

Just when he was starting to wonder where Rayn's people were, a swarm of them descended from every side. An emergency cart slipped into place between them, and Arren lowered Sandy onto it and slowed his pace to allow them to work while the move continued.

One doctor slid a scan plate low on Sandy's abdomen. Another tapped keys on a control board, pressing shoulder-to-shoulder with Tim to accomplish it. Readings were shouted out, most likely to comms in the walls Rayn was monitoring, as well as to the staff members directly preparing her for what would come next.

"Op One," Rayn's voice barked over a speaker they were passing. His voice echoed from others further down the line.

The staff members turned the gurney left at the next intersection, and Arren turned with it. No matter what Rayn said—conscious of his presence or not—Arren wasn't leaving Sandy's side.

No one asked him to. The entire team trooped through a fine spray and into the operating room. Dripping the foul-smelling antimicrobial liquid should have been uncomfortable, but it wasn't. Only Sandy mattered.

Sandy and our young.

Snips of conversation made it through the haze of his own desperation.

"—started en route. I've slowed it but—"

"How long has she been unconscious?"

"Ten milliliters. STAT."

"—distress."

"We will not lose her, Rayn." His *seir* warned.

"Doing my best, Raashh. Now let us work, or I'll have your hulking ass removed."

Arren shot a look at his *seir*, anticipating an explosion that didn't materialize. His *seir* snorted his disgust and paced the far end of the room, well out of the way of the medical team working on Sandy.

Fairly certain he wasn't going to be tasked with talking—or taking—his *seir* down while Rayn's team worked, Arren focused on his mate's pale, still face. Machines flashed warnings, and medical personnel stripped away Sandy's ruined *S'suuhhea* and covered her with sheets, top and bottom.

All of it likely took heartbeats, but it felt like hours to Arren. It was the worst torture a Xxanian male could suffer, he decided. His mate and young were at risk, and there was nothing Arren could do to save them.

"Arren? Arren!"

He snapped his head around to stare at Rayn.

"We need you to move."

His ridge plates rose in warning, and he bared his hunting teeth.

"Sparks has to make the incision. Just to the opposite side, but move. Now."

Incision? He rushed to follow Rayn's orders. If they were resorting to surgery, there wasn't a moment to lose.

There was no pretense at trying to hide the proceedings from him. Before Arren was situated across her body from his previous position, the slight human woman was making a precision laser cut.

Blood mixed with Xxanian amniot rolled down her abdomen. No effort was made to collect it for purification and return to her body. This was slash surgery, at its finest.

As if in answer to his fears of her losing too much blood, Tim strung up bags of blood, most likely synthesized from blood samples Sandy had given weeks earlier. He had them hooked into the IV and replacing what she'd lost in the blink of an eye.

A thin cry caught Arren's attention, and he whipped his head toward it. The first of his babies was halfway through the incision and already ramping up to a furious squall.

His *seir* appeared at Arren's back, rumbling the Xxanian welcome song. Arren joined in; Rayn and Tim did likewise without pausing in their work.

The young one was out and disappeared into the hands of a second female in a rush. Spark's hands were back in the incision before Arren could protest his child being whisked away from him that way.

They have to run tests, he reminded himself. *Let them.*

"Female," someone announced. "One point six kilos. She's coming in at a six. Strong responses to stimuli."

Arren watched his younger babe emerge in Sparks's grip. The young one was silent, and Arren's heart pounded in terror hard enough to make his head spin.

Breathe. For your Hauaa's *sake, breathe!*

Sparks handed the miniature babe to yet another female, then went to work with her flesh-knitting tools. "Second out," she informed Rayn.

He didn't look up from his own work, and he nodded grimly.

Breathe. The idea of going home without any of his family was inconceivable to him. It was horrific.

"Female," someone behind Sparks shouted. "One point one kilo. Three. Breathing but sluggish. I could use the *seir's* help."

It took a moment for Arren to latch onto the truth that *he* was the *seir* in question, not Raashh. He turned and slammed headlong into his *seir's* broad chest.

Raashh pushed Arren past the milling humans. "Go. Care for your young. I will protect your mate."

"I thank the brother warrior." It was out before Arren could think twice about the presumption of a Subdominant uttering the phrase.

He'd hardly caught his breath to question what the women tending to his young needed from him when one turned on him and stroked a stinging gel over the musk ducts on his chest.

Arren's ridge plates stirred to life as his musk started to flow.

In unison, the two women turned, each holding a tiny daughter wrapped in silk-lined flannel. They pressed the babes to him, faces nestled to his stimulated ducts.

"Cup your arms under them," one of them ordered.

Arren complied, confused by the command, and two squirming bodies were entrusted into his care. The humans scanned the med-disks attached to his daughters' chests.

"Six up to eight," one reported smartly.

"Three up to six," the other followed in her wake.

"Told you the *seir's* musk was the key," Tim gloated.

"Record it all," Rayn directed them. "I imagine Doctor Carew will need as much data as possible for his thesis conclusions." There was a hint of a smile in his tone.

"Ready to move to the nursery nest?" one of the attendants asked.

Arren looked toward Sandy, whispering her name, torn between his duty to his mate and the same toward his daughters.

"She won't wake for hours," Rayn replied. He looked over his shoulder at Arren, his expression solemn. "But she *will* wake. Sandy is strong and fighting."

"Marie was strong," Raashh countered.

"Marie wasn't here and in our care at the critical moments."

Raashh was still for a moment. "True. I cannot argue it."

And he blames himself for that.

Arren nodded to his *seir* and accompanied the women to the half-finished nest area. Already, they'd infused Raashh nest's scent into the medical nest.

Good. That decreased the chance of a tragedy like his own. *At least they are female. There can be no loss of a Dominant in this case.*

In a daze, Arren followed the commands of the medics surrounding him, learning how to care for his premature young.

Chapter Twenty-Two

Sandy took a deep breath, trying to right her senses before she opened her eyes. Throbbing aches in her abdomen had her reaching for her distended womb.

The mound of babies wasn't there. Memories of labor starting in the bathing pool rolled into ones of the thick, green amniot...and then blood coursing down her thighs.

I lost them. Sandy didn't question it. The room was too still and silent for babies to be within earshot. *As still as a centuries-old tomb.*

That was too much for her, and she started sobbing.

"Sandy?"

She opened her eyes, gazing up at Daveed. Her mind made unwanted connections. *I lost the babies, and Arren is in a killing rage.* Visions of him locked in a cell were searing, and she broke down in tears.

"Sandy? Are you in pain?" Daveed asked urgently.

Excruciating pain, and only Arren can understand it.

In the distance, a door slid open, and footsteps rushed toward the bed. Sandy turned her head toward the newcomer.

Dr. Rayn.

He scanned his gaze over the readouts on the screen above the bed, then focused on Sandy. "You're in pain?"

A hundred questions and statements fought their way toward her lips. At last, one emerged in a rush of sound and air. "I want to hold them. To...see them."

"The babies?"

It's bad. She nodded solemnly.

Rayn checked the readouts again. "We'd intended to move you into the nest when you woke, but if you're in pain—"

"What?" Nothing he was saying made sense.

"Are. You. In. Pain?" There was a demand for information couched in that.

"A...a little, I guess."

He sighed in seeming relief. "Why were you so panicked when you woke?"

Sandy pressed a hand to the soft patch of her abdomen, tears causing a lump in her throat.

To her surprise, Rayn smiled. "You have two beautiful daughters in the nest with Arren. We had to move them to the nest for the healing scents and sounds. Would you like to see them now?"

Catching her breath long enough to offer a verbal response beyond her, Sandy nodded.

Rayn tipped his head to Daveed, and Sandy looked that direction just in time to see her brother-in-law untucking the blankets and sheet on his side of the bed. Whispers of movement announced Rayn doing the same behind her. Her face burning in embarrassment, Sandy resigned herself to the fact that being carried from place to place was still a part of her life.

Daveed tucked the covers around her carefully and lifted Sandy into his arms. Rayn led the way out of her room and down the corridor.

The door to the nursery nest they'd constructed slid open, and the lush smells of plants and clove filled her lungs. Sandy sucked in a deep breath, starved for the nest she'd only recently become a part of.

As if she'd asked a question, Daveed offered information. "We hadn't finished the nest yet. Raashh has been bringing plants up from the far corners, and allies have had scentless plants sent to aid us. More arrive every hour. The nest will be complete in days, at the most."

"Why are allies sending plants?" *And what are scentless plants?* "Is it a Xxanian tradition when a baby is born?" If it was, she'd never heard of it.

His smile was grim. "Word is spreading that Raashh's nest has two young females in need of a stable, healing nest. None of them dare send their scents into the healing nest for infants, but none will chance us remembering a failure to aid us when..." He shot a narrow-eyed look at her that said he'd be blushing, were he capable of it. "When Arren considers males to sate your daughters' quickening."

That concept made the independent human woman in her balk. The idea of *anyone* choosing a sexual partner for her daughters wasn't something she could accept without a fight. *Arren and I will have to discuss that later.*

Daveed turned a corner on the winding path, and Arren was there, dozing on a dreaming mat, two blanket-wrapped babies on his chest. The breath caught in her throat at the sight of them.

Her brother-in-law settled her to the dreaming mat next to Arren. He stirred and opened his eyes, then extended his hand to stroke his fingertips along her cheek.

"How do you feel?" he whispered, seemingly intent on not waking their daughters.

"Sore."

Arren winced.

"But okay now that I've seen the three of you."

Sandy reached out and drew a fingertip along one tiny hand. Her daughter turned her hand and grasped on. Hard! Tears stinging her eyes, Sandy laughed.

Arren smiled widely. "I know the names we talked about, but the final decision is yours. If you don't think the names fit—"

She motioned to them with her free hand. "Which one was born first?"

"The one holding your hand. She's slightly larger than her twin, but the younger..." He chuckled. "She's our little fighter."

"Then the little fighter is Marie...Marie Janelle, for both of our mothers." Raashh had told her what a fighter Marie was. They'd originally intended to name each girl after a grandmother, but this seemed more appropriate to her.

"This one..." Sandy smiled as her daughter's grip tightened again. "...is Noelle Joy."

Daveed gasped. "Joy will be honored."

"Noelle for your brother?" Arren asked.

"Yes." Would that upset him?

"I'm sure he'll be pleased."

Better yet, Arren wasn't upset.

Marie started to cry, and Noelle picked up her cue.

"Just in time for the first feeding," Arren noted. "Perfect timing."

Daveed rose and made tracks the other direction, leaving Sandy to learn to nurse her daughters. In moments, they were both latched on. Arren settled behind her, creating a chair of his body, his arms supporting hers.

It was the very definition of family. *I never want to be anywhere else again.*

Chapter Twenty-Three

Two months later

"I suppose there is one excellent thing about this situation," Sandy offered brightly.

A smile curved Rayn's lips up, but he didn't look away from the panel he was working at. "And that would be?"

"I've always heard it's easier to handle a single baby after juggling twins."

All human sounds in the room ground to a heart-stopping halt. She looked from face to face, noting the unease. Several of the techs glanced from face to face, seemingly seeking something she couldn't name.

The hair at the back of Sandy's neck rose in warning. "What?" It was the most she could manage.

Rayn's jaw was tight in some powerful emotion. He sighed and rose from his chair, looking a decade older than he had moments before.

A long, tense moment passed in silence, before he started talking. "We'd hoped to avoid this discussion for a little longer."

"What discussion and why?"

"Because it's going to upset you, I'm sure."

Her heart hammered, and her head spun. Sandy eased back onto the pillow, certain now that she'd need the support. "Tell me."

"You can't have more children. I'm sorry, but the damage was too severe."

A hundred little comments Arren had made while she carried the girls echoed in her mind. He'd been ecstatic about their daughters, but he'd wanted to try for a son someday.

I can't give him a son.

Hundreds of questions tumbled and wrestled in her mind. Would he still want her? He couldn't have sex with someone else, and she was defective and couldn't give him the son he wanted. Would that make Arren bitter?

Would finding out she was barren send him into a killing rage? Was that really why Rayn hadn't wanted to tell her? Because Arren would be furious? Because his instincts would kick in and make him a danger to everyone around him?

As always, the thought of Arren locked in a cell while he vented off the rage seared her. "Arren." Tears stung at her eyes.

Rayn covered her hand with his own. "Stay here. I'll take care of it."

* * * *

Arren looked up at Rayn's approach, his heart stuttering at the doctor's grim expression. "Something is wrong. Something is wrong with Sandy."

He didn't question it. They were doing their weekly evaluation on her. Clearly, Rayn had found something that worried him, and that was bad news. Anything Rayn couldn't fix was unfixable. Every Xxanian crossbreed knew that.

Rayn motioned for peace, then looked toward Raashh. "Take the females. I need to talk to Arren."

Without the girls. He thinks whatever it is will push me into a killing rage.

Better that I'm not holding the girls, if that does *happen.* He handed the twins to his *seir* with a nod of thanks.

Rayn motioned Raashh away. His *seir* snorted his discontent, but he went, taking the girls to the far reaches of the nest. When they were well away, Arren found his voice.

"What is wrong with Sandy?"

Rayn sat cross-legged on the grass. "I told you she would live, and she will." He waved off Arren's protest. "I was trying to hide the extent of her injuries from her, to avoid her becoming upset, but she broached the subject, and my oaths demand I tell Sandy her condition if she asks."

Arren's ridge plates extended in frustration. "And what *is* her condition, Rayn? Since you have seen fit to hide it from me as well."

He didn't blush or otherwise show signs of embarrassment at being called out for such a dishonorable move. "She can't give you more young. Her womb was too badly damaged."

His heart ached at the loss...and for Sandy's suffering. He'd done this to her. Not purposefully, of course, but carrying his young had left her unable to carry again.

"Arren?" Rayn tensed, and Arren realized he'd come prepared to sedate him, if necessary.

"You will have no need of the tranq pad. I must see Sandy."

"She's very upset." He pushed to his feet.

Arren did the same. "I imagine she would be." And though Arren couldn't make this right, she was his mate, and it was his duty to ease her suffering however he could.

"We haven't sedated her. If you feel that's necessary, we will."

"I hope that won't be necessary." But who knew how Sandy would take the news that she was unable to carry again?

They made the distance to the exam bay in silence. Sandy looked up at their entrance, her eyes and cheeks swollen and red from tears.

She's shattered by this, and it is my fault. He'd pursued her. He'd made her his mate. Perhaps he'd even convinced Rayn to allow her to stay in the nest too long. Would she be able to have children if she'd been on SLAL when labor started?

Sandy sobbed, and he rushed to her side, gathering her to his chest, at a loss for the words to comfort her. Broken words left her lips, and he fought to make sense of them.

Apologizing. She's apologizing for not being able to give me sons.

"That doesn't matter," he soothed her. "We've brought two beautiful daughters to the nest. Daveed has provided the sons. The nest's future is secure."

"But I'm—" She sobbed again.

"What, Sandy? What do you think you are?" Whatever it was, it surely wasn't true.

"I'm...defective."

"No! You are not—"

"I am." Her throat bobbed.

Something is unsaid. "What do you think this means, Sandy?" *Please, don't let her withdraw from me. I couldn't stand it.*

She didn't answer him, and her throat bobbed again.

"Rayn?" he inquired, certain that the doctor would understand the unspoken question.

He nodded. "Room twelve is available."

Arren lifted Sandy from the examination table and went to the room Rayn had indicated. The door had been opened for them, in anticipation of their arrival. Arren used his foot to shove it closed behind them and took her to the wide bed at the center of the room.

He knew what this room was typically used for. Mating. Some males worried that their human mates might require medical care during mating and asked for such a mating room. And that was before one took Zondra and Evan Duncan into account. Couples who required medical intervention to mate used such rooms, by necessity.

Or the female who has spent nearly her entire pregnancy on bed rest in another of the rooms. He'd never seen her mate and had rarely glimpsed her...always from afar, of course. But the female had Rayn's attention, just as Sandy had, which meant she was Xxan or a Xxanian mate.

Once they were on the bed together, Sandy half-wrapped around Arren's body, he forged into the sticky situation. "What is it you believe I think, Sandy?"

Still, she struggled for words. "I...I don't know."

He pressed a kiss to her forehead. "I believe I made myself clear to you long ago."

Her eyes were wide and full of questions he could only guess the origin of.

"I told you the most important thing to me. Nothing is more important to me than having you as my mate."

"Even if—"

"My mother gave Raashh two babes and died as a result. You gave me two babes and live. Daahn's mate gave him only one child. Half of the elders stranded on Earth only produced one crossbreed babe with a mate. I don't think you understand, Sandy. You are already ahead of the curve, as far as Xxanian mating goes."

Her mouth moved as if she wanted to question something but couldn't figure out what to ask.

He drew her face up and sealed his lips to hers. At first, Arren believed she would refuse him. She didn't. Sandy's lips parted to his. After a moment, he pulled back.

"I believe you have forgotten what you are to me," he breathed.

Sandy moaned as he went to work on her robe. "You still—"

"Want you?" he asked.

She nodded.

Arren parted her *S'suuhhea*, then pulled up at his *S'suumea*. He eased into her body, mindful that she had suffered major injury two months earlier.

Rayn had apparently healed her well. Sandy rose against him, making the delightful little sounds she always had to encourage him.

The end came quickly. It had been too long for both of them. Arren reveled in the fact that she'd come for him.

One lazy kiss led to another, then a deeper one. Hands trailed over bodies. In moments, he was thrusting again, staking his claim on his mate. As if she was intent on doing the same, Sandy grasped as his buttocks and whispered pleas for more.

"If the babies didn't need to eat so soon, I would anoint you with my secondary this moment," Arren informed her. "You are mine. Always mine."

She nodded. "The girls sleep for a three-hour stretch," she reminded him.

They did do it, once a day. It was a new development, and they usually used it to get an unbroken sleep cycle while the girls slept.

He smiled. "I think we can pass on sleep this one time."

"Oh, yes." Arren thought she was agreeing with him, until her body started contracting. She repeated it over and over as a mantra, getting louder and louder each time.

Arren climaxed, his heart and lungs working hard in pleasure.

In the aftermath, they lay, entwined together.

Sandy combed her fingers through his hair. "That was so good."

"I wish we could stay like this," Arren agreed. He did, but their daughters would be hungry very soon.

She tipped her hips up, bringing his half-erect primary to full readiness again. "I think we have time for one more."

"I have heard the scent of sex makes for a happy nest environment, and healthy babies," he agreed, already working to grant her wish.

Sandy nipped at his chin. "Good. Then we're going to use your secondary in the nest tonight."

"As my mate wishes."

The End

Section 4:

Gabe

Crossbred Son

Prologue

"You can't be serious," Abby Jacobs croaked out.

Doctor Heston sighed. "Would I joke about something like this?"

Pregnant. I'm pregnant. "But you said... *All* the specialists said I couldn't have a child." *I didn't use protection, because they said it was impossible.*

His expression was grim. "It's nearly impossible, Abby. You still won't carry to term. I have to be realistic here. Chances are, you'll miscarry early, but you *will* miscarry."

The fledgling spark of excitement she hadn't even acknowledged yet extinguished.

"If you don't want to put yourself through this... If you can't face losing the baby later—"

"No. Are you crazy?" This was probably the only chance she'd have to have a child. Abby was going to follow it through, no matter the outcome.

"I'll set you up with Jules Bashaw. She's the best high-risk obstetrician in the area."

Her cheeks heated. "That would be good, but she's going to have to consult on this one."

Heston's brow furrowed in confusion. "Why would she have to consult? Are there other complications I don't know about?"

"Maybe."

He waited patiently for an answer.

"The father is Xxan...well, a Xxanian mix anyway. I think, all things considered, maybe SLAL should be consulted."

He straightened and took a step back. His gaze flicked to her abdomen and away, and his color faded a few shades.

Great. He's a bigot.

"I see. I'll make sure Jules knows it. I don't think she's ever handled a Xxanian birth before."

And I'll make sure she's not a bigot as well. "Thank you, Doctor Heston." *And goodbye.*

"I'll let Jules handle any prenatal vitamins. I don't know what will be safe for you...considering."

Abby exited as quickly as possible, the card for Doctor Bashaw in hand.

She'd only been home for a few minutes when her mobile phone rang. The caller ID announced an amorphous "Medical." *Which means it's probably Doctor Bashaw.* She flipped it open.

"Hello?"

"Miz Jacobs? This is Doctor Stephen Rayn from SLAL. Doctor Bashaw contacted me. I understand you are carrying a Xxanian mix young w...uh...baby."

Well, that was quick. "Yes. I am."

"We would like to bring you in for preliminary testing as soon as possible. Would you be available to take a shuttle to us this afternoon?"

There was a note of urgency in his voice that sent a shiver down her spine. "I suppose so. Where would I get the shuttle?"

"We can have a shuttle meet you at any of the hospitals or at the airport," he offered.

"Mercy?"

"Fine. Can you be there at two o'clock?"

"Yes." Her head was spinning at the speed of events. Abby resolved to lay down now, before she managed to collapse into sleep again.

"The front desk will have someone take you to the pad."

Abby nodded, then realized he couldn't see her. "Okay. Thanks." Her mouth went dry, and the feeling that she'd lost control of her life assaulted her.

"Miz Jacobs?"

"Yes." Her voice sounded strange in her own ears.

"Who is the *seir*...the father of your baby?"

"This is confidential, right?" *He can't tell Gabe. Chances are, I'm going to lose the baby, anyway.*

There was a moment of silence. "I don't understand."

"If Doctor Bashaw gave you a full update, you know there's almost no chance I'll carry to term...or even to a viable—"

"I'm going to do my best to make sure you do." There was a haughty undertone to that answer.

"I believe that, but you'll probably fail. I can't let you tell him, just to leave him hurt when I lose the baby." *This was why I left him in the first place. I can't give him children.*

"And if the baby doesn't miscarry? If he or she is born alive?"

"I'll cross that bridge when I come to it." Abby couldn't think about that now. If the baby lived, how could she ever explain to Gabe why she'd kept it a secret from him?

"Yes," he grumbled. "It's confidential. Now...who is the father?"

"Gabe Zhaahvan."

"Thank you. That helps us plan for your care."

"You're welcome. Thank you for helping."

"Keeping Xxan-human crossbreds alive is what I do, Miz Jacobs. I'll see you soon."

Chapter One

Six months later

The code coming over the comm unit sent chills down Gabe's back. *A woman and child being attacked. A Xxanian would never perpetrate such a heinous act.*

Steven Thomas, his partner, confirmed that they were en route. Gabe pressed the accelerator to the floor, and his partner grasped at the door handle reflexively.

"You know I love when you do this, buddy," Thomas informed him. "But you are going to get us both in deep shit with these antics."

"I'm Xxan. The chances of me actually wrecking the vehicle are—"

"Yeah. Yeah. Yeah. One in some hundreds of thousands, I'm sure."

That curved the corner of Gabe's mouth in a shadow of humor. It disappeared as the call site came into view. He pulled the vehicle to a screeching halt, slammed it into park, and was out the door before the dust cleared.

"Wait for backup," Thomas yelled after him, scrambling out the far door.

As if. Gabe was in the door and scanning for trouble coming his way before Thomas was around the front of the vehicle.

He didn't need the waitress motioning frantically toward the corridor with the sign for restrooms posted inside. The sounds of shouts and bangs announced which direction he should take clearly enough.

A baby's cry tightened down the muscles in his arms. What was wrong with humans that they did such things to the innocent?

Gabe bolted for the fray, cursing under his breath at the two men seated at the counter, looking as if they wanted nothing to do with the scene. Unless the perps had a handgun or other weapon, this was inexcusable.

Even if they do, there is no excuse those men can make to me. It would be better if Thomas took their statements. Gabe might be tempted to do something that would land him on suspension. Or worse.

His mind processed what he was seeing as Gabe barreled into the mob and started dragging them off the abused door. The woman had apparently managed to lock herself and her child in the ladies' room, and the three attackers were trying to break their way in to do more damage. From the looks of it, she had only minutes of safety before they would accomplish it. Already, there were gaping holes in the thin wood.

One of the men turned and attacked him with a hammer, probably taken from the tool belt at his waist. Gabe knocked the weapon away and took the man down with a punch to the ribs. He turned in time to see a second trying to attack his back with a heavy wrench in hand. The third was already in motion, into the restaurant, where Thomas ordered him to halt.

Too late to knock the weapon away effectively, Gabe captured the man's wrist in his left hand and grasped his attacker around the throat with his right.

The scent on the man's hand assaulted him, shocking Gabe to stillness, and he tongue scented in disbelief. *Xxanian scent. Not* just *Xxanian. My own nest.*

The young one's screaming tapered off, and sounds of the female soothing him whispered through the door.

It's a female and child. That made no sense. His sister was too young to have children. *And it's not Ariel's scent.*

It's male. His brother Geoff was no more mated than Gabe was. A woman Geoff slept with? The scent was Dominant, but it was...off for Geoff. *What in the* Seir-*God's name is going on here?*

"Gabe!"

Thomas's shout snapped him back to the present in time to see the attacker's blood-soaked right fist flying for his face. Gabe threw him against the wall and let him fall. He motioned Thomas to him and then turned toward the door.

"Annandale Police," he barked, well aware that his ridge plates were extended. "Open the door, please."

"Gabe," Thomas cautioned. "Settle down."

Settle down? With a female and child that smell of my nest behind that door, in an unknown condition? Of course, there was no way for Thomas to know that. *And no time to explain it.*

He forced his ridge plates back and knocked briskly at the door. "Police. Please, open the door, ma'am." Gabe didn't want to have to break the door down, but if she didn't open it, he would have no choice.

If she is Xxanian or a human female with a Xxanian boyfriend or mate, she may not be willing to emerge for a human officer. He rumbled out a soothing sound in Xxan, encouraging her to let him protect her.

There was a moment of silence. A sob followed. Then the lock clicked open.

Xxan. What is a Xxanian female doing in a café like this one? It's a given she can't eat what they serve. Meeting a human friend? Using the restroom to change the baby?

Assess the situation now. Get answers later. Gabe eased the door open, well aware that a Xxanian female protecting a young one might still attack.

The sight behind the door stopped him in his tracks. The female sitting on the floor—blood coursing down her face and matting her dark hair—wasn't Xxanian, but the young one in her arms—wearing the flexible, strapped sunglasses Xxanians put on their young—clearly was. She wasn't a stranger, either.

He knelt at her side. "Abby?"

The young one looked up at him, and Gabe tongue-scented to be certain before he spoke.

* * * *

Abby sighed in relief at the sight of Gabe. When she'd heard the Xxanian sound, she'd hoped it was him and not the other Xxanian they had on the force. But either would have been acceptable, in this case. If anyone would keep Michael safe, it would be a Xxanian male.

The Xxan are wired that way. Aren't they? Protect young, at all costs, even the young of another Xxanian.

"My son," he breathed.

Before she could respond to that, he was shouting out orders to someone.

"Thomas, get an ambulance here...and get backup." He pressed at the cut on her forehead hard enough to make Abby's head spin.

The other officer snorted. "You put them down alone. Why would we need backup now?"

"You'll need help taking them to the station."

The human officer appeared over Gabe's shoulder, a spare set of plastic handcuffs they used when they had more than one prisoner in his hand. "What? Where will you be?"

"Going to the hospital with them." He tipped his head toward Abby and Michael.

"Gabe, old buddy, I know—"

He motioned to Michael, his ridge plates extending. "This is my *son*, Thomas. He is not going anywhere without me."

Thomas paled, and he shot a glance from one side of him to the other. "Backup. Right away." He retreated a few steps, and the sound of the cuffs announced him restraining one of the men who had attacked her. "Believe me, pal. You move an inch, and he just may have to kill you."

Abby focused on Gabe with no small amount of difficulty. In the background, Thomas was following Gabe's orders, calling in an ambulance for her and more officers for the prisoners.

Gabe's ridge plates were in flux, a sure sign that he was brutally angry and trying to control it. "You should have told me."

"Not now, please." There was so much to explain, and her head ached too much to do it coherently.

He met her gaze and nodded. "But soon." It wasn't an order.

"Yes." It was about time she did the adult thing and faced her son's father.

Michael reached out for Gabe, and the man in question lifted the squirming baby from her arms with one big hand. Gabe's eye slits narrowed behind his dark glasses, and Abby followed his line of sight. There was blood on Michael's cheek. Gabe's muscles tightened down in preparation to spring.

If I don't do something, he's going to kill them all and end up in a lethal injection booth. "It's not his blood. It's not mine, either," she hastened to assure him. *Well, of course it's not Michael's.* Their son had the orange-tinted blood typical of Xxanian mixes, the same type of blood that ran in Gabe's veins.

Gabe looked at her, his gaze ranging up and down Abby's body. "Our son bit one of those *zhirrakkah?*"

She'd only heard Gabe use that term once before, when security had caught a rapist on campus. If she wasn't so sick to her stomach, Abby would have nodded in agreement to whatever foul term that was in Xxan. "Yes. The bastard grabbed for Michael, and I turned. He got a handful of my shirt instead, and Michael bit him. That's how we got this far."

Abby suspected her fear had set Michael off. The Xxan were scent oriented, and biting when she was frightened would likely be instinctual for Michael.

A smile pulled up at Gabe's lips, and he winked at their son. "Good boy. Always protect the females."

Michael looked at his father, his expression solemn. Then he started chewing on his fist.

Teething. Though Michael's hunting teeth had come in quickly, his human front teeth were taking their sweet time about it. *They aren't sharp.*

Thomas interrupted any questions Gabe might have had. "A few minutes, ma'am."

Abby let her eyes slide shut, too tired to respond to that.

* * * *

Gabe had never felt more out of place in his life. Here he was, sitting in a hospital waiting room, feeding his son—a son he knew nothing about—a bottle of expressed milk.

She must have stopped breastfeeding when Michael started getting teeth. Gabe prayed Abby didn't have scars from his son's hunting teeth. He'd heard it had happened to a few of the early human mates.

The young one dozed, sucking sporadically, his little fingers twitching in response to his dreams. His age was difficult to gauge. Gabe hadn't been around a lot of babies, crossbred or otherwise, so he wasn't certain how to tell. From what he'd seen, Michael had sprouted teeth, but he wasn't able to do more than pull himself along the floor, certainly not a full crawl.

Dozens of questions circling in his mind, he pulled out his mobile phone and dialed Aleeks Daahn's number from memory. Aleeks was the proud *seir* of a toddling young female and the uncle to both a female and a young Dominant. Surely, he would be able to guess the age of Gabe's son.

Aleeks answered on the second ring. "Problem, Gabe?"

I called early in the day, during Aleeks's work day. "Not a problem but a query. I am caring for"—*I don't want to involve anyone outside my nest in this, especially not before my own* seir *and* gran-seir *know it.*—"a young Xxanian mix. He has his hunting teeth but not his human teeth. He doesn't properly crawl, but he does sit up steadily and pull himself with elbows and knees or toes." He considered the contents of the bag. "He eats ground meat and vegetables. How old would he be...roughly?"

There was a moment of tense silence. "You are caring for a young one and don't even know his age?"

"It's a long story." *One I do not even know myself.* "His mother has a minor injury, and I am caring for the young one while the human doctors care for her."

"And the young one's *seir*?" he asked pointedly.

"Has been unavailable thus far. But that will change soon," he grumbled more to himself than Aleeks.

"He knows then?"

"Yes. He does," he snapped. "Will you help me or not?"

Aleeks sighed. "What generation? Do you know?"

"Third generation, which is why I asked you and not Daveed. Zondra's young would be the closest I know."

"I would guess somewhere between two and three months old then."

Two or three months. I've lost so much time with him.

"Is there a problem, Gabe?" he asked again.

"No. No problem. Thank you, Aleeks." He hung up before the astute young warrior could ask another question.

Two or three months. How long did Michael gestate? Did Abby know when she left me?

Even if she didn't, why didn't she tell me when she found out? Why didn't Abby trust me to be a proper seir *to our son?* Until she recovered, there would be no answers to his many questions.

* * * *

"We'll want to keep you here overnight for observation," the emergency room doctor pronounced.

"Not a chance."

He startled and met Abby's gaze. "Excuse me?"

"I'm nursing a baby, so no overnight and no drugs." She started to rise from the bed.

"Wait. I can't just let you walk out of here without knowing you have someone arranged to take care of you at home."

Her heart stuttered at the obvious answer. "There's a police officer in the waiting room named Gabe Zhaahvan. I'm sure he'll help out until I'm back on my feet." *For Michael. He'll at least do that for me. I hope.*

"And you'll stay here while I talk to him?" There was a warning couched in that.

"Won't move a millimeter."

Though he looked like he'd like to stay and argue with her, the doctor nodded and withdrew. He was gone so long, Abby started to fidget.

What if Gabe refuses? What if they keep me here? How will Michael get fed? Will they let me keep him with me?

The curtain slid back and the doctor came in, Gabe on his heels. Michael looked up at her, smiled, and let out a happy squeal.

She smiled. "There's my little man." Abby put her arms out, and Gabe settled Michael in them. She closed her eyes and inhaled his baby scent.

"I changed his diaper," Gabe informed her. "And he's had the last bottle of breast milk."

As if in confirmation her breasts ached to fill another.

"We should get you both home to prepare for his next meal."

Her heart rate eased a dozen beats or more per minute. "Thank you, Gabe."

He offered a tense nod but didn't make any further comments.

It's coming. We have to talk. Abby focused on the doctor. "Can I go now?"

"Sign the release, and you're free to go."

* * * *

Gabe tightened his fist around the steering wheel of his *Spice* coupe and bit back more questions. He'd held his tongue in check for the taxi ride to the station and the few moments it had taken him to check out and receive emergency leave for three days.

He'd promised to hold his questions until Abby was ready to talk, but how he was going to manage that was a mystery to him.

Abby looked back at Michael, strapped into the car seat Gabe had borrowed from the station. "Thank you," she repeated. "I couldn't do this without you."

You could have decided that at some point much earlier in the seven months we've been apart. "Right."

Her cheeks flushed, and she bit her lower lip. "I'm sorry."

"For?"

"For not telling you about Michael."

Apparently, she's ready. "Did you know when you left me?"

"No. Of course not."

His breath released in a rush. "You still should have told me."

Abby opened her mouth to talk, shut it again, then swallowed hard. "It wasn't that simple."

His anger spiked, and Gabe fought his ridge plates back. "Do you have *any* idea how dangerous it was to have a Xxanian child without support?"

"I *had* support. I had the best high risk obstetrician in the city and the doctors at SLAL." She visibly fumed. "Not that the human doctor had much to add to what SLAL did, but I still had her on the team."

"SLAL?"

Abby nodded solemnly.

"And they didn't contact me?" Someone at SLAL was going to pay.

"Patient-physician confidentiality."

"So you asked them not to contact me." He fisted his hands tighter.

"It wasn't that simple," she repeated.

"Then why don't you tell me what complicated it," he invited. Gabe wanted to understand. He needed to know she hadn't believed he'd be a bad *seir* to their son.

"*I* complicated it." Her breathing hitched, and Abby pressed her fingertips to her mouth, looking close to tears.

Gabe forced his hands to loosen. "Maybe we shouldn't discuss this now."

"No. We should. We really should. This discussion should have happened long ago, but I made a mess of it." She pressed a hand to the liquid stitches at her temple and shook her head.

He sighed. "Why didn't you tell me? Did you think I wouldn't be a good *seir*...father to Michael?" His heart thundered in apprehension at what she might say.

"No. I didn't think that. I'm sure you would be...will be a great father."

At least she's talking as if I have a future with our son. "What did I do to make you leave me?" He'd wondered that since the day she left.

"It wasn't you. It was me."

"The oldest line around," he growled.

"It was. You wanted children, and I—"

"If you didn't want a child, the time to make that decision has long since passed." Gabe looked at Michael out of the corner of his eye.

"Of course, I wanted children," she shouted.

Gabe pulled over to the curb, his head spinning too much to consider driving. It was disconcerting for a Xxanian warrior to be so marginalized physically. "Then why...? Why would you leave me? Was it the idea of binding?" He'd hinted at it with her shortly before she left. Had he scared her away?

Abby shook her head. "I would have loved to." Her breathing hitched again, and she wiped at her eyes.

"Then why did you leave me?"

"Because they told me I couldn't have children. Ever. The doctors said... Children were so important to you, and I. Couldn't. Have. Them." Her eyes pleaded with him for understanding.

"Oh, *Seir*-God. You thought that was more important to me than..." He cupped Abby's head and drew her to his chest. "No. I never wanted you to think that."

Abby vented tears into his shirt. From the back seat, Michael started to fuss. It was inborn, the discomfort at seeing a woman in distress.

"Let's get you both home," he whispered. "This can wait."

She nodded and tried to stifle her tears. Gabe pulled away from the curb and into traffic, his emotions reeling.

* * * *

Abby sipped at the hot chocolate Gabe had given her, holding the breast pump with the opposite hand. He'd been nothing but solicitous so far. Gabe had gotten her settled in the gliding rocker, a pillow beneath her feet; he'd thought of every comfort.

He stuck his head in the doorway, Michael on his hip. Gabe looked much more comfortable in the clothing he'd taken from the bag in his trunk than he'd looked in his uniform. Then again, his street clothes were probably *Spice* wear, specially formulated to be comforting against sensitive Xxanian skin.

Their son rubbed at his eyes, fussing little sounds escaping from his lips.

"I hate to ask," Gabe hinted. He tipped his head toward the quickly-filling bottle.

"Give me a second." Abby set the mug on the table beside her, turned off the pump, removed it from her leaking breast, and unscrewed the bottle. "Hand me a nipple and a second bottle from the shelf, please."

Gabe didn't move. Abby looked up at him, her mouth going dry at his fixed attention on her uncovered breast. Completely unwarranted, her body went wet and warm for him.

He turned abruptly, searched the shelves, and came back with a collar and nipple. Once she had it, he went back for a bottle. Gabe didn't look at her again. He took the bottle of milk with a muttered word of thanks and ambled away with Michael and the bottle.

Abby sat there, her body and mind in a riot. She hooked the new bottle up with shaking hands and started expressing again. Her gaze strayed to the doorway often, but Gabe didn't appear.

Of course not. If he is as confused as I am about what just happened, the last place he'll want to be is with me. But if that was true, why did she want him to come back?

* * * *

Seir-*God lives!* The memory of her lush breast had Gabe hard and aching. *Now is the wrong time. I don't know if there will ever be a right time again.*

Michael patted at the side of the bottle, and he kicked his feet. His eyes slid shut.

There has to be a right time for us. For all of us.

Abby had said she wanted to mate with him. *She did then. Does she still want to?* Her arousal said she wanted *something* from him, but it wasn't necessarily mating.

Sex had always been hot between them. What had started out as a chance encounter had led to a date. Three dates. Two years. And then it had ended abruptly.

In his arms, their son released the empty bottle with a sigh. He'd only dozed for a few moments earlier. Gabe suspected this would be a true nap.

He moved with all the stealth of a Xxanian warrior toward the nursery he'd found earlier. It was wholly unlike a Xxanian nursery nest, but it was cheery and welcoming. Gabe could easily understand how his son could be at peace here. It was a snug little home Abby had created for them.

Them alone. Without me. Would Gabe be welcome in it now? For longer than she needed him to help her care for Michael?

His heart aching at what might happen tomorrow, Gabe settled Michael in the crib, then tucked the blankets around him.

Chapter Two

Abby pushed the food around her plate and took peeks up at Gabe feeding Michael. He wasn't using the ground meat she normally did, and he wasn't using a spoon. In what she supposed was the Xxanian method of feeding a baby, Gabe was chewing cubes of meat and finger-feeding them into Michael's mouth, a process their son seemed to enjoy.

"You should eat, Abby." Gabe's voice was low and soothing.

She dropped her fork. "I don't have much of an appetite tonight."

He focused his disconcerting green-gold eyes on her. "Your head?"

"No. Just...everything else, I suppose."

"Do you want to finish the discussion? Would it be easier to do it now?"

Abby buried her face in her hands.

His hand stroked at her shoulder.

He moved. He's so quiet. I forgot how silently he moves.

"Abby?"

"How can you be so nice to me, all things considered?"

When he didn't answer, Abby looked up at him.

His brow was furrowed, and his head cocked to one side. "Shouldn't I be?"

She shrugged.

"Do you want to discuss it?" he offered again.

"Better now than later, I suppose."

Michael fussed from his highchair, bouncing and slapping his hands on the wood top impatiently. Gabe returned to the meat and vegetables he'd been feeding their son. Gabe didn't question her, leaving Abby to decide where to begin.

"I *did* want to become your mate," she assured him. Why she thought it would make a difference was a mystery to her, but it needed to be said.

"And you left me because you couldn't give me children." It was stated as a fact. "How long after you left did you find out you were pregnant?"

Gabe popped another cube into his mouth and chewed in precise little movements of his jaw, his muscles bunching and releasing. He pushed the meat onto his fingertips.

"Three weeks or so. I was sick. I was exhausted, falling asleep at odd times... It never even occurred to me that...that I was."

"Of course." He scooped the food into Michael's mouth and turned to look at her. "And why didn't you contact me then?"

She shifted uncomfortably and pushed her plate away.

"Abby? Why?" He hesitated a moment. "You didn't think I would turn my back on you, did you?"

"No. I did consider that you might think I was just coming back because of the baby, though."

Gabe sent her an incredulous look. "But?"

"But what?" It had been a straightforward comment.

"That was only part of your reason."

"How do you do that?"

He scowled. Gabe put a piece of broccoli in his mouth next.

Spitting the words out was harder than she'd thought it would be. How many times had she practiced this speech? Now she couldn't untie her tongue.

Gabe looked at Michael long enough to poke another mouthful of food in. That freed her tongue.

"They said I'd lose the baby. One of the human doctors... He wanted me to abort, because there was no way I could carry to term. I never went back to him and don't intend to," she hastened to add.

His head swung toward her, his expression horrified.

"I couldn't do it. A-abort, I mean. I had to try to carry Michael, but..."

"But?" he repeated.

The rest stuck in her throat, and Abby swallowed hard. Tears stung at her eyes. "I couldn't do that to you."

His eye slits narrowed, and his ridge plates stirred. "Do *what* to me?"

"Give you hope of having a baby, when the chances of delivering one were so hopeless. I had to try, but you... I couldn't do that to you."

"You didn't think I would want to know?"

"What could you do?" she wailed.

"Be there for both of you." There was a bite of something harsh in that.

Unforgiving. Abby hoped she was reading him wrong.

Gabe fed Michael another bite of meat, visibly calming himself. "And when Michael was born?"

"I don't know. I picked up the phone so many times, but I how could I tell you? How could I even begin?"

"You seem to be doing well enough now," he quipped.

"Now you *know* we have a son. I'm not telling you that. All I have to tell you is why it happened this way. Pitiful as it is, I'm trying to do that, because you deserve to know the truth."

"I deserved to be there from the day you found out you carried."

"Yes... Yes, you did." He'd deserved to be there before that, but Abby had screwed that up.

He didn't reply to that.

Her nerves jumping, Abby searched for something to say to fill the silence between them. "You should know that Doctor Rayn never gave up for a minute. He was determined that Michael would survive. Even when I didn't believe it was possible, he insisted it was."

Gabe stared at her, his expressions shifting and his ridge plates extending halfway and retracting again. She'd clearly said the wrong thing, but Abby couldn't fathom what it might be. She opened her mouth to ask.

He beat her to the punch. "Steven Rayn was your doctor?"

"They said he was the best there was with crossbred babies. How was I supposed to know—?"

Abby swallowed hard at his bland look. A look that seemed to proclaim: "You could have known if you'd just asked me." That went without saying.

"Well, isn't he?" she squeaked.

"Yes. Rayn is the best at saving the unsavable." He grumbled something she didn't catch.

And I'm not going to rock the boat.

Again, the silence grew into an oppressive cloud that even Michael seemed to perceive. Their son started to wiggle and fuss. Abby's hands itched to pick him up and cuddle him. She fisted them in her lap. If she did that, Gabe would think she didn't trust him with Michael, she was sure.

As it was, Gabe was monopolizing time with Michael. *He's making up for lost time. I have to let him...bond with Michael, or whatever the Xxan call it.* Knowing them, it likely had another word, considering what binding meant to them.

Or maybe not. Binding is binding.

But what if their parent-child binding is unbreakable, the way mate binding is.

Abby came to her senses, her hands halfway onto the tabletop. She forced them back to her lap. *I don't know what Xxanian fathers are supposed to do. I have to let him bond and hope it's not too late for them to form one.*

Gabe started cleaning Michael's face, and he didn't look at her. "If you have a spare blanket and a pillow, I can sleep on Michael's floor tonight."

Her heart aching, Abby forced herself to answer. "If that's what you want. Sure."

What? He's supposed to fall in bed with me after everything we've been through? Part of her wished he would. The rest knew that era of their lives was over.

Abby fled the table. By the time Gabe had Michael out of the highchair, the blanket and pillow were in Michael's nursery, and she was closed into her bedroom.

* * * *

Gabe looked down at the pile of linens on Michael's floor, swallowing down a roar, his ridge plates coming halfway erect. Michael looked up at him sharply, his ridge plates stirred, and his eye slits narrowed. Gabe forced his back and rumbled out a calming sound in Xxan. One fist went into his son's mouth, and he started teething on the knuckles.

He'd hoped Abby would argue with him, offer him somewhere else to sleep. When she'd sounded so hesitant, he'd been sure Abby would act on her continuing attraction to him and invite Gabe to her bed.

I'm dreaming. It's over. She's offering me a place in our son's life, but she's not interested in us as a couple anymore.

He looked down at Michael, offered a weak smile, then collected a fresh sleeper from the bureau and a diaper from the changing table.

It's soft. Spice Industries made the softest, most absorbent diapers around, and they sold them at a discount to Xxanian families, calling it a 'medial need' to have such diapers for crossbred infants. With SLAL aiding Abby, it was clear they'd arranged for *Spice* diapers for Michael. *Only the best for my son.*

"It's time for a bath, little man." It was long past time for a *seir's* first bathing of his son. Gabe pulled the bottle of clove bath gel out of his bag and carried baby and supplies to the bathroom.

He set Michael on the plush bath rug, and the baby clapped his hands on his thighs.

Gabe smiled widely. "Like your bath, do you? Well, that is normal for our breed."

His son cocked his head to one side and lost his balance. Gabe reached out and scooped him up. Michael squealed in delight and bounced in his *seir's* arms, seemingly speeding Gabe toward the bath.

"Just a minute, Michael. We have to undress you first."

That was easier said than done. Michael was in perpetual motion, moving an arm or leg, just as Gabe reached for the fabric to maneuver a limb out, rolling while Gabe was trying to work fasteners.

"How does your mother do this?" he inquired calmly. The warrior in him wanted to pin the squirming and flailing infant down and force his clothing off.

Not the right answer, Gabe. Definitely not right.

The tub had the prerequisite five or six inches of water for an infant bath in it long before Gabe lifted a very naked Michael to settle him inside. He stopped halfway at the sensation of the spreading wet spot on his shirt. A look of disbelief down at the tapering stream of urine later, Gabe scowled at his son, earning him a peel of laughter from the plump face.

"You think I deserved that, do you?" Gabe cocked one eyebrow up. "Can I assume you've similarly christened your mother?"

Michael clapped and reached for the water.

"I see. I guess that's all right then." Maybe this was a rite of acceptance Gabe didn't know about.

Or maybe young ones have no control over releasing their bladders.

He deposited Michael in the water and pulled his fouled shirt off, tossing it for the open hamper.

His jeans were halfway off when Gabe looked down again. His heart stuttered, and he reached for Michael, then pulled up short. When he'd seen the young one lying back in the bathtub, he'd flashed on the training tapes he'd seen about drowning.

"An infant can drown in less than two inches of water."

But Michael wasn't drowning. He was floating on his back, his arms spread wide, his feet kicking lightly. Gabe placed a hand to cushion Michael's head at the moment he would have hit the drain side of the tub.

Michael looked up at him, smiled, and scrambled to sitting again. He took a faceful of water, sneezed, then rubbed his face with a pudgy little hand. A moment later, he patted the water and looked up at Gabe expectantly.

"You're right. I'm doing this wrong. Aren't I?"

Gabe peeled off his damp jeans, tossed them in the hamper, and climbed into the tub with Michael. He picked up a lightweight washcloth and the clove bath gel and started bathing his son. All the while, he hummed the Xxanian welcoming song.

Chapter Three

From her bedroom, Abby heard the bath water gushing down the pipe. Gabe would be coming out of the bathroom with Michael soon. Though their son's baths were always amusing, she hadn't wanted to intrude on Gabe's time with Michael.

He's had little enough of it, and if he really wants nothing to do with me, he's not going to see Michael nearly as much as either of us want him to.

That bothered her. *A lot.* Abby paced the floor, her nerves jumping. If she had a larger apartment, she'd consider suggesting Gabe move in with them. Or she'd consider moving in with Gabe, if he offered, but neither of them had an apartment big enough for all of them.

Assuming he's in the same apartment I walked out of. She winced at that. For all she knew, Gabe had a new apartment and a steady girlfriend. He'd had seven months to find one, after all.

No. I won't think about that. Not right now.

Who am I kidding? It was all she could think about. Had Gabe found someone else? Would he choose that relationship over one with her.

Relationship? Now I know I'm demented. Gabe hadn't given the slightest indication that he wanted anything but a relationship with Michael. *Michael and answers.*

The door opened, and Gabe chatted his way to the nursery with Michael.

That's my cue. Abby let herself into the hall and ducked into the bathroom with the intention of brushing her hair and teeth.

The room smelled pleasantly of clove. That brought back potent memories of Gabe using his favorite clove bath gel on her while they had sex in the shower. Before she knew it, Abby was lost in daydreams of one of those times.

Gabe's touch was soft and knowing. He'd been her lover for well over two years. He knew how to arouse her, how to use the stinging clove to leave her shivering in pleasure.

Abby had no clue which time this was. She didn't care. If Gabe was with her, who cared which time it was?

She took a handful of the clove gel and stroked it up and down his hard cock, smiling at his groan of pleasure. There was no question what would come next. Gabe would rinse his cock off and lift her over it.

Gabe's sound of surprise shocked her to reality, and Abby turned toward him.

"Sorry. Didn't know you were in here." He stood in the doorway, wrapped in the informal *S'suumea*, a wet towel in his hand.

Abby's already aroused body weathered the blow badly. She wanted him. *Now. And there's no chance—*

Gabe let loose a growl and tossed the towel at the tub. She watched him cross the distance between them, shivering as she had in the daydream. He'd always been able to do this to her. One look, and she needed him buried inside her.

He grasped her by the back of the skull with one hand and slanted his mouth across hers. Abby opened to him, starving for Gabe. Their tongues danced and darted and hands explored.

Gabe dragged her against him, and Abby groaned at the length of his cock pressing to the meat of her belly. Her entire body trembled.

She reached for the fold of silk that would release the *S'suumea*, and Gabe pulled away. Her heart ached at the tension in him.

Abby took a step back. "Maybe I—"

"Shhh." Gabe cocked his head to one side and turned slightly.

He's listening to something. Abby did the same. It took a moment for her to lock on the sound he had, and she sighed in relief. "Don't worry. That's just the sound Michael makes when he's settling to sleep."

"You're sure?" There was an urgency to the question that offended her.

"Yes. I'm sure," she snapped in return. Abby turned to the sink and pulled down her toothbrush and toothpaste. The fact that his taste was in her mouth annoyed her. *How could he walk in and just expect—*

Gabe's hands settled on her shoulders, and he massaged them. "I'm sorry. It's new to me. Every sound. Every movement. I don't know what they mean yet."

That mollified her somewhat, but Abby was still stung. "You'll learn," she offered simply. A line of toothpaste deposited on the brush, she set the open tube aside and started brushing her teeth.

"Thank you for that."

"For what?" she grumbled around the brush.

"For giving me the chance to learn."

"I never intended to exclude you. I just..." She sighed and went back to brushing her teeth, at a loss to explain it.

"You just didn't know how to include me after excluding me so long," he whispered. "I do understand how hard that must have been. You've never been one who enjoyed confrontations."

Abby forced herself to spit in the sink when she wanted to sob, which would probably cause her to choke on the toothpaste. She rinsed the toothbrush, put it back in the holder, and rinsed her mouth with a handful of water.

Gabe's massage moved down her back. She considered telling him to stop, but some selfish corner of her mind missed this too much to follow through on the protest.

Instead, she wet the washcloth hung next to the sink with hot water, squirted some liquid soap on it, and started scrubbing her face.

"I could bathe you." There was a wistful undertone to Gabe's offer.

Her errant body responded. Abby avoided looking at him in the mirror, and she scrubbed harder at her face. She rinsed the washcloth used it to remove the layer of soap from her forehead and cheeks.

At the second rinse, Gabe spoke again. "You want it, but you aren't saying so. I don't know how to interpret that." The massage stopped, and Gabe's hands left her back, but he didn't retreat.

"You can interpret it that I have no clue what is happening between us. I hurt you before, and beyond not wanting to hurt you again, I don't want to get hurt again." It was blunt, all too true. After the day Abby had had, the last thing she wanted was to play games.

When he didn't immediately answer, she went back to rinsing her face. Gabe didn't move again until she was done drying her face and hands on the towel hung between the sink and shower. She deposited it on the hook, and his hand closed around her wrist.

His aroused body pressing to her back ripped a gasp from her throat. Gabe drew her arm around her stomach, his cradling it. His face nestled into her hair, and his answer caressed her ear.

"Are you with someone else?" He didn't give her a chance to answer. "I don't smell another man in your apartment, but that doesn't mean you aren't."

Her emotions rioted. On some level, Abby felt certain she should be offended by the question, but she wasn't. Even his possessive nature was endearing. "No. I'm not." *I haven't been since you.*

"Neither am I. There hasn't been more than the occasional one-night-stand for me since you left me." He paused. "And damned few of those."

"Then you've had more than I have," she quipped, stung that he'd slept with other women. *Be reasonable. I left him. Was he supposed to wait for me forever?*

He growled, and she shivered in response.

"If I asked you to mate with me—"

Her heart stuttered. "You're not asking."

Gabe took a step back and gently turned her to face him. "I'm telling you that the need to be with you is as powerful today as it ever was. I still...consider you my own. If you choose to let me, I will do my best to convince you to become my mate. If you don't intend that... That would the way to hurt me, Abby."

"But we can't," she protested.

He started to withdraw, his ridge plates fluctuating. She grasped his arms to stop him. Gabe had to understand what she was saying, and she was sure he didn't understand at all.

"You said mating takes three days, three days while we're both useless for anything else," Abby began.

Gabe's ridge plates retracted, but his expression was still sour. "What of it?"

"Michael."

Gabe swung a calculating look toward the nursery, then focused on her again. "I don't understand."

"Michael is nursing. We can't just—"

The smile curving his lips stole her ability to form words. "I didn't mean we'd mate today, Abby...or even this week or month. Even with my family to watch over Michael, we wouldn't want to interrupt his nursing. For one thing, the abrupt end to lactation would be agony for you." He reached up and scooped her shoulder-length hair behind one ear.

Responding to that was difficult. "So...when I stop nursing then?"

"Is that a 'yes' to letting me try to convince you?" he teased.

"I think that shower you offered sounds like a good start."

* * * *

Gabe bit back a smile at her breathless answer. Something told him Abby wouldn't appreciate it. He'd already irritated her once in the last five minutes. He wasn't game for a repeat.

Abby reached out and unfastened his *S'suumea*. She didn't let it fall to the floor. Instead, she folded it carefully—surprisingly in the correct way—and set it on the back of the toilet.

Taking his cue, Gabe slipped his hands beneath her nightshirt and worked it up her body. There were no panties beneath, and his cock jerked in pleasure at that fact. Her nipples were hard and swollen, practically begging for his hands.

Not too avidly. Her milk has a ready customer.

Speaking of which..."How long will Michael sleep?"

Her breath left her in a rush. "Five or six hours, most probably. Maybe seven, since he's just had a bath."

"Good."

Abby didn't question that.

Gabe removed her nightshirt and dropped it over his *S'suumea*. He tipped his head down and kissed her, turning the shower on and setting the temperature by feel.

The kiss was hot and hard. Her body brushed against his, smelling of aroused woman and Xxan.

Mine. My scent and my son's.

Abby had always fit Gabe as if she'd been crafted for him. She was tall for a woman, almost a full two meters of curves, making her a nice complement to his two point two meters. Her breasts were lush and heavy, even when they weren't full of milk, and her body sheathed him perfectly.

Perhaps not so nicely now. She has delivered a child.

He pushed that thought away. Abby was his. She'd been his from the moment he first saw her at the college party in their senior year. Within an hour of that meeting, she'd been in his bed, sheathing him for the first time. And the second. Third. Even for an oversexed young Xxanian Dominant, that night had been excessive.

No. Not excessive. Not nearly enough. That's why he'd gone back to her, again and again. Even now, he couldn't get enough of her.

When he was sure the water had settled on a comfortable temperature, Gabe guided Abby beneath the spray. The scent of Abby and clove was enough to steal his sanity.

Gabe forced himself to slow, to savor every touch as he massaged the clove gel into her skin and washed it away. There was no question where they were headed, no question they both wanted it to go this way.

But not rushing there. Not like we did the first few times.

He drank from her freshly washed skin, moaning at the fist closing in his hair.

Abby jerked her hips up at the first stroke of clove oil over her core, and she gasped. He knew from experience that the stinging oil aroused her nearly as much as it would a Xxanian female.

Or perhaps she is reacting to my touch. That thought settled in his cock, enflaming Gabe farther.

As if in confirmation, Abby started grinding against his fingers, breathless little sounds escaping her lips.

Not yet.

Gabe hastened to rinse the clove oil away, and Abby tipped her head back, her eyes sliding closed.

There was little question what she was hoping for, but Gabe wanted more than a rushed fuck in the shower. This woman was the *Hauaa* of his child, and she deserved a proper bathing.

He settled on his knees between her spread legs and started to feast on clove-flavored arousal. Abby's fingers tightened in his hair, drawing Gabe closer, asking with motions what she seemingly didn't have the air to ask with words.

Her sounds were sharp and her body's nectar pungent and drugging. In moments, he was thrusting his tongue into her, using the pebbled surface to drink in as much of her scent as possible.

Abby let loose with a shudder and a shout, her inner muscles clenching and releasing against his tongue. Gabe teased her with further strokes of his tongue and fingers, taking fierce pride in her responses. It was more than the instinctual delight in being able to sate a female you had a claim on speaking. It was the knowledge that he remained the only male that had made Abby shatter to his touch with such ease and precision.

And I will remain so. There could be no question of it.

* * * *

The shift in Gabe was subtle but undeniable, and Abby's heart rate ratcheted up a dozen beats a minute.

The air of determination was hardly new to her. Gabe had been in similar moods many times over the years they were together as a couple. It always promised mind-altering pleasure in bed...or wherever they were making love that moment.

She'd long ago dubbed the state of mind he was in 'his Dominant side.' Biologically, Gabe was always a Dominant Xxanian male. There was no mistaking that, even if one didn't know the innate signs of Dominant males, as compared to Subdominant males. But this was über-Dominant, when Gabe's nature was at its most base and potent edge.

He spun the spigot closed and rose slowly, capturing water from her body on his rough tongue. The slight indentation in the tip caught on one nipple, and she gasped in response. Gabe responded by circling the nipple, taunting her with pleasure to come.

Her mind numbly replayed his sexual appetite. It wasn't unusual for Gabe to last hours.

"Oh, stars burn," she breathed. She'd missed that almost more than she could bear.

A deep rumble in reply brought goose bumps up all over her body. Whatever Gabe did next was sure to rock her thinking mind.

There was a moment of stillness, and Abby came to the realization that Gabe was on his feet, towering over her. She looked up into his green eyes, sprinkled with flecks of shimmering gold. His eye slits were wide in arousal, his nostrils flaring, dragging in her scent. As if in confirmation of that, his cock bobbed her direction.

He seemed to be waiting for something, though Abby couldn't fathom what it might be. Before she could form the words to ask it, he posed a question of his own.

"I've showered you, Abby. Do I have permission to continue?"

The restraint evident in his tone left her trembling in anticipation. "Yes." *Anything.*

"I'm going to try to convince you to be my mate. No doubt about it."

Yes. She would agree to nearly anything he asked, if Gabe asked directly. That included binding with him. There were Xxanian mix formulas on the market, after all. Abby nodded, unable to form words.

A dangerous little grin curved Gabe's lips, and her breathing hitched in response.

Oh, this is going to be hot.

He hesitated. "I should collect a condom from—"

Abby shook her head. "No. I'm on a pregnancy block. The doctors insisted. At least six months, they said." It came out a series of gasped phrases, but he seemed to understand her.

Gabe stepped backward out of the tub and tugged a fresh towel off of the shelf. He dried her without a word, paying painstaking attention to every curve and hollow of her body.

By the time he was satisfied with her state of dryness—and the gathering wetness between her thighs, no doubt—his own body had air dried. Gabe hung the towel over the shower curtain bar and pulled her flush to his body.

His cock pressed to her hipbone and lower abdomen, already weeping fluids. The rising scent of his *Zhigaaal* went to her head, and Abby sought out the wells of musk on his chest, sampling them.

As always, that was enough to drug her senses. Spanish Fly had nothing on Xxanian musk.

Gabe scooped her into his arms and started walking. Once she was deposited in the center of her bed, he hesitated a moment, his gaze fastened at about her chest level.

"What's wrong?" she hazarded to ask.

One of his long, tapered fingers trailed slowly along her breast. He lifted it away, then brought it down in another position, and started over again.

Abby arched to his touch, stunned that so simple a touch could be so arousing.

"I apologize for our son," he breathed.

That shocked Abby out of her arousal somewhat. "What?" He wasn't saying he was sorry Michael existed, was he?

Gabe raised his head, his expression pained. "Had I been here, I would have trained Michael not to use his hunting teeth against you while he fed."

Abby snapped a look at the pale, white lines of scar tissue, her cheeks flaming. It was so not a sexy portion of her body anymore.

Gabe kissed at one of the scars as if in disagreement. "You might have had one scar, but not this many. I'm amazed you continued breastfeeding so long."

"It didn't take long. His hunting teeth erupted within days of each other. I think I got four or so of those on a single bite. I didn't even know he had that many teeth."

He swiveled his head, moving the backs of his fingers in an arc along the scars. "Five, I believe." A moment later, he shook his head. "Had I been here the first day he bit, I could have taught him not to. Now the bad habit is set. It would be very difficult to teach him not to bite at the breast that feeds him." He met her gaze solidly. "I apologize that our son caused you pain."

"He's a baby," she dismissed Gabe's concern. "Babies don't know better."

Her move to escape his piercing gaze ended with Gabe's hand cupped around her chin. "Xxanian children can be taught better." That sounded like a promise.

Abby swallowed hard and nodded her agreement.

Gabe lowered his head, laying a solemn, slow lick across her nipple. Then he went still.

* * * *

She shouldn't have been scarred. It was one thing no Xxanian male could stand, seeing permanent injuries on his females...mate or daughters or even granddaughters.

"Gabe?" A tremor worked down her body, most likely at his prolonged stillness.

Was she doubting her appeal? Preparing to retreat from him? As if in confirmation, her hand twitched up slightly as if she was considering covering her breasts.

No. Gabe took her breast in his mouth, working his tongue along the worst of the scarring, a solemn promise that he would never allow her to be so injured again. The slight sweetness teased at his senses and sent him to the other before he could cause her milk to drop.

Abby's breathing went ragged, and her fingers flexed against his shoulders. Moans escaped her lips. She trembled hard, a sure sign that she was in desperate sexual need.

How he'd missed this! Gabe reveled in her scent and the silk of her skin.

While some Xxanian males equated human females' sex sounds as 'prey sounds,' Gabe had never made that connection with Abby's sounds. To him, her sounds were all sensual woman.

My woman.

Those mews and moans spurred him on. Every one begged for him, told him she wanted him...told Gabe she craved his touch as much as he craved hers.

No one had ever touched him as Abby did. He prayed to the *Seir*-God that no other would, because Abby would become a permanent addition to his life. It was what he'd wanted from the moment he'd first set eyes on her.

In a daze, Gabe drank down the musk on Abby's skin, from her breasts to her throat, then sampled her mouth again. She moved closer, parting her legs in invitation.

That was enough to make him groan. He'd vowed to take this slowly, but the temptation was too much to bear.

As if adding fuel to the rising bonfire between them, Abby's hand closed around his cock, stroking purposefully. On one hand, he knew how enjoyable Abby's mouth and hands were. On the other, he wanted to hear her come for him again.

I want to feel her body milking my cock. It's not like I won't be ready again in short order.

While other women might merit once or twice a night, Abby could keep him hard and horny all night with little more than a glance.

Her hand worked at him as if she wanted to watch Gabe come that way. Her eyes pleaded for something entirely different.

He lifted her at the waist and settled Abby on the crown of his cock. Her hand retreated, and she nodded.

* * * *

As many times as they'd had sex, Abby hadn't felt anything like this before. Gabe lowered her onto his length, stretching her unused body around his girth.

Oh, stars burn! Oh, stars! The words stuck in her throat, crushed between gasping breaths.

"All right?" he asked.

Abby levered her eyes open, staring up at him, her mouth going dry. *All right?* That term wasn't even a pale comparison to how good she felt.

"Abby?" He cocked his head to one side, his green-gold eyes narrowing.

"Yes." She wasn't sure it was more than a gasp until Gabe nodded.

In the next moment, he was lifting her until only the tip breached her body, then sliding her down his length again. The first few minutes passed in torturous slowness.

As if something snapped, Gabe's motions became frantic. Abby gripped his arms, trying to mute her rising sounds as Gabe thrust into her like a wild man.

As if he's staking a claim on me.

Her attempts to quiet her sounds were a lost cause. Soon, Abby was screaming in release and begging for more. Gabe pinned her to the wall, bringing his mouth down on hers while he filled her to the brim with his heat.

The kiss went from manic to deep and toe-curling. He stroked his hands up and down her body, setting off aftershocks.

It has been far too long since I've been with him. Abby wasn't sure how she'd lasted this long without Gabe.

Finally, he left the kiss entirely and pressed his forehead to hers.

"Did you mean what you said?" he breathed.

"What?" *What did I say?* Her mind was so muddled, even replaying their discussions proved problematic.

A smile curved his lips up, a dangerously sexy look on him. "About wanting more?"

That set off a whole new set of aftershocks.

"Mmm. I'll take that as a 'yes. '"

"Oh, yes."

Chapter Four

Gabe let out a spate of Xxan language, and Abby smiled.

They'd made love most of the first night, and Gabe had taken care of Michael to allow her time to sleep. The previous night, they'd made love in the shower twice, until the water had gone cold. After they'd dried off, they'd spent the night in each other's arms.

"Don't stop," he begged. More Xxan followed.

As if. Abby added a squeeze at his cockhead at the top of each stroke, and Gabe's hips left the mattress.

It wouldn't be long now. She knew from experience that explosions of his native language meant he was close.

Gabe shifted as if he couldn't find a comfortable position. His chest heaved as his breathing degraded into short gasps.

Three. Two.

His shout of climax reverberated against the walls, and Abby thanked whatever deities were paying attention—hers, his, or both—that Michael was a sound sleeper. A heartbeat later, his cum was spurting over her abdomen and the sheets.

He loosened the grip he had on her sheets, leaving a matched set of fingertip-sized tears.

I forgot he does that. When Gabe got exceedingly excited, he tended to put his talons through the sheets. They'd replaced sheets at least once a month when they lived together. *And suffered more than one shredded feather pillow.*

His breathing calmed somewhat, but his cock remained ramrod stiff. He hadn't needed this little provocation since the first few months they were together.

And I love it.

A flash of something caught her eye, and Abby's mouth went dry. His secondary was emerging.

It's been so long. Her hands trembling, Abby reached out and touched the miniature cockhead pushing its way past the protective flap of skin located in the shadow of his primary.

Gabe moaned, but he didn't stop her. She rolled the pad of her thumb around the head, encouraging the secondary to grow.

It was a dangerous game. If his *Zhigaaal* started to flow, they'd be bound as mates at nearly the first touch. *Or is it the first touch?*

Abby knew she wanted that. She'd fantasized about it the first day Gabe came back into her life, but now she was sure.

It's not smart to do it now, while Michael is still nursing. Hadn't they decided that?

I don't care. There's formula. Dr Ryan will have a nurse tend to Michael while we bind.

The secondary was almost a thumb-length exposed. It would be so easy to—

"No." Gabe pulled her hand away, shaking his head adamantly.

The pleas stuck in her throat.

Gabe stared at her. He raised one hand and motioned for her to stay where she was. "Wait," he revised his order.

At Abby's nod, he left the bed. He was back a moment later, just as naked and delicious.

"You want to be my mate?" he asked. His eyes issued a challenge.

Answering that was easy enough. "Yes. I do."

He stood in the bedroom doorway, stroking his secondary up. When it was a hand-length, he rolled a specially-made condom from head to base.

Abby's hopes died a silent death.

"We will," he promised. "But not now. Not until we're prepared for it."

"I'm ready now," she countered. Abby was more than ready. Her body was in overdrive, asking for what he was currently denying her.

"You're not. Even if I called in my family to care for Michael...or SLAL, the switch to formula cold turkey would be difficult to both of you. I don't intend to mate with you when it's likely you will be in pain while we do it. Mating is supposed to be a...pleasant affair. Pun not intended."

Abby groaned and dropped back to the mattress.

"Abby?" he prompted her.

"You're right," she conceded. "I know you're right."

There was a moment of potent silence. Gabe appeared at the bedside, his expression intense. Abby swallowed hard. Before she could question him, he spoke.

"Believe me, I want this, but not this way. I want the best for you and for Michael."

"You're right," she repeated. "I understand."

"But you want to know what it will be like." It wasn't a question.

Abby's heart fluttered in excitement. "Yes, I do."

"I can't recreate everything." He paused. "But I can explain what will happen as we go."

She nodded eagerly. She'd always wanted to know what binding was like, but she'd been afraid to ask. If she asked, Gabe might get his hopes up, and that was something Abby had never dared inflict on him when she was sure she couldn't give him children.

Gabe stroked his secondary again, and the slim cock wrapped partway around his fingers at the move, becoming more expressive as he excited it. Abby's mouth watered.

"Some couples start with sucking, but the smarter ones start with other things," he informed her.

"How will we start?"

Gabe stepped closer to the bed, every muscle strung tight. He scooped up Abby's hand and brought it to the secondary. She stared up at him, seeking instruction.

"Rub here." He pressed her fingertips to the base of his secondary.

Abby complied, and Gabe let his head drop back, groaning. His *Zhigaaal* beaded beneath the condom. Abby licked her lips. One day, she would taste his concentrated musk.

More *Zhigaaal* escaped his secondary, and Gabe moved. He drew her hand away and knelt to the bed before her.

"Stroke your nipples," he ordered.

She hesitated a moment then did so, gasping at his heated look.

"Your nipples are hard, Abby."

She nodded, offering them to him.

"They'll be harder when you spread the *Zhigaaal* on them. They'll be sensitive, like you've put warming gel on them."

He leaned toward her, licked one nipple and then the other. Then he blew over them. Abby arched toward him, begging for more.

"Yes. Like that. Just like that. You'll want so much more. The *Zhigaaal* will make you crazy to have me inside you."

Gabe put a hand on her shoulder and eased her back to the bed. Abby spread her legs for him, and he stroked the condom-covered length up one thigh, then the other. He worked it back and forth, from her clit to her perineum, enflaming her entire body. Abby cried out, sitting up and reaching for him.

In the blink of an eye, Gabe had her by the wrists. "Most females fight at times, when they are in the grips of the madness the *Zhigaaal* causes." He hesitated and pressed a kiss to her lips. "But you will be doing precisely what I tell you to do. Won't you, Abby?"

If it means binding as his mate? "Yes."

* * * *

Both cocks bucked toward her, and Gabe tapped down the urge to finish what they'd started. He hadn't realized how maddening it would be to play at binding without allowing himself to do it.

Back to the lessons. Don't let the arousal dim.

Gabe released her wrists and knelt up. "Suck the secondary."

Abby didn't question him. She didn't hesitate. His secondary was nearly to the back of her throat before he could catch his breath. It was all Gabe could do to control his primary and keep it out of the way.

He allowed himself to fantasize. When they bound themselves, he wouldn't be wearing a condom, and his *Zhigaaal* would relax her throat muscles and soak into the porous tissues of her mouth and tongue.

That thought was enough to send him over. Gabe savored it, opening his eyes to the sight of Abby staring up at him.

He eased her to the mattress again and brought his secondary to her nether lips. Abby gasped, and he thrust up, being careful not to push too far. Without his *Zhigaaal* to prepare her, he would bottom out and probably hurt her.

"Gabe?"

He glanced up, trying to work his way to an explanation for her confusion. Realization made him smile. His primary wasn't inside her, as it hadn't been inside her when she sucked his secondary.

"Every infusion of *Zhigaaal* will help prepare your body and stoke your need. You'll feel drugged. You'll crave more."

"And?"

"You won't get my primary until you're prepared for it fully."

Abby nodded her agreement.

He held himself still while he rubbed up more *Zhigaaal*, biting back a wince at the burn against his sensitive cockhead. What it would do to Abby would be nothing short of pleasant torture.

I have to explain. "I'll fill you with *Zhigaaal*, and you will be crazy to have me inside you. I won't lie. You might feel like you'll go insane if I don't make love to you with my primary."

"I know the feeling," she complained.

Gabe collected cum off the head of his primary and used it to lubricate her anus as he would use his *Zhigaaal* while they bound. He moved his secondary to the tight ring of muscle and started working it in.

They'd played this game before, of course, but this time Abby pushed back, aiding him in. Her inner muscles gripped him tight, taunting him with another building climax. Her hips shifted, her muscles rippling along his length.

If she does that when we're binding, we'll both spend the three days exhausted and sore.

The secondary undulated, forcing deeper into her ass as it attained its full length. Abby screamed in pleasure, begging him for more.

Yes. She'll do that when we bind.

Gabe brought his secondary to her empty vaginal entry and thrust both cocks deep. Abby grabbed at his arms and gasped out something indecipherable. He let her move against him, though every instinct told him to pin her down and take control.

She vented cries at every movement of his hips, back and forth, driving them both on. At last, she shattered around him, and Gabe followed her over.

Abby was unnaturally still and quiet, and Gabe reached for her, panicked that he'd harmed her somehow. She shifted, moaning his name, and his heart rate eased.

"Are you all right?" he questioned her.

Abby sighed. "Three days of that?" she asked in return.

"Yes. That and much more."

Her hand stroked down his chest to his hip. "How often do you sleep during the binding?" Her voice announced she was on the edges of sleep already.

Gabe swallowed a laugh. "As often as you need to." No matter what torture waiting would be for him, the male always took his cues in mating from his woman.

She nodded and murmured something that sounded like agreement. With that, Abby fell asleep, still impaled on both his cocks.

She'll agree. There was no question Abby would allow Gabe to bind her when the time was right.

Thank the Seir-God.

Chapter Five

"You have to go back to work tomorrow."

Gabe looked up at her, turning and lifting his head from her abdomen to accomplish the task. Abby's fingers trailed through his hair, a gentle combing that he'd always found soothing. She wasn't focused on him. Rather, her gaze seemed directed inward instead of at anything in their current environment.

"You work every day," he reminded her.

"I work from home."

"True. I can't exactly catch criminals here." Just the thought of the scum of the Earth anywhere near Abby and Michael tightened the muscles that would raise his ridge plates.

Michael was lucky that she worked from home. Many children weren't so lucky, he knew.

Gabe wished Abby could do *all* of her work from home. It had been a trip out to the store to pick up supplies that had landed her in the café where they'd been attacked in the first place. Michael had needed to eat and have a diaper change while they'd been out on such errands. The café had been a convenient stop, though ill-fated.

Maybe I should offer to do her supply runs for her. Or accompany her, when I don't have work. There were plenty of cowardly humans who would attack a human female with a Xxanian infant, but few wanted to attack a Xxanian male protecting his mate and child. Bound or not,

Abby was his mate, and properly mated or not, Michael was his son.

And I've waited far too long to introduce them to my family. He opened his mouth to broach the subject.

"What will we do now?" Abby asked.

"What do you mean?" Was she asking what future they had?

"If you live the same place you did when..."

"I do." It came out rougher than he'd intended it, but the memory of her packing and walking out on him still hurt.

Abby winced. She took a moment, seemingly calming herself. "Why?"

Gabe turned on the bed, stretching out beside her while he tried to decode the strange question. "Why what, Abby?" he invited.

"You make so much more money now. You never let me contribute to the rent at your apartment. So...why haven't you moved on to somewhere larger?" She didn't look at him when she asked it.

That was a difficult question to answer. "I suppose..."

Her head swiveled around, and she stared at him, her eyes wide. "What? Why didn't you move?"

"I always hoped you'd walk back through the door to me."

Abby didn't seem to know how to answer that.

"If my *seir* hadn't beaten a woman's choice into me so soundly, I might have followed you and begged you to come back to me." It wasn't an exaggeration.

"I wish you had."

Her wistful tone stilled the need to balk at the implication that Abby would have preferred to see him beg.

"I would have had no excuse to hide the truth from you. And if you'd come looking for me and found me gone... You would have looked for me. You would have found out I was at SLAL."

"Damned right I would have." Gabe succeeded in keeping that lighthearted, when the concept of having to search for Abby made the Xxanian warrior in him stir in preparation for battle.

"So, what do we do now? Where do we live? How do we...arrange things?"

He laid a kiss on her forehead. "My apartment isn't large enough for all of us. I suppose I should start packing my belongings and terminate my lease."

Abby wriggled in what he would assume was apprehension.

"I would be most comfortable here with you, but that would be a short term option. As Michael grows, we will need more room."

"I agree." Her muscles eased.

Did she really believe I wouldn't come to her nest, if that was the only option we had? If she was most comfortable here?

"We could find a larger place, if you were willing to move into one. One with good schools and a safe neighborhood." *A Xxanian nest nearby.*

She nodded.

"Or, we could take the safest option and move into my family's nest."

Abby gasped, and her eyes widened. "But... Will your family...uh...?"

"Accept you? Of course."

"But they don't *know* us." There was an edge of panic in that.

"Which is what I want to talk to you about." *She gave me the opening. I have to take it.*

"What is?"

"I have to introduce you both to my nest, and I can't risk waiting too much longer to do that."

Abby stared at him, working at words that didn't emerge.

"How old is Michael now, Abby? Two months? Almost three?"

"F-four."

His heart stuttered. "Four?"

She nodded. "But he doesn't look it, because—"

"Four?" he demanded.

She cringed, drawing away from him on the mattress. "Yes, but—"

"*Seir*-God, he will set his scent without a firm nest scent unless we introduce him to the nest soon."

Gabe worked at that, making calculations and speculations. It would have to be this week. He didn't dare procrastinate on this. It was too important to give Michael a firm grounding in his nest. *And what will happen if he doesn't have it? He could end up like—*

326

"I didn't know." Her tone announced that tears threatened. "What happens if he doesn't have a nest scent?"

The possibilities were too dire to consider. *He could end up like Arren Rasshh.*

No. I will not allow that to happen to my son. "We can make it right, but we must act quickly. Are you willing to come to the nest with me today? If we expose Michael to the nest at least a day a week for the next few months, we can imprint the nest scent on him before it's too late."

Abby nodded. "If we moved into the nest, would it be better?"

Gabe took his time answering. "It would, but it would mean a concerted move. I can get my *seir* and brother to help move the necessary belongings... possibly other allies as well, but I don't want you to make that choice until you've seen the nest. If you can't live there, we will make the effort to spend a day or two there at a time while Michael acclimates to the nest."

"Okay. What do we have to do?"

"I have phone calls to make. I need *S'suuhhea* for you and *S'suumea* for Michael. I will arrange a gift of spice for my nest." His head spun in plans. Most of it would come from *Spice Industries*. With the Rasshh nest as allies, accommodating them would be a priority.

"I really didn't know," Abby whispered.

Questions warred for the right to be first to spring from his lips. Gabe took his time, prioritizing them into what he needed to know before he called for the clothing they'd pick up on the way.

She tried to tell me something. It was probably important. "Why does Michael appear to be younger than he is?" If he had a medical failing, his *seir* and gran-*seir* would never forgive Gabe for not being there to aid them. *I won't forgive myself for it.*

I couldn't have known it.

Abby swallowed hard. "Because he was premature."

Terror shafted through Gabe. "How far?"

"I carried him for a little less than three and a half months."

"Michael survived that?" The words were out before Gabe could think of something more appropriate to ask.

"Doctor Rayn said he's had a lot of experience with premature crossbred infants."

"He has." *Rasshh's young alone would account for that.* "How small was Michael at birth?"

"A little less than a kilogram and a half."

There was nothing Gabe could say to so shocking an answer. It was difficult to contemplate a babe so small. *He could have fit in my joined hands, I'd bet. I should have been there. I failed my family when they needed me most.*

"Gabe?"

"We must go today. Please say you'll accompany me."

Abby nodded. "Make whatever calls you need to, and we'll leave as soon as Michael has his lunch."

* * * *

Gabe lifted Michael from the car seat and hooked the bag of supplies over his shoulder. Beside him, Abby reached for the computer bag.

"Not now. My *seir* and I will collect the rest later."

She closed the car door and looked around the garage bunker.

Like most Xxanian nests, it was designed to deceive. It appeared to be a typical ranch-style house with attached garage from the outside, but this house was akin to a bomb shelter. It was a reinforced bunker: outfitted with blast doors, defensive systems, a hanger with two shuttles, a self-contained support system, and emergency escape tunnels. The tunnels of the main nest areas themselves were three stories beneath the surface and could be isolated from the outer shell.

Gabe guided Abby to the door, coded in, and escorted her into the *s'sanuea.* The garage door closed behind them, and he got down to business.

"We're going to dress appropriately. That means stripping off everything you have on now. Hang the clothing on the hooks, and place your shoes under the bench."

Abby shot a nervous look at the door to the nest, then complied. Gabe went to work on Michael's one-piece outfit.

Dressing them in the traditional Xxanian garb didn't take long. Each of them would only be wearing a single item of clothing—Michael's diaper aside—and proper wrap and folds were second nature to someone born and raised in a nest. Gabe had been aiding Ariel with her *S'suuhhea* since before she could walk and tying his own *S'suumea* since shortly after that age.

He took a moment to admire her. "You are beautiful." *And strong and confident. My family will love her.*

Abby was a stunning shade of embarrassed red, and she stared at him, shifting from foot to foot. "What now?"

"Now we enter the nest." He hesitated. "Don't try to introduce yourself or Michael to anyone. There is a tradition for bringing new family members to the nest. I have to introduce you."

She nodded. "Anything else I should know?"

"I'll have to teach you Xxan. Usually, we all speak Xxan in the nest, but everyone knows English. They'll understand you, but I'll have to do a lot of translating for you for now."

Abby groaned. "I have completely screwed this up, haven't I?"

Gabe gathered her into his arms. "We both have, and it's my job to make it right. Just let me."

A shaky nod was her only reply.

Best I can hope for. It wasn't ideal to walk in with Abby so obviously frightened, but it was better than chancing Michael.

Gabe hefted the bag and Michael, then offered Abby his arm. The internal door slid open for him, prompted by facial recognition scanners hooked to the defensive systems. It was a layer of security most of the nests didn't have. That way, even if someone got the code to open the outer door, he or she would be stuck in the *s'sanuea* with no way into the nest proper.

They stepped through, and the door slid closed behind them. The faint click announced the first of the blast doors securing at their backs. It was a sound that made Gabe feel safe. Behind doors like these, no one would try to kill his mate and son.

Not now. For now, he could only hope Abby would like the nest and choose to stay.

The first two downward sloping chambers were behind them before he sighted his *seir*. Abby stopped abruptly, as Brien stepped out of the shadows, the elder's *zuahhhbeahhh* in hand.

He surveyed their little group, then lowered the weapon. "The scanners showed three," he offered by way of apology.

"Safety of the nest, the women, and the young first," Gabe intoned, following his *seir's* use of Xxan.

Brien stepped toward them and offered his hand. "I welcome the brother warrior to the nest. I welcome all that come with—" He stopped speaking abruptly and focused on Michael. His tongue extended a bit to take in the baby's scent. "The elder will have questions," he grumbled.

"I know. I expect it." It was clear his *seir* had questions as well, but tradition said that the elder would be privy to all news first.

Gabe clasped his *seir*'s hand in a warrior's welcome.

"He's waiting for you." With one last questioning glance at Michael, Brien turned and led the way toward the center nest.

Abby hurried to keep up, and Gabe reeled her in. *A woman being added to the nest should never be rushed.*

When they reached the center nest, the family was assembled and waiting for them. Ariel and Geoff waited with their *Hauaa*, Geoff in a protective posture. Between that group and Gabe's little family, Brien stood with Zhaahvan.

Abby looked up at the elder...and up. She took a shuffling step backward, then planted her feet before Gabe could draw her to his side.

Zhaahvan cocked his head to one side and surveyed the visitors to his nest. "A most interesting pair, Gabe."

It was a challenge of bringing a young one to the nest, Gabe was sure. *Scent him, stars blaze you. Scent him, and you will know he belongs here.* "They are, Gran-*Seir*. A most pleasant surprise for me."

"Who is responsible for this young one?" His tone was gruff, a warning that he was highly displeased. Whether he was displeased with Gabe or with whatever male Gran-*Seir* suspected was the *seir* was unclear.

"I am."

Zhaahvan snapped a look at him, and his ridge plates stirred minutely. Gabe's did the same. He settled Michael in Abby's arms and took a step toward his gran-*seir* in challenge.

Slowly, with precision, the elder extended his forked tongue and drew in Abby and Michael's scents. A growl built in his massive chest, and Zhaahvan showed his hunting teeth. Abby sank back another step, her breathing rasping in and out in her terror.

"You hid a child from us? From your nest and elders?"

"No. I didn't know my son existed until three days ago. My mate was gone from my life before either of us knew he existed."

The elder snorted in displeasure, his ridge plates extending fully, his frills shaking in challenge. The rest of the family was silent. This was a judgment, and for the first time, Gabe feared his gran-*seir* might turn them away.

Then Michael will have my nest scent and not my family's. It is the old lizard's choice to accept us or not. Gabe squared his shoulders and prepared to tell the old buck precisely what he thought of him. That would most likely end in bitter battle, but if that was the elder's choice, so be it.

"And you were such a *worthless* male she didn't come to you to help raise your own son?"

Gabe bristled at the insult. "No. She was told our son would not survive and didn't want to cause me pain. She knew how important family is to me and was afraid of letting me tie myself to a woman who reportedly couldn't give me young, to force me to mourn a son who had no chance of surviving to see his first days." It still amazed him that Abby thought so highly of him.

Zhaahvan scented again in earnest. "I can detect no frailty in the young Dominant."

"The frailty is my mate's. She carries badly, but my son's presence proves she *can* carry and has already blessed the nest with a young Dominant." It was a half-truth, since the human doctor had determined Abby couldn't possibly carry so close to term again.

They told her she couldn't the first time. Maybe I should ask Rayn his opinion of her chances of carrying again.

His gran-*seir*'s voice snapped Gabe back to the continuing judgment. "You call the female your mate, but her scent proves that is not so."

"Only because our son is nursing. When he weans, we intend to bind. What sort of male do you think I am? I would not risk my son, even for this."

A moment of tense silence fell. "And you believe this female when she promises to mate?"

"I trust my mate is sincere. If you do not, we will leave this nest and never return."

Gabe's *Hauaa* gasped out a protest, and Zhaahvan's ridge plates retracted part way. Brien glanced at his mate, made a soothing sound, then shot a glare at Gabe.

Gabe forced back a wince. He hadn't meant to distress his *Hauaa*, but a show of his strength had been warranted.

"Perhaps I should see the young Dominant and his *Hauaa*," Zhaahvan suggested.

"Perhaps you should." Gabe didn't pretend all was forgiven and forgotten. That wasn't a Xxanian warrior's way. He back-stepped to Abby's side.

She grasped his hand, trembling more than a little. *"He won't accept us. Will he?"*

The elder snorted, and she jumped minutely.

Chapter Six

Zhaahvan took a long stride toward them and reached one taloned hand toward Abby. Her heart pounded in fear. Moments ago, he'd clearly been arguing with Gabe. What if he didn't approve of them?

He won't try to hurt Michael, will he? Or me? This is my fault, after all.

Michael shifted in her arms, and Abby remembered what had happened the last time a man got this close when she was scared.

"No. Be careful. Michael will—"

Her son moved like a little streak, his mouth opening wide and closing on the elder's hand.

Abby winced in anticipation of a violent reaction to the bite. *Why isn't Gabe doing something?* Whether he believed they could teach Michael not to bite or not, it was essential she try. She reached for Michael's cheeks. "No, Michael. No biting."

The rumbling from the elder couldn't be anything but laughter. He brushed her hand away and stroked the back of a talon along the extended ridge plate on the right of Michael's throat. Sounds she didn't recognize left the big warrior's lips, and Michael turned his head stubbornly, no doubt widening the tear.

"I'm so sorry," she began. "When I'm scared, he tends to—"

Gabe chuckled. "It's all right, Abby. Gran-*Seir* approves of Michael. Young ones rarely display their Dominant traits so vividly at this age. He will be showing that bite to all his contemporaries with pride. Trust me."

"I can't let him—" Abby reached for Michael again.

Zhaahvan's free hand circled her wrist, and he guided her hand away gently. The sounds he made had the tone of an order.

Gabe translated for him. "Gran-*Seir* says Michael will let go when he is content his warning is understood."

"But it will scar," she protested.

"I'm sure that's his intent." A sly smile curved Gabe's lips.

I will never understand Xxanian men. It was a given, and it was nerve wracking.

Before she could reason with them that she had to teach Michael how to live in a human world, her son let go with a glare at the elder, yellow-green Xxanian blood dripping from his mouth.

Zhaahvan tipped his head, offered a rumble, and reached his uninjured hand toward Abby. Michael moved to strike again, and Abby raised her hand to block him with a warning shout of "no."

In a blur of motion, Gabe's hand was between her fingers and Michael's mouth, and he had a finger hooked inside the baby's mouth. "No, Michael," he offered calmly. "*Hauaa* is never to be injured. Your mother is precious." He slanted a soft look her direction. "So precious."

Her face burned in pleasure. "I'm sure he didn't mean to hurt me."

"But he would have, and the lesson for it would have been harsh. This is a kinder way to teach him not to bite you." His gaze trailed to her breasts and away again.

The scars. She nodded. "I understand."

Gabe lifted Michael from Abby's arms, and she shot him a questioning look. His eyes slanted toward the elder towering over them. "Gran-*Seir* wishes to meet you."

He turned back to the elder and shifted Michael in his arms, switching back to Xxan. The only words she understood were her own name and Michael's.

Abby looked up at Zhaahvan again, her heart skittering at his proximity. A soothing rumble not unlike the one Gabe had used at the café reverberated between them. His uninjured hand came up, and he cupped her cheek, his talons combing through her hair. His scaled skin was cool and smooth.

His voice emerged in stilted English. "Welcome, li-ttle daughter."

She nodded, forcing speech. "Thank you."

A long string of Xxan language trilled off his lips, and Gabe started translating for her.

"You do the entire nest honor by bringing such a strong young Dominant to us."

Zhaahvan tipped his head to one side and started speaking again.

"But you should not have tried to raise a young Xxanian without his nest elders. Michael is a babe today. Tomorrow, he will be stronger and faster than you are. We must teach him now and teach him well, so you are not injured by him when that is so. The young warrior will not know his strength."

Abby swallowed a lump in her throat at the fact that she'd underestimated the difficulties of raising Michael alone. "I think I understand." *It had never been my intent to raise him alone.* Though, after so many months of indecision, Abby couldn't state with certainty that she ever would have found a way to tell Gabe about Michael either.

The elder's voice was getting more soothing by the moment. Abby closed her eyes, abruptly tired.

"And still this is the fault of my race. We did not know this was a possibility. We put you at unconscionable risk."

Abby shook her head in denial. They hadn't. It had been a misunderstanding.

"We did. Gabe will bathe you daily for—"

Gabe erupted in a spate of Xxan language, and his gran-*seir* replied.

"Daily for three months. My apologies. I was not aware that the young one had already injured you. Or that you had been injured by those who hate our kind. Both are inexcusable."

Abby forced her eyes open. Something told her to continue addressing Zhaahvan. "Bathing?" She knew the Xxan used bathing in ritual, but she didn't know what it meant to them.

The elder tipped his head to Gabe, and the latter started explaining.

"The private clove bath daily is ordered for a period of time for several reasons. Yours... It would be a mixture of apology for the injuries against you and to strengthen the bond between us with...intimacy."

Her cheeks heated at the unspoken implication. *It's sexual.* Abby nodded. "I see."

"We can use the bathing pools upstairs for some of them, but the first will be in here in the center nest...after a family bath of welcome for you and Michael."

Her heart stuttered. "Family bath? Everyone?" *Naked? In the pond together? Not a chance.*

Gabe shook his head. "Zhaahvan will enter the pool with us, as will my *seir.*"

She started to protest.

"Clothed, for your comfort."

Zhaahvan let out a sound akin to a snort and grumbled something in Xxan. Gabe answered, and the elder made several soft snuffling sounds.

"We will bathe Michael first, and my *seir* will remove him from the pool and dress him again. Considering the time, he and my *Hauaa* and sister will feed him."

"And your gran-*seir* and the two of us?" she asked.

"In the deep water, where no one can see, I will remove your *S'suuhhea.* Gran-*Seir* will bathe your neck and back. Then he will leave the pool, and we will finish the bath alone."

"How often do we...do a family bath?"

"When you come to the nest the first time. When you present a new child to the nest. And when you are injured. Those are the only times we do this."

Her stomach squirmed at the idea, but Abby nodded. If this was what being mated into Gabe's family meant, she could accept that. "Well then... I suppose we should get started? Just let me know what I'm supposed to do."

Gabe smiled and kissed her cheek.

* * * *

He could hardly believe Abby was so at ease with the situation. He'd been told most human mates were less sure about the bathing rituals the Xxan indulged in, though there was nothing sexual beyond the mated pair involved.

"It is simple enough."

With that, he released a now-calm Michael into Zhaahvan's hands. His son looked up at the massive elder and patted his unarmored chest, prompting a barking laugh from Gran-*Seir.*

Zhaahvan snuggled the young one under his chin and started the soothing rumble used with infants. Gabe and his *seir* joined in, and Gabe laid a little hand to Gran-*Seir*'s neck, his fingers rubbing up and down along one of the ridge plates in the elder's throat. The other hand went to Michael's mouth, and he started sucking on the side of his fist.

Brien reached up and drew off Michael's *S'suumea.* He dropped the rectangle of silk to the grass, then removed the diaper. Gabe tensed for the usual fountain of urine open air brought out in Michael, but his son must have relieved himself in the diaper.

Zhaahvan led the way to the pond and stepped in, still clothed, Brien on his heels.

Gabe broke off the rumble and offered a warning...in English, to avoid translating again for Abby. "Michael likes to swim. We'll have to be cautious around the pools. If he can reach them, he will go in."

Both elder males turned to shoot him looks of disbelief, the rumble dying out abruptly.

Gabe didn't have to question what they were thinking. Most Xxanian children liked water, but few were natural swimmers, and most wanted an adult with them when they braved the pools before the age of one. Swimming so young was a much more human trait than they were accustomed to.

"He's good, but I worry."

"I took him to infant swim classes," Abby inserted. "He likes the water so much. Of course, I had to find a pool without chlorine and a class that would accept Xxanian children. Doctor Rayn helped with that."

Zhaahvan squatted, bringing Michael down to the surface of the water. The babe kicked his feet, splashing and squealing in delight, then turned belly down and started using his hands to create big arcs of water toward Brien. The elder lowered him into the water and let him go, seemingly amazed. Michael flipped to his back, arms spread, and started kicking for the far wall.

"Brien," Zhaahvan barked.

Gabe's *seir* chased Michael down and scooped the happy young one up again. He shot a look of worry at Zhaahvan.

The elder grunted. *"I propose a motion tracker."*

Gabe swallowed a laugh. "A sensible decision, Gran-*Seir*." And a choice no Xxanian elder likely thought he'd have to make to safeguard a young one of his nest.

"How old is Michael?" his *seir* inquired.

Gabe bit back a wince. *"Four months."*

Abby shifted uncomfortably at the potent silence, proving even humans could feel the rising tide of a battle-ready Xxanian warrior, extended ridge plates or not. "What is it?" she asked.

"Michael's age," Gabe replied.

Her cheeks went darker than the red of her *S'suuhhea.* "Oh."

I have to explain this. "My mate's frailty meant that Michael was born very early. Premature." Some words just didn't have a Xxanian equivalent. *"He slept in the womb for less than three and a half months."*

Beside him, Abby wiggled in a show of nerves. She looked from Gabe to the elders and back again.

Zhaahvan walked to Abby and scooped up her hands. He tipped his head down in a bow and brought the back of her fingers to his forehead in a show of respect. At last, he focused on her fully and spoke in English. "Four moons." He strode back into the pool and lifted Michael from Brien's hands.

Abby watched him, seemingly stunned. "I don't understand," she admitted.

Gabe smiled. "I had better order another case of clove."

* * * *

Words stuck in Abby's throat. She forced them up. "I understood *that* part."

Gabe searched for a translation into English for the Xxanian saying. "There is no pain deeper than a mother's love tested."

She gaped at him.

"Gran-*Seir* recognizes how hard it must have been for you to carry and care for Michael, believing he would not survive, despite all you did for him. It is a pain he cannot conceive of. He respects your strength as...something of a female warrior."

Tears stung at her eyes, and she nodded.

"Gabe," his *seir* reminded him.

He nodded and stripped off his *S'suumea.*

Abby forced herself not to protest. Of all the males in the pool, he would naturally assume she wouldn't mind seeing him naked. It seemed as if it was expected for this sort of event.

Gabe took her hand and guided Abby into the pool. The water was warm and heavy in the scent of salt and minerals, the type of water high-end spas charged big money to access.

The silk clung to her thighs, her hips, her abdomen...Gabe helped Abby to her knees, so the water reached to her upper chest.

Brien crossed the pool to them, Michael bouncing in his arms and waving to her. When Gabe's father reached them, he dropped to his

344

knees. Zhaahvan settled in the water next to his son.

All three men spread clove oil on Michael, bathing the baby with care, while Michael kicked and splashed, laughing and wiggling in Brien's arms.

The low hum rose in intensity, and Brien took his leave with Michael peeking over his shoulder. Abby watched him go, waiting for the protest that Abby wasn't coming with him, but Michael went along silently, seemingly content with the additions to his family.

It's probably scent based. So much of Xxanian life is.

"He'll be fine, Abby," Gabe assured her.

"I know. I've just never had someone I could leave Michael with...until now." No one Michael would allow himself to be alone with, certainly. Save the staff at SLAL.

Gabe cupped her face, and Abby focused on him. She managed a weak smile.

A slight stirring of the water was her only indication that Zhaahvan had moved. Then his hand was wrapped around the back of her neck, spreading clove oil and massaging gently. His skin was softer than she would have anticipated before she met him.

The elder grumbled something in the Xxan language, and Gabe reached up to untie the *S'suuhhea*. Abby's breathing hitched and she reminded herself that there was no way Zhaahvan could see her in the murky water.

Gabe pressed a kiss to her lips, and she let her eyes slide shut. The silk peeled away from her body, and droplets of water rained down as he tossed it away.

Zhaahvan moved on to washing her back, while Gabe started spreading the clove oil along her cheeks and chin. Before the elder's massage of her back muscles was complete, his grandson's attentions had moved to the front of her shoulders and her chest.

Abby bit back a moan, well aware of the elder at her back. Still, she arched into Gabe's touch, encouraging him as he cupped her breasts, bringing them to a potent sensitivity with the stinging oil.

Zhaahvan's hands left her body at her waist and moved to her upper arm, as Gabe moved down her ribcage to her abdomen. The elder's attentions seemed to speed. He finished with her right arm and moved to the left when Gabe had barely reached her pubic curls. Gabe shifted, teasing her inner thigh with the length of his ready cock, reminding her that they were expected to make love in the pool.

Zhaahvan made quick work of her left hand and moved away with a snuff and grumble that meant nothing to her.

Gabe's lips parted hers, and Abby wrapped herself around him, her entire body alive to his touch. He lifted her by the waist and brought Abby down around his cock, groaning into her mouth.

Part of her argued that Zhaahvan couldn't even be out of the water yet. The other half argued that it didn't matter. He expected them to have sex in the pool, and he couldn't see more than her back and the kiss they were engaged in. Some until-now-unheard part of her mind even argued that she didn't care if the elder watched them, as long as Gabe didn't stop what he was doing.

There was little chance of that. The heat between them skyrocketed, from thrust to thrust. Their sounds rose, echoing off the cave walls. Hands explored. Their movements became more vigorous, churning the water.

Climax choked off her voice. Then it exploded out in a scream of pleasure. Gabe pressed her hips down, seating deep inside her, his cum filling her with heat that sent her senses into a spin.

Abby sagged against Gabe, exhausted, gasping for breath. He stroked handfuls of water over her, washing away much of the remaining oil. It had the added benefit of arousing her all over again, and Abby moaned, half in acceptance and half in the realization that she was too tired to launch into another sexual encounter yet.

Gabe laughed heartily. "Food first," he ordered.

He didn't set her off his lap. Instead, Gabe lifted Abby into his arms and pushed to his feet. He carried her from the pool, settled her in a large chair that would easily seat Zhaahvan, and started to dry himself with a fluffy bath sheet.

Abby looked around for another, and Gabe made a sound that drew her attention back to him. He moved his finger back and forth in a negative motion. She settled in the chair and watched Gabe dress, admiring the way his body moved.

* * * *

Gabe looked up, his heart stuttering at the sight of Abby licking her lips. *Seir*-God help him, if they weren't expected to eat with his family, he'd carry her directly to a bed or satellite nest and make use of that tongue. And his own.

We are expected to dress and eat with my family. Gabe took a calming breath and wrapped his *S'suumea* again.

That left Abby to be cared for. He picked up the towel and stalked toward her, feeling every gram the Dominant male he was.

She raised one foot and planted it on the edge of Zhaahvan's chair, pushing herself to the high back. Abby swallowed hard, her breathing coming in ragged little movements of air in and out of her lungs.

He didn't question that she wasn't frightened of him. Her nipples were hard and begging for his mouth, and her scent was enough to render him rock hard again.

Gabe eased her foot up and started drying her from bottom to top. Abby arched up in the chair, inviting Gabe to prove his Dominance in a way a Xxanian woman never would. Though inviting his gran-*seir*'s ire by making love on his chair would be sweet mischief, Gabe restrained himself.

When Abby was dry, he wrapped her in a fresh *S'suuhhea* and lifted her to her feet. Abby hesitated, then raised a hand and massaged at the well of musk on his chest. Gabe captured her mouth in a searing kiss.

He pulled away, cursing traditions. "We're expected to eat with my family now."

Abby nodded. "And then?"

Gabe wouldn't have stopped the smile if he could have. "Michael will need a feeding. After that...I suggest we allow my parents to settle Michael to sleep for us."

She nodded again.

He led her to the dining area, where the family had congregated to wait for them to dress. Gabe's *seir* and *Hauaa* had Michael between them.

Gabe didn't waste time. He started introducing everyone to Abby, pointing them out as he went. "This is my sister Ariel, my brother Geoff, my *seir* Brien, my *Hauaa* Jana, and...of course...my gran-*seir* Zhaahvan."

Abby tipped her head to each of them in turn. Her brow furrowed. "What is a *Hauaa*?"

Jana smiled. "It's the Xxanian term for a mother. You'll find most Xxan prefer the term. There is a blessing couched in the term...an almost spiritual connotation to bringing forth life."

Abby seemed stunned by the concept. "I think I understand."

"We should eat," Brien suggested. He smiled down at Michael. "I believe our young Dominant is losing patience."

Gabe chuckled at Michael's attempts to reach the tray of meat and nodded his agreement. He glanced at Abby, wincing at the fact that she didn't eat a Xxanian diet.

She smiled and plucked a cube of meat off the tray. Gabe watched her eat it in amazement.

Abby glanced at him, her cheeks darkening in a blush. She swallowed the mouthful of meat and offered an answer to his unasked question. "I craved this when I was pregnant with Michael. I still have a taste for it."

Jana spoke up from across the room. "While you're nursing, you should make an effort to eat *z'haahn*. It will strengthen the milk you make for a young Xxanian."

That said, the entire family started eating in earnest. Brien chewed food for Michael and finger-fed the young Dominant.

It was several minutes before Zhaahvan offered a comment from his place at the head of the room. *"Your mate is most responsive, Gabe. Even moreso than fully mated females usually are. It was all I could do to leave the pool in time."*

Brien darkened, and Geoff shot the elder a look of disbelief.

Gabe smiled. *"Then you will not question that someone to watch over my son after his final meal would be necessary."*

No one answered, a sure sign that no one did.

Chapter Seven

Gabe strode into the station house, dropped the car seat he'd borrowed at Anderson's desk, and continued directly through to the locker room. Though he had come to work in uniform, he had something important to attend to.

The inside of his locker was largely unadorned. Aside from pictures of his *Hauaa* and Ariel, Gabe hadn't found the need to indulge in memorabilia of loved ones or sports teams or pastimes he enjoyed.

Now he had another thing he wanted to see whenever he opened his locker. Gabe rearranged the pictures of his *Hauaa* and sister to place the picture of Abby and Michael in the center and at eye level.

It was a recent picture, obviously taken in a studio designed for Xxanian customers. The lights had been low enough to allow Michael to go without his sunglasses. Still the equipment had captured the blue of his eyes—so close a match for Abby's—with the flecks of stunning gold his son had inherited from Gabe.

He was so captivated by the scene that Thomas was next to him before Gabe realized anyone had entered the room.

Bad form for a Xxanian warrior.

"Good picture," his partner intoned.

Gabe smiled, taking the compliment to heart. "Yes, it is. We'll have to do another soon." *One with me in it.* Of course, Michael would grow quickly. Most Xxanian couples opted for a continuous stream of pictures, due to a Xxanian child's growth rate.

Thomas opened his locker and started changing his clothing. It took a moment for the silence to strike Gabe as odd. His partner was something of a chatterbox, always sharing some story about the latest sporting event or what his family had done this time.

A glance in Thomas's direction revealed his partner's stiff posture. Something was seriously off with the human today.

"Is there a problem, Thomas?" Gabe inquired, the skin over his ridge plates itching in warning.

His partner shot a quick glance past Gabe, then turned back to the buttons on his uniform shirt without comment.

Gabe followed his line of sight to the picture of Abby and Michael. He swung the locker door shut, second guessing his choice to put a picture of them up, though it made little sense to do so. It was a natural thing to take comfort in the sight of loved ones.

Stay calm. There has been no overt threat to them. This was Thomas, after all. They'd been partnered for over a year. Gabe knew him.

Do I? "Might as well spit it out, Thomas. What's bothering you?" The last thing any officer wanted to do was head out with trouble brewing between him and his partner.

There was a moment of tense silence. Then Thomas looked at Gabe directly, his expression unreadable. "Did you know?"

"That I had a son? No. It's a long story. Probably take me half the shift to do justice to it," he admitted.

The tightening of Thomas's jaw said the answer wasn't to his liking. Before Gabe could question that, he'd continued his questioning.

"Not that. Did you know Xxanian's could have babies with human women without...?"

"Binding?"

He nodded once, a jerk of his head.

"No. It's never been an issue before." Though there was still some question of whether or not crossbred females could become pregnant to an alpha human male without an infusion of *Zhigaaal—Thank you Zondra for that uncertainty!*—there had never been question of the reverse.

Thomas's expression said he expected more of an answer.

Gabe obliged him. "Women that are straightforward either want to bind or don't. If they don't, they are on pregnancy block. Those that aren't straightforward typically reek of deception, which we find highly unpalatable. If we fuck them, we use protection of our own."

"Which was *she*?"

Gabe's ridge plates stirred at the unspoken implication that Abby had deceived him...or that Gabe had knowingly let himself be deceived. "Straightforward," he snapped in return.

"Pregnancy block doesn't fail, buddy." The accusation was impossible to miss.

"No, it doesn't, but doctors do not always diagnose accurately, either."

Another oppressive silence followed. Gabe reined in his instincts. Humans had the most infuriating ability to make a Xxanian Dominant want to strike out.

"So...she...?" For the first time, Thomas looked uncertain.

"Abby was told there was no chance she could have a child. She believed it. I knew she was sincere when she said there was no possibility of her becoming pregnant, though I mistakenly thought she meant she was on pregnancy block. We can't scent it as we can the typical hormonal preventatives."

"Then why—?"

"It's a long story. I can tell you the whole thing today. Unless you'd rather...?" Gabe's heart ached at the fact that he might have lost his partner over some indefinable offense or species discomfort.

"What? Switch partners?"

To Gabe's relief, he sounded offended by the suggestion.

"You must be kidding. Do you have any idea what our combined success rate does for both our careers?"

Gabe bit back a laugh. "Not a clue," he lied.

Thomas snorted and rolled his eyes, then went back to buttoning his uniform shirt. "Yeah. I believe that. Not."

* * * *

"All this time, she's been raising Michael alone and trying to figure out how to tell you?"

354

The question came out muffled by the bite of hamburger Thomas was choking down, but clear enough for Gabe to pick out the words...more or less.

Gabe closed the now-empty temperature-controlled unit he carried his lunch in, nodding in answer. He could skip lunch, but he'd always enjoyed the social interaction with Thomas. Since the only 'fast food' option for a Xxanian was sashimi, he brought his lunch four days out of five and treated Thomas to oriental food the fifth.

"Damn. That must have been hard for her."

"Yes. Very hard, I'm certain." *Too hard.* A human mother raising a human child alone was hard enough. A human *Hauaa* raising a Xxanian-mix child alone was inconceivable. More than ever, Gabe wanted to do something special for Abby.

"You do realize the trouble this is going to cause, don't you?"

The abrupt change of subject caught Gabe off guard and sent warning tremors down his spine. "What trouble?"

Thomas swallowed another mouthful of burger. "You know humans." He shrugged and took another bite.

Some days, all too well. Some days, not nearly well enough. "I suppose so." But he still wasn't following the connection between Abby's pregnancy, his son, and human troubles. They'd already jailed the men who'd attacked Abby and Michael, and she'd agreed to take one of the men with her or leave Michael at the nest when she ventured out, to avoid a repeat.

Thomas set his burger down and stared at Gabe, his expression starkly serious. "When the elders started taking human mates and crossbreeding, what happened?"

Gabe considered that. "It took the humans a few bindings to react to it, but that's when the guerrilla attacks against Xxanians started." They'd been bloody and brutal, and they'd only escalated when Earth's military moved to protect their new Xxanian allies. "But there hasn't been an attack like that in at least...two decades."

"Because there haven't been any more accidental bindings, and it was believed that it was impossible to create a bastard crossbreed." Thomas raised his hand to still Gabe's boiling temper. "I'm not calling your son a bastard, but *they* will. And once word gets around that it's possible for babies to be conceived out of binding, there is going to be a whole new shit-storm. Excuse the term."

"Why would word...get around?" Suspicion burned in his gut.

Thomas leaned toward him, his usual easy-going nature chillingly missing. "Because these things always...get around. It's all over the station already. Your emergency leave paperwork listed the reason for your leave."

"Caring for my mate and son."

"But the rest of your paperwork has you listed as unmarried...unbound. What's your next step? At the end of our shift?"

They'd discussed this already. Realization dawned on him. "Changing my benefits paperwork. Listing Abby and Michael as my beneficiaries and adding them to my medical."

"But your paperwork still shows you as unbound. Even if you married Abby today...human marriage, you're still unbound. No Xxanian that had been through binding would neglect to...well, no offense—"

"None taken. You're correct about that. A Xxanian would take every possible measure, human and Xxanian, to make sure every man on Earth and beyond knew his mate was his woman. Not even the smallest doubt would be left to chance."

Thomas waited for his response.

Gabe nodded. "I'll suggest to Zhaahvan that the other elders might need to know this information. Not only because of the human threat, either."

Thomas winced. "So no one else makes the same...oversight you did?" he guessed.

"That would be prudent." This was sure to cause the same sorts of repercussions Andy Daahn's mating did. *May the* Seir-*God and human gods all protect us.*

* * * *

By the time Gabe made it back to the nest, his nerves were jumping. Once Thomas mentioned the rumors circulating, Gabe became all too aware of heads turning his direction as he walked through the station.

He'd dismissed it earlier as officers simply noting that he'd returned to duty. By late afternoon, he was struck by the averted eyes, whispered comments to coworkers, and sideward glances people tried to mask.

It is the subtle undercurrent of human society that you must be wary of.

How often had his gran-*seir* warned them of that? Xxanians never made a secret of their intentions. Though a Xxanian warrior might lay in wait and ambush an enemy, it was always an ambush the enemy should have known was a possibility. Unlike humans, Xxanians never wore a false face and stabbed one that perceived the Xxanian as a comrade in the back.

But humans do. That raised issues Gabe hadn't concerned himself with earlier. He could trust no one human, save those tied to Xxanian nests. He would have to be vigilant.

That thought made the click of the blast doors all the more comforting. Inside, there was little chance of successful attack against those he loved and protected.

Chapter Eight

"Zhaahvan! Captain's office."

Gabe looked up from the fasteners on his leg armor. "On my way." He buckled down the last strap, offered Thomas a shrug, and headed toward the central office suite, his helmet tucked under his arm.

The officer on Captain DeMarco's door waved Gabe through. He knocked and waited for DeMarco's shout of "Enter." to let himself in.

"You called, sir?"

DeMarco didn't look up from his paperwork. "Close the door, Zhaahvan."

He did so, and the sounds of the bustling station house tapered to a comfortable buzzing. DeMarco didn't address him promptly, and Gabe bit back the urge to clear his throat and hint at an explanation.

I would do that with Xxanian elders. But human supervisors were not Xxanian elders.

At last, the Captain pushed the paperwork away and looked up at Gabe. He sighed, his expression weary. "I'm going to have to put you on paid leave, Zhaahvan."

"Has there been some complaint against me?" There were only so many reasons the Captain would make such a decision.

"Nothing past the usual."

Gabe nodded, relieved. 'The usual' meant ridiculous claims of police or Xxan-Human brutality that physical evidence and witnesses didn't bear out.

"Rhaazhaa was killed this morning."

The news hit Gabe like a gut shot. Still..."His nest and mine are not closely allied. I will not be called upon to honor him at the pyre." Though Mattew's gran-*seir* would be furious at the loss of his only gran-*vvaashee*, Rhaazhaa wasn't likely to request aid from Zhaahvan, no matter what his plans.

DeMarco winced. "You don't understand. Rhaazhaa didn't die in the line of duty. He was targeted. You will be, too."

Gabe straightened, fighting his ridge plates back. "My job—"

"This isn't about your job, Zhaahvan. This is about keeping you alive to raise your son."

He opened his mouth to protest the assumption that he was incapable of defending himself.

"And it's about keeping Thomas alive long enough to *have* a son."

His stomach clenched at that pronouncement. "I don't think I understand." He hoped he didn't.

"Rhaazhaa and his partner—"

"Greete," Gabe recalled.

"Yes. Rhaazhaa and Greete stopped for breakfast after their shift."

As Thomas and I have lunch together halfway through ours. He nodded dumbly, sure he knew what was coming next.

"When the anti-Xxan guerillas opened fire, Greete tried to protect his partner with his personal weapon."

"They killed him as well," Gabe guessed. He glanced at the steady-stream of work going on outside the bullet-proof glass. "No one knows yet." News like this traveled fast. *How could no one know?*

"It happened in grid six-beta."

Across town.

"I just got the call half an hour ago. Within an hour, it will be all over the station."

"And you want me gone by then."

"Thomas is young, Zhaahvan. He won't let you go to a more experienced partner. He won't back down if...when you're attacked."

Gabe considered that. "I think you're right."

DeMarco seemed relieved. "You won't fight me then?"

"No. I'll change out and—"

"Wear the armor home," he ordered.

Gabe hesitated, then nodded. "Will do."

"Good. Let's sign the paperwork."

By the time Gabe returned to the locker room, Thomas was nowhere in sight. *He's probably in the briefing room.*

Gabe reasoned it was better this way. If his partner didn't see Gabe leaving, he wouldn't ask questions. Gabe wouldn't be forced to explain that he was leaving to save Thomas's life.

Thomas would hear about it in the briefing. By then, it would all be over, a 'done deal.'

Dispirited by the turn of events, Gabe opened his locker and started packing everything into his duffel.

He paused with his hand hovering over the photos of his family, torn. He didn't want to have to have the pictures on him if he was ambushed, but destroying them wasn't an option. At a loss for a better idea, Gabe folded them in half, slid his hand inside his body armor, and deposited them in his shirt pocket.

The empty locker room was a depressing sight. Without question, he knew his life as a police officer in this city had ended.

Maybe I can get a job in security at a Xxanian company. He didn't doubt *Spice Industries* would consider him an asset. As long as Gabe was working and providing for his family, he could live with not being on the force, he was sure.

One last glance around convinced Gabe it was time to go. He settled his helmet on his head, positioned the mic, locked the face plate, then headed for his car. For the first time in his life, he was glad his gran-*seir* had insisted on the military-grade safety systems in his vehicle...and at the nest.

* * * *

"You're serious, aren't you?" Abby felt her face pale. He'd only been on leave from the police for a day, and Gabe was already giving orders to keep her in the nest full time.

Gabe winced. "There are three dead already, Abby. I do not intend to add you or Michael to that number."

"I've already agreed to leave Michael here at the nest when I go out. I've already agreed that we'll move here permanently."

He sighed and scrubbed a hand over his face. "If they see you leave the nest, they'll assume you are a mate or prospective mate. They will do their best to kill you, Abby, to keep the population of crossbred Xxan down. They've killed two Dominants and a human officer who got in their way. Please, I need you to understand."

She nodded. "But we have to collect our belongings. At least some things from the apartment. How will we—?"

Gabe waved her off. "I'll arrange a detail of Xxanian warriors to do it. We'll get everything we can. We may only be able to get in once, so we'll have to take the most important things first."

Abby considered that. "I'll make a list."

"Include where to find everything. We won't be searching, so if you say something is in a closet, we'll probably grab everything from that closet, just to be sure we don't leave it behind."

"O-okay. I can do that." Her heart thundered at his stark and serious nature. This wasn't like Gabe. He was rattled.

"In the meantime, the elders have already arranged to have deliveries for Xxanian nests accepted by the shipping department at *Spice Industries*, checked, and moved to the nests by shuttle.

"If you want to shop at *Spice*, you can likewise go by shuttle. Gran-*Seir*'s shuttle will be available to transport the women and Michael at all times. But only to secure locations, like *Spice Tower* or SLAL."

"I don't understand," she admitted. "Your coupe has military-grade systems." Was it that *Spice Tower* lacked a bunker garage? She'd thought they had one.

"There are military-grade weapons that can destroy it. The shuttles have the advantage of maneuverability."

"How can you go back to work?"

He seemed pained by the question. "On duty with the police? I can't. Not at this point. Maybe not ever."

Abby placed a hand on his arm, at a loss to comfort him. All he'd ever wanted was to be a police officer, and a bunch of bigots stole it from him.

He took a calming breath and continued. "I'll be working with the *Spice* security force, overseeing the new delivery measures and the influx of shuttle traffic at the tower. I can go to work by shuttle."

A potent silence fell between them, and Abby wrapped her arms around him. In all the years she'd been with Gabe, all the specists spewing hate at the two of them...even after the attack on her and Michael, she'd never realized the extremes the anti-Xxan guerillas would go to.

"Be careful," she begged him.

"I will. I have to. I have a son and mate to come home to."

There was an unspoken vow in that. No matter what Gabe had to do, he wouldn't leave Abby alone to die when her mate was killed. She wasn't sure whether she should take that unspoken vow as crushing her dreams of mating or making them come true.

Chapter Nine

Gabe sat in the back of the second transport van, watching the city streets pass by through the heavily-tinted, bullet-proof glass panels. They'd chosen their timing well. It was after work hours on a Friday evening. The streets were full of traffic, and no one would notice a couple of nondescript vans.

Of course, someone would notice when they all filed out of those vans. Every one of the Xxanian Dominants aiding Gabe with the move wore body armor and impact helmets. The males who would be protecting the vans and doors additionally carried weapons.

Gabe had planned this move with Abby, putting her mind as much at ease as he could with the fact that the Xxanian team he'd assembled could strip down the most important things from her apartment and get them away in less than twenty minutes. Abby had been incredibly picky about what she wanted them to bring first. If there couldn't be a second trip—for whatever reason—they would be sure to get the things she considered most important.

Sirens screamed in the distance, moving the same direction they were. Gabe listened, endeavoring to separate the overlapping sounds.

Police. Fire. Ambulance. It's a trifecta. He itched to help, but he was still officially on leave and was unlikely to go back at all.

"Behind us," one of the other males decided.

"And ahead," Gabe corrected him. *It must be something big.*

"We're blocked ahead," Jaee Vhheaa, the driver of the first van, announced over their headsets.

Gabe launched to his feet and scanned the road blocked by emergency vehicles over Marcus Raashh's shoulder. He pressed the transmit button. "Turn right here, Jaee. Two blocks down, turn left. We'll work our way down the backstreets to her apartment." He released the button.

"On our way," Jaee responded.

Jaee made the right, and Marcus followed in his wake.

"Blocked," Jaee reported when he reached the alley Gabe had wanted him to use.

Gabe muttered a handful of curses in Xxan, then connected to Jaee again. "Two more blocks. Then make the left. We'll go around."

Thankfully, that worked. The street Abby's apartment building opened onto was a one-way street, so he had Jaee overshoot it and then make another left, so they could come down the cross street her building cornered on and turn in right at their destination.

"Blocked," Jaee reported again, more than a block from their destination. "Looks like one *huzhaah* of a fire."

Gabe pulled his visor up to get a better look, his heart stuttering. He sank to the floor of the van, heartsick. Fire poured out of the windows of Abby's apartment and those on the two floors above. Part of the roof had already collapsed.

A hand closed on his shoulder. "It's hers, isn't it?"

Since Marcus's question had gone out to the entire crew, Gabe answered in kind. "It's her apartment." His fingers felt numb against the button. "Head back to the nest. There's no way we can salvage anything from this."

He peeked up again as Marcus turned away, his heart stuttering at the gaping hole in the brick face halfway down the length of Abby's apartment. This hadn't been a fire. It had been an explosion. Gabe didn't question that it had been set.

"What are you going to tell her?" Jaee asked.

"The truth. What else can I tell her? How? Isn't that the question?" How was he supposed to tell Abby that all her most precious belongings were gone?

Gabe shuddered at a more disturbing thought. *What would I have done if Abby and Michael had been there?* His killing rage would have shaken the foundations of the tentative peace between humans and Xxan.

* * * *

"They're coming back in, Abby," Ariel informed her.

Abby rushed into the center nest though she reasoned that the men would need at least a little time in the *s'sanuea* to change clothing. Then again, it wouldn't be practical to move her belongings in dressed in *S'suumea*.

What will they have to remove?

As if in answer, Gabe strode into the center nest, barefoot and unarmored but still dressed in the uniform he'd been wearing beneath, his *seir* and more than a dozen similarly-dressed Xxanian warriors at his heels. It took a moment for their empty hands to resonate with her. Something was wrong, and the hair at the base of her skull rose in warning.

"Gabe?" she questioned.

He crossed the cave to her, looking pained. Gabe took her hands in his and sank to one knee, pressing his forehead to the backs of them. "I'm sorry, Abby. We were too late."

She glanced up at the other males, noting their bowed heads. "Too late? Too late for what?"

Gabe hesitated and looked up at her, seemingly at a loss. Finally, he started talking.

"There was an attack."

"On *you*?" Abby felt the blood draining from her face at the thought of them under attack.

"No. Your apartment. The cowards—"

"Then you can't go there," she decided. "Not even when the attack is over." Nothing was worth that.

Gabe shook his head. "There's no reason to. It's...gone, Abby. The entire building will be gone by the time the fire is extinguished."

A lump lodged in her throat. "You're saying someone set the fire?"

"There is no question of it."

Abby's knees started to shake, and Gabe helped her down to the thick grass floor of the center nest.

"I will replace everything I can," he promised. "Nearly as perfectly as I can, but your precious mementos— I am sorry, Abby."

She wrapped her arms around him, shivering hard. *Gone. Everything is gone.*

Gabe stopped speaking and scooped her into his arms. He paused for a moment and offered a word of thanks to the other warriors who'd gone with him. Then he carried Abby up the stairs to the human-style bedroom they shared.

Everything is gone. Except Gabe and Michael. Thank the stars none of us were there.

His warnings about going out alone had seemed somewhat irrational. *Until now.* Something told Abby she would think twice about walking the streets of the city ever again.

Chapter Ten

"Someone to see you, Abby," Jana announced.

She looked up from the screen, shocked by the pronouncement. "There is?" Who would visit her? Abby didn't have family, and she'd lost her only friend when she announced she was keeping the Xxanian child she carried. Since she lived at the nest, who else would come to see her?

Jana smiled and waved her toward the center nest. Her heart pounding, Abby followed her. Ariel was currently babysitting Michael, so there was no reason to stop and pluck him from his playpen in the upper bedroom that doubled as her office. That left her hands disconcertingly empty.

It wasn't just some*one* to see her. It was a crowd of someones. There were at least a dozen women, all dressed in *S'suuhhea*, at the center of the room and half that many men in *S'suumea* congregated at the exits to the room.

Standing guard. With the threats against the Xxan and Xxanian mates and children, they don't trust their women are safe, even here.

One of the women approached, her hand out but not for a handshake. At a loss, Abby offered her own, and the stranger squeezed it but didn't release her.

For a moment, neither of them spoke. That gave Abby a chance to examine her.

The woman was at least fifteen years older than Abby was. Her hair was in an intricate up-do that left honey-colored curls cascading around her elfin face.

"Joy," the other woman stated.

"Excuse me?" Abby asked. Was this some strange greeting between the Xxan she still hadn't learned.

She chuckled. "My name. Joy Rasshh. It's good to meet you, Abby, and I am sorry to intrude on your work."

Stifling the wince proved impossible. Abby nodded and offered a smile that she knew was strained.

Joy wasn't interrupting much. *Well, besides the end of my life's dream.*

Once the news services reported her name in connection with the firebombing of her apartment, some eager beaver dug up her ownership of *Ideal Ideas*. In the last three days, she'd not only lost a large proportion of her and her son's belongings; she'd lost more than seventy percent of her business.

Corporate accounts she'd fostered in the last year—even after she'd surrendered her offices and started working at home to care for Michael, when finding child care had proven impossible—had pulled abruptly, stating that her services were no longer required. Though a few of her accounts had increased their orders—most likely out of pity—it couldn't make up for the loss of the larger accounts.

Face it. In a world full of humans, the Xxan are the minority.

"Thank you." It was the only response she could think of to make.

Joy tipped her head. "Come meet the others," she invited.

Why not? What else do I have to do besides raise my son?

They walked down to the group of women, and the introductions started. There were only two names she recognized besides Joy's: Zondra and Miri Daahn. Miri carried a baby in a sling around her shoulders, Zondra had a young girl she'd guess to be about twice Michael's age on her hip, and the four Daahns wore matching *S'suuhhea.*

Geoff appeared in the doorway to the eating area and cleared his throat for attention. All chatter between the women stopped, and they moved toward his position. Joy hooked an arm through Abby's and guided her along with them.

The room was set with all the cushions—save Zhaahvan's—pulled into a ring in the center of the room. The trays of meat in the middle contained more food than Abby had ever seen in one place.

To her surprise, none of the males joined them, even the elder of the nest, save the babies and toddlers. Ariel set to work feeding Michael, leaving Abby nothing to do but try to socialize with a roomful of women she'd never met before. It wasn't a situation she was accustomed to. She'd always avoided these types of events.

Whatever this type of event is.

Zondra spoke up first. "We are so sorry for your loss."

"Loss?" What in the world was she talking about?

She motioned to a stack of boxes and bags against the far wall. "We were told you lost almost everything in...in that deplorable attack." Zondra reached across and covered Abby's hand with her own. "I am so glad you and Michael weren't there when it happened."

"So am I." Abby glanced at the pile. "What is...?" She motioned up and down, at a loss to comprehend it.

Miri spoke up. "It is our way to send gifts when a new mate joins an ally's nest...and when a new young one does."

"But we—"

"You and Gabe are mates in the eyes of the Xxan, though the situation precludes formal mating. As such, we send gifts as allies of your nest."

Abby swallowed a lump of emotion and nodded. "Thank you."

Another woman inserted herself into the conversation. "And when an allied nest has need, we help. Whatever we can do to help. Not everything stacked there is new. We've collected old toys and clothes Michael might be able to use. Things like that."

Abby searched frantically for her name. Sarah? Stacie? Susan? Oh, it doesn't matter. "Thank you."

There was a moment of silence between them.

I should say something. Anything. "Do you get together often?" *That was stupid. Why did I choose to ask that?*

Jana laughed. "Not nearly as often as we'd like to, I'm sure."

Zondra cut in again. "Mostly those of us with young ones of about the same age. My Siri is not much older than your Michael is. Perhaps we could have them play together."

"And my Lewis," another woman added.

Miri nodded. "Amanda is only a few months younger than the others."

"A play group," Abby mused. "I've always wanted a play group for Michael, but..." She shrugged.

Zondra made a noise that spoke of disgust. "I know. You would think Xxanian children had cooties."

The laugh bubbled up, and there was no stopping it. Tears leaked from Abby's eyes as she laughed harder.

"It's good to hear you laughing again." Jana smiled and wrapped a hand around Abby's shoulders.

Abby squeezed her tight. *Is this home? Is this what I've been missing all these years?* She suspected it was.

* * * *

"Abby," Joy called out. "I understand you have a profitable little business."

Some of the happiness seeped out of Abby's heart, and she sighed. "I did. I'm not sure I will have one for much longer."

Conversations on the other side of the ring stopped abruptly, and the women gaped at her.

"It's not this anti-Xxan thing, is it?" Stacie asked, seemingly incredulous.

Abby motioned vaguely. "When accounts that were throwing more and more your way suddenly say they don't need your services anymore... There's really only one thing you can assume."

"Damned bigots," she cursed. "I am so glad the Xxan aren't that way."

"Some are," Miri stated.

From the way Zondra hugged her sister-in-law, something told Abby there was a story there.

"Well, you don't need to worry about the accounts you lost," Joy informed her.

"Oh, I know I don't *need* to work," Abby replied. "I know Gabe and the nest are more than willing and capable of taking care of us, but my business was always my dream."

"And I'm not telling you to give up on that," Joy offered patiently. "I'm telling you that you have other clients, if you want them."

Her meaning was crystal clear. "I can't accept nepotism. Just because our nests are allies... That doesn't mean it's your duty to keep my business alive."

Joy laughed and pulled the messenger bag she'd been carrying into her lap. Without a word, she opened it and handed over a thick folder, passing it through Jana.

Abby opened it and started flipping through the pages. It was a full profile on her company, from the looks of it. "How did you get this so quickly?"

"I didn't. I'd already been looking into a contract between *Ideal Ideas* and *Spice Industries.*"

Abby's mouth went dry. "For how long?"

"Ever since you signed *Koltrane* as a client."

Five months. "Wow."

"As you can see, my brother-in-law is rather...exhaustive in his research when we choose to take on a new business partner."

Zondra broke in. "After that nastiness with Sandy's former boss, can you blame him?"

Joy nodded her agreement. "Arren and Sandy send their regards. They would be here as well, but their girls are still on medical lockdown. You know Doctors Rayn and Carew, I'm sure. At least they're at home now." She wagged a finger, her gaze far away. "Once they are allowed to, they'd make excellent additions to the play group."

A niggling memory ate at Abby. *Rasshh?* "The other preemies," she recalled. "They were in lockdown on SLAL much longer than Michael and I were." The Rasshh twins had had a special nest area, while she'd stayed in a bedroom with Michael. She'd never seen them, though she knew they'd been on the space station for more than a month together.

Joy nodded. "At any rate, I've been looking at adding a gift basket option for *Spice Industries.* Arren was particularly intrigued with the idea of dealing with you when he learned you were raising a Xxanian young one and buying our products for Michael. Of course, he was frustrated by the lack of information about which nest you were connected to or how you could come to be in possession of a Xxanian child." Her smile said she rather enjoyed Arren's frustration.

Another story there. Abby forced her mind back to the main issue. "The gift baskets?" she prompted.

"We would pay you to design a whole range of options for us, and we would employ our own staff to produce them—to your standards of course. You would have complete creative control. Every time one sells, you would get a commission from it."

"Just your own products?" It was always best to know the scope of a new project.

"Not at all. There are human mates and human business partners our customers might want to purchase for. We would keep a store room of any products you add to the baskets, so they'll be on hand when we need to make a basket."

"Free reign? All the suppliers I usually work with?"

"Plus *Spice Industries*," Joy reminded her. "Ideally, we would like to start with a minimum of about a hundred designs and add more seasonally."

"That's a huge undertaking," Abby breathed.

"You could still run your own designs as well, but the anticipated earnings from this venture would more than make up for it, if you moved your existing client base over to the new system."

"No. I do personal designs for them."

Joy tipped her head.

Abby considered it. "It's definitely close to what I've always wanted," she conceded. "Staff to assemble the bulk designs and freedom to create personalized ones."

"And a discount on all *Spice* products you want to use in your personalized designs," Joy reminded her.

"Better than I'd anticipated then."

"Is that an agreement?" Joy asked, seemingly excited at the prospect.

Bring out your businesswoman face. Abby smiled widely. "Send me a contract. I'd love to see the proposal." Something told her it would be more than fair.

Epilogue

Seven months later

Abby led Michael off the shuttle, the toddler hopping on two feet at the end of his mother's arm.

Doctor Rayn's rich laughter lit his crinkled eyes. "Let me guess. He wasn't doing that yesterday."

One particularly hearty bounce nearly pulled Abby over on top of him, and she sighed. "I swear he went from cruising to walking to running nearly overnight."

"Most Xxanian children do. Especially Dominants like your son."

The young Dominant in question stopped short. Abby tipped her head down, intent on asking what was wrong.

Michael stood, one tiny foot raised, swiveling it back and forth. His blond head was bowed in serious consideration.

The first hop on his left foot was tentative. The next several were increasingly robust. He looked up at Abby and smiled widely, showing both his human incisors and canines and his Xxanian hunting teeth.

Abby offered a weary smile. "That's good, Michael."

Rayn's Xxan was slow and smooth. *"Come, young Dominant."*

Michael stopped hopping and stared at the doctor. He cocked his head to one side, hesitated a long moment, and released Abby's hand. Hopping on his left foot, Michael reached Rayn's side. He grasped the doctor's hand, switched feet, and started testing his prowess on the right foot.

"Hauaa *comes,*" her son pronounced in Xxan. He'd quickly become bilingual and had started using both English and Xxan words within days of each other.

Abby sighed and trudged after them. Exhaustion weighed her down. Even with Gabe's family running herd, keeping up with a Xxanian toddler was a full time job. *Plus some.* More than once in the last few months, she'd kicked herself that she'd ever believed she could do this alone.

Michael vaulted up on the far examination bed with the agility of a gymnast. Then he crumpled in that careless way children had.

Abby stopped beside the closer bed. It was tempting to climb up on it and take a nap while Michael had his appointment.

"*Hauaa*, watch!" Michael commanded, switching back to English again.

He jumped hard on the bed, two corpsmen bracketing their arms to catch him in case his fledgling muscle prowess failed him or he misjudged his position. Rayn stepped back and let Michael play, a smile curving his lips.

"That's good, Michael," she repeated. *Encouraging children is necessary. Isn't it?*

Just watching him landing and rebounding made Abby's head spin. She closed her hand around the safety bar on the edge of the bed.

"Abby?" Doctor Rayn inquired.

She looked up and met his gaze. The deep blue of his eyes was clear and crisp, but everything else was swimming and indistinct.

The pounding of Michael's feet slowed, lengthened...and Abby's heart rate seemed to slow to match it. Colors muted and then faded to sepia tones.

Michael went still, coiled in a crouch, his eye slits narrowing and his ridge plates extending. Movement came from every direction, and a fierce growl followed her into darkness.

* * * *

Gabe rushed through changing his clothing. It had been a long shift, and he was more anxious than ever to see Abby and Michael.

They might not be home yet. Abby had said the check-up at SLAL would be "quick," but there was still travel time to consider. Travel time and the overprotective SLAL doctors. Given the chance, Rayn could turn even a routine physical examination into a two-day event.

The fact that they might not be within the nest couldn't dampen his spirits. His mate was happy, settled in the nest with the rest of his family. Her business had blossomed into a thriving endeavor. His son was flourishing, both physically and emotionally.

The *s'sanuea* left behind, Gabe padded through the nest, savoring the plants caressing his bare feet and the wind brushing against his face.

He'd made it nearly to the center nest when the taint of battle pheromones hit him solidly. His heart pumping the same into his own body, Gabe sprinted the rest of the way.

His *seir* and gran-*seir* snapped looks at him. Neither held weapons, but their scents said there was danger to the nest.

He scanned his gaze over the women lounging near the bathing pool. The fact that they were here said there was no imminent danger.

But Abby and Michael aren't here. What if they are in danger? Visions of space pirates or anti-Xxan guerrillas raised his ridge plates. "What is it?" Gabe demanded in Xxan.

"Come," his gran-*seir* ordered. He turned toward the tunnel that led to the elder's shuttle.

"What has happened to my mate and son?"

His *seir* answered. "Abby is ill, and Michael will not allow the SLAL doctors to render aid to her. They prefer not to drug him to accomplish the task, and there is no reasoning with the child, so they called for us to remove the young Dominant before he injures more of their people."

A series of human curses escaped Gabe's mouth. Under normal circumstances, he might be concerned about his gran-*seir*'s reaction to the slip. The dual grunts of agreement attested that no one begrudged Gabe his reaction.

Aboard the shuttle, there were no wasted words. One moment, they were Earthbound, and the next, they were winging toward space at a reckless rate of speed.

Gabe winced, then reminded himself that Rayn would have warned the rangers on duty that a Xxanian medical emergency had been declared. Far short of stopping them, the military would give the incoming Xxanian vessel a wide berth and even clear traffic lanes for them.

That meant they made the usual forty-minute journey in less than half that time. The shuttle bay doors opened for them without the usual radio chatter, and Zhaahvan set the family shuttle down neatly on the pad next to a military model, most likely the same shuttle that had transferred Abby and Michel on board.

Gabe was out the door and halfway across the bay before one of the younger scientists appeared.

"This way," he shouted. He turned and ran, knowing full well the Xxanian warriors behind him would more than keep pace.

They breached the doorway to a large exam room, Zhaahvan and Gabe abreast and his *seir* a few steps behind.

The scene stole Gabe's breath. Abby lay on the floor, sprawled in a prone position, her head turned toward the doorway, a trickle of blood drying on her lower lip. Michael was squatted next to her, blood on the talons of his right hand and his chin.

Gabe and his gran-*seir* moved together, both advancing on the young Dominant. He turned toward them with a hiss. Only a heartbeat later, he straightened and reached for Gabe.

Zhaahvan scooped him up instead, and Gabe eased down next to Abby. At the first movement of the doctors, Michael growled and reached two handfuls of talons toward them. They stopped short, and Zhaahvan hummed soothing sounds to the toddler warrior.

"Abby?" Gabe called softly.

She didn't move. He reached for her, stopped just shy of touching her, and looked up at Rayn. Having not witnessed what happened, he wasn't certain it was safe to move her.

The doctor nodded. "Lift her onto the bed, please." His gaze darted toward Zhaahvan. "Take Michael out, if you would." Rows of liquid stitches on the doctor's hand and arm explained Rayn's hesitation at having Michael in the room.

It was typical of Rayn. He'd been the first one to Abby's side. That meant he'd been the first to taste Michael's fighting skills.

Gabe lifted Abby and turned her, wincing at the bruising on her face. The ruckus from behind him was impossible to mistake. Michael was intent on staying and was fighting to make that a reality.

"Hauaa!"

A grunt of pain said the toddler was in Brien's hands and not in Zhaahvan's.

"Seir! Hauaa!"

Gabe settled Abby on the examination bed. "Go with Gran-*Seir*, Michael," he ordered.

It was a lost cause, of course. Michael was having none of it.

The growling from Zhaahvan brought the fight to an abrupt halt. Gabe glanced back, slightly surprised to see his *seir* bleeding from deep furrows in his arm.

Michael had given up the fight and clung to Brien, his eyes wide, wild, and locked on the elder.

Zhaahvan offered sharp sounds of correction, then switched to speech. *"Your* Hauaa *needs doctors now. You will sit on that bed."* He motioned to the empty but rumpled bed across the room. *"You will allow the doctors to aid your* Hauaa. *I will sit with you. If* Hauaa *needs protection, your seir and I will attend to it. Understood?"*

A meek nod was Michael's only reply. Zhaahvan scooped Michael from his son's arms and jerked his head toward the far corridor.

Doctors for his injuries. As always, the elder protected his entire family, young and old, male and female.

That thought shot Gabe's attention back to Abby.

Rayn and his staff were already hard at work around her. They spaced themselves around Gabe. None of them asked him to move; they knew that wouldn't happen. With his mate at risk, Gabe wasn't about to leave her side.

One of the younger males worked at the bruising on her face, healing the damage with the wand locked between trembling fingers. Another operated the scan plate and read off the status of every area of her body to Rayn, as it glided downward.

Though he wanted to know what had happened, Gabe didn't interrupt them. It was more important that Abby be cared for than his desire to know be slaked.

The running litany stopped abruptly. Everyone around the table looked up, including Gabe.

"What is it?" Gabe demanded before Rayn could.

"She's...uh... She's carrying. That's why she..." He motioned up and down at Abby.

He didn't need to be more specific. Abby had collapsed. The unexpected event and the doctors' reactions to it would have confused and unnerved Michael.

I did *tell him to protect his mother. Seir-God help me, I never thought that would backfire on us.*

Rayn didn't waste time. "You all know the procedures. Tim, you were here for Abby's last pregnancy. We have a head start this time. Let's not waste it."

The medical team scattered, unnerving Gabe. *They* knew the procedures. He, on the other hand, had no clue what would be involved in his mate's care.

Rayn stopped short in the process of strapping a band to Abby's wrist. He stared at Gabe for a moment, then went back to work and started speaking.

"She has to stop nursing Michael. We'll give her an injection to dry her milk quickly and painlessly." He nodded toward the head of the bed.

Gabe turned, gaping at the sight of a female medic expressing Abby's milk. *What in the* Seir-God's *name is this?*

Rayn continued. "We don't dare do this for long. It's a damned miracle that expressing for Michael hasn't sent her into a premature labor already, considering Abby's condition.

"Jude will take just enough to allow us to synthesize milk for Michael. Over the next few months, we'll start cutting *Spice Industries* formula into the milk, so he'll wean from the synthesized milk before he has to change formulations." He shot a look at Jude. "Try...formula three, for a start. That should be about right for him."

Gabe's head spun at the complexity of the situation. "Can Abby come home, or must she stay here?" She'd stayed at SLAL for most of Michael's pregnancy, he knew.

Tim returned with a tray of medications. "Using Michael's pregnancy as a guide? I'd say she'll probably be safe at your nest for the next month and a half, since she'll have family members to watch over her. After that, a nest here would be best."

Gran-*Seir* cut in with his opinion. "I will order scentless plants to be delivered tonight. The sooner we infuse them with our nest scent and transport them here, the better."

Gabe nodded his agreement and continued. "What can she do? Or not? Can she...?" He stopped short of asking something as crass and selfish as whether or not she could have sex with him while she carried. If expressing milk was too strenuous an activity for her, surely sex was.

Tim and Rayn locked gazes, twin smiles on their faces. Tim chuckled and went back to filling a hypo.

Rayn answered for them. "Moderate sexual relations may actually help."

Gabe sighed, shooting a glance at his gran-*seir*. The old buck wasn't going to like a further delay in their plans to mate, but if Gabe's young and Abby depended on such a delay, it couldn't be avoided.

Rayn's eyes narrowed. "What is it?"

Better to say it than leave it unsaid. "We'd planned to mate when Abby was done nursing, but I guess that will have to—"

"Oh, no," Tim interrupted him. "In fact, the biological changes that binding will cause in Abby may make carrying this time easier. As long as it is accomplished gently, and she's monitored while you bind..." He tapped the band on Abby's arm. "That may be the single best thing you can do to help her deliver a healthy young one."

Inappropriate as it might be, Gabe's body reacted to the news and hardened. If the doctors noticed it, they hid it well.

"As for the rest..." Rayn intoned. "There will be some things Abby cannot do, but those are concerns for a month from now."

* * * *

Abby came to consciousness slowly, confused by conflicting sensations. She was in a bed, but it clearly wasn't her bed in Zhaahvan's nest. She was wearing something made of silk, which further indicated she wasn't in her own bed. While she wore a *S'suuhhea* in the center nest and satellite nests, even for sleep, she and Gabe slept nude in the human-style bedroom on the level above.

A roll of her head from side to side on the pillow was enough to convince her she was in a bed at SLAL...but not a hospital bed. It was probably the bedroom she'd used when she was pregnant with Michael.

I'm at SLAL. Still *at SLAL.* The last coherent memory she had was bringing Michael up for his one-year physical. But what happened to land her in a bed, hooked up to monitoring, was a mystery to her.

Michael. She opened her eyes and shot to sitting, scanning the room for her son.

A soothing rumble reached her a moment before Gabe's arms wrapped around her. She relaxed into his hold. If Gabe was here, Michael was most likely with his family. That meant he was safe, and she could certainly use the rest.

Obviously. There was little doubt that she'd passed out. *Time to build more sleep into the schedule.* Of course, that would be easier if Michael slept more.

"Better?" Gabe asked.

Abby snuggled into his shoulder and turned on the bed to wrap herself around him. "It is now."

"Why didn't you tell me you were fatigued?"

She yawned. "Keeping up with our son makes that SOP. I can't imagine how people manage with more than one, especially Xxanian families."

There was a tense moment of silence. Abby opened her eyes and looked up into Gabe's stony face.

"What is it?" Had something happened to Michael? Her heart pounded in outright fear.

"You *did* say you'd always dreamed of a big family, right?"

"Well, yes. But I always knew that was—"

His raised eyebrow stopped her short.

"Isn't...it?" *Oh. Shit.* One of the reasons Rayn hadn't let her stay at home alone when she was pregnant with Michael was that there was no one to watch over her and get her help if she collapsed. *Keeping up with a Xxanian child isn't the only thing that causes this level of fatigue. Carrying one does, too.*

She'd been due for another pregnancy block shot today. Had it worn off early? She would have to ask Rayn that question.

Gabe's voice dragged her back to the present.

"You know how I feel about this, but if you feel you can't—"

Abby smacked him on the chest hard enough to make the sound reverberate through the room. "Never suggest such a thing."

His smile was slow coming but wide enough to show his hunting teeth. It was a rare indulgence for a Xxanian male, she'd found. "Well then...There are some things we should attend to."

She let her head drop to his chest. "Let me guess... Doctors Rayn and Carew are already putting the brakes on everything I do."

Gabe eased down to the mattress with her nestled to his shoulder. "Only a few things. They've moved Michael to synthesized breast milk and *Spice* formula."

"That's good, I guess." It would be an easier transition than it would be going to formula cold turkey.

"You make no outings without a male member of the family. Not even by shuttle."

"Oh, you like that one, I'm sure," she accused.

He didn't deny it. "The females may or may not be able to help you if you collapse."

As much as she hated to admit it, that was true. "Go on then," Abby conceded.

"The last thing is more...personal."

She groaned. "Let me guess. No sex?"

"The opposite."

Her head spun at that pronouncement. "Massive amounts of sex?" That didn't sound like something Rayn and Carew would prescribe.

"In moderation, but one particular thing..." He winced. "This is not how I wanted to do this."

Abby tightened her grip on him reflexively. It was disconcerting to see Gabe so uncertain. "Wanted to do what?"

"They believe binding will help you carry easier, and—"

"They didn't tell me that the last time," she fumed.

"You didn't want to tell me the last time. They were working within your comfort zone. Would you honestly have bound yourself to me, if you weren't sure Michael would survive?"

Finding the words to refute it was impossible. He was right about that. Abby shook her head in response.

"So... Are you going to mate with me?"

"Do you honestly believe I'd refuse? Of course, I'm going to mate with you. Do we have to wait for some reason?"

"We should probably get a meal in you first."

Her mouth watered at the thought of the spiced meat Xxanians and human women pregnant with Xxanian crossbreds ate. "Are you going to feed me properly?"

Gabe groaned, most likely at the thought of how mouth feeding between mates normally turned to hot sex. "You better believe it."

The End

About the Author

Brenna Lyons wears many hats, sometimes all on the same day: former president of EPIC, author of more than 100 published works, owner of Fireborn Publishing, columnist, special needs teacher, wife, mother...and member in good standing of more than 60 writing advocacy groups.

In her first ten years published in novel-length, she's won 3 EPIC e-Book Awards (out of 15 finalists) and finaled for 3 PEARLS (including one Honorable Mention, second to NY Times Bestseller Angela Knight), 2 CAPAS, and a Dream Realm Award. She's also taken Spinetingler's Book of the Year for 2007.

Brenna writes in 26 established worlds plus stand-alones, poetry, articles and essays. She's a bestseller in indie/e fantasy and horror, straight genre and cross-genres thereof. Brenna has been termed "one of the most deviant erotic minds in the publishing world...not for the weak." (Rachelle for Fallen Angels Reviews) Milieu-heavy dark work is practically Brenna's calling card, with or without the erotic content.

She teaches classes in everything from POV studies to advanced editing, networking to marketing. Brenna enjoys hearing from people who read her work and can be reached by e-mail.

Website: http://www.brennalyons.com/

Facebook:
http://www.facebook.com/brenna.lyons

Email: brennalyons4168@live.com

Also by this Author

Hunter's Tales
Maher Men
The Blutjagdfrau Chronicles
Veriel's Tales I: Crossbearer Turned
Veriel's Tales II: Losing Regana

URBAN GRIMM
Catch Me, If You Can
Three Wishes
Temptation of Eve

WEREWOLF U
Werewolf U
Younger Daughter
Alpha Son
Never Alone
Her Christmas Wolves

ANGEL-WING SAGA
Sons of Heaven: Beldon
Sons of Heaven: Unexpected Mates
Daughters of Man: Prize Match
Daughters of Man: Claiming a Princess

COLOR OF LOVE
The Color of Love

KEGIN SERIES
Conquest
The Last of Fion's Daughters
Last Chance for Love
Rites of Mating
In Her Ladyship's Service
Matchmaker's Misery

KIELAN SERIES
The Lady's Lowborn Lover
Time Currents

Cubed

STAR MAGES
Written in the Stars
The Master's Lover

DAN AIDAN FAIRIES
Fairy Dreams
Monsters of Myth Anthology

XXAN WAR
Daahan Rising
Raashh Decisions

MYTHOS SERIES
The Punishment of Phoebus Apollo
Black Sail

IT'S ALL GREEK TO ME...
All's Fair...

SANCTUM
Dream Walk

GRELLAN WAR
With Great Power

BLOOD MAGES
Enslaved

CARSON COUSINS
All I Want for Christmas is You

FATES WAR
Fates Magic

Beyond the Veil
Mine for the Night

Once in a Blue Moon
Overtime Pay
Stay With Me
The Fire God's Woman
Nevermore
Bride Ball
Undead in Blue
Mama's Tales
Unexpected Daddy
We Shall Live Again
May the Best Man Win
Marked
And It Was Good
Monsters of Myth Anthology

Available from **Under The Moon**

Evil Overlords Union Issue #1 Anthology
Undead Embrace
"Playing Games" in *Forbidden Love: Bad Boys*
"Marked" in *Forbidden Love: Wicked Women*
"The Master's Lover" in *Forbidden Love:*
Sacred Bands

Available from **Logical Lust**

"Mine for the Night" in *The Cougar Book*
Anthology

Available from **Coming Together Charity Anthologies**

INSTINCT SERIES
"Foundling" in *Coming Together: Into the Light*
Anthology

"Claim Mate" (available separately and as
part of the *Coming Together: Against the*

Odds Anthology)
"The Fire God's Woman" in *Coming Together:
Under Fire* Anthology

Available ***self-published***

Snapshots from a Poet's Life

Award-Winning Books

EPPIE/EPIC eBOOK AWARDS WINNERS
Coming Together: Against the Odds- 2010
Time Currents- 2010
Coming Together: Into the Light- 2011

EPPIE/EPIC eBOOK AWARDS FINALISTS
Fion's Daughter- 2004
Collected Poems: Book One- 2005 (now titled
Snapshots of a Poet's Life)
Renegade's Run- 2005
Rites of Mating- 2006
All I Want for Christmas- 2006
Phaze in Verse- 2008
*"The Fire God's Woman" in Coming Together:
Under Fire*- 2009
Three Wishes- 2010
Matchmaker's Misery- 2010
The Cougar Book- 2011
The Master's Lover- 2011
Bride Ball- 2011

DREAM REALM AWARDS FINALIST
Last Chance for Love- 2003

PEARL HONORABLE MENTION
Night Warriors- 2004

PEARL FINALISTS
Schente Night- 2003 (now included in *The
Last of Fion's Daughters*)
König Cursebreakers- 2004 (now titled *Will of
the Stone*)

JOYFULLY REVIEWED BEST BOOKS OF
2010
Written in the Stars- 2010

SPINETINGLER'S BOOK OF THE YEAR 2007
NOBODY: An Anthology of Dark Fiction- 2007
(Brenna's pieces of the anthology can be
found in *Beyond the Veil*)

TRS's CAPA FINALISTS
Ultimate Warriors- 2004 (Brenna's portion is
now available as *With Great Power*)
Written in the Stars

LOVE ROMANCE AND MORE CAFÉ BOOK
OF THE YEAR RUNNER UP
Last Chance for Love- 2008

ROAD TO ROMANCE REVIEWERS' CHOICE
AWARD
Prophecy: Revelations- 2004

LOVE ROMANCES REVIEWERS' CHOICE
AWARD
Black Sail- 2003

ROMANCE JUNKIES BOOK CLUB STAFF
PICK
TYGERS- 2003

FALLEN ANGELS ROMANCE
RECOMMENDED READ
Devon's Price-2005 (now available in *Bearing
Armen*)

JOYFULLY RECOMMENDED READ
Fairy Dreams- 2008
The Last of Fion's Daughters- 2009

TREBLE HEART FINALIST
Prophecy: Revelations- 2003